# Heather

By
Lane McFarland

Please visit Lane McFarland's website at
http://www.romancingtheeras.com
to learn more about her and her books.

# HEATHER

## (The Daughters of Alastair MacDougall ~ Book II)

Heather
**Dedication**

This book is dedicated to my husband,
Ken, and my son, Kenneth.
I thank you for your patience while
my head was buried in my computer,
for your tremendous support
and loving encouragement.

Special thanks to Tessy, my mentor,
who stuck with me from  the first rough sketch
of my story to my final beta read.
Bless your heart for helping me through
this journey!
Thank you for your sweet spirit & your
constructive criticism and coaching.

I am so grateful to Lexi (my editor),
Becca (my beta reader) and my
critique partners in Hearts Through History
& Celtic Hearts for their wonderful
suggestions, comments and
tremendous support.

# Chapter One

*MacDougall Castle*
*Kilmarnock, Scotland*
*October 1298*

Warning bells clanged throughout the castle. Heather MacDougall straightened and shaded her eyes from the afternoon sun. Horse hooves clattered on the wooden bridge as a MacDougall warrior galloped through the large worn gate, passing the guardhouses on either side.

"They're coming!" he shouted.

Her pulse quickened. English soldiers had been spotted in the area last week. Were they bearing down on the castle?

The women she'd been sorting vegetables with stood, their widened eyes focused on the warrior. Heather hiked her brown woolen skirt, weaved around baskets of leeks and turnips, and ran into the outer bailey with the women close behind.

The horse slid to a halt, and the man jumped from the saddle. He jerked his head right and left, his gaze searching the people working in the yard. "Mistress MacDougall!"

"I'm here," she shouted, as she hurried to him.

Beathan, Da's captain, tossed his pitchfork, jumped off the wagon next to the stables and strode toward them. Warriors darted from barracks lining the outer bailey walls. The blacksmith and his helpers stepped from their stall against the stone enclosure.

Bent over, hands on knees, the warrior panted. "Armed men…heading this way."

"English?" she asked.

He shook his head as he straightened. "Nay, Symon Fraser."

Her stomach plummeted. "Symon?"

"Aye, m'lady. Yer cousin's marching on MacDougall Castle."

She swallowed hard. When Da cast Symon out of the clan over a year ago, he threatened retribution. Apparently, the day to carry out his spiteful vengeance had arrived.

"How many?" Beathan asked.

4

The man raked his fingers through his road-dusted brown hair. "I don't rightly know. Dozens."

Men appeared in the stable's doorway, craning their necks to see the disturbance, while others from the guardhouse joined the growing throng.

Da hobbled from the mason's quarters. "How long before they get here?"

"Within the day, Laird."

Heather whirled around and addressed the crowd. "Bring the tenants and animals behind the walls. Beathan, organize the men to prepare for attack. Lock and secure the gates, and man the walks with archers."

The group dispersed, running in different directions.

Da grabbed her arm.

"Did ye get the vegetables picked?" Voice breathless, eyebrows raised, a long-lost light flickered in his old brown eyes.

"Aye, we got the last of them in."

"That's my lassie. Ye never know how long a siege will last." He patted her back and scuffled toward the armory, his face animated with the anticipation of battle.

Her chest squeezed. A glimpse of the father she had known resurfaced. How she'd missed that man. With his frequent confusion and random memory loss, his spirit had dimmed, and his eyes no longer sparkled with excitement. Guarding the secret of his illness, the weight of battle once again fell upon her shoulders.

She bolted to the stone stairs leading to the great hall. Beathan, her steadfast friend and confidant, met her midway up the steps. His bushy dark brows drew together over piercing grey eyes. Brown wavy hair, damp with sweat, brushed his broad shoulders. "We haven't finished work on the main gate. I don't know if it'll hold."

She rubbed her forehead. "If they break through, lower the portcullis and trap them before they reach the inner wall. We'll pick them off from the towers."

"Aye, we'll guard the inner passage."

An older woman with a worn brown cloak draped over her hunched shoulders, grasped the wooden railing with gnarled hands and struggled up the main stairs. Several young lads snaked past her and other residents hurrying into the great hall.

Heather wiped her face with the back of her sleeve and glanced at Beathan. "I'll secure the keep and see to the women and children before I join ye."

Da bustled through the yard toward the castle gates, strapping his sword around his waist.

Her shoulders sagged. She wanted to grab her father and safely sequester him inside the keep, but she could not prevent his participation. He was Laird. While the clan accepted her leadership within the castle walls, they would not understand Da's absence.

Beathan followed her gaze.

"Close the portals! Bar the gate!" Da jumped, kicking one foot in the air and throwing his knotted fist over his head. "We won't let the bastards in!"

"Please watch over him," she whispered.

"Ye know I will." Beathan gently squeezed her arm and ran to the tower.

Heather's mind raced as she dashed up the stairs. Would they be able to hold off Symon? How many men had he amassed? Chest heaving, she rushed into the great hall.

The MacDougalls' aging healer, Muire, sat at a long trestle table shelling peas with several women.

"Prepare for attack," Heather shouted. "Ready the keep!"

The women gasped, and Muire's head snapped up, her brown eyes wide. "Attack?"

Heather paused at the table. "Aye, Symon's leading a group of men to the castle."

"Oh, no." Muire and the women stood, peapods falling from their laps. Strands of white hair had escaped Muire's bun, sticking out at odd angles. "It's been so long since we've heard anything from him, I assumed his threat was mere words."

"Nay, he hasn't given up. Ye need to prepare for the wounded. I'm afraid we're in for a long night."

Heather

"I'll see to it straight away." The old healer headed toward the solar while serving women cleared the table of bowls filled with peas, discarded hulls and shells.

Heather ran down the dark narrow corridor off the main hall and entered the kitchen. Women cleaned worktables, grabbed trays, cooking utensils and linens, and hurried to storage. Heather caught a lad's arm as he raced past. "Tell the men to heat tar and pitch. We'll throw it over the walls and see how they like that."

The lad's blue eyes lit up, his head bobbing. "Aye, I'll take care of it," he replied, and ran from the room.

"Mistress Heather? What should we do with the vegetables?" A servant stood in the middle of the floor surrounded by baskets overflowing with freshly-picked turnips, leeks, and carrots.

"Store them in the stock rooms. And have someone bring in the containers from the courtyard."

With preparations underway, she ran up the stairs to her chamber. She lifted her gown over her head and dropped it on a chair in front of the cold hearth. How many times had she donned a man's clothing, bound her breasts, and prepared to fight for her clan?

She threw open the worn wooden chest at the foot of her bed. Her hand trembled as she gathered the long, cream-colored strip of linen folded on top of her brown trews and tan tunic. She slipped out of her soft chemise. It fluttered to the floor around her feet, and she went through the familiar ritual of wrapping lengths of material around her breasts. God willing, Symon's diabolical band would meet resistance as they never expected. She would lead the clan's fight to the death. They would never relent to her cousin's domination.

Heather slid into the trews and tossed the tunic over her head before securing her long blonde hair in a black scarf. She grabbed her sword off the bedside table and darted down the stairs.

Servants ushered inhabitants into the main hall. Children cried, clinging to their mothers. Several lasses arranged straw mattresses in rows while others deposited blankets and stoked the fire in the hearth.

Heather hurried out the front door and onto the landing at the top of the bailey stairs. Her sister, Lindsey, dressed in lad's trews with her auburn hair stuffed into a grey woolen cap, threw a rope around a horse's neck and led him through the confusion. "Bring the animals to the stables," she shouted over the noise.

Two lads coaxed cattle and sheep into the pens at the back of the bailey. Ducks and geese squawked and waddled through the crowd while panic-stricken residents flooded into the courtyard, dragging carts loaded with their belongings.

"Place yer things in the barn and gather in the great hall." Heather motioned for them to follow and took an old woman's elbow, trying to clear the area as men prepared for battle. She ushered her into the keep with anxious residents trailing behind.

~~~

Laird Alastair MacDougall marched down the ramparts and supervised men securing weapons, strapping swords and quivers to their backs. Lads ran from the blacksmith's quarters, arms loaded with bundles of arrows. They hurried to the warriors positioned along the walls and distributed the barbed shafts while others sharpened blades, dispensed flails and pikes.

Alastair and his men had worked long and hard, training for the inevitable day of defending MacDougall Castle. However, it never occurred to him he would be defending his home against Symon. His beloved wife would turn in her grave as her nephew waged a battle against her family.

He would keep Symon from breaking through their defenses. Why did he attack them? Alastair strained to evoke memories, but nothing came to mind. Why could he not remember?

His chest constricted. He feared the clan no longer respected his leadership. What would become of him? What would become of his people?

Heather

He swallowed past the lump in his throat. Thank God for his daughter. Heather was the son he never had. Already the men obeyed her as if she were laird. She and Beathan held the clan together, covering for his forgetfulness.

Tense hours passed while darkness descended. Torches, their flames shooting into the sky, lined the grey stone walls of the castle. With Beathan at his side, Alastair fingered the pommel of his sword. Watching. Waiting. His fingers wrapped around the hilt, the leather creaking. He would stand strong and prove he was as good a leader as he always had been.

He peered into the blackening night, the outline of trees barely visible against the moonless sky. They were out there—somewhere. "Symon waited until the cover of darkness."

Beathan stared through the arrow slits in the walls lining the battlements. "Aye, he's too cowardly to face us in the light of day."

Alastair looked at Beathan. "Do ye think Darach Graham rides with him?"

Beathan's head jerked toward Alastair. His forehead wrinkled and he paused. "Nay, Laird. Ye remember Darach passed away a while ago."

Alastair cringed before turning back to the loopholes. "Aye, I remember."

His eyes focused on the dark woods in front of the castle. How could he forget the neighbor he had been feuding with had died? He shook his head. That was when Robert Graham had kidnapped Alastair's daughter, Cameron. How could he forget the endless days and long nights he had worried over her?

*Beathan must think I've lost my mind.*

Alastair cleared his throat and pushed away from the wall. "I'll check on the men."

~~~

Wrought iron candelabras, nearly as tall as Heather, resembled sentries standing guard the way they were positioned around the great hall. She went about the room, and with trembling fingers, lit tallow candles in each of them until the room was aglow. "Rena, please hand out food and water, and perhaps some of yer sweet cakes."

"Aye, mistress," the elderly cook replied and ambled down the corridor leading to the kitchen.

Heather handed the torch to a lad. Dark smoke wafted from the spitting flame. "See to lighting any candles I might have missed."

The residents huddled around the hall. The normally boisterous and happy group stood quiet and somber. Mothers kept their children close and listened for sounds of battle. Children bunched next to their mother's legs, their innocent eyes wide with fright. Heather retrieved a blanket from a stack on the table and placed the warm quilt around a woman's shoulders.

"All will be well," she encouraged. She tried to smile, but her face was stiff and awkward. Praying she did not portray the fear welling inside her, she patted a small girl's back. "Stay close to yer mum."

Heather straightened and massaged her temples in slow circles. *Ye must step in and run the keep, help yer father lead the clan.* Mum's dying words echoed through her mind. Her shoulders slumped with the weighty responsibility.

"Mistress?"

Heather blinked.

A woman stood in front of her, wringing her hands.

Heather put a hand on the woman's forearm. "I'm sorry, I didn't hear ye. What were ye saying?"

"Rena's honey cakes are ready. Did ye want me to pass them out?"

Frightened faces and blank wide-eyed stares peered at Heather. "Aye, see the children each get one. Mayhap the treats will help take their minds off what's to come."

~~~

In the dead of night, flaming arrows shot over the walls and ignited fires within the bailey. Hooks from scaling ladders flew over the battlements and clanked against the crenels, fastening to the stone structure.

10

# Heather

Symon's men stormed the outer walls and battered the main door with massive logs. The wooden gate heaved and splintered with each resounding *boom!* The sound reverberated through Heather's ears. They must be stopped.

She scurried up the steep grey stairway, her legs aching, her breathing labored. Her toe caught a step and she stumbled. Her knee smacked the rough rock. Pain shot through her leg and tears stung her eyes. She rubbed her shin and scrambled up the remaining treads.

Men lined the ramparts, their arrows fixed on targets beyond the castle. She peered around a crenel. There must be a hundred men. Oh Lord, like ants on a mound, they ran from all directions. How had Symon amassed such a large following? She and her archers must take out the villainous procession before Symon managed to break through their defenses.

Legs set apart, she stood on the granite ramparts surrounding the top of the castle. She jerked an arrow from the quiver on her back and nocked it. Her right hand tugged the string taunt. The bow creaked. Her other hand dropped lower with her eyes trained on the barb pointed at the throng.

MacDougall arrows pelted the attacker's, but the fiends held their shields high and the futile blows bounced off the raised armor.

She swung the dart to the right. A hefty man with blond hair rushed the front gate.

*Symon!*

She aimed at him, but he threw a shield over his head. She couldn't take the shot. "Damn!"

The group hammered the worn door with a battering ram. Frantically, she searched the crowd seeking an opportunity to dispatch the men, but the attackers' armored shields protected their heads and bodies.

Men's frenzied shouts from inside the bailey rose. "Bar the doors!"

Her shaking aim veered left to a burly man cloaked in animal skins. His fist gripped a mace over his head as he roared a battle cry and charged up the hill to the bridge. The squeak of wood sounded in her ear. Her chest expanded with rapid

11

breaths. Pain burned her right arm, the tension of her bow resisting her grasp.

She waited for the right moment. Sweat trickled down the middle of her back. She relaxed her fingers and her arrow whistled through the air.

*Sfit!*

The barb struck her target's chest. He dropped the mace and clutched the protruding shaft before crumpling to the ground.

She reached over her shoulder, grabbed another arrow and nocked it. She swung left. With shields knocked aside, an opening cleared. Now was her chance to staunch the men storming the castle. Her right arm pulled the string tight, her burning muscles straining, shaking.

*Sfit!*

The shank protruded from the man's gut. He lost his hold on the battering ram and grasped at the arrow. Elation soared through her body. She nocked another and sent it flying into his partner. The man screamed and grabbed the dart protruding from his neck.

MacDougall archers rained barbs into the onslaught, the arrows jutting from their attackers like porcupine quills. Where was Symon? He had disappeared in the melee. She yearned to sink her arrow into his chest. If only she had managed to get a shot off at him earlier, perhaps she could have slowed their progress.

Frantic shouts ascended from the bailey. She leaned over the ramparts and studied the ground below. Lads, sloshing water from their buckets, ran through the courtyard to extinguish blazes, while men worked to reinforce the main gate.

Several struggled with containers of hot oily tar. "Grab that side, and we'll hoist it over the wall," a man yelled.

It took three to maneuver the cumbersome barrel. Struggling with the heavy caldron, they dumped the scalding dark pitch over the side, drenching the men scaling the walls. Painful screams rent the air as attackers dropped from the ladders.

"It worked," a man shouted.

Another threw his fist in the air. "We got 'em!"

"Hurry, we've got more barrels." Two men ran to retrieve another tub.

"Over here, bring it down the line," Beathan shouted, waving and motioning. "They're trying to get over the top."

The men inched across the rampart.

"One…two…three!"

They dumped the barrel, once again drenching men with the scalding, sticky tar.

Heather peered through the stone crenellations at the horrific scene beyond the gates. Wounded and bleeding men helplessly exposed, cried in pain. Flames from grass fires flickered, turning into a blaze upon reaching the spilled tar. Men covered in the black pitch screamed in agony, rolling in the grass, desperate to remove the burning substance. Bodies with protruding arrows littered the ground.

Symon's uninjured men scattered and fled into the dark woods.

She hurried down the narrow staircase and into the outer bailey. Smoke billowed from the servants' quarters and flames shot out of the chapel windows. She held her sleeve against her nose and ran to access the damage.

Beathan accounted for the MacDougalls. "Six men injured and two dead."

Her chest clenched. "Two dead?"

"Aye, mistress, Gabriel and Thom."

"Oh, no." Both men, still in their prime, had wives and young children. What a tragic loss.

"The gate held, but it's damaged. I don't know if it'll last much longer," a man reported.

"Enough! We can't let the bastards in!" Da shook uncontrollably, his eyes wide. He grabbed a fist full of his grey hair. "We can't let them in!"

Heather clutched his arm. "Da."

His confused eyes turned to her.

"We'll handle the problems—one at a time."

He searched her face, and his arms dropped. His frame sagged, and she embraced his hunched shoulders. Oh, Da. His illness accentuated frustration and irrational behavior. Her heart cleaved in two. Her strong, robust father was now a weak, feeble old man.

"Fergus, organize a group to reinforce the gate," Beathan shouted over the noise. "Randall, get more tar. John, replenish the weapons and —"

"Fire! Help!" Frantic screams interrupted Beathan. Flames shot out of the stables, leaping high into the dark sky.

Heather ran to the trough. She grabbed a wooden bucket off the stack next to the barn, filled it with water and hurried into the stables. Horses shrieked, their eyes wide and nostrils flared. Lindsey and several boys frantically beat the flames with heavy blankets. Heather emptied her bucket, having little effect on the hot fire.

A blazing beam hurtled to the ground, cutting off access to the horses. Heather jerked on a wooden gate, but a log wedged against it and held it closed. Flames leapt up around her, the heat on her face scorching. Sweat trickled down her temple. Her heart pounded. She kicked the timber and yanked on the door. Splinters tore into her hands, but the gate wouldn't budge.

"I've got to get the horses out," Lindsey hollered, and jumped onto the wooden enclosure and scrambled across stalls to reach the animals.

"Are ye mad? Ye'll get trampled." Heather couldn't let her younger sister do this by herself. She hoisted herself on top of the railing and followed Lindsey.

Her foot slipped.

She sucked in air and flung her arms to the side for balance. The rickety timber wobbled, swaying under her feet, threatening to crumble at any moment.

Just a few more steps…

Flames licked at her, singeing her trews. The burn seared her calf, and she slapped her leg, then leapt from stall to stall and onto the dirt floor.

"Unlatch the gates!" Lindsey yelled over the noise.

Breathing hard, Heather grabbed one of the wooden doors and flipped up the bolt. The gate swung wide and several

14

horses ran into the open corral. Coughing, she hurried to the next stall and freed more animals.

Lindsey scrambled to the center of the pen. Throwing a cloth over a horse's head, she sprang onto his back and dug her heels into his sides. He lurched forward, and she steered him to the back of the barn, bursting through the doorway.

Heather wrenched open another worn gate for more panicked animals and jumped to the side as the horses' massive bodies collided with each other. Frantic to flee the burning building, the animals' powerful hooves churned the dirt floor.

Several men yanked busted wooden slats and enlarged a gap in the damaged stable wall. Heather grasped a horse's halter. The beast reared, the rope cutting into her hands.

"Whoa. Easy there." A thick course cloth draped the wooden fence. She snatched it and threw it over the frightened animal's eyes, then hauled him to the back of the stables toward the opening. Jerking the fabric off, she slapped the large animal's rump, and he bolted. Her rope-burned fingers stung and she rubbed her sore hands against her trews.

Timbers creaked and groaned as blazing embers and debris fell around her. It was only a matter of time before the structure collapsed. Choking on thick, pungent smoke, she waved her hand in front of her face and searched for trapped horses. Tears blinded her, and she wiped her eyes with the back of her sleeve. Another look—all the animals were free from their stalls but frantically bolting around the paddock.

Lindsey ran back in and grabbed another horse's halter. He reared and backed up, dragging her sister across the dirt floor. Lindsey hung on as a lad ran to help. He threw a covering over the beast's head, seized the bridle, and Lindsey sprang onto its back. The boy slapped the animal's hindquarters, and her sister and the horse lurched through the opening the men had cleared.

Burning debris floated in the air, the smoke gagging. Pulse racing, Heather swiped her forearm across her eyes and scrambled onto the wooden railing. She climbed across a downed beam and dropped onto another horse. Her legs trembled as she dug her heels into his sides and steered him to the back of the barn. They burst through the opening, leading dozens of horses racing out around them. Black smoke billowed from the barn as men rushed to extinguish the flames.

Coughing, Lindsey coaxed the large warhorses to the back of the bailey.

Heather followed. "Are ye all right?"

"Aye, h–help me get them to safety."

Fergus and three lads were corralling the beasts into a makeshift pen when a resounding crash reverberated through the bailey. Distraught, Heather turned and watched the barn crumble to the ground.

A screaming war cry rent the air.

*Oh Lord, what more can we endure?*

# Chapter Two

*Near Kilmarnock, Scotland*

Images of the bloody battle played out beneath a moonless sky. Flaming arrows rained upon the exposed Scots, their battered shields no longer protective. Mutilated limbs and disfigured corpses blackened from fire mingled with animal carcasses. Visions of mangled and burned bodies littering the field seared Alec Campbell's mind, while the quiet stillness of the night failed to extinguish the howls and pleas of the dying.

He lay on a pallet, arm pillowing his head, staring into the vast darkness dotted with stars. The cold, hard ground against his back was a strange solace, an anchor reminding him of his survival.

*Falkirk.*

Only a city name, but one that inflicted terror, sadness, and determination in his troops. His men had fought gallantly to defend their homeland against the English, but hadn't stood a chance against Edward's archers.

Vengeance coursed through his body. He lost many good men that July day. Slaughtered. Their deaths would not go unpunished. His warriors would regroup, and like the mythological phoenix, they would emerge stronger than before.

A shrill whistle broke the silence. He jerked up on his elbow.

A horse galloped into the clearing. His captain, Eric, jumped to the ground and strode toward him. "Fire's coming from the MacDougall's."

Alec rolled to his feet. "Soldiers?"

"Can't say, but flames are shooting high over the castle."

Alec buckled his sword belt around his waist. "Mount up!"

His men scattered, stuffing sleeping blankets into their satchels and securing their belongings.

Alec wrapped his brown woolen cloak around his shoulders and strode to his horse, his breath a fog in the cool night air. He swung onto Aeton's back. "Kilmarnock is too far west for Edward's men to attack. It makes no sense."

Eric stepped into the stirrup and settled on the saddle. "Nay, but it's just like the scum to strike in the middle of the night."

"Let's ride. Stay alert." Alec led his men out of the clearing and onto a dirt road. The dark night did little to assist their journey. His tired eyes tried to focus on bleary shapes through the trees. Smoke hit his nostrils. He kicked Aeton into a gallop. God willing, they would arrive in time to aid the MacDougalls.

Red and orange flames leapt into the sky, dark plumes billowing from the burnt structures. Bodies lay scattered across the ground, arrows protruding from their lifeless forms. Cries from those still alive filled the bitter, choking air. Memories of Falkirk flashed before his eyes. Warriors, wounded and bleeding, begged for death to come quickly.

His gaze darted through the carnage for surviving marauders anxious to attack him and his men. Who were these assailants? The ragtag band of ruffians and dark skinned swarthy giants were cloaked in animal skins.

A stout iron-grilled portcullis blocked the entrance to the castle. Alec peered through the bars. Dozens battled within. The piercing clank of steel against steel rang out as clashing swords collided. A slender lad ran across the ramparts, firing arrows into the bailey. A man hoisted himself onto the battlements and took one of the boy's barbs in the chest, falling head first over the wall. The lad turned and shot another in the throat—his aim excellent.

"Open the gates," Alec shouted as Aeton pranced with excitement. "'Tis the Laird of Glencara. We bring aid."

Alastair MacDougall and Alec's father were lifelong friends, the two clans strong allies. He hoped the lad recognized him.

The boy peered around the crenels, his eyes narrowing on Alec. The black scarf around his head matched the soot smearing his face.

"Raise the gate," the lad called, his voice nay deeper than a lass's.

# Heather

A man charged the boy. "Look out," Alec shouted.

The lad turned at the last minute and ducked as the enemy swung at him. The attacker's force propelled him forward. He slipped, and the boy rammed his elbow into his foe's back, shoving him off the wall. The man yelled, his arms flailing wildly as he pitched over the side.

Heavy chains grated as the MacDougalls tugged on ropes, raising the heavy metal door, spikes at the bottom inching up little by little. Alec charged under the gate and into the bailey. He jumped from Aeton and onto the back of a brute attacking a boy clad in the rough garments of a stable hand. Alec dragged his dagger across the fiend's thick neck. The assailant fell to his knees, and Alec kicked him to the ground.

The boy nodded then ducked another strike.

Why were these men attacking the MacDougalls? Many wore dark furs, matted and dirty. Their filthy faces and unwashed bodies were smeared with soot and grime.

A snarling bellow sounded from behind, and Alec spun toward the noise. A man yelled and charged, his lips pulled back over blackened and rotting teeth. He brought down his sword, aimed at Alec's head. Alec thrust his blade to block the strike.

"Umph!" Vibrations rippled down his arms. His grasp on the hilt slipped, but he managed to knock his adversary's weapon to the side. Grip restored, he swung, slicing the animal pelt covering the swine's chest. Blood spewed from the wound and the man dropped his weapon. Eyes wide, he grabbed his torso before crumbling to the ground.

Smoke caused Alec's eyes to water as his gaze swept the fighting. The lad from the ramparts swung his sword, both hands gripping the hilt. His blade knocked the weapon from the hand of a man twice the lad's size. The lad's backward swing of his sword slashed across his enemy's abdomen. Blood and entrails oozed from the gash.

A beefy opponent roared, advancing toward Alec. He deflected the blow and sidestepped the assailant. The challenger's momentum drove him forward. Alec swung around and smashed the back of the man's skull.

Alec ran through the smoke-choked bailey, searching for Laird MacDougall. Across the yard, his father's friend struggled to fight an opponent half his age. The old laird fell and hit the hard ground. The enemy raised his sword, the sharp blade poised to kill. Alec couldn't reach MacDougall in time.

The young lad suddenly appeared in front of his laird. The boy swung left, then right. The attacker backed, holding his blade high to deflect the blows. The boy grasped the hilt with both hands and thrust it. The assailant stumbled, the lad gaining the upper hand. But when another joined the assault, the lad was outmatched.

Alec raced behind the young warrior. "Put yer back to mine!"

The boy jumped behind Alec.

Two fur covered monsters advanced. "Come on, mon. Ye'd best give it up. Ye have nay chance," one of the aggressors taunted. The other laughed. The men lunged in unison.

With both hands clamped around his sword's hilt, Alec deflected their blows. The muscles in his shoulders and arms tightened, burning. He swung his blade, knocking one miscreant into the other. When one of the men stumbled, Alec's sword pierced his gut. Alec snarled, jerked his dagger from his belt and sank it into the other's neck.

After wrenching his blade free, he and the lad circled together as one.

"Oomph," the boy blew out and reeled against Alec's back.

He pushed away from him. Alec spared a glance over his shoulder. The lad was too agile for the heavier attackers. He dodged and weaved, tiring them, then bore down, driving them back with determined strokes.

One of the men caught Alec off guard. Alec jumped back, but the man managed to hit his chest. God's blood that was close. A burn spread down his torso and blood seeped through his shirt. "Ye whoreson!"

With a strong thrust, Alec plunged his blade into his opponent's gut. His chest's stinging laceration was a constant reminder of his unforgiving inattention.

Heather

The fight ended abruptly. Alec turned to the lad, but he was nowhere in sight. His chest pinched with sudden protectiveness. He searched the carnage, afraid he'd find the young boy lying amongst the bodies.

He squinted against the acrid smoke and wiped a dirty sleeve across his face. Alastair's captain held the lad by the shoulders. Thank God. The lad pulled away, twirled his dagger between his fingers and stuffed it in his scabbard. Alec couldn't hear what was said, but the boy shook his head and ran into the keep.

"Owww," Alastair emitted a growl as he struggled to sit up.

Alec knelt beside the old laird, whose sweaty, grey hair lay plastered to his head. Streaks of dirt traversed his wrinkled face, droplets sliding down his stubbled cheeks. Blood soaked his tunic, and his dark eyes squinted from pain.

"Laird MacDougall?"

Alastair's weathered forehead creased.

"I'm Alec Campbell. Ye might not remember me, but I'm Grant Campbell's son."

Alastair's eyes narrowed. "Why would ye think I didn't remember?"

Alec stiffened at his sharp tone, but given the circumstances, considered it understandable. "No reason other than I doubt ye were expecting to see my face tonight."

Alastair's captain dropped next to them. "Laird? Are ye all right?"

"'Tis but a wee scratch."

Alec looked from one to the other. "What was this about? Who were those men?"

"It was Symon." Alastair's face scrunched, his breath short. "I—I don't know what was wrong with him."

Alec frowned. "Yer wife's nephew?"

Beathan grasped Alastair's arm and looked at Alec. "Last year, Symon attacked the Graham clan, and the laird banished him." He turned to Alastair. "Let's get ye inside so Muire can tend ye."

21

"I'll take him." Alec leaned forward and placed his arm around Alastair then lifted him to his feet. A burning pain shot through Alec's abdomen. Damn bastard got him better than he first thought. Thick wetness dribbled down his torso and gathered on his tunic.

What was Symon thinking? Did he hope to kill Alastair and take over the castle? Blood poured from the old man's side, soaking his dirty, tattered shirt. He groaned, and his sagging body leaned on Alec. The laird's grimaced face grew pastier, his breath laboring with every step.

Sweat dribbled through Alec's hair and slid down his face. He shoved his shoulder under Alastair's armpit, providing more support for the aging laird and dragged the hefty man's dead weight to the stairs. They made their way up the long flight of steps and into the main hall, Alec all but carrying the man.

The wounded had been placed on tables lining the room. Several lads brought in makeshift beds for the overflow. Men stretched out—many bleeding, suffering severe wounds. Women weaved between straw mattresses, arms full of linens. Other servants ran with buckets of water, and an older man stoked the fire in the massive hearth.

Alec maneuvered the crowd, guiding Alastair to a table against the wall. He grasped the man's torso and eased him down on a nearby pallet. The laird groaned, and his sooty, sweat-streaked face strained as he clutched his side.

The old healer frowned as she ran a hand over his thinning hair. "What shame and disgrace Symon has brought upon ye."

"I'll leave ye to treat him while I help Beathan." Alec straightened in time to see a woman glide down the stairs and into the great hall. When a servant touched the woman's arm, the lass quickly swept something off her head. Beautiful, blonde tresses fell around her shoulders and down her back.

*Heather.*

His chest constricted. How long had it been since he last saw her? Three years? Would she remember him? Would she remember his kiss?

## Heather

The maid rubbed her mistress' cheek, and Heather wiped the same spot with a cloth. When the servant nodded, Heather hurried toward him.

Did she stuff a black scarf in her sleeve? His eyes narrowed.

"Laird Campbell, welcome to MacDougall Castle." She extended a hand. "Yer timing could not have been better."

"Mistress MacDougall." He bent and placed a kiss on her knuckles. Calluses covered her once soft palm. He straightened and studied her blue eyes. "Why so formal?"

"It's been years since we last met. I'm afraid that young lass ye knew grew up."

The gorgeous azure depths of her eyes mesmerized him. "Aye, she grew into a beautiful woman."

A flush spread over her cheeks and she withdrew her hand. "I understand we've ye to thank for our lives."

"One of yer da's men—a young lad—is who ye should thank. He saved Laird MacDougall from certain death."

Something akin to caution flittered across her eyes. Had he not been watching closely, he would've missed it.

She crossed her arms over her waist. "My da's fortunate to have many good men defending the castle." Her eyes widened, and she reached out. "Ye're hurt. Forgive me, I didn't notice."

Alec caught her hand and rubbed her skin with the pad of his thumb. "'Tis nothing to worry over."

"If ye'll permit me, I'll tend ye and yer men so ye can be on yer way. I'm sure ye're anxious to return home."

Was she eager to be rid of him?

He hesitated. "We are ready to be home, but we'll repair yer keep first."

Her back stiffened. When she smiled, it didn't quite reach her lovely eyes. "Thank ye. If ye will excuse me, I need to see to Da."

"I understand."

Heather slipped past him. Her hips swayed as she stepped around a lass carrying blankets and hurried through the hall to her father.

Alec exhaled and raked a hand through his hair. He was needed out-of-doors. Rubbing the stinging cut on his chest, he marched past the injured. As he strode down the grey steps and into the bailey, his thoughts turned to the slender lad with the black scarf.

Why did he feel something was amiss? Why was the lad spirited away? And why did Heather make light of his fighting?

~~~

Heather rushed toward Da, her pulse racing. The effect of battle on her nerves paled in comparison to the feelings Alec invoked. Her hands trembled as she smoothed the fabric of her soft woolen gown over her stomach. This was the first time she had seen him since his father's accident and the rampant rumors surrounding the attack on Glencara Castle had reached her ears.

He had changed. Years of battle had honed his muscular body. Slight creases etched the corners of his penetrating grey eyes. With braids on either side of his face, his brown shaggy hair skimmed his broad shoulders. Dark whiskers covered his strong jaw and swept his upper lip.

She still felt his solid back—a wall of protection— against hers. How she wished things were different. How she longed to turn to him and ask for help, but the rumors could not be ignored. Many men voiced their opinions on how the unexpected raid on Glencara had enabled Alec to conveniently step into the Laird's role. Where was he during the onslaught? Was it true he had instigated the attack, then was not there to defend the clan?

She sighed and shook her head to clear her thoughts, then quickened her steps, anxious to see how Da fared.

Heather gasped at the deep gash in her father's side. Blood dripped from the wound and onto the floor. He was quickly fading. She grabbed a cloth and held it firmly against his injury. He moaned, and his head rolled from side to side. Sweat trickled down his drawn face, and he grimaced.

# Heather

Muire brushed her white hair back with her forearm and began threading a needle. "Clean around the cut, then I'll stitch it closed."

Heather snatched a cloth and bowl from one of the side tables and ran to the large stone fireplace. Flames licked the bottom of a pot suspended by the swing bar. She scooped a ladleful of water into her bowl and hurried back to Da.

She dipped the cloth in the water, then dabbed at the grime. The grunge tugged his skin, and her nose wrinkled in sympathy. Despite her attempt to be gentle, his eyes scrunched and sweat dribbled down the side of his face. Patting the moisture dry she whispered, "I'm sorry, Da. I didn't mean to hurt ye, but I needed to remove dirt around the wound."

His head shook. "'Tis all right, lassie."

Muire leaned over him. "Now, Laird, this will pinch a bit." She spoke softly as she began the task of sewing his ragged flesh together. "A few more stitches, and I'll leave ye to rest."

Moments later, she straightened and addressed Heather. "Take the brown leaves I set out, and crush them in a small amount of water. It will make a sticky poultice ye can spread on his side. I'll prepare a potion to alleviate his pain."

Heather grabbed a bowl off the table against the wall. She made the salve and applied the tacky mixture to his wound.

Muire handed Heather a mug containing the pain draught. "Get him to drink this if ye can. I'll check on him shortly."

She wiped her hands on a cloth and turned to treat the man lying next to Da.

Heather slipped a hand under her father's damp head and helped him raise it. She held the concoction to his cracked lips. "This should help ye." He managed to swallow the contents, and she laid him back down. "Try to rest."

She gently dabbed his face again with the cloth. He caught her hand, holding it tight. His tired brown eyes drooped, and his pale face strained with pain. "Lassie, I'm all right. See to the others."

Heather hesitated before she patted his weathered hand and nodded. "Verra well."

A pitiful cry, followed by a shriek, bellowed behind her. She swung to the sound. Young William, with an arrow lodged in his shoulder, struggled against two men.

"Nay, nay!" His pleas fell on deaf ears. They held him down while another man broke the shaft. He raised a mallet and slammed the broken end, thrusting the barb through the lad's thin shoulder.

Bile billowed into her throat and threatened to spill. She ran to him and wrapped her arms around the boy, cradling his head while he sobbed. "Oh Will, I'm so sorry," she whispered.

"It had to be done, mistress," one of the men said, shaking his head. "We had to remove the arrow."

"Aye, John, I know."

Will's head rolled into the crook of her arm. The poor lad had passed out. Her throat clogged with emotion.

Why had Symon done such a terrible thing? Hatred filled her soul. He had inflicted pain and suffering on innocent people who never caused him harm.

"Tis guid he's oot. This'll hurt." Another man poured a small amount of whisky into the opening.

Will's eyes flew open, and he screeched, his torso rising from the table. Heather grasped his shoulders, and held her head against his dark hair. "Shhh, hold on lad."

"It'll have ta do til Muire can tend it," John said.

Sobs shook the lad's body as she eased her grip and stroked his cheek's still soft baby skin. William was so small, but he fought bravely. Pallets lining the room held many injured men. *All* had fought bravely. Her stomach roiled. What senseless destruction.

She couldn't let the clan down with useless emotions. Trying to gain control of herself, she inhaled and smoothed William's hair. She prayed they had fatally wounded Symon. He did not deserve to live. Given the opportunity, she would ensure he suffered retribution for his actions. After tucking a blanket over William's shoulder, she stood and turned toward Muire who was tending one of Da's warriors.

26

Heather

The healer tied a sling around the man's broken arm. "Keep this in place, and be careful not to move it."

He grimaced and held his injured arm while awkwardly tugging on his shirt back on.

"Let me help ye." Heather eased the tunic over his blood-encrusted shoulder, careful not to scrape his red aggravated wounds.

Muire stretched her back, wrinkles lining her weathered face. "After Will, I believe that will take care of the last of them."

Heather nodded. "He caught an arrow in his shoulder."

"Poor dear." Muire shuffled to the boy and once again, threaded her needle.

Heather mixed another bowl of salve for Will and placed it on the table with more force than intended. Fury gushed through her body, and she trembled. "Did anyone see what happened to Symon? Did we get him?"

"He wasn't in the yard after the fighting ended."

Heather whirled around at Beathan's words. "He got away?"

The captain strode over to her. "I'm afraid so."

She exhaled loudly through her nose. "Post lookouts. I would not put it past him to return."

Beathan paused, hands on hips. "Laird Campbell has already seen to it."

Heather stared at him. "He did?"

"Aye, he has everything under control."

She grabbed his arm. "We *do not want* him to have everything under control. He and his men must leave." Alec discovering the clan's vulnerabilities was the last thing she needed.

"But they'll help us rebuild. With so many wounded, we need them."

"I don't care. Don't ye see? If Alec Campbell gets wind of Da's problem, he'll take over, or worse yet, others will hear and MacDougall Castle will be swarming with miscreants. I need not remind ye of what happened when I placed my trust in Richard's hands."

"Nay, I remember well enough." Beathan's shoulders sagged, and he rubbed the back of his neck. "I'll have the men to do what they can to hurry the repairs along." He strode from the room.

Alec was inquisitive about the young warrior. She would have to be on guard. It had been three long years since she last saw him. While at that time she felt she could confide in him, she had been fooled before. After her former betrothed blindsided her and attempted to use her to advance his holdings, she learned she could only place her trust in a select few inside her clan. Many opportunists sided with the English, pillaging and conquering their neighbors. No, she would not be deceived again.

After seeing the residents cared for, Heather stepped into the bailey. Her muscles ached, and tension racked her tired body. Hands on her lower back, she stretched. Light touched her face as the sun peaked over the horizon sending splays of red streaking across the morning sky—a beautiful backdrop ironically displaying heartrending destruction.

Smoke wafted in the cool morning breeze, white plumes curling over charred remains. Most of Lindsey's stables lay in ruins. The once sturdy timber structure consisted of blackened and scorched sticks rising out of ashes and debris. Bitter steam drifted past her nose. Men picked through the rubble, salvaging what they could.

Lindsey slowly climbed the stairs and embraced Heather. She stepped back, holding Heather's hands. "How's Da?"

"I don't know. He was badly wounded. Muire tended him, and the men took him to his chamber. I'm hoping he'll rest and that fever doesn't set in."

"Heather?"

She turned at Alec's deep voice. He marched up the stairs.

"I cannot thank ye enough for yer help," she said.

"I'm glad we were camped close by."

Fresh blood seeped through his shirt. He had to be in pain. "Please come in the hall and let me tend yer wound."

28

Heather

Blake snatched his cap off his head and stepped beside Lindsey. "The horses are skittish, but they'll be all right."

"Thank ye." Lindsey hooked her arm through her friend's. "Let's get something to eat. It's been a long night."

Heather and Alec climbed the stairs with Lindsey and Blake following. She steered Alec between the pallets of injured to a table in front of the large hearth and patted the worn oak surface. "Sit and let me see to yer cut."

Alec leaned against the table and tugged his tunic over his head.

Her breath caught. His massive chest and muscular arms gleamed in the candlelight. Dark hair traversed his rippled bronze torso and the brown circles encasing his nipples. A ragged laceration crossed his chest. The red, aggravated wound was not deep, but dried blood mixed with dirt smeared the injury.

Suddenly realizing she ogled him, she swallowed and blinked. She must compose herself. What must he think of her gawking?

Clearing her throat, she grabbed a cloth off the table, dipped it in the water basin next to him and tried to concentrate on cleaning the gash. Her fingers trembled, and her insides tightened at the feel of his warm smooth skin. As if she had consumed too much ale, a tingling flush spread through her body.

"I missed ye." His deep voice rumbled in his chest.

Her fingers stilled. "I missed ye, too." With her gaze focused on his wound, she wiped more dried blood off his massive chest. "I've been worried about ye."

"Have ye now?"

"Aye, I have." She glimpsed a twinkle in his eyes. His look caused the sides of her mouth to turn up of their own accord. He was so handsome. She longed to bend forward and place her lips on his grin. Instead, she dried the cut. Thankfully, it was not severe, but she applied some of Muire's poultice to ward off fever.

Heat radiated off his naked skin, and she restrained from running her palms over the sculpted muscle. Her stomach

29

flipped over like a young lass's, full of excitement. But other than for this fleeting moment, that delightful feeling was not meant for her future. If she could not protect the clan, she would be forced to marry. Too many disreputable land-seeking miscreants would love the chance to acquire MacDougall lands.

She took a deep breath and exhaled while wiping the excess ointment off her hands. "I'll wrap this linen around ye to keep the cut clean and stop the bleeding."

Alec held his arms over his head, and she moved closer. The warmth of his body seeped into her as she wrapped the material around him. If only she could lean into him, absorb his strength, encase herself in his strong embrace. If only she had her life to do with as she wanted.

~~~

Heather was more beautiful than Alec remembered. She snipped the cloth and tied the ends of the bandage. Candlelight reflected golden strands in her hair. She had changed since he last saw her—a few years older, more alluring and poised. As with all Scots, she had experienced her share of sadness.

He touched her shoulder until she raised her head. "I'm sorry for the loss of yer mum."

Her melancholy gaze dropped. "It's hard to believe it's been two years. I miss her terribly."

"I've no doubt ye do. She was a lovely lady."

Heather stroked the binding and quickly changed the subject. "There, all done. Sit here and rest while I fetch ye something to eat."

She gathered the soiled cloth and water basin off the table, and hurried to the kitchen. Alec enjoyed the sway of her hips as he dropped his tunic over his head.

Eric stepped beside him and plopped onto a bench next to the table. "She's a bonny lass."

Alec stroked his scratchy beard as she disappeared down the hall. "She is that."

"I thought ye were heading home to yer betrothed?"

Alec's head jerked toward his captain's grinning face. "Ye know I do not wish to discuss Robena—or my betrothal."

"I do." Eric nodded. "But ye'll have to face it sooner or later, my friend."

Alec's eyes narrowed. Damn Eric. Always bringing up subjects Alec would rather let lie. "All is secured?"

Eric leaned back against the table and stretched his legs. "There's a good bit of work to be done, but the gate is in place for now."

Alec paused. "We'll stay until we can shore up their defenses, though I don't think Symon will be back any time soon."

Heather entered the main hall carrying a tray of food and ale. She paused to speak to a servant while balancing the serving dish on her hip. Her hand tucked an errant wheat-colored lock behind her ear, and a smile broke across her face, lighting her blue eyes. How he longed for her to smile at him that way.

As if she heard his thoughts, she lifted her head, and their gazes met. His pulse strummed in his ears, and his chest clenched. Why did she have such an effect on him? She said something to the servant and started toward the table where he sat with Eric.

She placed bowls of hot frumenty in front of them. "This should fill yer stomachs."

"Ahh, it looks good." Eric shoveled the creamy thick porridge into his mouth.

Alec took the offered bowl. "Thank ye." When she turned, he asked, "Won't ye join us?"

"I've already eaten." She stacked dirty utensils and tankards on her tray. "We have plenty so eat yer fill. If ye'll excuse me, I'll have rooms and baths readied for ye before I retire. It has been a long night."

Alec touched her arm. "Thank ye again."

She stared at his hand before lifting her gaze back to his face. "Ye're welcome. Let me know if ye need anything."

Alec could not take his attention off the lass while she checked on inhabitants in the main hall. She handed her tray to a servant before stooping next to a small lad and hugging him. The youngster's mother sat beside him and took Heather's hand. Heather smiled at the two before she stood and moved to the next person.

She genuinely cared for the MacDougall clan and tried to bolster their spirits. The effects of Symon's attack were devastating, but the MacDougalls remained resilient, vowing to rebuild and reinforce the structures of the keep. Heather shouldered a great responsibility, but she appeared to thrive on it.

His thoughts turned to Robena, and his gut twisted. How he wished he had not promised to marry her. *She will make a good match for the clan.* Da's words still echoed through his mind.

Everything Alec did was for the good of his clan. He had trained under the best warriors, learning to defend Glencara. He fought many hard battles in the name of freedom for his people—anything to atone for his indiscretions.

Could he ever make amends with his conscience?

He closed his eyes. *No.* Each time he saw his da's lifeless legs, the events of that day resurfaced. So when Da insisted he wed Robena, Alec had agreed. After all, he vowed he would never give his heart to a woman, so it didn't matter that he wasn't fond of her. However, after seeing Heather again, that promise haunted him.

~~~

Heather slipped inside her chamber, relishing the quiet solitude. She leaned against the door, her thoughts on Alec. She inhaled, remembering his male scent of leather and ale, his smile and the crinkles around his eyes, the dimples in his bearded cheeks.

Her pulse quickened. Although soot, ashes and blood splattered him from head to toe, his handsome face unnerved her. She had never met a man who made her feel the way Alec did.

She relived running her hands over his muscular chest. It had been difficult to keep from sliding her palms across his brawny shoulders, along his massive arms. She swallowed hard, envisioning the dark hair tapering down his taut abdomen, disappearing into his trews. Her breathing grew shallow imaging his hands on her. Remembering the kiss they'd once shared.

She dropped her head back against the door. Such thoughts only tortured her. Last night she had run away from him as if he scorched her with his eyes, his touch. What was she fleeing?

A dream she could never have. She would never surrender her heart to another man. Not after Richard ripped it from her chest and planted humiliation deep into the pit of her stomach.

She had been a fool to believe his words of admiration, his praise over her idea to better prepare the women of the keep to defend themselves. Wanting to surprise him, she had slipped into the back of the barn to wait while he spoke to his men. Had she not stretched out amongst the bales of hay and listened, she never would have guessed his intentions. But that fateful afternoon, he had revealed his true feelings. *What man would want a wife who wields a sword and masters the bow? Once I'm ensconced in the clan, I'll simply shove her aside.*

His men's laughter still rang through her ears.

Heather pushed away from the door and stoked the fire in the hearth. She sank in a chair. Bracing her forearms on her thighs, she stared into the flames.

Lowrens McLaughlin had shown interest in MacDougall Castle for quite some time. On more than one occasion, he had mentioned joining their clans. She shook her head. Mum had promised she and her sisters would not be forced to marry, they would have a say in who they wed. Well, if she died an old maid, it would be better than marrying a man she didn't like.

Determined to protect her father and the clan, she would continue to secretly lead the men on assignments for the rebellion. She would not let MacDougall Castle succumb to pressure from McLaughlin. At the first sign of Da's condition, Lowrens would descend upon them, overthrow her father and force her to marry him, securing the clan for himself.

Greedy men eyed MacDougall lands and more than one worked to convince Da to marry her off to them. She refused to wed an old laird or a man she did not care for. Not to mention, her da needed her here. He relied on her and she would not let him or the clan down. She prayed the prying eyes would not discover his forgetfulness or the clan's vulnerability.

If only she knew Alec better. At one time, she trusted him without question, but many months with tragic circumstances had passed since she last saw him. Rumors circulated over his reckless words, an insult to a rival clan. After inciting an attack, he couldn't be found to defend his father's castle. His absence caused his people to suffer a severe blow, his da crippled.

Disquiet seeped into the corner of her heart. If his own clan could not trust him, how could she? She would not take the risk of getting close to him and have him witness Da's infirmity. She could not take the chance he would inadvertently expose her clan. If word got out about Da, she'd be at the mercy of the next attack. That could be their undoing.

She must convince Alec to leave. And she must keep Da's secret at all costs.

# *Chapter Three*

A loud knock sounded on Heather's bedchamber door. A serving lass, holding a candle, stuck her head inside the room. "Mistress? Are ye awake?"

Heather rose on her elbow, her sleepy eyes trying to focus. "What is it?"

The candle flickered and the girl cupped her hand in front of the flame as she scurried over to the bed. "Laird MacDougall has a fever."

Oh, no. How she dreaded hearing those words. "I'll be there directly."

The lass slipped from the room and shut the door.

Heather flopped back on the bed and threw her arm over her eyes. What would become of the clan if Da died? She could not keep his death a secret, and it would only be a short time before scroungers besieged MacDougall Castle.

*Alec.* How she longed to turn to him, unload the responsibilities consuming her. She sighed and shook her head. Even if she could trust him, she could not stand to watch disgust fill his eyes when he learned of the things she had done. Who would blame him? No man would want her after the atrocities she had inflicted—the lives she had taken.

Richard's red splotched face filled her mind. His nose scrunched as if he smelled manure while he relayed the tale of the Scottish Laird's wife who had taken up arms. His ridicule of the laird commanded by a female struck a sensitive nerve, the similarity to her situation too close.

Her throat constricted. No, with Beathan's help, she would find a way to manage the clan.

After dressing, she slipped down the stairs and into her father's chamber. Da thrashed about, mumbling and cursing an invisible enemy. Muire hovered over him, inspecting his wound.

"Och." The healer wrinkled her nose. "Tis not good. The gash is festering." She reached into her basket of herbs on the bedside table. "Boil water so I can clean it."

35

Heather emptied a pitcher of water into the heavy pot suspended over the hearth and stoked the fire until flames leapt, licking the underside of the container.

*Festering.*

She wrapped her arms around her waist and studied Da. Would he be able to withstand a high temperature and a decaying wound? His chest barely rose with shallow, raspy breaths. His face flushed, and his wrinkled and stained clothes were damp with sweat.

The water simmered. She poured a small amount into a bowl and gathered clean linens from the chest at the foot of Da's bed. She stepped beside Muire as the healer snipped the thread and pressed around the gash expelling a thick, yellowish substance.

Heather cringed, her nose wrinkling. "Will he be all right?"

Muire paused. "I can't say for sure. He's not as young as he used to be, but he's still a strong man."

Heather prepared a poultice and while Muire applied it, she bathed her father's face with cool water. He muttered unintelligible words, but every now and then, his tortured thoughts were clear.

"Rosie, don't leave me." His head rolled from side to side, beaded perspiration trickling down his pinched face. "Don't leave…"

Heather's chest squeezed. She patted his shoulder, trying to comfort him. "All will be well."

His eyes shot open, and he stared at her. "Rosie? Is it ye?"

He grasped her arm, whispering incoherently, his glassy eyes intense with pain no one could heal.

Her throat constricted with unshed tears. "Nay, Da, it's Heather. Shhh…rest easy."

Her voice sounded unsteady as she witnessed her father suffering the pain of his injury and the sorrow of his loss. His steely clutch on her arm eased, and his eyes slowly closed.

"It's the fever making him talk nonsense." Muire tossed her cloth on a bedside table and unrolled her sleeves. "With his confusion and ye favoring yer mum, he does not realize what he says."

Heather dropped onto the bench by his bed. "Oh Lord, please be with him. He needs yer strength," she whispered. "We *all* need yer strength."

She rubbed her forehead. How long must they endure hardships thrust upon them by fiends, whether they be English or misbegotten Scots? Would there ever be a time of carefree abandon, living in a world free of violence and strife?

The night dragged on with Da flaying about, oftentimes cursing and ranting, other times begging for Mum. Heather bathed his hot flesh. She waved a large cloth over him, fanning the air, desperate to bring down his temperature.

Muire clutched a bowl of her special potion. "Lift his head so I can pour this brew into his mouth. If he can get it down, it will help him fight the fever."

Heather propped her father's head and Muire tipped the mixture to his lips.

"That's it, Da. Drink." When he drained the contents, Heather eased him back.

She sat with him throughout the day, bathing his face and arms with cool water. Muire continued to apply her salves to his wound and by late afternoon, his fever finally broke, and he rested comfortably.

Muire rubbed Heather's back. "Ye've had a great deal on yer shoulders, and ye need rest. Why don't ye return to yer chambers?"

"No, I'll be fine. I want to stay with him a while longer." She tugged the blanket over his shoulder. "Please go tend to yerself and the others."

Muire gently brushed the hair off Heather's face. "Verra well, but call me should ye need me. I'll send someone to relieve ye shortly." She slid her hand down Heather's arm. "He's through the worst of it. Time will tell how well he heals."

Heather lightly squeezed Muire's hand. "Thank ye."

The old healer kissed Heather's cheek, collected her herbs off the table and shuffled from the room.

Heather sat on the edge of the bed and touched Da's cheek with the back of her fingers.

His eyes sprang open. He placed his hand over hers and winked. "I just saw yer mum."

Heather straightened and shook her head. "Oh, Da..."

"No, no, now listen to me." He held up a hand, silencing her. "I know I'm getting forgetful, but I'm a strong man. I can still lead my clan as I always have. And Rosie told me to believe in ye, to trust in ye," he croaked, crinkles around his old eyes creasing. "She says I will always lead the clan with ye beside me. Yer mum and I know we can count on ye, daughter."

Her heart sank. Was the fever causing him to imagine things? Or was this another bizarre behavior, another sign of his mind slipping?

She stroked his wrinkled, weathered hand. "Aye, Da. Ye can always count on me."

"I know I can." His heavy eyelids fluttered shut. "I know I can."

She sat back, rubbed her forehead and massaged her aching temples. Would he truly be able to depend on her? Every time she donned the lad's garb, she prayed she was not leading Da's men to their deaths. Not to mention the physical rigors of battle that took their toll on her body. Each assignment grew more dangerous than the last. Not only did she receive scrapes, cuts and abrasions, but she did not have the fighting skills, strength or stamina of a man. While she controlled her arrows with precision from the safety of the trees, she inevitably emerged from her hiding spot and engaged in the battle. Groaning, she shook her head. How long could she continue to lead the men and fool neighboring clans?

She had no choice. It was up to her to keep the miscreants at bay. She would not let Symon, Lowrens, or anyone else seize MacDougall Castle and force her to marry him to secure MacDougall lands. That could not...nay, that *would not* happen.

Several minutes later, the door opened, and Lindsey and Fergus slipped inside. They padded across the room and stood next to the bed. Shadows from the hearth danced across their bodies. Only the crackling and popping of firewood broke the silence.

Lindsey's brow wrinkled. "How is he?"

Heather tucked a blanket around Da's leg. "He had a bout of fever earlier, but he's resting comfortably now."

Fergus rubbed the black and white stubble dotting his chin. "He's a strong one, he is. He'll be fine. Don't ye worry. He'll be up in no time."

Lindsey glanced at Heather. "Ye must be tired. Don't ye want to lie down for a bit?"

"I am tired." Heather tugged her soft wrap around her shoulders. "Muire's sending someone to sit with him. Please let me know if ye need me."

"I will. Now go rest."

~~~

The day was unusually warm for October. Alec tossed several burned boards onto the pile of wreckage and wiped sweat from his upper lip with his forearm. It would take weeks to repair what Symon had destroyed. "Once we clear the area, we'll have a better idea of what needs to be done. While we'll have to rebuild the barn and surrounding buildings, we might be able to salvage the smokehouse."

Beathan wiped a soot-covered cloth across the back of his neck. "Aye, it doesn't appear to be completely ruined."

"I'll take Eric and several others to cut the trees we need." Alec studied the burned rafters. "We'll need a number of horses to haul the timber."

"Lindsey!" Beathan yelled.

The lass stuck her head around the corner of a blackened stall. Straw stuck through her worn cap and smudges of dirt smeared her face. "Aye?"

"Bring yer horses around. Laird Campbell needs them to tote logs."

She sauntered down the aisle toward them, her gaze skimming the damaged rafters before settling on Alec. Dressed in a lad's brown trews and tan tunic, her hands rested on her

39

hips, her brows raised over her piercing blue eyes. "What are ye planning?"

"For the most part, we'll put the structure back as it was." He stepped to the right and pointed to remnants of the roof beams. "We'll have to replace those struts, but we can add several new stalls in the area underneath."

"No. We had enough stalls before the fire. I don't want ye to do that." She opened her arms and rotated in a circle. "I need this area to exercise my horses."

"Our plans include enhancements to yer *da's* configuration."

Lindsey's arms dropped to her sides. She shook her head and stepped in front of Alec. Auburn hair piled underneath a grey cap escaped in curly strands around her freckled face. "Ye don't seem to understand. This is *my* stable, and *I* have the last word on how it's laid out."

Alec's jaw clenched, and his arms crossed his chest. He and his men worked tirelessly to rebuild, and she expected him to listen to this insolence?

Beathan stepped between them and placed his hand on Lindsey's shoulder. "She has a point. We can leave this area open."

Several men paused in their work, observing the difference of opinion. He could argue the merits of additional stalls, but this battle was not worth fighting. "All right, if that's what ye want."

"Verra well, I'll bring the horses around." She spun on her heels. With her shoulders pinned back and her head held high, she strutted down the dirt aisle. She added a swagger to her step, obviously reveling in gaining her way.

Dodging smoldering debris and burned boards, Alec strode from the stables. Lindsey and Blake rode lightweight horses around the side of the barn while leading a number of massive warhorses. She easily maneuvered the smaller animals. They were fast and agile.

Alec rubbed his chin, his mind mulling over possibilities. This was the type of horse he needed for their plans to battle the English. Perhaps he would speak to Alastair about procuring some of the beasts.

# Heather

Later that evening, he guided the horses dragging the last of the heavy logs into the bailey, as Heather stepped onto the landing. He hadn't seen her all day, and she was balm to his tired eyes. He devoured her image as if he were starved. Her beautiful thick hair, pert nose and lush mouth enticed him. Even in his fatigued state, his pulse beat fast in anticipation of an evening in her company.

Heather motioned toward the stairs. "Come in and eat. I know ye must be exhausted."

"Thank ye. It has been a long day," Alec replied, and he and his men made their way into the main hall. Servers placed bowls of thick beef stew on the long oak tables.

He sat and turned up a tankard of ale. The refreshing liquid slid down his parched throat, a welcome relief from the choking, smoke-filled, charred remnants of the barn. After draining the contents, he wiped his mouth on the back of his sleeve.

Heather waved to a serving girl. "Bring more ale, please."

"How's yer father?"

Heather took the pitcher from the lass and filled his empty mug. "He's better. Still weak so he slept most of the day."

She placed the jug on the table and sat on a bench across from him.

"It was a bad injury, and it'll take time to recover." He ran a slice of bread around his trencher and soaked up the gravy, then plopped the dripping morsel into his mouth.

Her forefinger rubbed the rim of her cup. "Aye, Muire says it will take a while before he's up and about."

Fergus, sitting at the end of the table, winked at Heather. "I keep telling ye the laird is strong for his age. Ye wait and see. He'll be good as new."

Alec set his tankard on the table. "I'd like to see him in a couple of days, if he's up to it."

"I know he'd like to thank ye for all ye and yer men have done." Heather tried to stifle a yawn. Her eyes drooped and dark circles lined her creamy skin.

41

He rested his forearms on the table. "Ye've had a long day."

"I think we all have." She yawned again and stretched. Her back arched, and the gown's bodice pulled tight. A jolt shot straight to his loins. When she straightened, wisps of blonde curls caressed her cheeks, and a golden mane cascaded across her shoulders. He longed to run his fingers through the silky tresses.

"I have a bath readied in yer chamber."

He swallowed hard, tamping down the urge to grasp her and bury himself in her sweetness. "It'll be good to scrub away the dirt and climb into bed."

Images of climbing into bed with her flooded his mind. His cock twitched, and he groaned inwardly. He wouldn't get much sleep tonight.

She picked up the tray of dishes at the end of the table. "Well, if ye'll excuse me, I think I'll retire."

"Verra well, lass. Goodnight."

Her hips swayed as she left the room.

Lindsey sat farther down the table from Alec. "Where's yer cousin Logan?" she asked. "He's well?"

Alec swung his head to face her as he took another swig of ale. Her question struck a nerve. He longed to know the answer himself. "He was fine when I last saw him. He decided to stay and is still leading a group fighting the English."

"I see." Lindsey studied her stew while pushing pieces of carrots around her trencher.

Alec noted her disappointment. His cousin and Lindsey had shared fun times before the English changed their lives—a carefree time long gone.

She stood. "I'm tired. I'll see ye on the morrow."

Alec bid her goodnight and before long, the room emptied.

He threw his legs to the other side of the bench and faced the hearth. The fire burned low. Balancing his mug on his thigh, his back leaned against the table. He hadn't seen the young warrior—the lad who fought so bravely. What had become of him? When Alec questioned Beathan, the man acted as if he had no idea of whom Alec spoke. Beathan had returned to his work, bending away from Alec, his eyes hooded. Why did Alec feel Beathan hid something?

Alec drained his mug. He didn't know, but he aimed to find out.

~~~

Heather descended the stairs and strolled into the bailey. Over the past few days, men rebuilt the stables and the sound of saws cutting wood and mallets pounding nails rang throughout the keep.

She stepped into the barn, her eyes adjusting to the dim light. The smell of freshly cut wood wafted past her nose. Hammers clanged against iron spikes. Men shouted, some guiding horses dragging bulky logs. Masons chiseled slabs of stone into blocks, providing a solid base for the massive timber. Several men plastered mortar around the structure to hold the heavy foundation in place.

"Whoa!" Alec's hand went up. He and Eric had hoisted a heavy log on their shoulders, and they rolled it into place.

It took great strength to maneuver the wood, but Alec made the task appear effortless. MacDougall men ran to do his bidding, each one eager to please the Laird of Glencara. She raked her teeth across her bottom lip. He commanded with ease and the men from both clans accepted his leadership without question.

"Secure it to the beam," Alec ground out while he and Eric strained to hold the wood in place. Sweat trickled down his temple as Blake and several others wrapped ropes around the log and fastened them to the brace.

Alec grabbed the timber and tried to shake it, testing the sturdiness. "Good job."

He slapped the wood and glanced around the barn. His gaze locked with hers, and a now familiar quickening rushed through her stomach.

She stepped forward and pointed to the rafters. "What about throwing a beam through the middle? It would give us an easy way to hoist grain across the barn to the stalls."

Alec wiped the sweat with his arm as he examined the wooden strut. "Aye, it's an idea. We'll consider it." He slapped Eric on the shoulder and called down the aisle, "Beathan, we need to wind up the construction plans."

She stepped closer. "I'd like to join ye."

Alec paused. His gaze lingered on her mouth then rose to her eyes.

"I have other ideas, and I want to hear what plans ye've made."

"Meet me in the solar." He bowed slightly, tugged his gloves off and strode to the back of the barn.

Heather hurried into the keep. She wanted to be included in the plans for the barn and storage building without Alec becoming suspicious of her interest. She dashed to the kitchen, grabbed several tankards and a large pitcher of ale.

Alec, Eric and Beathan were standing around Da's desk when she entered the solar.

"We've got most of the materials we need to finish," Alec announced.

Heather placed the tray on a side table, poured the refreshing drink into mugs and handed them to the three men.

Alec accepted the tankard. "Thank ye."

"Ye're welcome." She fingered several documents scattered about the desk. A map of the castle lay on top.

"Tomorrow we'll patch the walls." Alec pointed to a drawing. "Eric discovered cracks running about twenty feet long that need to be repaired."

She traced a line on the diagram. "One of the guardhouses is above this. Are ye telling me the tower is unstable?"

"Nay, but if the wall isn't repaired soon, it will be." He addressed Eric over his shoulder. "Take the men ye need to get it done."

Eric nodded. "We should have it repaired within the week."

Alec set his tankard on the table and looked at Heather. "We're rebuilding the stables, adding a different, more open, configuration for the stalls."

"Does Lindsey know what ye're planning?"

44

Alec grunted. "She's in the thick of it. There's not much that goes on in the barn she's not aware of."

Heather couldn't help but smile. Her younger sister was a force to be reckoned with when it came to her horses.

They discussed the restoration with Alec assuring Heather he would consider her ideas. He refilled his tankard and extended his hand toward the hearth. "Will ye join me?"

Her heart fluttered as she slipped into one of the chairs.

Alec dropped on the seat next to her, stretched his long legs before him and gazed over his tankard. "Ye've been busy. I've hardly seen ye."

His smoky dark eyes drew out nervous energy, and she smoothed her skirt over her legs. "With Da still abed, I've tried to step in for him."

Beathan moved around the desk. "And ye're doing a good job."

Heather smiled at him. He had been a tremendous help. What would she do without him?

"Repairs are moving along? The barn's almost finished?" She held her breath. It *had to* be finished soon.

"It's close. We should wind up in a few days."

"Ye will head to Glencara then?"

Alec rested the heavy tankard on his thigh. "Are ye so ready for us to leave?"

Oh dear, was she that obvious? "I only inquire as ye and yer men are understandably ready to return home." She cleared her throat. "I don't want to keep ye any longer than necessary."

He paused, and his gaze searched her face. "I want to be sure yer clan is secure before we head out."

"I thank ye, but we'll manage."

His brow rose. "Until Symon shows up again?"

"I appreciate all ye've done, Laird Campbell. We certainly needed yer help, but I can manage until Da is back on his feet."

"How will ye defend the castle? Women don't know anything about strategy, but perhaps yer young warrior will appear to fend them off?"

She straightened. He had some kind of nerve.

Beathan casually placed his hand on her shoulder, a reminder to choose her words carefully. She bit her lip, wanting to retort, but instead, she changed the subject. "Do ye play chess, Laird Campbell?"

She would show *him* strategy.

Alec eyes widened. "I do."

"Would ye care for a game?"

The corners of his mouth tugged upward. "*Ye* know how to play?"

The arrogance! "I've enjoyed the game for many years."

Beathan placed his empty tankard on the table. "Watch out. She's good."

Eric stood and yawned. "It's time for me to retire."

"Please don't leave," she said. "I didn't intend to break up yer meeting."

Beathan rubbed his neck. "Ye didn't, lass. It's been a long day."

"Verra well. Goodnight," she called as the men left the room.

She slipped to the side cabinet and removed an old chess set from a large drawer, then placed it on the table between their chairs.

Alec leaned back, observing her placement of the black chess pieces on the board. "Where did ye learn to play?"

"My da taught me." She set her queen and king on adjacent squares. "Contrary to what ye might believe, I can read, write and even perform basic calculations. Da even schooled me in the intricacies of warfare."

He lounged in the chair. His long muscular legs encased in brow trews relaxed. His tunic, open at the neck, revealed dark hair peeking out. He leaned toward the table and placed the white chess pieces opposite her on the board. "Indeed?"

"My mum saw to it my sisters and I were educated. Da not only agreed to have Brother Martin provide lessons once a week, he granted all of us our wish to live our lives as we desired. That's why Cameron devoted her life to the healing arts, Lindsey has managed Da's stables for years now, and my youngest sister, Elsbeth, set out with the sisters of the abbey to protect orphaned children."

Alec's dark eyes focused on her. "And what of ye, Heather? How do ye wish to live yer life?"

His intense gaze mesmerized her as if he could read her thoughts. "I oversee the castle's household chores, and care for its people."

His eyebrow quirked. "That is yer dream? To run yer da's castle?"

Heather cleared her throat and sat back. Time to change the subject. "I'll let ye start."

He hesitated, then responded, "All right."

He advanced a pawn two spaces.

Heather made a similar move.

"And just what intricacies did yer da teach ye?" He slid his rook across two vacant squares.

She studied him. Did he ridicule her? Most men scoffed at a woman's knowledge of the art of battle. Richard's sneering face loomed before her, but Alec's gaze was intent. He appeared genuinely interested.

"Never let yer enemy know what ye're thinking." She hesitated, the words she recited with Da rambling through her head. "Never let them see ye nervous. Hold them close enough to know their weaknesses then call their bluff."

Alec's eyes narrowed. "Ruthless words for one so soft."

She moved another pawn, aware of his attention upon her. "As with the Goddess Athena, I strive to use reason over brawn, but it's not always effective."

His booted foot brushed her leg. Her gaze shot to his face, but he did not seem to notice he had touched her. With heightened nerves, even the bump of his trews against her leg jolted her senses. Her fingers shook. She abruptly reached for her bishop, and her hand collided with his. The black piece clattered to the board on its side.

His head tilted. "Did I misstep?"

She straightened. "I beg yer pardon?"

"I did not yet make my move."

Pinpricks crept up her neck and she grimaced. Totally captivated in the sensations he caused by the mere sweep of his leg against hers, she lost concentration in the game. So much for her formidable battle words. With one touch, he disconcerted her, causing irrational feelings to course through her body. "I apologize. Please continue."

She pulled herself together and studied the board as they progressed, strategically positioning her pieces and focusing on her next move. Each time she glanced up, his eyes were fixed on her, not the chessboard. Perhaps she could distract *him* for a change.

Arching her back in a stretch, she thrust her chest toward him.

She heard his intake of air. She had him.

Just a couple more well-placed moves. "It's yer turn."

He inspected the board and straightened, puzzling over how to situate his pieces. "Yer beauty has me at a disadvantage, lass."

He expertly moved his knight.

Why hadn't she seen that opening? Her teeth raked her bottom lip as she considered her options. She had to take a defensive position and move her queen out of harm's way.

He grinned as she struggled with losing her rook. After several strategic moves, he sat back. "Checkmate."

She could not believe it—she had him a few moments earlier. Her arms dropped to her sides, shoulders hunched.

"Well done," Alec said.

Heather lifted her gaze to meet his.

"Ye're quite a player."

"Obviously not quite good enough. I'll have to practice with Da."

Alec enveloped her hand in his warm, callused palm. He stroked the back of her knuckles. "Ye can practice with me anytime."

Her heart slammed against the walls of her chest. Her breathing grew erratic. He brought her fingers to his mouth, his gaze never leaving her face as he kissed the back of her hand.

"The winner exacts his reward." He stood and moved around the table, tugging her to her feet. She should not get this close to him, but her resolve dissipated, her longing to be in his arms too great.

Although he smiled, his piercing eyes bore into her. Her knees wobbled when he tugged her into his strong embrace, lowered his head, and gently brushed her lips with his mouth.

His heavy, rough stubble grazed her cheek. She closed her eyes and breathed in a whiff of ale mixed with charred wood smoke. Heat spread from his large body, engulfing her in his essence. She ran her hands along his powerful arms to his broad shoulders. His chiseled, well-honed muscles bunched underneath her touch.

Her pulse quickened. The overpowering effect frightened her. No man commanded such a response in her. He exuded dominance and strength. She should be in control, but her traitorous body acted of its own accord, relishing in the safety and security his hold invoked. She must push him away — keep him at a distance.

He slowly eased his tongue into her mouth, and desire flooded her body. Her legs buckled, and her head reeled at his assault on her senses, thrilling passion coursing through her veins. His hands roved her back and lower to her bottom.

A knock on the door startled them. She guiltily broke away, smoothing her hair.

Muire stuck her head inside. "Excuse me, Heather, but yer father asks for ye."

Heat crept up her neck and over her face. Her mouth and cheeks tingled from Alec's scratchy beard, and she suspected Muire recognized the telltale signs.

Heather ran her hand down the front of her gown. Trying to compose herself, she cleared her throat and glanced at Alec. "Thank ye for the chess game. I'll challenge ye to a rematch."

He bowed slightly. "I look forward to it."

## Chapter Four

Over the next few days, MacDougall Castle recovered. Heather resumed her daily routine, working with the servants to air the main hall and erase memory of Symon's attack.

"Fergus, will ye have someone move these tables and benches against the wall?" She wrinkled her nose and waved her hands in front of her face. "And ask someone to dispose of these old rushes and bring in fresh ones."

Shortly afterward, several men arrived and cleared the room of furniture while boys carried armfuls of musty, withered rods out-of-doors. She grabbed a broom and swept away the filth and debris. Several women joined her, and dust billowed as they removed the dirt and grime. After the boys replaced the stale rushes with fresh reeds, Heather sprinkled the area with sweet-smelling herbs and instructed the men to return the furniture. She was determined to rally the clan, erase what she could of the attack, and move forward.

Wiping her hands on her gown, she glanced around the room and sighed. "Bring a ladder and take these tapestries down. Soot has made its way onto them and everything reeks of smoke. Ye'll need to hang them out-of-doors to air."

Several boys scurried to remove the large wall hangings and dragged them into the bailey.

Once finished, Heather inspected the main hall. A sweet fragrance of lavender wafted in the air, freshened tapestries adorned the walls, and polished furniture gleamed. Cleaning the hall of soot and eliminating the smell of smoke further diminished the remnants of Symon's attack.

Satisfied with her progress, she slipped out of the keep and down the grey stairs leading into the inner bailey. She tilted her face to the sun, relishing its rays warm against her skin as she strolled across the gravel pathway. Tugging her wrap tighter around her shoulders, she glanced to her left at the armory. Men sharpened weapons, forever preparing for battle. Her chest squeezed. What she would give to live in peace—never fearing the neighboring clans overtaking her vulnerable people or soldiers storming the castle. Would that day ever arrive?

# Heather

Pushing fanciful dreams aside, she made her way to the kitchen. She ducked through the wooden opening and into the dim room. A single beam of sunlight streamed through the smoke-filled space as women, gathered around worktables, diced carrots and leeks. Two lasses hurried past her carrying a large caldron and another followed, her arms laden with clean linens. Heather stepped aside to let them pass before she slipped behind Rena.

The old cook poked a knife at a charred hog suspended on a metal rod over flames. Heather placed her arm around the woman's shoulders, leaned toward the open stone hearth and breathed in the aroma of roasting meat. Fat dripped into the fire and sizzled, sending steam up the blackened stone chimney.

"Laird Campbell brought in this large boar."

Heather stilled. "He did?"

"Aye, he and his men went hunting before dawn." Rena's old eyes turned dreamy. "He's quite a man, ye know. He thinks of everything."

Even the kitchen servants were enamored with Laird Campbell. It would not do for him to linger at MacDougall Castle much longer. If he did not leave soon, she risked losing the authority she had worked so hard to garner with her clan. Over the past two years, she had proven herself capable of managing the keep and the men protecting the castle. But her rule had not come easy.

Rena rotated the spit. "And I have bread and the honey buns ye requested baking."

"After the evening meal, we'll pass out the treats to the children and ask them to join me by the hearth for a story," Heather said. "They have had a hard time of it lately."

"Aye, they would enjoy that. 'Tis nice of ye to think of them."

"Will ye have a bathing tub sent to my chamber? I'm covered in dirt."

"I'll ask the lads to fetch it directly, mistress."

"Thank ye, Rena." Heather strolled past women shelling peas and dicing carrots as she made her way from the kitchen and back into the keep. She climbed the staircase,

51

hands on her lower back, and stretched as she stepped into her chambers.

Before long, several boys rushed in with her bathing tub and buckets of water. They filled the wooden container and steam rose from the surface. She smiled with anticipation as she ushered them from the room, thanking them before closing the door.

The warm water did wonders for her sore muscles, and she relaxed in the luxurious heat. Leaning against the tub, she thought of Alec. Memories flooded her mind—his passionate kiss, his strong body pressed against hers. She closed her eyes, reliving his hands cupping her bottom, lifting her against his stiff manhood as his mouth played havoc on her senses.

Her stomach tightened, and she squirmed, her feelings for Alec warring against her mind's voice. Her life was no longer hers to live as she desired. She had responsibilities to her father and clan, and could not entertain thoughts of a future with Alec. But sooner or later, she would have to chose a husband or risk one being thrust upon her. While she didn't want to believe the widespread clamor over Alec's actions, she required a man she could count on without question.

Not to mention, he would look upon her with disgust once he learned of her role, of the men she had killed for the rebellion. As Richard voiced, what man would want a wife who wielded a sword and mastered the bow, filling adversaries with deadly arrows? Her shoulders slumped. A young lassie's fairy tale dreams of love were lost to her.

Stoically, she washed her hair and stepped from the tub. Wrapped in a drying cloth, she sat in front of the hearth, the warmth from the fire comforting. She drew a comb through her hair. Her hands trembled in anxious anticipation of seeing Alec this evening. She relished the short time she had with him. Doesn't she deserve some measure of happiness? Why should she deny herself a wee bit of joy?

She could remain in control and not let their flirting get out of hand. After all, Alec would soon leave for Glencara.

When she entered the main hall, light from candles lining the walls flickered, and a welcoming fire blazed in the hearth. Women hurried in from the kitchen with trays of food.

Two carried a large platter of the roasted boar. They placed the meat on one of the long trestle tables as the clan's men, women and children arrived. Heather took a serving dish of carrots and leeks from Betsy and placed it on the table's end. She removed a cloth from underneath the dish and rearranged several loaves of bread to make room for more platters.

A deep chuckle caught her attention, and she straightened while wiping her hands on the linen fabric.

*Alec.*

His hair was damp from a recent bath, and his grey eyes twinkled with laughter at something Eric said. He slapped his captain on the back and took a swig of ale. His eyes locked with hers, and she suddenly became nervous, aware of her appearance. She tucked a stray hair behind her ear and smoothed her blue woolen gown over her stomach.

Dimples pressed into his handsome, dark-stubbled face. Her insides warmed, and she returned his smile.

~~~

Alec's pulse pumped an extra beat. Even from across the room, uninhibited joy radiated from Heather's eyes. Her thick, wheat-colored hair hung to her trim waist—hair he longed to run his fingers through. He stared at her plump breasts pushing against the bodice of her gown. Groaning, he shook his head. He'd thought of her all day. What was it about her that drove him to distraction?

She stepped over to him. "Good evening. Please take a place at the table, and I'll have someone serve ye something to eat."

"Thank ye." Alec sat, and his men filed in around him.

Serving girls passed out trenchers, and Heather helped arrange platters of roasted venison and leeks on the tables. Only the sound of clicking utensils could be heard as the men devoured the meal.

Eric licked his fingers and wiped his hand on his sleeve. "My compliments to yer cook."

Alec set his tankard on the table. "Aye, 'tis excellent."

53

Heather settled onto the bench in front of them. "Rena will be pleased ye enjoyed it."

The servants brought more platters of steaming vegetables and freshly baked bread to the tables. After the men finished eating, women cleared their empty dishes and trenchers.

The subdued atmosphere from the attack and the hard work of reconstruction, hung heavy in the hall. Heather skimmed the faces of the quiet children. "Come, we've got time for a story before ye go to bed." She waved, coaxing the lads and lasses forward as the cook brought out a tray of honeyed buns. "Rena made special treats for ye."

The children each took a sticky-bun from the tray and raced to the hearth. They sat on the floor around Heather's feet as she perched on a stool. Several lassies scooted close, their eyes wide with excitement while they stuffed their mouths. "I'm going to tell ye a story about a cockatrice."

"Tell us, tell us!" the youngsters shouted, bouncing up and down.

Alec stretched out his legs, his mug balanced on his thigh as he waited to hear Heather weave her tale. Upturned, expectant faces displayed the children's undivided attention, each one focused on their beautiful mistress.

Lindsey joined the group on the floor.

"Who has heard of the cockatrice?" Heather asked.

Most of the children shook their heads, but one young lad yelled, "I've heard of them!" His dark head bobbed enthusiastically. "My da told us about them."

"What's a cocktree?" one of the little lassies asked.

Alec chuckled and took a swig of ale.

"It's a *cockatrice*, and they've been around for quite some time, but few people who have seen them actually live to tell the tale. Ye see, the monster changes ye to stone just by looking at ye."

The children gasped and Heather paused. The fire crackled and popped, shadows creeping across the walls.

"The cockatrice is a hideous creature with the head and legs of a rooster and the body of a dragon. It has large wings to carry it across the land, and it roams the countryside searching for unsuspecting travelers." She scrunched her face.

Although she hoped to portray a monster, she could not have been more lovely. Not only did her appearance stop his heart, she was beautiful to the core—always thinking of the children, forever comforting her clan. Just the kind of woman he longed to have at his side.

She spread her arms wide as if she were gliding and leaned down, pretending to swoop upon the children. Several of the girls huddled together. Heather sat up and gazed across the group.

Wide-eyed, they listened to her every word. "Not so long ago, a cockatrice terrorized a small English village called Wherwell. The men tricked the monster into the dungeons below the priory. They kept the fiend locked up, but frightened townspeople demanded it be killed before the monster turned anyone else to stone."

The little girls nodded in agreement.

The corners of Heather's mouth hitched. "They were at a loss as to how to deal with this cockatrice as it roared and raged in anger at being imprisoned."

She threw her hands over her head and growled loudly. The children's eyes grew wider as she continued. "The townspeople were too frightened to get close enough to kill it. But there was one man who came up with a plan to rid the town of the monster."

Heather glanced at each child. "It's said that only one thing will kill a cockatrice. It must see its own reflection. With that in mind, a villager named Green bravely stepped forward with a mirror, but no one would volunteer to try the theory. Who would want to face that hideous monster armed with a simple mirror?"

She lowered her voice ominously. "Green knew it had to be done, so he eased the mirror into the pit."

"Did it work?" a wee lass asked.

"Aye, the beast thought the mirror was another cockatrice and fought its reflection until it was exhausted. Green then jumped into the dungeon and killed the monster!"

The children cheered and clapped.

Heather held up a hand for silence. "I warn ye not to get too excited as they say the cockatrice in Wherwell was only one of many that roam the moors hunting unwary victims."

As Heather paused, Eric grabbed Lindsey around the shoulders and roared loudly, "Grrrr!"

"Ahhhh!" Lindsey leaped up and twisted around, her eyes wide. The children jumped and screamed alongside her.

Heather gasped and placed her hand on her chest.

"Eric!" Lindsey shouted.

"Haaa!" he teased and ran with her fast on his heels. The boys and girls hollered and helped Lindsey chase his captain around the great hall.

Alec stood and placed his mug on the table. "Ye weave quite a tale, mistress."

~~~

Alec's warm, strong hand engulfed Heather's, and he brought her from the stool to stand before him.

"I hope that between the sweet buns and the scary story, I haven't given their parents a long night."

He chuckled while running his thumb over her wrist. "Would ye care for some fresh air before ye retire?"

Her heart bumped against the walls of her chest. "Aye, I would like that."

Alec entwined his fingers through hers, led her out the back steps and into the yard. She swallowed nervously. She didn't quake so when facing an enemy in battle. Why did this man cause such an erratic response?

An autumn chill cooled the air, adding to her trembling. He led her out the castle walls, and waved to a man patrolling the ramparts. The guard nodded as they continued down the road. The bright moon cast its light, throwing shadows off tall trees from the dense forest surrounding MacDougall Castle. They strolled in silence.

Alec squeezed her fingers. "The children love their mistress."

Heather grinned. "I love them as well."

"It shows."

56

## Heather

They followed the trail that bordered thick woods. Their footsteps fell on a soft cushion of pine needles. Stars filled the dark, clear sky and a light wind encircled them. She tugged her wrap tighter around her shoulders and followed Alec down the path.

"Tell me about yourself, lass."

"There's not much to tell. Since Mum's death, I've run the castle, keeping the accounts straight—"

He stopped and faced her. "No, tell me what ye like to do. Tell me about yourself."

No one had ever shown an interest in her, what she liked or disliked. The idea he was interested thrilled her. "Well, I enjoy a swim in the loch."

His brow rose and a playful gleam twinkled in his eyes. "I should like to take ye for a swim in the loch."

Pinpricks crept up her neck, tingling across her cheeks. She quickly added, "And I enjoy drawing…and sewing…and gardening."

He winked and continued down the path, her hand ensconced in his, butterflies fluttering in her belly.

"The barn is coming along. I took yer advice," he said. "We added a beam across the middle that supports a pulley with ropes to move heavy sacks of grain or bales of hay."

"That's wonderful. Thank ye."

"Yer sister seemed pleased."

"I have no doubt. She wants everything to be just so for her horses."

"Blake is a big help to her. The men listen to her opinion." Alec shook his head. "And she definitely expresses her opinion regularly for them to hear."

Heather chuckled. "Aye, that's my little sister."

He tugged her hand. "It's not often ye see men following a woman's lead."

Heather stiffened. His face, hidden in the shadows, was unreadable. "What do ye mean?"

"Those men follow her orders without question. The stable hands are a close group. Each man watches out for yer sister and would seemingly do anything for her. They admire her." He stopped and faced her. "And ye, Heather. They listen to ye above all others."

"As I've said, Da has tremendous support and admiration from his men. They know with his injury, we're doing all we can to hold together and repair our clan."

"All but the young warrior I've yet to see again."

Her stomach plummeted. Why did he have to keep bringing up the *young warrior*? She searched his face. Was he on to her?

"The day of the attack, I fought with a slender young lad." He leaned back from her and his gaze raked her up and down. "He was about yer size and he shot an arrow with precision."

He stepped behind her, lifted her hair and piled it on top of her head. His warm breath caressed the back of her neck causing fine hairs to stand on end.

She shivered. "Ye describe many of Da's warriors."

Alec let her hair fall around her shoulders and skimmed his hands down her arms to interlace his fingers through hers. He pulled her back against his chest, surrounding her with his heat and rested his chin on her head. They stood in silence.

She cringed. If he knew the truth, would he caress her like this? Or like Richard, would he deceive her into believing he cared for her in order to acquire Da's land?

"Are ye keeping something from me, Heather?"

Her breath quickened, and her pulse thumped so fiercely he had to feel it. "Why do ye question me?"

He paused a few seconds. "I worry for yer safety."

The breeze blew around them, leaves rustling in the trees above their heads. Heather closed her eyes and leaned against the solid wall of his chest. She must calm down or she would certainly appear suspicious. "I appreciate yer concern, but we'll be fine."

"Ye do not trust me."

Did she trust Alec? Where was he when the Campbells were attacked? Some said his absence suggested he was behind the strike, and with his father no longer able to lead the clan, Alec stepped into the role of Laird. Was he so different than any of the other men eyeing MacDougall Castle?

"Trust is something earned, not freely given."

He stiffened ever so slightly. Had she not been so aware of his strong body pressed against hers, she would not have noticed. "An accomplishment I strive to attain."

Laughter caught their attention as three lads ran by with two large dogs on their heels.

Alec lightly squeezed her. "Come, let's walk."

The moon lit their path as they wound down a worn trail toward the dense forest. "Where are ye taking me, m'laird?"

Alec chuckled deep in his chest. "To a place where I can have ye all to myself."

All to himself? Her pulse pounded in her ears, and her breath quickened.

He continued farther into the thick trees. The path exposed a clearing surrounded by grey boulders. A cold stream trickled over rocks and stones to feed a small pond. She inhaled the fresh air while stepping into the opening.

"It's been many years since I last visited this spot. When I was a wee lass, I came here often. This was my special place."

"Yer special place?"

She tugged him to a wild thicket and pulled back some of the undergrowth. "If ye look close, ye'll see a secret cave. Whenever I upset Mum or Da, I would hide here."

"I cannot imagine ye causing them grief."

She grinned. "Oh, I caused my share of grey hairs."

"And did ye hide here often?"

"Only when I did not want to be found—no one knew about my hiding place."

They strolled around the pool's edge before stopping next to a small waterfall.

"Verra lovely," she whispered, closing her eyes to the sound of water cascading across boulders and trickling into the basin.

Alec kissed her forehead, and she opened her eyes. Her breath caught at his darkening gaze. His nostrils flared—his desire for her evident. With his hand under her chin, he brought his mouth down on her lips. Senses heightened, she breathed in a hint of ale on his breath, felt his stubble scrape her skin. His strong arms enveloped her, and she snuggled closer to him, to his warmth. He deepened his kiss, slowly inserting his tongue into her mouth. Lost in the sensations he invoked, she melted into his embrace.

His hands wandered across her back. She knew this could not lead to anything. She had her clan to consider. But for a few short moments, she could pretend things were different. What harm could possibly come from a few caresses? A few stolen kisses?

When he ran his palms down to her buttocks, his hardened member pressed against her abdomen. A hand eased across her waist and inched up to cup her breast. Her breathing became erratic and her nipples pebbled, straining against her gown.

~~~

Alec's heart hammered when Heather eased her arms around his neck, her soft breasts pressing into his chest. His cock swelled painfully against his trews. He untied the ribbon at the neck of her gown and when she didn't protest, eased her dress open and placed kisses across her supple, white shoulders.

He breathed in a fresh scent of lavender. Her soft hair brushed his face and he buried his nose in the silky tresses. Hearing her sigh encouraged him, and he cupped her breast, her taut nipple outlined in the fabric. He pushed his hips into hers, only to strain against the clothing separating them. God, he wanted to strip away her gown, lose himself in her...

His eyes sprang open.

*What the hell am I about?*

He was not free to be with Heather. He had to stop, *now,* before he totally lost control.

When he leaned back, her eyes narrowed and her brow knit in confusion. He grazed his lips against her kiss-swollen mouth, her cheek and eyelids. Leaning his forehead against hers, he took a deep breath and exhaled slowly. He had not meant to do this. *Damn it!* He was committed to another. He closed his eyes, savoring one more moment of her soft body nestled so sweetly against his.

It took every ounce of strength to pull away before he ripped her gown off and made love to her on the hard ground.

~~~

Heather reeled from the sensations Alec invoked. She longed to feel his naked skin against hers, to surrender to his warm palms caressing her, wrap herself in his strength. She might never again have the chance to lie in the arms of a man like Alec. If she did not succeed in protecting her father and clan, she would be forced into a loveless marriage. She grasped at the fleeting happiness in Alec's embrace, yearning to make love with wild abandon...just this once.

"Ye're driving me mad. I'm hard with wanting ye, and I know ye must feel my desire." Alec kissed the tip of her nose. "But I'll not dishonor ye." He stepped back and a cold emptiness enveloped her. "I need to get ye back to the keep before I do something we'll both regret."

Regret?

Would he regret lying with her?

She tried to smile, but tautness clutched her cheeks, and her face grew stilted. Her fingers trembled as she tugged her gown over her shoulders and tied the ribbon. Afraid she would see pity reflected in his eyes, her gaze dropped to the ground.

"I did not mean to ravish ye. It was not my intention when I brought ye here." He held her hand and stroked her skin. "I only wanted a wee bit of time alone with ye."

She scrunched her eyes briefly. *Don't explain. Don't make it any worse than it is.* She misread his intentions. "It's getting late. Perhaps we should head back," she replied, her tone terse.

Alec brought her hand to his warm mouth and placed a kiss on her palm. "I hope I haven't offended ye."

Chest clenching, she shook her head. She had thrown herself at him. What would he think of her willingness, no, her eagerness to toss her clothes aside, only to have him come to

61

his senses and stop his advances? She should have been the one to halt their heated caresses.

Her face burned. "No, I'm just tired."

"It has been a long day." Alec placed her hand in the crook of his arm. "I'll escort ye inside."

They walked in silence until they reached the bailey stairs. "Goodnight, Alec."

She spun toward the keep. When he didn't release her arm, her head whipped around.

He stared at her for a moment before he bowed. "Goodnight, Heather."

~~~

Several days later, Heather sat with Da. He grew stronger with each passing day, however, he appeared to have aged years overnight. His white hair was thin and the deep wrinkles traversing his weathered face accented dark shadows marring the skin around his eyes. Purplish-yellow splotches stained his whiskered cheekbones, and calloused, gnarled fingers grasped the bedding. His chest rose and fell with heavy breaths, but at least he rested comfortably.

A knock on the door broke her thoughts. She slipped across the room, careful not to disturb Da.

Alec stood on the other side of the door.

She raised her eyebrows. "Good evening."

"Good evening, lass. I'd like to speak to yer father if he's up to company."

"I'm sorry, but he sleeps—"

"He does not sleep," Da rasped. "Come in, Alec. Come in."

Her father struggled to prop himself up.

Damn.

Her heartbeat quickened. She had no choice but to let Alec in. Lord, please don't let Da have a lapse of memory now.

She opened the door wider. "Apparently, I was mistaken. Please come in."

Alec strode past her and entered the room. "How are ye, Laird MacDougall?"

Her father's eyes lit, a sparkle appearing in the brown depths. He patted his torso and winked. "I'll be fine in a few more days and I've ye to thank. I would not be here if ye had not arrived."

Alec sat in a chair next to the bed. "I'm happy to see ye're recovering."

Heather closed the door and crossed the room. Da was more animated than she had seen him since his injury. He laughed and threw his head back at something Alec said. He obviously enjoyed talking to Alec, but her nerves stood on end at the thought of what Da might say with his random loss of memory.

"I'll be up before ye know it. Beathan tells me ye're rebuilding the barn and smokehouse."

"Aye, we've made good progress. It won't be long before we'll have it back in order."

"Ye've done so much for us. I don't know what would have happened if ye had not come along."

"Ye have a young warrior in yer midst who saved yer life. It was not me."

Her stomach dropped. Oh, no. Not again. Why does he keep bringing up the lad?

"A young warrior?" Da's eyes widened. "I don't know which one ye speak of."

She smoothed the blankets around her father's legs. "Da's got many young warriors amongst his men, and we appreciate ye and yer men lending them a hand."

Alec leaned against the back of his chair. "We were heading home when we spotted smoke rising from yer stables." He turned toward Heather. "I'm glad we were camping close by."

Thank God, he dropped the subject.

"We are forever in yer debt," Da replied.

"I do have some business to talk to ye about."

Heather's back stiffened.

"Business? What can I do for ye?"

Alec's dark grey eyes grew serious, intense. "Ye might have heard we suffered a severe blow at Falkirk. We lost many good men. The English forces were too strong, their numbers immense." He stood and paced, raking a hand through his hair. "William Wallace disbanded his forces and is on the run, but he still organizes attacks. We're changing strategy. That's where I need yer help."

Heather's heart lurched. Oh, no. What would he ask of her father?

Da's eyes widened and he sat straighter, his face alive with excitement. "Ye want me to join ye?"

Alec faced him, hands on hips. "Nay, not in battle, but ye can help in another way. We cannot match their strength in numbers, and our weapons are crude in comparison. We can't continue our full frontal attacks or we'll lose every time. We plan to strike in small groups, hitting hard, disabling their forces and fleeing into the forests. We need quick, agile horses for this type of assault. The English are weighted down and ride massive warhorses they cannot easily maneuver."

Heather leaned forward. Lightweight horses? Attack and flee? She had not thought of such a strategy, but his idea did merit consideration.

Da stroked the white stubble on his chin. "I see."

"Yer stable houses a number of the verra horses I need. I would purchase them from ye, if ye're willing."

"If it would help rid us of the English scum, I would be honored if ye'd take them."

Alec's shoulders relaxed. "I thank ye. I think this will help us defeat them."

"Good, the sooner the better. I'll speak to Lindsey on the morrow. Ye can take what ye need."

Alec described the battle and their ultimate defeat at Falkirk. "The English are starving, their troops depleted. If we can strike soon, we can take advantage and finally push the Sassenachs off our land."

A knock on the door interrupted Alec. Heather stepped across the room to find Becca wringing her hands. "Mistress, Rena says to tell ye she has an issue of *utmost importance*," she tossed her head from side to side, "and she needs ye in the kitchen."

"Uh, I'm busy at the moment." Heather could not leave her father alone with Alec. There was no telling what he might say while she was gone.

"Nonsense, daughter." Da waved a hand. "I'll visit with Alec while ye take care of the kitchen." He then addressed Alec. "I've missed yer father. Tell me, how is my good friend faring?"

Alec sat again. Grand. He intended to stay.

"Missives from my sister tell me he's still bedridden, but relatively healthy otherwise. I haven't seen him in a number of months."

Shaking her head, she had no choice but to leave. It would appear suspicious if she refused, so she slipped from the room and hurried down the hall behind Becca. When she entered the main hall, she spotted Beathan sitting at the long trestle table. Thank goodness. What would she do without him?

She ran to him and clutched his arm. "May I have a word with ye?"

He wiped his mouth with a cloth. "Aye, what's amiss?"

"Please go to Da's room. He's alone with Alec, and I'd like for ye to be with him," she whispered.

He rose from the bench and patted her arm. "Aye, I'll head there directly."

~~~

A knock sounded on the door. Alec glanced up to see Beathan peering inside the room. "Laird, I wanted to check on ye. Do ye need anything?"

The captain strode across the floor and stood at Alastair's bedside.

Laird MacDougall's brow furrowed. "Don't be fussing over me. I'll be up in no time."

Beathan chuckled. "I can see ye're getting stronger."

Alec stood. "Aye, but it's getting late, and I should let ye rest. I don't want to wear ye out as ye're beginning to heal."

"Before ye go, I'd like to offer ye a proposal."

A proposal?

When Alastair continued, his voice was hoarse. "I'm not as young as I used to be. This attack from Symon made me realize I'm getting older." He inspected his wrinkled hands. "I need someone who can step in and protect the MacDougall clan, someone who can take control and provide the leadership I can no longer give." He raised his sad eyes. "I would ask ye to consider my Heather."

Alec's gut twisted. He couldn't marry Heather with his betrothal to Robena. Oh, Lord, how he wished things were different.

"I'm most honored ye would want me fer yer daughter. If I were not so involved in this rebellion…." He paused. "Nay, that is not the reason I can't marry her. I'm not in a position to offer marriage. I'm betrothed, Alastair. I'm sorry. If circumstances were different –"

Alastair held up a hand. "I understand. No need to explain." A few stilted seconds passed before he spoke again. "I'm tired. Perhaps we'll speak again later."

Alec nodded, strode from the room and down the corridor. Marrying Heather was the last thing he expected Alastair to ask. If matters were different, he would welcome the proposal. He admired the beautiful kind-hearted lass, but he was not free. Hell, he didn't want to marry Robena, but he had promised. His vow to his father reverberated through his mind. How he wished he could take back those words.

"Laird Campbell?"

Beathan's voice stopped Alec in midstride as he marched through the great hall. Alec faced him, hands on hips as the MacDougall captain stormed over to him.

"I've seen how she looks at ye, and I ask ye to stay away from her. Do not give her the wrong impression and play her a fool."

"I beg yer pardon?"

Beathan crossed his thick arms over his chest, his dark eyes challenging. "I think ye understand exactly what I'm saying."

# *Chapter Five*

Alec wanted to refute Beathan's comments, deny his attraction to Heather and tell the captain he was wrong. He would never play on Heather's emotions...

Well, not purposefully.

Is that what he had done? Had he given her false impressions?

His gut churned. Was he so callous he did not consider how his actions appeared?

Alec strode through the hall, down the stairs, and into the cool night air. He took a deep breath and tilted his head back. He stared at the stars, but didn't see them.

Beathan was right.

He'd have to stay away from her, finish the repairs and head home. He could not lead her to believe there might be a future between them.

How could he stay away from her?

He was drawn to her as if he had no will of his own. She constantly invaded his thoughts. He longed to be with her, hear her voice, her laughter, and witness her compassion.

His shoulders sagged under the weight of his atonement. He exhaled loudly.

He would not hurt her.

Vowing to find strength to resist her, he made plans to leave as soon as possible.

~~~

Two days passed and on the morning of the third, Alec marched out of the newly constructed barn and over to a large barrel of water. He pulled off his shirt and dunked his head inside the cool, refreshing liquid and rinsed away sweat and grime stuck to his skin. When he straightened and shook his hair, water flew in all directions, droplets sliding down his chest and abdomen.

Men and women milled around the bailey. Eric tossed a hammer in a crate and strolled across the yard. "The barn's almost ready?"

Alec studied the wooden building and swiped his shirt across his face. "We should finish in a few days. The smokehouse is close as well."

Movement out of the corner of his eye caught his attention. Lindsey stomped toward them, her hands balled into fists at her sides.

Shite. What the hell did she want?

Eric chuckled. "Watch out. She has ye in her sights."

She stopped in front of Alec and jammed her hands on her hips. "Da says ye want my horses for the rebellion."

He'd had about enough of the redheaded lass. He tossed his shirt over his head and thrust his arms in the sleeves. "We agreed I would purchase some before I leave."

"Those horses are bred for pleasure, not war. They're small and delicate. I don't know if they can even carry ye or yer men." The corners of her mouth turned down, her nose wrinkling as if assaulted by a foul odor. Her eyes raked him up and down before she turned her icy glower on Eric.

After long days of backbreaking work and sleepless nights brooding over Heather, Alec was in no mood to put up with Lindsey's disrespect. Hell, not only had he been told to stay away from her sister, this meddling lass constantly inserted herself into his business. Well, he was tired of dealing with her spoiled pig-headedness.

Avoiding Heather made him miserable. His unwanted betrothal irritated like a swelling boil set to burst, and he was ready to unleash his pent up fury and frustration. He crossed his arms over his chest and fixed the most menacing glare he could muster on her. "They will do."

Her eyes, mere slits, shot sparks of anger. She spun and stalked off, calling over her shoulder, "Ye'll need to go through *me* if ye want them."

"Small and delicate horses?" Eric chuckled.

Alec shook his head. "Let's get back to work. I'm anxious to finish and be on our way."

68

# Heather

~~~

Heather's heart ached. Throughout the week, Alec's men worked alongside Da's to finish rebuilding and repairing the damaged structures. Alec made himself scarce, rising early and retiring late, taking his meals when she was not in the hall, and sleeping outside with his men.

The last evening they spent together repeated itself over in her mind and she searched for what might have caused his sudden absence. Had her eagerness to fall into his arms offended him? Did he think her willingness wanton and shameful?

Her stomach twisted.

She missed him—longed to be near him, hear his deep laugh, and feel his arms around her. She huffed. If she was to see him, it would be up to her to seek him out.

Intent on confronting the barrier he erected, she marched across the bailey carrying a tray of tankards. A young lad followed, his arms straining under the weight of the refreshments. She stepped into the new stables.

Sturdy beams, spaced roughly ten feet apart, crossed the wide expanse of the wooden ceiling. Each end rested on equally thick logs erected with braces for support. The high-pitched roof soared above. A straight ladder ran from the ground up to a platform constructed midway for storage. A large pulley hung over the raised area with ropes strung to each side of the building. Alec had taken her advice and had created an easy means for hauling hay and grain. The stables appeared more open and spacious. Windows had been cut to provide fresh air and light.

It would not be long before the construction was complete.

Alec would soon leave.

She should be relieved the work was almost finished. So far she had managed to hide Da's illness. The sooner Alec left the less chance he would have to discover that secret. Conflicting emotions collided, squeezing the breath from her lungs. When he departed, the resulting void of his absence would smother her.

The lad placed the platter on a bench, and she filled the mugs. "Please rest and have some ale."

Men dropped their tools and hurried over. She handed a tankard to Eric, and he downed the drink in a quick gulp then wiped his mouth on his sleeve. He set his goblet on the tray. "That tasted good. Thank ye, lass."

"Ye're welcome to more." She casually searched the area for Alec.

A man held out his empty goblet. "I'll have more."

Heather refilled his mug. "Any others?"

She glanced around the barn and finally found Alec.

His grey eyes darkened, and his brows drew together. What caused his hostile expression?

After serving the men, she accepted their thanks and gathered the empty mugs. Fine hairs on her neck rose. She felt Alec's gaze, but when she looked in his direction, he averted his eyes.

Why does he stay away? What had she done? His avoidance hurt. But…wasn't that what she wanted—for him to hurry the repairs along and leave? Was it not best he stay away? Was he not, once again, being the sensible one?

With the recent turmoil, he had been her haven. When she was with him, she forgot the hardships, absorbed his strength and confidence. His nearness made her pulse thump wildly and her hands tremble. He provided her a chance to forget her many weighty responsibilities.

But, now he ignored her. She raked her teeth across her bottom lip. It was time to do something about it. Squaring her shoulders and raising her chin, she marched across the barn, wove between the stalls and working men, and stopped before him.

Several nails stuck out of his mouth as he hammered one into a log. His long hair was tied in a leather thong and his bearded cheeks were smudged with dust and dirt. He gazed down at her and raised a dark eyebrow.

"What would ye think about holding an All Hallows Eve Festival?" Heather blurted. "The weather is lovely, and it might help to lift everyone's spirits to celebrate before Cailleach Bheur arrives."

He removed the nails from his mouth and shook his head. "Ye're asking me? Why?"

"I'm asking for yer help in setting up the activities. We'll need tables and benches carried to the south field, not to mention organizing and directing games for the children."

One eye squinted and he cocked his head to the side. "Let me get this straight. Ye want me to ask my men to lay down their tools and help direct *games*?"

"Aye."

His eyes searched her face, and she held her breath. He leaned against a wooden support beam and crossed his massive arms over his chest. "That sounds like a wonderful idea, Heather. The children would surely enjoy it."

"I'll have Rena bake sweet cakes, and Lindsey and I can come up with games. Josh tells a great story about Cailleach Bheur and All Hallows Eve. Perhaps we'll have a dance in the evening."

"An autumn festival? That would be fun," Lindsey sang out as she strolled down the aisle.

"Will ye help me?"

Her sister climbed on a stall gate and sat on the top rail. "Aye. What would ye have me do?"

"I'd like yer help with the games for the children while others bob for apples." Heather rattled off other activities.

Alec chuckled then turned back to work.

"So I can expect help from ye and yer men?"

He glanced over his shoulder while positioning another nail. "We'll be there."

With his agreement, her spirits rose. She looked forward to a carefree day of fun.

A carefree day with Alec.

~~~

The last day of October arrived. The sun shining through a cloudless blue sky warmed the fall air. Heather supervised the festival preparations. Squeaky wagon wheels caught her attention, and she turned toward the noise.

Her breath caught.

Alec steered a team of horses carrying barrels of water. The animals struggled to pull the heavy weight, but with persistence, the cart slowly rolled to a stop at the top of the field.

He stood in the wagon. "Where would ye like these?"

Heather waved, motioning to the side of the grassy meadow under the shade of a large tree. "This is a good spot. Place them in a row, one next to the other."

He jumped to the ground and hoisted a barrel off the cart, water sloshing over the rim. Beathan, Blake and several others ran to help carry the heavy containers. Once the drums were in position, she tossed in apples, and they sprang to the surface.

"Last year one of the smaller lads fell in headfirst." She chuckled. "We'll be sure to hold them tight this year."

"A bit over zealous?" Alec's grey eyes twinkled. He rolled up his sleeves, exposing thick, muscular forearms.

Her heart fluttered. How she had missed his presence. "Aye, he didn't care for his older brother besting him."

"Eric, help me with the tables and benches," Alec called over his shoulder as he marched back to the wagon. Eric jogged over and leaped onto the cart. Alec flicked the reins, and the wooden wagon lurched forward as the team started down the hill.

"I'm here to help." Fergus shuffled toward her with a limp in his gate. A snaggletooth grin reached his dark eyes.

"I placed a box of scrap cloth on the table next to the benches. There are sticks and a ball of twine in the bottom. Would ye help the children make kites?"

"I'll see to it directly," he answered and headed to the table.

Lindsey strolled to Heather, her arms full of large fruit. "I found gourds we can use for a game of ninepins and bowls."

Beathan and Blake erected Da's old tournament platform for the evening's music and dancers. Alec drove a wagon filled with tables and benches onto the field. He, Eric

72

and several others carried the furniture, while Heather directed the arrangement to the right of the stage, under a worn tan tent.

Laughter and squeals of arriving children filled the afternoon air. They ran onto the field, anxious to play games and take advantage of the last of the autumn weather.

Alec and Eric returned, the cart loaded with the last of the benches. Blake helped them empty the wagon and place the furniture around wooden tables erected under the tent.

Fergus patiently helped several lads with their kites. "Let me show ye how to weave string around the sticks." He held the wood together with one hand and wrapped twine around the pieces with the other. "Now, ye try it."

One of the young boys worked diligently with the sticks and twine, only to get his fingers wrapped in a tangle of string.

"Let me help ye." Fergus's gnarled, but surprisingly nimble fingers, twisted the cord around the wood. "Pick out some cloth, and we'll attach it to the mount."

Soon colorful frames caught the wind as the lads hollered and raced down the field, holding their kites high.

Alec addressed another group of boys. "Who wants to play a game of bowls?"

"We do! We do!" the lads shouted, jumping up and down.

"Gather around." Alec clutched a leather ball made from a sheep's bladder and pointed to a row of gourds. "Try to roll the ball as close to the gourd as ye can. Don't hit it, or the throw won't count."

One of the lads hopped up and down. "I've played this game before, and our team almost won!"

Alec dug the heel of his booted foot in the ground, indicating the starting points. "All right, I want two teams to line up on either side of these lines. The group that has the most shots landing closest to the gourds will be the winner."

The boys lined up, eagerly awaiting their turn.

Watching Alec, a warm feeling spread like honey through Heather's body. His expression no longer dark and brooding, he appeared genuinely pleased to oversee the games.

A boy's shot went awry.

"Whoa!" Alec ruffled the lad's hair. "Ye'll have another try at it."

Heather's chest filled with delight. She grabbed some gourds from Lindsey's pile and placed them in rows before hurrying to the assembled lasses, ready to play ninepins. Anne was first. "Roll this ball and knock down as many of the gourds as ye can."

The wee lass stepped to the line, her dark curls bouncing around her shoulders. With concentration, her tongue peeked out of the side of her mouth. She pitched the ball and managed to knock down four of the gourds.

Heather clapped. "Wonderful!"

Anne jumped and spun around in a circle, her arms wide. "I did it!"

The other children cheered and laughed. After each took a turn, Heather declared one of the lassies a winner and awarded her a new red ribbon for her hair.

The afternoon grew late, but the children wanted one last game—a tug of war.

~~~

Alec sat on a table, his feet resting on a bench with his forearms braced on his thighs. Heather laughed and hugged a lass to her side. How he missed hearing the sound of her voice, smelling the faint scent of lavender drifting from her blonde hair. How he missed the feel of her soft skin and looking into the depths of her blue eyes. She was a soothing balm to his tortured soul. She made him forget—the war, the atrocities inflicted upon his brother Scots, and aye, the bloodshed by his blade—just for a moment.

Heather hiked her brown woolen skirt and hurried to him. She placed her hands on his. "Will ye help with the tug of war?" Her eyes sparkled. "It's a tradition between the lads and lassies."

He wanted to wrap his arms around her, nuzzle her neck and bury his face in her thick tresses. "Aye, I'll help."

"To make it a fair fight, ye will lead the girls, and I'll lead the boys."

## Heather

He squeezed her hands and winked. "Sounds like a challenge. Care to place a wee wager on yer team?"

Her eyes narrowed, and she tilted her head to the side. "Just what kind of a wager did ye have in mind?"

He stroked her wrist in small circles. "If ye win, I'll honor yer wish."

Her gaze locked onto his.

"If I win, ye'll honor mine," he added, the sound of his voice came out husky and seductive.

"Hmmm, I'm not sure what I'd be agreeing to, m'laird."

Thoughts of his most fervent wish flashed through his mind, but he tamped it down. He could not have what he truly wanted. He could not secure a future with Heather—have her in his life.

He brought her knuckles to his mouth and whispered. "Just the first dance."

Her nostrils flared and her eyes darkened to a deep sapphire. "It would be my pleasure."

Alec's insides warmed at the tone of her sensuous voice. She smiled, and his stomach flipped over. He looked forward to holding her in his arms, spinning her around the dance floor.

He hopped off the table and clapped his hands. "All right, all the lassies come with me!"

Squeals and laughter rose as a dozen or so little girls gathered around him.

Lindsey dug her heel into the ground making two lines and secured a ribbon in the middle of the rope. "The group to move this flag over their line will be the winner!"

With a troop of lasses at his back, Alec and his team tugged the rope, inching the suspended cloth closer to their line.

Heather faced him, leaning back, her feet digging into the earth as Alec's team wrenched them forward.

"Pull!" She yanked on the rope, but she and the lads struggled against Alec's powerful hold.

"We're winning!" a lass yelled.

The ribbon crossed the line, and Lindsey jumped up, declaring Alec's team of lasses the winners.

The lads behind Heather dropped the rope, propelling her forward. Eyes wide, she stumbled and fell into Alec's outstretched arms. He wrapped her in his embrace and swung her around. The girls hollered and ran around Heather and Alec, before Alec fell in the grass with Heather in his arms. The boys piled on them, laughing.

Alec tickled several children. They giggled and raced away, then came back for more.

Heather sat in the midst of youngsters and Alec's pulse pounded. Her eyes lit, an unfettered happiness traversed her beautiful face. Tendrils of blonde hair escaped her blue ribbon. Her innocent, exuberant expression was one he would always remember.

"Time to make yer costumes for All Hallows Eve," Lindsey called. The children scurried to her. "Here's some fabric ye can use to create fairies, ghosts and goblins." She rummaged through the stacks of material and handed pieces to the children. "We've also got berry dye ye can use to color them, and when ye're ready, Fergus will cut holes for yer eyes and mouth."

Heather squeezed Alec's hand, her skin soft against his palm. "Thank ye. Thank ye for making this such a special day."

"Ye're welcome, m'lady." He stood and brought her before him. "I look forward to our dance."

"As do I." Her breathless voice caused his gut to clench. She wanted him as he wanted her. If only he could have her...

After the children finished with their costumes, Josh yelled, "Gather around."

He waved, beckoning the children to the large bonfire. The setting sun cast shadows over his face. The children sat wide-eyed.

Alec spun Heather, placing her back to him, and wrapped his arms around her waist. She leaned her head against his chest, and he kissed her temple. She felt so good snuggled against him. He dipped his nose to her soft hair and breathed in a familiar whiff of lavender. His arm rested beneath

76

her breasts. How he longed to inch his palms up and fill them with her sweet flesh. His loins tightened. He took a deep breath and focused his attention on Josh.

"The blue hag will walk the earth tonight." The storyteller paused. "All must be abed as she drums her staff across the land and moors, freezing the ground as she goes." His eyes grew wide. "Her fangs have grown long." He grabbed invisible teeth and ran his hands down the imaginary tips. "She has three hideous faces, and when she rises from her cave, she can see far and wide as she brings the snow storms of winter!"

The fire crackled and hissed. The wind whipped through the flames and red sparks flew into the black sky. "This night, when some say the dead walk the land, ye might see Cailleach Bheur galloping across the moors on the back of a large black wolf, swinging her magical staff made from the flesh of humans!"

Alec chuckled and squeezed Heather. "They'll not sleep a wink tonight."

Josh dramatically swung his arm over his head, portraying a scene of terror.

The children gasped.

"Ye must run to yer homes and dress in the costumes ye made to scare away the spirits wandering with Cailleach Bheur at MacDougall Castle."

He jumped up and coaxed the children to their feet. "Hurry, Hurry!"

The lads and lassies leaped up, screaming as they raced away.

Heather and Alec clapped while watching them run across the field. She stepped next to Josh and grasped his arm. "Thank ye. That was wonderful."

He chuckled, holding his wide girth with his beefy hands. "It was good fun."

Heather addressed several serving women. "Please bring out the food. Everyone can eat when they're ready." She then turned to a group of men gathering with musical instruments. "And Jake, please set up on the platform." She waved a hand, indicating an open space in front of the raised wooden stand. "We'll leave this area open for dancing."

Alec moved toward her, but Beathan blocked his path. "Do I have to call ye out?" His dark eyes glared, and his forehead wrinkled. He stabbed his finger in Alec's chest. "I thought I made myself clear. Stay away from the mistress or ye'll answer to me."

~~~

Men positioned their musical instruments on the stage while women brought food from the kitchen. Heather supervised the placement of platters of meat, bread and dishes of carrots and leeks on the tables. She brushed her hair from her eyes and searched for Alec. Where was he? He'd stood behind her just a moment ago. She turned right then left. He was no longer on the field. How strange.

Lindsey yanked a woolen cap off her head. Thick auburn hair fell around down her back. "I'm ready for a bath."

Heather wrapped her cloak around her shoulders. "Aye, I am as well," she replied, her gaze still on the emptying field.

Alec must have gone ahead to freshen up for the dance. She wondered why he didn't say anything before he left.

Lindsey and Heather strolled up the hill and through the castle gates. The pounding of horses' hooves clattered on the wooden bridge leading into the outer bailey. Heather whirled around. Who would be arriving? They weren't expecting anyone.

Men rounded the corner and came into view.

Lowrens McLaughlin.

Her heart sank.

He dismounted and approached them while pulling off his gloves. Taking their hands, he placed a kiss on the back of each one. "Mistresses Heather and Lindsey, it's good to see ye."

Heather's back stiffened, her revulsion barely contained. "Master McLaughlin," she answered. "What brings ye this way?" *Nothing good, I'm sure.*

"Lowrens, call me Lowrens, lass."

Heather withdrew her hands from his sweaty clutch.

"I heard yer father was injured and stopped by to see how he's faring." His snake-like eyes, devoid of compassion, searched her face.

She would wager he hoped Da was *not* faring well. "That is verra kind of ye. He's fine."

"Ah, I'm happy to hear it." He looked at Lindsey and back at her. "May I have a word with him?"

No. The simple word hovered on the tip of her tongue. What did he want with Da?

A stilted silence passed. His brow rose.

"I'm sure he'll be happy to see ye," she replied. "We were just heading inside."

Lowrens placed his hand on Heather's back. Her skin crawled. Once in the keep, her sister excused herself while Heather quickened her footsteps, hurrying up the stairs to avoid his touch.

She knocked on Da's door and stuck her head inside to find him propped up in bed. "Master McLaughlin is here to see ye."

"Lowrens McLaughlin?" Da hesitated. He frowned, his brow drawing together. "Show him in."

Heather opened the door, and Lowrens brushed past. As if on second thought, he turned. "Thank ye, Heather. We'll spend time together later."

*Not if I have anything to do with it.* She shivered and watched him slither into her father's room. After closing the door, she hurried down the hall frantic to find Beathan. She could not leave Da to fend off the scrounger alone.

She ran through the great hall, down the stairs and into the bailey. Two women strolled past, their arms laden with soiled laundry. Blake led a chestnut mare into the stables. As he passed, she spotted Beathan carrying a water bucket in each hand.

She dashed across the yard. "Beathan!"

His head jerked toward her and he paused.

She caught up to him. "Will ye sit with Da and Lowrens McLaughlin? I would do it, but I loathe to be near that man."

Beathan nodded. "After I deliver these to Lindsey, I'll see what McLaughlin is up to."

She clutched his arm. "Ye will let me know why he's here?"

"I will," he said over his shoulder and disappeared into the barn.

What could McLaughlin want? Her gut churned. How had he heard about Da? There was something suspicious about his sudden appearance. Did he hope to take advantage of Da's injuries and weakened state?

She stepped into the stables. Where was Beathan? He must hurry.

Da's captain jogged down the aisle. "I'm heading there directly."

Relief poured over her. Beathan would protect Da and keep McLaughlin at bay. She followed him into the keep. When he jogged upstairs, she veered left toward her chamber and opened the door to find her old nursemaid bent over, rummaging through the chest at the foot of the bed.

A fire blazed in the hearth against the wall, and candlelight flickered from candelabras positioned around the chamber.

Heather padded across the floor and sat on the edge of the bed next to Lanie.

"I've ordered ye a bath, and I was searching through yer gowns." The woman held up Heather's royal blue dress. "What about this one? Ye've always looked so pretty in it."

Heather fingered the soft material. The last time she wore the garment was when she first met Alec years ago at Da's annual tournament. Memories of his passionate kiss flooded her mind, and her insides warmed. That was the night he told her she was beautiful. Perhaps he'd feel the same tonight.

"That one will be fine."

Lads deposited the old tub in front of the hearth and filled it with hot water. After they left, Heather stripped and sank into the warmth, the heat loosening her tired muscles. What fun she'd had. With troubled times of war and destruction, the clan rarely experienced a day of carefree abandon. And she rarely experienced the thrill of being with a man. Not just any man, but a man she longed to be with.

However perfect the afternoon might have been, warning bells reverberated through her brain over McLaughlin's untimely visit. He was trouble, and she was thankful Alec was here. Lowrens would be on his best behavior. He would not cause discord and risk raising the wrath inflicted by Laird Campbell. But, when Alec departed they would once again be at the mercy of neighboring scoundrels.

Lanie held out a drying cloth. "Time to get ye ready for the big dance."

After donning her gown, Heather brushed her hair and before long, she was ready.

Lanie clasped her hands before her chest. "Ye're a striking young woman."

"Thank ye, Lanie." Heather kissed her aging nursemaid's cheek, picked up her wrap and headed below stairs.

Laughter and cheerful shouts drifted from the festivities as she strolled down the worn dirt path to the south field. The cool night air caressed her skin, and she tugged her wrap tight around her shoulders. Torches, their flames shooting high in the dark night, lined the grounds. Clan members surrounded tables holding Rena's delicious food, and ale flowed freely as evidenced by raucous laughter emanating from the boisterous crowd. Musicians strummed their instruments, and a few couples danced to the melodies.

Heather wound through the throng to the tables where the kitchen servants continued to replenish dishes of meats and vegetables, hot breads and desserts. They had worked in the kitchen all day, preparing the festival's feast. Two lassies dressed as fairies squealed and ran from a goblin. Heather jumped back as they weaved around her, through the revelers, screaming and laughing at the same time.

Muire chose a slice of cheese and plopped it into her mouth. "The day was perfect. The villagers thank ye for yer thoughtfulness."

Laughter roared and Beathan slapped Blake on the back.

"'Tis good to see them enjoying themselves after all we've been through," Heather replied.

"Mistress, where do ye want this?"

Heather turned at the strained voice. Two lads struggled with a platter holding a venison roast. "Oh heavens, follow me."

She guided the boys through the crowd to the table. They placed the meat at the end, and she rearranged the dishes of carrots and turnips around it.

Afterwards, she and Lindsey walked through the crowd visiting with their clan, but Heather's eyes sought Alec. Surrounded by his men, he stoically drank his ale, never acknowledging her, let alone approaching her. As the hour grew late, the festivities wound down.

What about their dance?

Had he changed his mind?

Was he back to ignoring her?

Pride kept her feet from racing to him and pulling him onto the platform.

"Lindsey, would ye like one last turn around the floor?" Blake extended his arm toward the stage.

Lindsey hooked her arm through his. "I would."

"Mistress Heather?"

Heather briefly closed her eyes and took a deep breath before turning to face Lowrens McLaughlin.

His beady, black eyes leered, brazenly inspecting the bodice of her gown. His thin, shoulder length brown hair lay plastered to his head. He grasped her hand with his sweaty paw and kissed her knuckles. His thumb stroked the back of her hand. "Yer father appears well. We had a nice visit."

Bile rose in her throat.

"Would ye care to dance?"

Although she had misgivings about Lowrens, she really had nothing concrete she could point to as to why she felt that way. She should be happy to dance with him. What was wrong with her? Alec obviously did not want to have anything to do

82

with her. What was it about him that caused her to act like such a fool?

Her face stiffened, but she nodded and let Lowrens lead her up the steps to the platform. He leered at her as they glided together in time with the music. As they slid around the dance floor, Alec stood and stormed off the field. She craned her neck to watch him leave. Her chest squeezed.

Lowrens twirled her around, then pulled her too close and brushed his hand down her back to rest at her waist. When he ran his meaty palm lower to cup her bottom, she'd had as much as she could stomach.

Distraught over Alec's strange behavior, she shoved against Lowrens' chest. "I apologize. It's getting late, and I'm verra tired. If ye'll excuse me, I think I've had enough celebrating for one day."

His eyes smoldered with undisguised desire. "As ye wish. I'll escort ye back to the keep."

She shook her head and placed her hand on his forearm. "Oh, no, please stay, and enjoy the rest of the festival." She backed away. "Goodnight."

~~~

After taking a dive into the cold water of the loch, Alec entered the camp where his men had gathered around a fire. He dropped his satchel on the ground and sat beside it. Eric handed him a cup of ale, and Alec swallowed it down, his thoughts still on Heather and Lowrens McLaughlin. Why was he here? Did Alastair offer his daughter to him as well?

When McLaughlin had taken her hand, Alec's blood boiled. He wanted to jerk him away from her, but Beathan's words resounded through his ears. Alec had no right to interfere. He held no claim on her, and that realization hit his chest like a battle axe.

He exhaled loudly and raked a hand through his hair and down the back of his neck. "It's time we head home. Our work is finished," he announced.

"It'll be good to get back to my wife," Ian spoke up.

Everyone around him agreed.

83

"Tomorrow morning, I'll arrange to purchase the horses we need, and we'll be on our way." Alec tossed the remnants of his cup into the fire. "Get some rest. We head out early."

As he lay on his makeshift bed, his thoughts were once again flooded with Heather. Hell, when were they not? He tugged her worn ribbon out of his pocket, remembering the day she gave it to him.

Brandon McLeod had ridden into the MacDougall's bailey after the tournament to recruit men for the rebellion. Heather had given her ribbon to Alec as a token of affection, and he had held it with him throughout numerous battles and skirmishes. It kept him going—gave him something to grasp in his darkest hours. The simple fabric was a reminder of what he fought for, an anchor in the violent turmoil of King Edward's injustice.

How could he leave Heather? Would McLaughlin step in? Had he already convinced Alastair of a perfect union between their clans?

He groaned and flipped onto his side. Sleep eluded him. He tossed and turned throughout the night. The sun finally crested the horizon with streaks of pink and purple. He rose from the hard ground and once again, made his way to the cold water of the loch.

~~~

Alec walked into the great hall and locked eyes with Heather as she sat next to her father at the dais' long table. Her gaze dropped to the trencher in front of her. He strode across the room and addressed the old laird. "Ye appear rested."

"Aye, I'm tired of lying about. 'Tis time to get back to work."

Alec sat down the table from Heather. "Lass, ye're doing well?"

"Aye."

She barely glimpsed at him. Guilt struck his core. He had not kept his promise of the first dance. He tried to ignore his feelings toward her—tried to stay away and as Beathan pointed out, not continue to give her the wrong impression.

While struggling to keep from hurting her, he feared that is just what he had done.

Alastair broke off a piece of bread from a loaf. "Beathan tells me the repairs are complete. I was just going to have a look."

A lass served Alec a plate of smoked mutton. "We finished last evening."

"That is indeed good news. I appreciate all ye've done for us."

Heather's eyes fixed on him. "Aye, thank ye, Alec."

Alec speared a slice of meat, ran it through thick gravy and plopped it in his mouth. They ate in silence. Only the clanking of utensils rivaled the tension strung tight between Alec and Heather.

He cleared his throat and wiped his mouth. "Now that the repairs are finished, we'll be heading home, and I'd like to settle with ye on the horses."

Heather's head jerked up, but she quickly dropped her gaze back to the table. Her finger circled the rim of her cup, and her shoulders appeared to droop...or was that his imagination?

"Horses?" Alastair asked, his brow wrinkling in confusion. He crammed a spoonful of porridge in his mouth.

Alec paused. What did he mean? "Aye, the lightweight horses ye agreed I could purchase from ye." He glanced at Heather and then at Alastair. "Have ye changed yer mind?"

"No, Alec. Da was not sure which horses ye referred to." She touched her father's hand. "Why don't ye finish yer breakfast and then Alec can pick out the horses he needs for the rebellion."

What was amiss? Heather appeared to be protecting Alastair, stepping in and answering for him. Not to mention the way her father looked to her for the answer.

Alastair nodded. "Aye, eat up. We'll go to the stables shortly."

Heather stared at her trencher, pushing food around her plate. The pain in her eyes pierced Alec's soul. Pain he caused. He wanted to take her in his arms and ask her to be his, to arrive home with the bride of his choice on his arm. He swallowed hard. He could not waste time on frivolous fantasies. His leaving would be best for both of them.

The MacDougall's captain strolled into the keep, wiping his face with a cloth.

"Beathan?" Heather called out.

He paused before crossing the room to the table. "Aye?"

"Would ye go with Da and Alec to the stables? Da's selling some horses to Alec for the rebellion."

"I'd be happy to help." He grasped Alastair's shoulder. "We'd do anything to rid the English from our soil."

They finished eating and made their way through the bailey. Alastair beamed when he stepped into the barn. Chuckling, he clapped Alec on the back. "I could not have done a better job myself."

He ambled through the new building, inspecting and commenting on the superior workmanship.

"Now, about those horses," Beathan spoke up.

"Huh?" Alastair frowned. His dark eyes blinked rapidly, and he appeared confused.

Why did the old laird hesitate? Did he not want to part with the animals, but feels obligated?

Beathan touched Alastair's shoulder and coaxed him to the back of the barn. "The horses ye're selling Alec for the cause."

"Oh, aye, aye." Alastair motioned for Alec to follow. "Let me show them to ye." He shuffled down the dirt aisle. "Ye're welcome to as many as ye need."

Alec singled out eight horses and tugged a bag of gold pieces out of a leather pouch tied on his belt.

Alastair placed his hand over Alec's. "No, take these horses in payment for all ye've done."

Alec hesitated, but recognized pride in the old man's eyes and closed the pouch. "Thank ye."

"Crush 'em, Alec. Crush 'em and run 'em out of Scotland."

Alec grasped Alastair's hand. "We'll do our best."

Heather

A loud bang came from the adjacent stall where Blake worked alongside Lindsey.

"Lins, cool down. There's nothing ye can do about it."

Alec glanced over the wooden fence. Lindsey slammed her fist on a bale of hay, her face an angry red. "If I were a *man* he would have to answer to *me* about taking them. I bred them. I raised them, and he's going to just take them from me."

"I understand, but he needs them. It's for a good cause." Blake ran his hand down her arm. "We can breed more. He won't take them all."

Beathan and Alastair shared a look. "Lindsey, that's enough," the old laird asserted.

She turned back to her work mumbling under her breath, slamming tools and kicking hay around in anger.

Alec shook his head. She was one spitfire he would not miss.

~~~

Later that morning, Alec tugged the girth under Aeton's belly and tied it off as his men broke camp and packed their belongings. Constant thoughts of Heather's gentle touch, comforting voice and warm smile invaded his mind. He wanted to see her, be with her one last time before he left. His gut churned. He owed her an explanation.

Eric strode down the stable's main aisle toward Alec. "We're ready to head out when ye are."

"Have the men line up." Alec secured his satchel onto the saddle and patted Aeton's rump as he stepped around the horse. "We'll leave shortly."

He marched from the barn, across the bailey and through the narrow gate to castle's herb garden. Heather stooped over late blooming plants, her fingers digging in the rich soil. As he approached, she gazed up at him, her eyes wary.

"I've come to say goodbye."

She straightened, twirled her dagger between her fingers, and stuffed it into her pouch.

His eyes narrowed. *Where have I seen that move before?*

"Godspeed, Alec."

She shoved an errant lock from her face. One of the ribbons she enjoyed wearing secured her hair. Her soft skin tinged pink from the sun and the cool morning air brought a rosy red to her lips.

"If ye need anything, get word to me, and I'll be here as quick as I can."

"Ye don't need to worry about us. We'll be fine. I do thank ye for all ye've done."

Alec stepped closer and placed his hands on her shoulders. She pulled back, but he held on, his fingers sliding down her arms until he grasped her hands. "Lass, if only things were different —"

She shook her head, her brow furrowed, and eyes displayed the pain of betrayal.

He couldn't stop himself from drawing her into him and kissing her. She shoved against his chest, but he held tight. His hands roamed her back, and he reveled in the feel of her against him. When he lifted his head, her stormy eyes questioned him.

"Why did ye do that?" she whispered. "Ye have avoided me on and off for days, and right before ye leave, ye do this? Why?"

Alec backed away and shoved a hand through his hair. When he looked at her, confusion clouded her eyes. "I want ye in my life, Heather. I'm drawn to ye. I want to be with ye, have ye by my side, but I cannot marry ye. Not now when I'm needed to help with the rebellion."

He raised his face to the sky and exhaled loudly. "I don't want to play ye false." He hated the words he had to utter. "I stayed away from ye because I can't have ye. I'm betrothed to Robena McMillan."

She straightened. Her eyes widened, and she stepped back, blinking and shaking her head. "Betrothed?"

"Aye."

Her mouth fell open. "Why are ye just now telling me?"

"I couldn't bring myself to…"

"So ye led me along?"

"No. I mean, I didn't intend to hurt ye. If things were different, I would relish marriage to ye."

"I never said anything about ye marrying me."

"No, *ye* didn't."

She studied his face. "Did my father ask ye to marry me?"

Alec stood motionless. With her da always asking her for guidance, Alec thought she knew.

"Did he?" she demanded louder.

"Aye."

Heather placed her hands on her head. "I can't believe he did that. He knows I cannot marry ye."

*Cannot?* "Why not?"

She wrapped her arms around her waist. "It doesn't matter."

When he stepped closer, she backed away and held up a hand. "No, don't. Just leave. Please... just leave."

*Shite!* The pain emanating from her blue eyes pierced his heart. He wanted to wrap her in his arms, tell her he would end the loathsome betrothal. Instead, he nodded and left the garden.

~~~

Alec stepped into the keep and disappeared from sight.

A tear slid down Heather's cheek. "Betrothed to Robena," she whispered.

She dropped onto the bench, and put her face in her hands. Bile bubbled in her stomach. Da offered her up on a golden platter, only to have Alec refuse.

He is marrying Robena—the hateful, arrogant Robena.

A few minutes later, she dried her eyes. What did it matter *who* he married? She had known she would never have a future with Alec. But hearing him utter the words of his upcoming nuptials was a bitter taste to swallow.

Her breath hitched. She had grown fond of him. Images of him playing with the children, chasing and tickling them, of him pulling her closer in the tug of war, of his arms around her flashed through her mind.

She shook her head and looked to the heavens. A short time later, the sound of galloping horses departing MacDougall Castle pierced the quiet garden.

Alec left taking her heart with him.

# Chapter Six

*Road to Glencara*
*November 1298*

Alec's gut churned. Heather's crestfallen blue eyes had stared at him through thick black lashes. Innocence shattered, her shocked face paled. He hurt her, and he hated himself for it.

*Shite.*

And what of McLaughlin? Could Alec watch the scoundrel step in and make her his wife? Did he have a choice?

Flecks of white lather hit his arm. He reined Aeton in and patted his sleek neck. "Forgive me. I did not mean to run ye into the ground."

Alec shaded his eyes from the afternoon sun, his gaze searching the hillside. They were inside Campbell land—almost home. "We'll rest the horses a bit. Water is just ahead."

Alec guided Aeton to a secluded spot and slid to the ground. His men followed, leading the animals to a small lake. While the beasts drank, Alec removed the water skin from his saddle and took several swigs.

Eric stretched and rubbed at the small of his back as he eyed Alec. "Ye've been quiet. I don't think ye've uttered a word since we left the MacDougalls."

Alec grunted.

"It wouldn't have anything to do with Mistress Heather, would it?"

Alec shot a glare over his shoulder at the taunt. "Keep yer thoughts to yerself and out of my business."

He strode away, marching through the woods, down a path winding into the forest. Damn Eric. A parasite burrowing under his skin could not have irritated more. He slapped a branch. Leaves fluttered to the ground as he brushed past and rounded a boulder.

Two horses stood in front of an abandoned shack. He froze, his gaze darting around the yard. Easing his sword from the sheath, he crouched low and made his way to the animals. They shifted and nickered. "Easy."

He ran his hand over the rump of one of the beasts. The saddle sported an English military water skin with King Edward's emblem etched in the worn brown leather.

It was silent inside the hut. A busted window stood agape, a door slightly ajar. He inched through the brambles, eased closer to the shack and peered through the window. An English officer's uniform and sword lay across a broken chair. Alec nudged the door with his foot.

It creaked, and he held his breath. When nothing stirred, he opened it wider and slipped inside.

A man lay on a bed with a young woman cradled in his arms. They appeared to be sleeping, but that was soon to change.

Alec lowered his blade to the man's chest. The soldier's eyes sprang open. "I would not move if I were ye."

The girl gasped and yanked a blanket over her naked breasts.

"Who are ye?" Alec demanded. "What are ye doing on Campbell land?"

The man glared.

Alec nudged him with the sharp tip of his sword.

The soldier's dark menacing eyes squinted. "My name is Barclay Taylor. I'm a Commander in Edward's army."

"What are ye doing on my land?"

Emotion flittered across the soldier's face. He obviously did not want to divulge information.

The girl slid to the edge of the bed and Alec jerked his head toward her. "Don't move another inch, or I'll run him through."

Her head bobbed, her eyes wide.

"Do not hurt her. She's innocent."

"I don't intend to harm her unless she gives me reason. Now for the last time, what are ye doing on my land?"

Barclay tilted his head toward the girl. "I came to be with her."

Alec's eyes narrowed. His blade's pointed tip dug into Barclay's flesh and blood trickled down the man's chest. "Where are the rest of yer troops?"

"I came alone."

"Please don't kill us, Laird Campbell," the lass squeaked.

Alec studied her. "Who are ye?"

"Skena. I live in the village at the base of Glencara with my mother Maria."

Maria managed the kitchen, cooking and cleaning, and had raised his cousin. Logan's mother died giving birth to him, and Maria brought him into her home, cared for him as if he was her own. "Get dressed. Slowly."

She slipped off the bed and gathered her clothes.

"In here. Do not leave this room."

Skena threw her gown over her head. Her dark gaze darted from Barclay to Alec.

"Don't do anything foolish. He'll be skewered in two by the time ye reach me."

Skena shook her head and backed against the wall.

Alec focused on the commander. "Now, ye, get up."

Barclay eased off the bed and stood nude before him. "Throw me his clothes."

Skena tossed his pants to Alec. He checked for weapons and threw the clothing at Barclay. Once he dressed, Alec motioned for the commander to sit.

"Please, Laird Campbell." Skena scooted next to Taylor, and he placed an arm around her, holding her against him. "I carry his child. We love each other."

Alec tilted his head. A babe—an innocent life created amongst the hatred between their countries. Innocence be damned! He should kill the Sassenach and be done with it.

Skena's wide, hazel eyes beseeched him. "Please…"

Alec exhaled. "Commander Taylor, get yer arse off my land, and do not come back. I don't want to regret I let ye go when I had the perfect opportunity to run ye through. Do ye understand?"

"Oh, thank ye, laird," Skena wailed. "Thank ye."

Barclay's eyes fixed on Alec's. "Your act of forbearance will not be forgotten."

"Leave before I change my mind."

The commander grabbed his shirt and tugged it over his head.

When Alec picked up Barclay's sword, he studied the commander. Was Alec making a fatal mistake? How many of his brother Scots would perish below this blade?

Taylor straightened and extended his hand. Stilted seconds passed before Alec relinquished the sword.

When Skena slipped into the commander's embrace and wept, Barclay rubbed her back. "Shhh, we will be together again." He glanced over her head. "I request another favor."

Alec raised his brow. After freeing the man, he asked for another boon?

"Will you permit Skena to work in your keep where I would know she and our babe will be safe?"

Alec considered the request. He owed this man nothing, but Barclay being in his debt could not hurt. "I will see to it."

Barclay extended his hand. "If I can ever be of assistance to you—"

Alec grasped Taylor's grip while assessing him, the commander's dark eyes trusting. They both nodded in unspoken understanding.

Barclay kissed Skena's forehead and left the hut. A few moments later, Alec sheathed his sword, and he and the maid followed. Taylor tipped his hat and galloped away.

"Come with me." Alec helped her onto the horse and took the reins. He recognized the Campbell emblem on the side of the saddle and raised his brow.

The wench simply grinned and shrugged her shoulders.

Alec shook his head and led the horse out of the woods and into the clearing. He approached his men, and they stared wide-eyed.

"Don't ask." Alec swung onto the saddle and turned Aeton toward Glencara. "Let's go."

~~~

Pink and purple hues splashed the evening sky as Alec led the group through Glencara village. Cold biting wind swirled around him and he tugged his cloak tighter around his neck. Small hovels lined the road. A golden glow of tallow candles slipped through the wooden slats, illuminating warmth from within. The men's horses trotted down the road and through the gates leading to the keep while Skena turned right, heading toward her cabin.

When they trotted into the bailey, several stable lads ran to greet them. Alec dismounted and handed Aeton's reins to one of the boys.

"Alec!"

He turned toward the keep. Ainslee raced down the long flight of stairs. Her dark hair bounced around her shoulders, and her green eyes shined with unshed tears. She threw herself into Alec's outstretched arms.

His chest squeezed. How he had missed her.

"Thank God ye're home," she whispered.

Alec laughed and twirled her about. He loved his sister and longed for her cheerful face. He hugged her tight before setting her from him and inspecting her from head to toe. "Ye've grown a foot while I was gone."

"Ye're just saying that."

He cupped the side of her face. "How have ye been? How is father?"

Ainslee's smile waned. "We're doing well. Da is in his chambers and I know he'll be pleased ye're home." She steered him up the stairs and into the great hall to the worn table set with steaming food. Servants hurried into the room from the kitchen, their arms straining under the weight of a large venison roast. Men, women and children roared with welcoming voices and laughter. Squeals of joy echoed through the hall.

"Why don't ye sit and have a bit to eat?" Ainslee asked. "Ye must be famished."

Eric and his men devoured Maria's cooking and the thirst-quenching ale. Whiffs of roasted boar, sweet glazed fruit and freshly baked bread wafted past Alec's nose. His stomach growled, but he longed to see his father. "I want to visit Da first."

"Verra well, I'll walk ye to his room." She hooked her arm through his and started toward the stairs.

"So tell me the news. What has gone on while I've been away?"

The corners of her mouth turned down. "Nothing much has changed. I heard that shrew ye're betrothed to complains ye've stood her up. Alec, I know she's trying to stir up trouble. Clyde, the traveling merchant, told me she no more wants this match than ye do."

A loud screech interrupted them. Ainslee and Alec stopped in mid-stride and turned to the noise.

Megan raced across the room, her russet hair falling in ringlets around her face, the wide expanse of partially-exposed bosom jiggling over her low cut bodice. "Alec, my darling," she cried before launching herself into his arms.

Ainslee stood back as his old leman kissed him soundly on the mouth. He disengaged from her grasp, but Megan ran her hands up and down his chest. Eyes twinkling, she purred, "I cannot believe ye're finally home."

"Megan, I was on my way to see Da."

"Oh, of course. Perhaps we'll *visit* later?" She winked and wiggled her shoulders, thrusting her ample breasts toward him. "I'll give ye a fine welcome home."

Her white globes were perilously close to spilling over her bodice. "Perhaps."

With his hands on her shoulders, he stepped around her and continued up the stairs. Ainslee caught up with him and he hugged her to his side as they climbed the steps.

Candles, ensconced in dark recesses lining the halls, cast shadows across the cold hard floor. With no way to warm the corridors off the main room, damp air permeated the castle. A chill seeped through Alec's clothes and he shivered. He strode down the passageway and knocked loudly on the heavy wood door to his father's room.

"Enter," his father bellowed.

When Alec opened the door, Ainslee raced into the room. "Look who's here," she announced.

Da peered up from a parchment in his lap. Furrows etched his weathered face, his bushy white brows raised in surprise. Cloudy grey eyes shining, he held his arms wide. Blue lines marred his thin skin, his swollen fingers gnarled. "Son, my God, it has been a long time. It's good to finally have ye home."

"It is indeed good to be back." Alec leaned over the bed and embraced his father. When he straightened, tears misted Da's eyes.

Alec's chest squeezed. He had missed his father.

"Sit, sit." Da waved a hand toward the bench and Ainslee plopped down. "Ye appear well, son. I want to hear all about yer adventures."

Alec chuckled and slid next to Ainslee. "I dare say we had our hands too full with the rebellion to be adventurous."

The corners of his father's mouth turned down. "I heard of our loss at Falkirk. I thank God ye were not injured."

"We had a rough go of it." Images flashed before his eyes of the wounded riddled with protruding arrows, missing and mangled limbs, blackened and burned faces, too many screaming in agony. Lifeless bodies and animal carcasses were strewn across the blood-soaked field—symbolic of Edward's design to annihilate the Scots—permanently carved into his memory.

"What went wrong?"

Alec exhaled. "William Wallace's strategy is what went wrong. It was a brutal, bloody battle. He placed groups of warriors together, crouched in a circle with their backs to each other, their shields held high for protection. When the English charged, Wallace commanded the defensive formation to rise, bringing their pikes and lances forward to spear the horses carrying the soldiers." Alec sighed and shook his head. "At first, it appeared to be working, but we hardly stood a chance once Edward brought in his archers. Blazing arrows filled the sky and rained down on the immobile formation. They were slaughtered."

Da frowned. "Did we lose any men?"

"Aye, we did—Abraham, Hugh and Keith." Alec rubbed the back of his neck. Sounds of their desperate pleas for death resounded through his head. Powerless to save his men, he had ended their misery. Now he must face their grieving families.

"What about Logan?" Ainslee asked.

Alec turned to his sister. "After Wallace's command to retreat, most clans returned home, but our cousin decided to stay and continue the fight. When I last saw him he was heading into the southeastern territory where a number of English have been crossing Scotland's borders and landing on our shores."

Da scowled. "I wish I could have been there to fight with both of ye."

His father could not have joined the battle. His useless, shriveling legs—useless due to Alec's immature and reckless actions—lay motionless. His stomach churned. "It would not have mattered. We were no match for them. We cannot continue the game of racing into battle against their massive numbers and advanced weapons."

"We cannot give in to them." Da's voice rose.

"No, we won't give in. We've come up with a new strategy, a plan to strike their convoys as they come onto our land. Brandon McLeod garners support from the clans in our region. We'll take out as many English trains of food and supplies as we can. The idea is to strike hard and fast before they know what hit them."

"A sound plan," Da agreed. "Have ye worked before with McLeod?"

Alec leaned back on the bench. "Aye, ye'd like him. He's a natural leader. Men follow him without question."

"Will ye return to battle soon?"

"I plan to stay put for a while, but I'll return when Brandon calls."

"It'll be good to have ye around." Da paused. His eyes darkened, and his bushy brows drew together. "I would like ye to settle down with Robena. Ye cannot keep her waiting forever."

Alec focused on the bedclothing, the silence heavy in the air. Finally, he raised his eyes and glared. "I'll see to it, but there is no hurry."

"No hurry? Ye've been promised to her for over two years, son. Ye need to do the honorable thing."

Heather

"Ye know I have no desire to marry her. I gave my vow, and I will see it through, but I have important business to conduct before I travel to the McMillans."

"It's for the clan that I ask ye to consummate this union. We have a tenuous relationship with the McMillans as it is."

"I'm well aware of the situation, and I will marry her, but at a time of my own choosing," Alec ground out with frustration.

Ainslee glanced at Alec and then at their father. "Da, I know ye must be tired, and Alec, ye've got to be hungry."

Thankful for the diversion, Alec stood and touched his father's shoulder. "We'll talk again tomorrow."

"Welcome home, son."

Aye, *welcome* home.

Alec followed Ainslee from the room, and shut the door behind him. He stalked down the hall, his father's words ringing through his ears. Robena McMillan. How could he marry her when his thoughts centered on Heather?

Robena's father was not a man to be trusted. His loyalties swayed with the drifting wind. He would think nothing of turning his neighbor or brother in to authorities if it advanced him politically. However, Da was adamant in his opinion on the subject of uniting the two clans. With their marriage, Alec would bring the clans together, eliminating hostilities between them and securing their relationship.

Shouts and laughter drifted down the hall, but Alec was in no mood for merriment. His gut churned with the duty he faced. How do ye tell mothers, wives and children, their loved ones were killed? How do ye console them, when there is no hope of ever seeing those fine men again?

Ainslee continued into the great room as he exited out a side door, strode down the steps and into the bailey. Cold wind sliced through his cloak. The austere weather matched the bleakness of his soul. He tugged the collar around his neck as he marched across the yard and into the barn.

Stable hands scurried in the dim light. One struggled with a heavy sack of grain while another rolled a barrel on its side toward the storage area. The lad raised his brow. "M'laird? May I help ye?"

"Nay, carry on." Alec marched down the aisle to Aeton's stall. A stable hand had stripped the horse of his saddle, brushed and rubbed his sleek dark coat. Alec stepped into the pen, and the horse tossed his head and whinnied. He patted the gelding's neck. "Ye're enjoying that grain, aren't ye?"

Running his hand over Aeton's withers, he stepped to the other side of the pen. His worn satchel, rolled up blanket, and wineskin lay on a shelf. He opened the bag and extracted Abraham's red and black plaid.

Dread descended over him as he fingered the man's belongings—a dagger, a necklace with a metal charm, and the small reed pipe he liked to play around campfires. Images of the red-haired man blowing into the instrument while lads sang to the tunes flashed through his mind. He exhaled. Abraham would be sorely missed.

He grasped the hilt of Abraham's heavy sword, took a deep breath and trod out the door to the man's family.

~~~

Alec dropped onto a bench in the main hall. A feast covered the table. A serving girl piled roasted beef and carrots on a trencher and placed it before him. Yearning to blot out visions of tear-streaked faces and sounds of grief-stricken wails, he poured a large tankard of ale and downed it in a gulp.

His men's laughter and shouts of boasting prowess pervaded the smoky hall. Two men played the flute in celebration of the troops' return. Eric twirled a lass around the floor. Her long red hair and brown woolen skirt swung as he wove her through the dancers.

Ian's guffaw caught Alec's attention, and he turned toward the sound. Surrounded by a brood of children, the man held his wife in his lap and leaned back with a burst of laughter. Ralf, sitting across the table from Ian, kissed his woman, his hands roving her assets. Alec chuckled. After two years, they were either oblivious to those around them or they did not care.

Heather

What would it be like to come home to a wife and children? Images of Heather embracing lads and lasses, weaving tales and caring for their happiness passed through his mind—her soft hands grasping his, her innocent smile brightening her eyes. But when those eyes turned wary, and hurt emanated from the azure depths, his gut knotted.

He rubbed the back of his neck. He was tired. After a long day, he headed to his bedchamber. Too many months had passed since he left Glencara, and it was good to be home. He entered his room to find lads filling a wooden tub with steaming water. Megan stretched out across his bed, her head propped on her hand.

"Thank ye," Alec said to the lads before they left and closed the door.

Megan's gaze followed him as he trod into the room and tugged his shirt over his head. He dropped it on a bench in front of the fireplace, removed his sword from his belt, and propped it against the wall.

She slipped off the bed and strolled to him, sliding her gown over her hips and depositing it on the floor. "Let me help ye."

Kneeling before him, she tugged off his boots. As she straightened, her breasts brushed his legs, then his abdomen. Her fingers stroked his chest while she placed kisses across his torso, her fingers untying his trews. "I missed ye."

Megan had been his mistress for several months before he left for the rebellion. But as he studied her, he did not have the same lustful thoughts he once held. He could not help but think of Heather's wheat-colored hair and big blue eyes, the sway of her hips and how the bodice of her gown hugged her breasts. Closing his eyes, he envisioned her, how she responded to his kiss, how she molded to him when he held her against him. His manhood stirred.

Megan began sliding his trews down his hips, but he grabbed her hand.

"Not tonight."

"What? But ye've just arrived." Her lips pursed in a pout as she rubbed her palm against the growing bulge between his legs. "And I can feel yer obvious desire for me."

"Leave me."

She drew her frame up. "Ye cannot mean that. After I have waited all these months for ye to come home, and ye want me to go away?"

"Aye." He brushed past and stepped to the tub of hot water. "Shut the door on yer way out."

"Ye will not set me aside so easily," she yelled as she grabbed her clothes, then stomped from the room and slammed the door behind her.

~~~

Alec, anxious to work with the lightweight horses, summoned his men before dawn on the field south of the castle. Streaks of red filled the sky as the sun's light crept over the horizon. A breeze blew across the dew drenched grass and the three dozen warriors who were focused on his commands.

He addressed the troops. "We'll engage the English on *our* terms, in places of *our* choosing. Edward's soldiers are heavily clad, wearing bulky cumbersome armor. They have no choice but to ride warhorses in order to carry their weight and in doing so, they give up speed and agility."

He signaled to Eric who brought one of the MacDougall horses in front of the group. Alec took the reins and paraded the chestnut animal down the line of men. The beast pranced, tossing his head, his dark mane bouncing. "We'll use these light horses to carry us into battle, enabling us to strike hard and fast, in places advantageous to a quick escape where the large destriers cannot easily follow. I want ye to train and work with these animals. I'll teach ye maneuvers to put ye in good stead when we're called on our next assignment. Any questions?"

Alec slapped the reins in his hand. "All right, let's get started." He mounted the horse and held his arms in the air while steering the beast around in a circle—first turning left and then right. "Work on commanding yer horse without using yer hands."

102

Heather

He squeezed his legs and the horse trotted forward. He moved his feet toward the animal's chest, and his mount slowed. He brought the beast to stand next to Eric while never touching the animal with his hands.

The men cheered and clapped. "How'd ye do that?" one called out.

"It's all about using yer legs to let the horse know what ye want." Alec removed the bow from his shoulder and nocked an arrow. "With yer hands free, ye can attack or defend."

He stretched the string taut and the wood squeaked under the tension. After loosening his fingers, the arrow sailed through the air and struck one of the targets placed on the side of the field.

The men hollered with excitement.

"We've eight horses for ye to train on." Alec addressed Ian, Eric and Ralf. "Each of ye take a team and run them through simple commands." He glanced at the line of men. Their faces lit. They nudged each other, chuckled and pointed at the animals. He could not help but smile at their enthusiasm. "Those who are not working with horses, do drills with swords and bows."

"Line up," Eric shouted, and the men ran to organize their groups.

~~~

Over the next four weeks, Alec worked his men well into the night only to rise early the following morning to begin again. He repeated the rigorous schedule day after day, the bitter winter adding hardship to his training regime. The men groaned over his strenuous commands, but he was determined to build a resilient force.

He spent his nights in front of the hearth, his legs stretched before the fire. On this evening, as with so many others, ale filled the long hours. The familiar warm flush spread through his body, the numbing drink his loyal companion.

He fingered Heather's worn blue ribbon. *Come home safely*, she had whispered. Even at a young age, she had been a beautiful lass. Alec smiled remembering her, remembering those carefree days gone by.

The fire popped loudly and a log rolled in the grate, bringing his thoughts back to the present. He glanced around the large room. All was quiet. Everyone had retired for the night. He leaned over, grabbed the poker, and shifted the logs.

Staring at the red sparks swirling up the chimney, he considered his life as a warrior and the rigors of battle. He thought about his home, void of the love of a wife and children. He thought of Heather and had regrets about his shortsighted decision to outright reject Alastair's offer of marriage. But what was he to do? He had given his vow to marry Robena and join the two clans.

He would do anything to take back that promise. Marriage to her would seal his fate, condemn him to a life of misery. He'd be on constant guard in his own home, never trusting those around him. Aye, it might halt future attacks on Glencara from the McMillans, but at what cost? He could not bring a snake into his bed while he watched Heather marry another man.

Like McLaughlin.

"Shite!"

Alec downed the contents of his mug. The ale burned a path from his throat to his gut. He set the tankard on the table, strode across the room and up the stairs to his chambers.

"Ye're back." Megan sashayed toward him.

Alec held up a hand. "Don't start. Ye need to leave, and I don't want ye in my private chambers again."

"Why not?" She grasped his arm. "Ye've not even lain with me *once* since yer return." Her bottom lip poked out, and she ran her palms across his chest and down his abdomen. "Ye know I can give ye what ye want."

Her fingers continued to slide lower to the front of his trews, and she squeezed his manhood.

"No."

"Is it because of Robena? She'll never know. Besides, ye're not the only one who will lie between her legs."

Alec grabbed her wrist and jerked her toward him. "What do ye mean?"

Megan winced and pulled on his fingers.

He loosened his grip.

"Just that she spreads her thighs for many men. I don't see why ye cannot lay between mine if she's not faithful to ye." Megan walked her fingertips up his chest. "She mocks ye, Alec. Laughs about how she'll bring ye an illegitimate brat."

Alec stared into her eyes. He was not surprised at Megan's words. He had suspected for some time Robena was no innocent. He scowled, stepped back, and turned from her. "Leave me."

Megan rushed around him and grabbed his shoulders. "Ye cannot mean it. Please don't turn me away."

He exhaled and shook his head. "I don't wish to hurt ye, but I do not desire ye in my bed."

Megan recoiled, her eyes narrowing. "Ye will be sorry ye tossed me aside. Many dream of becoming my man, and I'll not hold my charms from them any longer."

She jerked away and once again, gathered her clothing, then stormed from the room, slamming the door.

Alec marched to the washstand and splashed water on his face. He placed his hands on either side of the table and leaned forward. Droplets dripped off his hair and into the bowl. Considering Megan's words, he growled and grabbed a drying cloth off the chair.

Although he agreed to marry Robena, he would not put up with infidelity. If he found Megan's words to be true, he could end their betrothal with a guilt-free conscience. Even his father could not expect him to unite with a whore.

The irony of him marrying to protect his clan hit him full force. Wedding Robena McMillan would bring nothing but poison into the fold. He would pay her a visit, and as Laird of Glencara, he would make a decision he had put off too long.

# Chapter Seven

*MacDougall Castle*

Heather stepped into the dimly lit barn and admired the improvements Alec made to the structure. The area was more spacious, allowing ample room for Lindsey to work her horses. Sturdy beams ran across the ceiling holding the rafters in place, and the pulley she requested was ready for use.

She strolled past the large wooden logs secured by massive spikes and rope. Trailing her fingertips along them, she envisioned Alec hoisting the heavy timber on his shoulder and maneuvering it into place. Would she ever be able to walk through the barn without thinking of him? Although he left only a month ago, she missed him, which made her question her sanity. Aye, he had torn her heart asunder, but she longed to see him—be with him. He was forever on her mind.

Casting those thoughts aside, she strolled down the aisle to where Lindsey worked with a colt. Heather stepped onto the bottom rung of the wooden stall and leaned against a post to watch.

Her sister coaxed the young horse in a circle, never touching him, but instead, speaking softly. The animal tossed his dark head, which sported a white strip between his eyes narrowing at his nose, and a short black forelock that bounced between his ears. He followed at her shoulder, his little tail flicking. She turned left and the horse moved alongside her. When she stopped, the colt stopped. She chuckled and hugged his neck. "Verra good."

Heather clapped and Lindsey's gaze shot over the animal's back. "Oh, ye startled me. I didn't see ye."

Heather climbed the fence, threw her legs over the top railing, and dropped into the pen. "He catches on quickly." She ran her palm along his sleek coat and patted his black chest. "Ye're a fast learner, aren't ye boy?"

"Aye, he's verra bright."

"Ye're teaching him to follow verbal commands?"

"I prefer to have him know what I want without using a whip."

106

## Heather

Heather inspected the horses in the adjacent pens. "How many have ye trained?"

"Every one," Lindsey stated proudly. As if on second thought, she turned and her eyes narrowed. "Is there a reason ye're so interested in my horses?"

"I need to talk to ye, Lins."

"That sounds serious."

Heather hooked her arm through her sister's. "I trust what I'm about to tell ye will be held in strictest confidence. Ye cannot repeat this to anyone." They strolled a few paces before she faced Lindsey. "Do I have yer word?"

"Aye. Whatever is the matter? Ye're worrying me."

Heather paused and raked her teeth across her bottom lip. "I have been leading the men on assignments for the rebellion."

Lindsey frowned. "Leading the men? What do ye mean?"

"I have been the one directing Da's men into battle."

The cap on Lindsey's head appeared lopsided with straw poking out here and there. Auburn curls escaped, and tendrils framed her face. Her gaze searched Heather's eyes. "I don't understand."

Heather stepped a few feet away. "With Da's confusion, Beathan, Fergus and I agreed he could no longer lead the men, but neighboring clans must see the MacDougalls on the battlefield."

She stood still, her blue eyes intense. "Oh, my God. We all knew ye led when the castle was in danger, but to take on assignments for the rebellion?"

Heather rubbed her forehead. "It's not as if I have conducted many raids." She dropped her arm. "I know it's risky, but dressed as a lad, no one suspects anything. The clans see the MacDougalls, not the Laird's daughter. If word got out we could not be counted on, they would suspect our clan vulnerable. Lowrens McLaughlin would be breathing down our necks in no time. The night of the festival he asked for my hand. Da rejected his proposal, but I don't know how long Da will remember what he said, and to whom. I will not marry

McLaughlin. I'd rather die an old maid than risk having to spend my life with someone I don't care for, let alone loathe."

Lindsey's eyes narrowed. "Why did ye not tell me sooner?"

"I didn't want to worry ye, but I have no choice now. I need yer help."

Her sister's stance relaxed. "What can I do?"

"Ye're not going to like what I ask, but we could use yer horses. We'll have an advantage if we ride them. Da agreed to hunt down an English convoy heading into the heart of the country. Yer horses are small and agile, and they would enable us to strike and retreat quickly."

Lindsey turned away. "I cannot believe what I'm hearing. *Ye* leading the men?" She suddenly swung back to Heather. "What of Da?"

"I told him he and Fergus must stay here and protect the clan. So far he's agreed without question. He knows he's losing his memory and it frightens him."

"But ye could be killed."

"It's a risk I have to take. Fergus, Beathan and I handpicked the most loyal of Da's men. It took some convincing, but each one feels devoted to Da for various reasons. They took an oath to fight with me, help me protect MacDougall keep. No one wants to see Da cast aside. And no one wants to see the clan fall into the hands of Lowrens McLaughlin or Symon. They'll keep Da's secret."

Lindsey crossed her arms over her waist. "Ye can have whatever horses ye need, but I would like to train with ye. I can teach the men how to handle the lighter animals. They're not like the warhorses the men are accustomed to riding. These horses have a sensitive mouth, and it does not take much coaxing to get them to do what ye want."

Heather threw her arms around Lindsey. "I knew I could count on ye."

"There's one more thing."

Heather straightened. "What is it?"

"While we're confessing, I need to tell ye…I have been a runner for Hamish."

## Heather

A runner? Heather stared at her sister, searching her blue eyes. "I beg yer pardon?"

"I deliver messages to our brother Scots."

She grasped Lindsey's upper arm. "When?"

Her sister rolled her shoulder, breaking out of Heather's grasp. "Do ye remember my visits to Clara's?"

Heather's brow knit. "Aye, ye visit her quite often..." Her voice trailed off.

Lindsey nodded.

Heather's pulse skipped a beat. Her younger sister risked her life to deliver messages? If she was caught, she would be lucky if the soldiers only killed her. "Oh Lins, I had no idea. Why did ye not tell me?"

Lindsey shrugged. "I guess we have both been keeping secrets."

~~~

A glow emanating from a low fire in the hearth lit the dark bedchamber. Heather tucked a blanket around her shoulders and stared into the flames. She would lead the men today. They would follow her command in destroying the English procession—a dangerous task and one she did not take lightly.

Her thoughts turned to Alec. How she yearned to confide in him, to shake her weighty responsibilities. How she longed to wrap herself in his strength, revel in his protection and love. She scoffed. He was betrothed. Robena would be the one to lie in his arms, mother his children, and remain at his side.

Her chest clenched.

There was no reason to continue these torturous thoughts.

A breeze wafted down the chimney. The fire popped, red glowing coals flickered to life, flames curling around the charred wood. The early morning was quiet and peaceful. If only she could describe her life in the same light. She sighed. It was time to be up and dressed. "Please, Lord, see us through this assignment. Watch over and protect us."

She slid out of bed, poured water in the basin on her table and washed her face before pulling on a pair of leather breeches. They fit her thighs and hips snuggly, but her oversized shirt and cloak would provide cover.

She fumbled through the chest at the foot of her bed for the soft wraps, the long lengths of cloth that would minimize her bosom, conceal her curves. She wound the binding around her chest and took a deep breath to ensure the material was not too tight. When she placed her tunic over her head, no one could see the outline of her breasts or the curve of her hips.

She brushed her hair, twisted it into a knot and secured it on top of her head. A dark scarf hung on the inside of her trunk. She tugged it from the hook and wrapped it around her head. When she studied herself in the mirror, a lean lad stared back. Once she smudged her face with soot, she would blend in with the other warriors.

She strapped her knife to her belt, then slung her bow and quiver of arrows over her shoulder and picked up her sword. While straightening the straps across her chest, she glanced around her bedchamber. Her gown lay across the foot of her rumpled bed and her wrap was draped over a chair. She closed the chest and took a fortifying breath before she marched from her room, trotted down the stairs and out the door.

Sunlight crept over the horizon, and a fine mist hung in the cool morning air. Only a few servants were afoot at this time of day. Da's men milled around the bailey, packing the last of their supplies.

Heather strolled across the yard and into the dim barn. "Good morning."

As always, Lindsey helped with the animals. "I saddled yer horse."

"Ahh, thank ye." Heather dropped her satchel on the ground next to her mount. She tied her sword onto the saddle, picked up a rolled blanket and secured it as well.

Lindsey slid her hand down Heather's back. "Promise ye'll be careful. Don't take unnecessary chances."

Heather glanced over her shoulder and grinned. "I never do."

110

Heather

Beathan marched down the main aisle toward her. "The men are ready."

"Let's be on our way." Heather hugged Lindsey and climbed onto the saddle. "Take care of Da."

"I will," Lindsey whispered. "Godspeed, sister."

~~~

Mist swirled around the horses' hooves as they ambled down the worn path. In order to avoid unwanted attention, Heather led the group through the dense forest. The soft undergrowth muted the sound of their hoof beats. Water from last night's rain dripped from the trees and dribbled down her neck. She shivered and tugged her grey woolen cloak tighter around her shoulders.

They rode all day before finally coming to the crossroads, their land-marker. The sun had dropped low, filling the evening sky with hues of blue and pink. Darkness would soon be upon them.

"Set up camp," Heather called to the men.

"There's a flat area to the right." Beathan pointed to strand of trees, a creek running alongside. He nudged his horse, and she and the men followed.

Before long, they had the animals unsaddled and brushed down. Heather climbed on a large boulder, stretched out her tired legs and opened her wine skin. Beathan dropped next to her and handed her a hunk of bread and cheese. Her belly growled, and she welcomed the light meal.

He leaned back, swigging a flask of ale. She was glad he was with her. He had been like a big brother, always watching out for her, always there to lend a hand, catch her when she fell. As her steadfast confidant, she grew up around him and had not considered him in any manner other than a close friend.

Her gaze traveled across his brown hair and down his rugged, whiskered face. He was a handsome man, one she could rely on and trust without a doubt.

Perhaps she should plead with him to become her husband, rule by her side.

111

He smiled while biting into his bread. "How do ye fair?"

"I'm fine." She sipped her wine.

His eyes narrowed. "Ye had a faraway look."

She broke off a piece of cheese. "I was thinking of what a help ye've been to me, and I thank ye."

Beathan stopped chewing and nodded. "Ye're welcome, Heather." He resumed eating and reached for his flask again. "We'll do well."

He chugged down the remainder of the ale and wiped his mouth on his sleeve.

"I hope ye're right. Hamish said Brandon expects the soldiers will pass through here tomorrow evening. I would like to have everything in place by mid day. The sooner we start, the more time we'll have to set up, and the more time we'll have to ensure we don't make mistakes."

~~~

A shrill whistle of warning broke the silence. The soldiers approached. Heavy hooves bearing down on them vibrated the ground. Heather nodded at Beathan. He raised a hand and made several circles in the air, signaling the men to get ready.

Heather focused her attention on the gap in the path between the large boulders. They would allow a half dozen or so through the opening before her men would pounce on the unsuspecting soldiers.

The clank of metal and the squeak of leather echoed through the gap before the first man cleared the opening, then the second, and the third. Massive horses hauled two large wagons down the dirt path. Lindsey would be pleased to have those animals in her stables.

Heather hid behind a boulder with an arrow nocked, aiming at the procession. She drew it tight, and as the sixth man cleared the gap, she let it fly.

It hit him squarely in the chest. He clutched the shaft and toppled to the ground.

112

Heather

With the yells of the descending MacDougalls, horses shrieked and shied away. Heather nocked another arrow and sent it slicing through the air.

*Sfit!*

Her target screamed and gurgled before he fell to the side.

The unsuspecting, heavily clad soldiers encumbered under weighty armor, fell prey to her warriors. Grunts and shouts filled her ears as she grabbed another arrow from the quiver on her back and let her gaze skim the battle. Her fingers eased and the barb whistled through the air and sank into another soldier's neck.

Beathan jerked a man from his horse. He landed on the ground, and her captain smashed the soldier's face with his booted foot. William and Thomas yanked another to the dirt as Heather shot the next man who appeared between the boulders.

A bloody scene played out. They would take no prisoners, nor would they leave witnesses to alert future convoys.

Although everything suddenly fell quiet, Heather's pulse hammered in her ears. She searched the area for her men. "Beathan, William, David and Brian, — five, six, seven," she trailed off, her finger in the air as she counted, "eleven, twelve." She sighed with relief. When she jumped from the boulder, she stumbled over a dead solider. One of her arrows protruded from his chest. His unseeing eyes stared and her hand flew to her throat. She scrunched her face, her gut churning. She would never get used to that sight.

Beathan grasped her shoulders, his intense eyes studying her face. "Mistress?"

She clutched his strong forearm and swallowed hard. Once she caught her breath, she nodded. "Secure the food and supplies, and let's get out of here."

"I'll gather the horses."

Heather scrambled across the rocks to the wagons. The animals were tense, spooked from the fray. Jonathan stroked the nose of a large horse harnessed to the first cart.

"As soon as he calms, lead him around the bend and circle back." Heather glanced over her shoulder at the other wagon. "I'll ask Randall to drive that one."

"He's a bit jumpy, but he'll be all right." Jonathan patted the horse's neck and climbed onto the wagon's rickety seat.

"Randall, drive that dray behind Jonathan. I want to head home quickly."

"Aye, mistress." He flicked the reins on the rump of the horse. The wagon jerked and creaked, inching down the rocky path.

"Discard the bodies, and clean the area," Heather ordered. "We can't leave any evidence."

William and David searched soldiers' pockets for documents or anything of value. They jerked the men's boots off and stripped them of their warm cloaks before dragging their bodies into a thicket.

An English saber lay in the grass. Heather picked it up and turned it over, testing the weight and balance. An intricate design etched the heavy ornate blade and wire wrapped the leather grip.

Beathan whistled low. "Impressive."

Heather inspected it once more then handed it to him. His brow shot up.

"Take it. Ye deserve it. It's too heavy and cumbersome for me anyway."

Beathan grasped the sword and sliced it through the air. "Thank ye, Heather."

She gazed over his shoulder at the men. "Round up the horses. I'm anxious to be home."

"Aye." Beathan glanced at the darkening sky and trotted off calling, "If we hurry, we can arrive home by midnight."

" Home," she whispered. Images of Symon's attack flashed through her mind. "I just hope we arrive to find it as we left it."

## *Chapter Eight*

*Glencara Castle*
*December 1298*

"Riders coming!"

Alec turned as horses' hooves clattered on the wooden bridge leading into the bailey. Brandon McLeod led several men into the yard.

"My friend," McLeod called and dismounted. He tugged off his gloves and extended his hand. Creases splayed the edges of his brown eyes and grey streaked his dark hair. "It's been a long time."

Alec grasped Brandon's hand. "Aye, too long. What brings ye to Glencara?"

Brandon brushed dust off his trews with his gloves. His eyes darkened. "I have business to discuss."

"Verra well, come inside."

The men strode through the bailey, up the stairs to the keep and into the solar. Alec poured two cups of mead and handed one to Brandon.

His friend sipped the drink and closed his eyes. When he opened them, he smiled. "Aye, that's good."

Alec held up the decanter. Brandon nodded and extended his mug. Alec refilled it, placed the bottle on the desk and sat in his chair.

"I need ye to destroy a band of soldiers northwest of here near Argyle. We expect Edward's food shipment to travel through that area and we need it stopped. The MacDougalls recently ambushed a convoy and it severely hurt the English. We have it on good authority the soldiers are close to starving."

Alec's legs lay across the edge of the desk, his feet crossed at the ankles. He swirled the amber liquid in his mug. "Ye say the MacDougalls captured the shipment?" How could Alastair organize and coordinate an attack? Perhaps the young warrior led his men. "Alastair suffered a bad injury not too long ago. I'm surprised he was well enough to take on such an assignment."

"I'm not aware of his injury, but last month they stopped a band of soldiers escorting food, weapons and supplies. It was a decisive blow." Brandon balanced his mug on his thigh. "I'd like ye to join forces with Robert Graham. Between the two of ye and the MacDougalls, we'll have the southwest corner covered."

"I'll see it done."

"Good, I knew I could count on ye." Brandon drained the contents of his cup.

Alec stared into the amber liquid. "I've not heard from Logan. Have ye any word from their group? He led the forces near Dumfries."

Brandon set his empty cup on the table. "There have been a number of skirmishes in our southern area. Some have been successful, but there is an English contingency stationed just over the border in Northumberland. A man named Arnold Collins is the commander who controls the garrison. He's brutal, Alec." Brandon leaned back in his chair. "I'll ask around. I'm scouting ports along the Firth of Clyde to guard potential landing sites. If I learn anything, I'll get word to ye."

"I worry as to why we haven't heard from him." Close as brothers, he had grown up with Logan. He prayed his cousin was too preoccupied with successful raids to send word. Other alternatives were too painful to consider.

Brandon stood. "I'd best head out. Hamish will inform ye of future duties."

Alec's legs dropped off the desk. "Aye, we'll watch for him."

"I anticipate supply wagons and reinforcements to pass soon. Ye need to be in place by the end of the week."

"We'll be there."

After seeing Brandon off, Alec motioned to Eric. They made their way back to the castle. "We travel to the McMillans tomorrow. It's time I confront this situation with Robena. Afterwards, we'll head to the Grahams to garner Robert's support. Tell Ian and Ralf they ride with us."

Eric's brow rose. "I didn't realize ye were ready to fetch yer bride. Do ye want me to send word to the McMillans?"

Alec shook his head. "No, I'll arrive unannounced."

"Unannounced?" Eric whistled low. "Verra well."

Alec continued into the main hall where serving girls set out the evening meal. The aroma of savory stew wafted past as he walked down the line of tables and into the kitchen. A lass stirred a caldron over the fire in the hearth against the back wall. Two lads poured buckets of water in the barrel next to her.

Bent over a worktable pushing a rolling pin through dough, Maria concentrated on making bannock. Oat flour sprinkled her grey hair and dough stuck to her elbows. When she glanced up, her mouth dropped. It was not often he visited the kitchen.

"I would have a word with ye."

Maria wiped her hands on a cloth while approaching him, her eyes wide. "Aye, m'laird, what can I do for ye?"

"Ye have a daughter, Skena?"

"Aye, is there something amiss?" she asked, her dark eyes concerned.

"No. I would like for ye to move her into the keep. Train her in managing yer chores." Alec surveyed the busy room. Several women cut vegetables at the wooden worktable while two others placed platters of roasted boar and smoked fish on trays. "Ye can use the help."

Maria's head bobbed. "Thank ye, m'laird. She'll be pleased."

Alec nodded and left the room. When he entered the hall, Ainslee sauntered up to him and looped her arm through his. "Brother, ye've been far too busy training. I haven't seen much of ye since ye returned."

"We have to be ready to strike our enemy and defend our home."

"I understand, but must ye work every day? Can ye not take a day or two of rest?"

Alec extracted his arm from her grasp and sat at the table. He reached across the food for the pitcher of ale and filled his large tankard.

Ainslee plopped onto the bench beside him. "I worry about ye. Ye're driving yerself too hard."

Refreshing liquid slid down his throat. He stabbed a piece of meat and seared her with a dark stare. "There is nothing to worry about."

He continued to eat in silence, the subject closed.

Eric and Ian joined them.

"Lass," Eric acknowledged Ainslee as he sat next to her, then turned to Alec. "Everything's ready. I asked Kirk to continue the training."

Alec nodded. He had intended to visit Graham since he departed MacDougall Castle last month. He not only needed Robert's support in battle, but he'd ask him to keep an eye on the MacDougalls. Guilt weighed heavy as he feared he left them unprotected. Aye, he restored the buildings and shored up their surrounding walls, but he could not shake the grim feeling Symon lurked close by. His scowl deepened, and he pushed away from the table.

"Be ready at dawn."

~~~

The trip to McMillan Castle took two long days. As the sun set on the evening of the second, Alec raised his hand to stop. To the left, thick trees, their branches devoid of leaves, stood like sentries guarding a secluded riverbed. Large boulders blocked the view of the road, an area where they could watch for intruders. "We'll make camp ahead."

The night grew cold and damp. The men huddled near a small campfire seeking the meager warmth it offered. Alec poked a blazed log and sparks swirled into the dark night. Flames danced, casting shadows across the men's faces.

Alec rested his forearms on his thighs and addressed his men. "As ye know, we travel to the McMillans to fetch Mistress Robena."

The men grumbled.

"It's Da's wish to unite with their clan." Alec paused and pinned each man with a stare. "And it's *my* wish we do what is *best* for our clan."

The men nodded in agreement.

118

"Once we arrive, I'll assess the situation and decide what course of action to take. If nothing is amiss, we'll deposit Mistress McMillan at Glencara and ride to the Grahams." Alec leaned back and swigged his ale.

"McLeod still works with William Wallace?" Eric asked.

Alec swiped his sleeve across his mouth. "Aye, although Wallace disbanded, his commanders still include us in their military tactics. Wallace asks the clans to organize their own army of sorts, striking quickly and often, taking advantage of the starving and depleted English forces."

"'Tis a good plan," Ian offered. "It might work."

"Aye," Ralf agreed. "What would our lives be like without *Sassenachs* breathing down our necks?"

An existence without constantly being on alert, training to protect and defend against English soldiers? If Edward's advance into their country indicated things to come, the Scots would be forever on guard.

Alec rolled out a plaid. "Get some rest. I want each of ye vigilant tomorrow."

The men settled on the hard, cold ground, sleeping as close to the fire as safety permitted. Alec tossed and turned, dreaming of Heather, her beaten face crying out to him. He struggled to reach her, his legs unmoving as if mired in quicksand. Symon's hands circled her throat. She clutched at his fingers, her frightened eyes beseeching Alec's help. Her mouth worked, but no sound uttered. Her blue eyes dimmed, and her limp body crumpled to the floor.

"No," Alec shouted and jerked upright.

His men leaped up, weapons in hand.

Alec ran a hand over his face, then glanced at Eric, Ian and Ralf. "'Twas only a dream, go back to sleep."

He rolled off his pallet and strode to the river. Staring at the dark rushing water, his heart slammed against his chest, his soul cloaked in ominous foreboding.

~~~

Light broke the horizon with red streaks painting the sky. Dew dripped from leaves and a light frost covered the ground. Alec rose, impatient to resume their journey. He kicked the ashes of their campfire. Smoke wafted and he tossed in the remnants of his cup's mead. The men snatched hunks of bread and cheese while they packed their belongings.

Alec grabbed Aeton's reins and swung onto the saddle. "Time to head out."

He led the group from the woods, continuing their swift pace to the McMillans. As miles stretched, his mind raced with thoughts of his pending surprise. What would he find? Would he witness Robena in the arms of another man? If not, how could he break their betrothal? His gut churned. He might be forced to escort her back to Glencara—a march to his death.

The midday sun rose overhead and warmed the ground. Aeton's sides heaved. A small stream from a loch ran alongside the road. "Rest yer horses."

Alec dismounted, strode to the water, and squatted. While Aeton drank, Alec splashed water on his face.

Eric stooped on the grassy bank and dipped his hands into the water. "We should be there shortly."

Alec wiped his face with his forearm, droplets dripping from his hair. "Aye, the sooner the better." He grabbed a cloth out of his satchel and rubbed it over his head. "Ye know I loathe the idea of bringing Robena into our clan. Hell, the servants dread thinking of her firm hand and unreasonable temper." He shook the fabric in his fist. "I won't have them abused if it means I must lock Robena in her chambers!"

He shoved the cloth back in his bag.

Eric stood. "Yer da seems unwavering on the subject."

Alec bent, picked up several pebbles, and tossed them up and down. He pitched one in the water. "He's convinced this alliance is what we need, and he's too damn stubborn to see the truth of it. The only thing we'll accomplish is to bring a snake into our nest."

He skimmed another pebble across the stream.

Eric stepped forward. "What will ye do?"

Alec paused. "I'll make good on my word and marry her if I believe it's for the best."

"And if it's not?"

Alec pitched another stone. "I'll end it."

Eric stared at him, lines creasing his forehead.

Alec returned the glare. "I know ye think that might cause war between our clans. But I won't bring poison into Glencara to ward off a possible attack from the McMillans."

His friend's stance eased, and he rubbed the back of his neck. "Nay, ye're right. No one wants the McMillans in our midst."

"We have to strike a food shipment in the northwest woods. Brandon asked us to gain Graham's help and leave for the corridor by the end of the week." The sun had started its decent. "Our time is running out."

He threw the remaining pebbles in the loch and grabbed Aeton's reins. "Mount up."

Several hours later, Alec crested a hill and surveyed the town below. Dark clouds settled over McMillan Castle. People worked in the surrounding fields and wagons moved in and out the castle's front gate.

He nodded to his men, and they started toward the keep. Alec dismounted at the edge of the village, and his men followed. He walked Aeton down a dirt path, sidestepping puddles in the road. At first glimpse, the McMillans appeared to be thriving, but a closer look told a story of waste and slovenly men, inebriated early in the day with many passed out along the road.

Dirty faces of children in threadbare clothing watched Alec with widened eyes. Barking dogs ran between them, snarling and biting at each other. Three women gathered at the well stared openly at Alec and his men when they passed.

"I'm available if yer coin is good, honey," a buxom woman called from across the yard.

A woman next to her cackled. "Ye don't need coin to lie between my thighs, handsome."

The men ignored the lewd comments and made their way to the stables. An older man with white tufts of hair surrounding his otherwise bald head threw his rake to the side and shuffled to Alec. "Wha' can I do fer ye?"

"We need to board our mounts." Alec handed the man several coins. "Brush them down. Give them oats and fresh water."

The man jingled the gold pieces in his hand, and his eyes lit. "Aye, m'laird. I'll take guid care of 'em fer ye."

Alec removed his sword from Aeton's saddle and strapped it to his belt. Eric, Ian and Ralf did the same before the old man led their horses down the aisle and disappeared into a stall.

The smell of manure overwhelmed Alec and he wrinkled his nose. "Filth seems to be a common theme amongst the McMillans."

"Aye." Eric picked up his foot and shook his leg to dislodge muck stuck to his boot.

Alec stepped out of the barn and started across the bailey. "Stay vigilant. I need not remind ye we're in the devil's den."

Several men leaned against the wall surrounding the bailey. A burly man nudged the one standing next to him. A few moments later, they pushed away from the wall and sauntered toward Alec.

"Who are ye, and what do ye want?" the gruff man shouted. Others in the bailey turned at the commotion and stared.

Alec ignored him and marched toward the keep, but the McMillans stepped in front of him, blocking his path. The smell of unwashed bodies, perspiration and sour ale assaulted his nostrils.

"Ye had best stand aside," Alec snarled.

The man smirked. Blackened rotting teeth matched the stench of his breath. "Who are ye to order me around?"

"I'm Laird Campbell of Glencara, here for Mistress McMillan."

"Is that right?" The man pushed Alec with a beefy hand. "I donnae recall her inviting guests."

In a flash, Alec slipped his dagger from his belt and held it to the man's throat. "I said to back away or feel my blade."

The stunned man's eyes widened. "Ye had best watch yerself."

"Are ye threatening me?"

The man's eyes darted to his right and left. His men were held in equally compromising positions. Alec put pressure on his knife, and the man swallowed hard. Shaking his head, he responded, "Nay, ye can go on yer way."

Alec shoved him. "After ye."

The assailant turned as Alec's men released the others. He nudged his cohorts before stalking off, his dark beady eyes looking over his shoulder.

Alec sheathed his dagger. Hostile faces of men and women milling in the bailey watched him and his men. "Stay alert."

He squared his shoulders and continued into the keep. Alec, Eric, Ralf and Ian strode into the main hall. Men and half-dressed women lounged on cushions scattered about the room. Dogs fought over scraps of rotting meat discarded on the filthy floor rushes. The putrid stench of decaying food and excrement hit him full force.

An old woman hobbled over to them. "May I help ye?"

"I'm Alec Campbell, Laird of Glencara, and I'm here to see Mistress McMillan."

The woman's mouth dropped open. "Laird Campbell?"

"Aye."

The woman wrung her hands. "But the mistress did not expect ye."

Hands on hips, he surveyed the main room. His nose wrinkled with disgust before turning back to the woman. "Nevertheless, I'm here. Please inform her I wish to speak with her."

"Aye, m'laird," the woman replied. "Come with me."

She turned and limped off. Alec and his men followed her down a dark corridor lined with flickering torches to a room at the end of the hall. She knocked loudly on the closed door and waited.

Moments passed.

She knocked again.

Finally, a man shouted, "Enter."

The maid stuck her head inside the chamber and stammered. "M...M'laird, madam, ye have visitors."

Alec brushed past the old woman and advanced into the room.

Robena, her dark locks framing her creamy face and green eyes, lounged on a chair, her legs stretched out, her feet resting on a stool. His gaze landed on her bulging abdomen. She jerked her tan wrap tighter around her stomach and straightened.

"Laird Campbell? Why, we had no idea ye would be here today," Herbert McMillan asserted, glancing at Robena, then back to Alec. He heaved his rotund frame off the bench. His ruddy face grew splotchy, his pudgy cheeks shaking. "Yer disrespect is incredible."

Alec laughed. "Ye don't deserve respect." He turned to Robena. A stilted moment passed. "Whose child is it?"

Robena glowered, but she did not utter a word.

"Have there been so many ye do not or mayhap cannot know for sure?"

Robena slapped her palms on the arms of the chair. "Ye whore-son! How dare ye act betrayed. This is all yer fault." She rubbed her swollen abdomen. "Ye left me to wonder if ye were coming for me. Ye left me to wonder if ye were even alive. I had no word from ye, so I turned to others to console my loneliness."

Alec chuckled deep in his chest. "Verra dramatic indeed, mistress. Have ye been rehearsing?"

"Ye will not speak to my daughter in this manner," Herbert asserted.

"Ye're quite right. I have only one more thing to say." Alec faced Robena. "I'm freeing ye from our betrothal."

Robena gasped, her red lips pursed. "Ye cannot do that."

"I just did. Enjoy yer life, madam." He tipped his head toward them and spun to leave.

"Ye will regret humiliating my daughter, Laird Campbell. I will allow no one to treat her with such little regard. I demand retribution."

Alec stopped in midstride. In two steps, he grabbed a fist full of Herbert's tunic and jerked him forward, the man's flabby cheeks jiggling. "Ye will get no compensation for yer daughter's whoring ways, and if ye know what's good for ye, ye will heed my warning to stay off our land."

He shoved MacMillan from him. The man tripped and fell backward, landing on the filthy floor. Looming over him, Alec sneered. "Ye had best thank yer maker I do not seek reparation from yer clan. However, having been saved from a hellacious existence with yer daughter is compensation enough for me."

He pivoted on his heel and stormed from the room.

Ian, Ralf and Eric followed him from the keep and into the bailey. Alec took a deep breath and let it out slowly. Relief washed over him. He raised his face to the sky. The weight of the chains binding him to Robena fell away. "Let's get our horses and be on our way. Watch yer backs."

The four men purposefully strode across the bailey and into the barn. The stable master ambled down the aisle. "Ye're leaving already?"

Alec marched toward the man. "Aye, we need our horses."

"They're in the back stalls."

After saddling the animals, they mounted and Alec led his group from the barn. He nudged Aeton and trotted past the line of McMillans eyeing him with hatred. They cleared the gates and continued down the road for a good distance before Alec grinned. "Damn, but it does feel good to free my neck of that strangulation."

"Ye're so sure yer da will not be angry over this broken strangulation?" Eric asked.

Alec shook his head. "Even Da would not have me marry into that hellhole. He worries McMillan will attack, but I say let him. I won't be held prisoner for the rest of my life to prevent a possible strike from Herbert McMillan." Alec nudged his horse into a trot while calling over his shoulder, "And if he attacks, I'll kill him."

Eric nudged his horse next to him. "Ye expected as much, didn't ye?"

"Aye, I wasn't surprised at what I found, and I thank God I was not trapped in marriage to her."

Eric chuckled. "Ye're one lucky man."

Ian rode alongside them. "What will ye do now?"

"We'll stop at Glencara and get fresh supplies. I'll talk to Da about Robena, and then we'll be on our way to the Grahams."

Thunder rumbled in the distance as Ralf caught up to the men. "Looks like we might be in for a storm."

"Pick up the pace," Alec shouted as he spurred Aeton down the road. "If we beat the bad weather to the south bend, we can take shelter in the caves."

As large raindrops splattered the ground, he recognized the hollowed out caverns in the side of the mountain. He slid off the saddle and led his horse to a worn path winding up the hill. Rocks and pebbles rolled under his boots, but he secured his footing and climbed up the steep slope. The men cleared the cave's entrance as rain fell in earnest.

Alec's eyes adjusted to the cavern's dim light, the sound of rain echoing against the cavern walls. While the cave was not deep, the cavity would protect them from the tempestuous weather. Charred remnants of a campfire, sticks and debris scattered the dirt floor. Cold air swirled around him, his breath a fog as he guided Aeton to the back wall. His men followed, tugged saddles from their mounts, and dropped their satchels on the ground.

Ralf held up a worn grey sack. "We've got plenty of bannock and beef jerky left."

"What? None of Rena's sweetmeats?" Eric teased as he stooped and gathered sticks into a pile.

"Nay, he ate them before she could get them into the bag," Ian chimed in.

"Och, ye're just jealous the cook's sweet on me." Ralf straightened and placed his meaty paw on his chest in mock indignation. "Can I help it if she is constantly stuffing me with her tarts?"

Heather

Alec chuckled while rummaging through his saddlebag. He extracted his wine skin, turned the container up, and gulped several mouthfuls of the refreshing drink.

Eric started a fire, and tenuous flames flickered around the dry wood. Kneeling next to the blaze, he fed it with sticks, a few pieces at a time. Alec handed him a hunk of bread and headed to the opening of the cave.

A clap of thunder crashed and the wind picked up, tossing tree branches and sending leaves swirling. The deluge carved rivulets through a dirt path snaking down the side of the mountain. Cold spray peppered his face and trickled down his neck.

He leaned against the cave opening and took another swig of wine. Although the turbulent storm raged, calm swathed his soul. After seeing firsthand what Robena and the McMillans were about, he knew he had made the right decision in ending their sham of a betrothal. He hoped his father would understand. Da wouldn't expect him to be saddled with a whore, even for the sake of peace.

His thoughts turned to Heather. Would she consider him for her husband? He smiled, remembering her compassionate manner with the children, the stories she told and the sweet treats she had baked for them. He thought of her beautiful thick hair and the ribbons she loved to wear. Unlike Robena, Heather's beauty ran through her core. Not only was she pleasing to the eye, but she was loving and caring. She would make a good wife, the perfect Lady of Glencara.

His brow knit in a scowl. Why had Lowrens McLaughlin paid a visit to Alastair? Were the clans closely linked? Thoughts of Heather and Lowrens dancing across the platform at the festival bore into his mind. His chest clenched at memories of the brute holding her close, his hands roaming her back. Did she enjoy the man's embrace?

Thunder cracked, and the ground vibrated. He watched the torrent of rushing water and prayed he would arrive at MacDougall Castle in time to thwart any plans Lowrens might have set in motion.

# Chapter Nine

Alec pounded up the bailey steps and into the keep. Although cold and tired from his ride to the McMillans, he was anxious to put the subject of his betrothal behind him. Da would not be happy with his decision, but blast it all, he'd made the right one. He would not compromise his principles or the well-being of the clan over a potential threat from Herbert McMillan. Prepared for battle, he strode through the main hall.

Ainslee placed a platter of cabbage and spinach on a trestle table. She straightened and watched him cross the room. "Where is Robena?"

"At McMillan Castle," Alec called over his shoulder. *Where she belongs, living amongst the debased pigs.*

His sister wiped her hands on a cloth and ran after him up the stairs. "Why did she not come back with ye?"

Alec marched down the corridor, the thud of his boots loud on the stone floor. Torches secured in sconces lined the dark passageway, the flames casting shadows across the walls. He knocked on Da's door and waited until he heard his father answer before treading into the room with Ainslee tagging behind.

Da sat in a chair before the hearth. A brown woolen blanket, littered with wood shavings, draped his shriveled legs. His head jerked up, and he lowered a partially whittled figure to his lap.

"Ye're home so soon?" His steely eyes narrowed as he fingered the short blade in his hand. "I did not expect ye and Mistress McMillan for several more days."

Alec stopped in front of his father, arms crossing his chest. "I returned home alone."

Da's chin dropped. "Son …"

Alec held up a hand. "Let me explain."

His father's mouth tightened into a thin line. He sighed dramatically, his shoulders sagging. Ainslee slipped into a chair next to him.

"I intended to bring her back as my bride. I considered what ye said, and I decided to go to her..." He paused. "Unannounced, to assess the situation."

Da leaned forward, his eyes narrowing. "Ye did not inform her ye were coming?"

"No."

His father's white brow creased, and he flopped against the back of the chair, crossing his arms over his chest. "That action alone might cause a battle."

"Herbert McMillan does not concern me. If he attacks, his clan will be met with ruthless force. I will not cower from his threat of retribution."

Da shook his head from side to side and agitatedly brushed the shavings from his lap. "Ye insulted him." His grey eyes turned steely. "Ye have once again brought a fight to our clan and I am no longer able to defend it in your absence."

Pain shot into Alec's gut as if his father rammed a dull sword through him.

He swallowed hard, choking on the strangling emotions. "I will not let the clan down. I have done everything I could to atone for my lack of judgment."

Da grunted. "Ye marrying McMillan's daughter was part of the penance. She is a beautiful woman. What man would not desire her as his wife? I fail to understand yer actions."

"I wanted to uncover the real Robena, see her unprepared and caught off guard before I brought her into our home. And I daresay I saw her integrity firsthand. Her belly swells with another man's child."

Ainslee gasped. "Robena is with child?"

"Aye. I had heard rumors of her improper behavior. As Laird of Glencara, I won't marry that whore and comingle with her disorderly, untrustworthy and filthy clan."

Da's mouth hung open. "Ye're sure of this?"

"I witnessed her protruding belly. There is no mistake."

His father's ashen face turned to the hearth, and he stared into the flames.

129

Stilted moments passed. What the hell was Da thinking? Even *he* could not condone Robena's illicit behavior.

Finally, his father broke the silence. "I'm sorry, son. I had no idea. Herbert has been a threat for many years, but ye're right. We have never bowed to any clan, and we won't start now. I fear my own interests blinded me to the truth. I'm getting old, and I'd like ye to marry before I die." Eyes beseeching, he added, "Ye're a warrior first and foremost, but ye are Laird of a clan that needs yer heirs and a lady to run the keep when yer sister marries."

"I agree and have decided to ask Laird MacDougall's daughter, Heather, to become my wife."

Ainslee inhaled and her hands flew to her mouth. "Oh, Alec! That is wonderful news."

Da's head tilted. "Alastair's daughter? Isn't Heather his first child?"

"She is."

"Tell me about her. I have not seen her since she was a wee lass."

An image of Heather drifted across his mind. "She's caring and works hard to run MacDougall Castle. She keeps the records and manages the servants, but she always finds time for others." Recalling her imitation of the cockatrice, he chuckled. "She has sweet treats baked for the children, and she loves to weave scary tales to wee ones around the hearth at night. Ye will like her. She's a most gracious lady."

Da grinned and winked. "Do ye love her?"

Alec straightened. *Love?* He had not thought of loving a lass since he was an inexperienced buck. All too quickly he had learned the cruelties of betrayal and unfaithfulness. He would never fall into that trap again.

"I enjoy her company." End of subject. He marched across the room to the door. "In the morning, I travel to the Grahams. I plan to stop by the MacDougalls on my way home."

"If ye're bringing Heather here, ye must tell Megan to leave," Ainslee said.

"Megan? We have not…been together for years."

Heather

"Regardless, she'll not be happy to hear yer news, and I would not put it past her to cause trouble for Mistress MacDougall."

~~~

Alec and Eric rode into the Graham's bailey with Ian and Ralf close behind. Several lads ran to greet them and take their horses. Alec dismounted and tugged off his gloves.

The clank of hammers striking metal rang out as Robert worked alongside several lads repairing a wagon wheel. He straightened, his eyes narrowing. A broad smile broke across his face. He stepped over to the men while wiping his hands on his trews. "Alec, it's good to see ye."

Alec grasped Robert's hand and nodded at the others around the wagon. "It is good to see ye as well. It has been a while since I was here last." Alec surveyed the bailey. "All seems to be well."

"We're managing." Robert clapped Ian's shoulder and addressed the others. "It has been a long time. Eric and Ralf, I'm pleased ye're still in one piece."

Ralf chuckled. "I have a new scar or two, but for the most part, still in one piece."

Robert turned to Alec. "Have ye seen many English?"

"That's why we're here. Brandon McLeod asked for our assistance, and I told him I would pay ye a visit."

"Verra well, come inside." Robert extended his arm toward the keep and led the way across the yard. Several lads, sloshing water from containers, hurried into the barn. Two women, their arms full of linens, strolled past.

"This way." Robert guided them into the great hall. Orange flames blazed in the large, stone hearth. The rushes on the floor emitted a pleasant spicy fragrance, and heavy wooden chairs surrounded the welcoming fireplace. "Please make yerselves at home."

Robert removed several mugs from a side table and splashed a liberal amount of mead into each while Alec and his men soaked up heat on their backsides before the welcome fire.

Alec accepted the drink. The burning amber liquid cut a path to his belly, and warmth spread through his body.

Cameron glided into the room, her dark waist-length tresses swaying behind her. Although she was another MacDougall delicacy, she could not rival Heather's beauty.

He and his men stood, and Robert offered his hand to her. "Gentlemen, ye know my wife, Cameron?"

She scrutinized Alec, her green eyes cool and wary. "Good evening."

Alec took her hand and kissed her knuckles. "It has been a long time, m'lady."

"Laird Campbell, welcome to our home. Ye appear well."

"As do ye. Let me congratulate ye on yer marriage." He raised his cup to Robert. "Best wishes to ye both."

His men chimed in, toasting the couple.

Robert placed his arm around Cameron's waist, and she patted his hand. "If ye will excuse me, I'll have food prepared for ye."

Alec caught the stern look she gave her husband and was quite sure she would not be pleased when she learned the purpose of Alec's visit.

The men watched her leave before Robert addressed Alec. "Tell me what ye know."

Alec dropped on a bench and leaned forward, arms braced on his thighs. "Brandon seeks help in taking out an English convoy. They'll bring a food shipment through the northwest pass near Argyle sometime late next week." Alec sipped his mead. "Brandon has had these processions taken out over the past few months, and it appears to be working. We have it on good authority, the soldiers are starving."

Robert sat across from Alec. "Hamish informed us Brandon is organizing these attacks."

"Our plan is to take advantage of the narrow opening on the other side of the pass. The deep glen will block their retreat. If we surround them, they'll have no choice but to file through one at a time. We'll strike as they enter the gap."

Robert downed his mead. "I'm with ye. What do ye need?"

# Heather

~~~

The next day, Alec and his men joined Robert and Cameron to break their fast around a long oak table.

"Good morning." Robert speared a slice of meat and plopped it into his mouth.

"Aye, it is," Alec replied.

Cameron, her back stiff and eyes sharp, held her toddler, Douglas, in her lap. His little mouth worked the gruel she fed him, a sticky lump dropped on his dimpled chin and landed on his chest.

Alec took a bite of oatcake. "He's quite a lad. He favors his mum."

She shot an icy glare at Alec over the babe's dark head. Tension radiated across the table. Obviously, Robert had shared his purpose with her. Cameron, a healer, did not like battles of any kind, particularly when her husband was involved.

With the exception of clanking utensils, Eric's slurping and Douglas's cooing, an uncomfortable silence hung in the air. Alec addressed Robert. "I need to speak with ye about the MacDougalls."

"What about them?" Cameron's nostrils flared. "Ye are not involving my father in this."

"No." Alec wiped his mouth on a cloth. "I only ask ye to keep an eye on them. Did ye hear they were attacked by Symon Fraser several months back?"

"Aye," Cameron breathed out. "Heather sent word."

Alec's fingertips rubbed the rim of his cup. "The foray was underway when we arrived. Yer cousin stormed the gates bent on revenge, from what I understand. We held him off, but I worry he'll return."

Robert growled, "That whoreson. I would like nothing better than to end his miserable life."

Douglas's little fist smeared gruel across his chubby cheeks. Cameron wiped the baby's mouth. "Symon tried to kill Duncan and Robert's brother Androu."

"What the hell is wrong with him?"

Robert leaned his forearms on the table. "He dreams of conquering, of the grandeur and power of a laird. From appearances, he doesn't care which clan he presides over, whether it be Grahams or MacDougalls."

Symon was a rotten bastard. Alastair had brought his wife's young nephew into the fold when Symon was homeless. He'd cared for him, trained him and treated him as one of his own. "I worry he's not finished with yer family."

Robert leaned back in his chair. "I'll keep an eye on them."

Cameron's hand patted Alec's, and her eyes softened. "Thank ye for being there."

She held a slight resemblance to her sister—her smile, the way she touched him with feeling. His gut twisted. How he missed Heather.

He stood and dropped his cloth on the table. "We'll stop in and see to them on our way home."

Eric's head jerked up. His brow rose and a smirk spread across his face.

Alec extended his hand. "I thank ye for yer support." When Robert grasped it, he added, "We'll see ye next week."

Alec nodded at Cameron. "Good day, m'lady."

~~~

Thunder rumbled in the distance as Alec led his men down the dusty road. Fat raindrops splattered the ground. The wind picked up and blew freezing, stinging needles into their faces. They quickened their pace, but several hours passed before they finally entered the MacDougall's bailey.

Flames from torches lining the yard whipped in the turbulent wind, and the MacDougall flag slapped against the staff overhead. Men patrolling the ramparts grasped their cloaks around their shoulders and took shelter from the onslaught behind grey crenels. Lightning streaked the black sky, silhouetting skeletal, leaf-bare trees bent in the tempest.

Lads ran to take their horses as the men dismounted. Alec raced up the stairs two at a time, with the others close behind. They made their way into the keep, shaking off water as they went.

134

Fergus shuffled toward them. "Welcome back. Please come in and make yerselves comfortable next to the fire. I'll let the Laird know ye've arrived."

Alec and his men handed their cloaks to a lad and a few minutes later, Alastair strode into the room, his voice booming. "Alec, 'tis good to see ye. What brings ye this way?"

Alec grasped the older man's weathered hand. "We had business not far from here so we took the opportunity to see how things fared for ye before returning home."

"Ah, we're well."

"That is good news. I'm pleased to hear it."

Heather strolled into the room. Her beauty took his breath away. She wore a light blue, woolen gown matching the color of her eyes. The bodice hugged her hidden treasures, and her thick hair was secured with one of her ribbons. His palms itched to loosen the silken tresses, run his fingers through the heavenly mass and down to cup her adorable bottom.

"Gentlemen, welcome." She studied each one, her gaze settling on Alec.

His chest tightened. He was concerned how she would receive him after their last encounter, but relief poured over him at her amiable greeting. "Good evening, m'lady."

She extended her hand toward the hearth before taking a tray from a serving girl. "Please have a seat and help yerselves to some cheese."

She paused in front of each man as he took a wedge. The closer she drew to Alec, the faster his pulse beat. Her gown brushed him and a jolt tingled up his leg. Like an untried lad, his pulse raced with excitement. "Thank ye."

"I will leave ye men to talk."

Alec stood. "Please stay. We won't be long."

She hesitated. Wariness flittered across her lovely eyes, but she nodded and slid into the chair across from him. He could not keep his attention off her. He barely heard what was being said around him. What was it about her that captivated him so?

"Lindsey appreciates the improvements ye made to her stables," Heather commented. "Every day she makes use of the open area to work with her horses."

"She definitely knows her mind when it comes to those animals. She has quite a herd." Memory of Brandon's praise of the MacDougall's assignment flashed through his mind. He leaned back in the chair and glanced at her father. "And I hear ye garnered more horses from yer successful raid on the convoy last month."

Alastair's eyebrows drew together. "Convoy?"

The old laird turned to Heather and she clutched his arm.

"It's all right, Da. He knows ye help with the rebellion." Her blue eyes rounded on Alec. "Lindsey houses those warhorses in her stables if ye care to see them."

"Perhaps." Alec took another swig of ale. Alastair continued to look to Heather for answers and she always jumped in with a legitimate response. He could not put his finger on what was afoot, but something was—of that he was certain.

The conversation turned light. Alastair regaled them with stories of growing up with Alec's da. Alec found himself laughing at the boyish antics. What a refreshing change to the bleak subject of battling Edward's forces, planning and scheming, carnage and destruction. For a few short moments, he had a glimpse of another world—living in peace, enjoying simple pleasures.

The MacDougalls enveloped him and his men in gracious hospitality, but as the evening grew late, Heather stood. "If ye will excuse me, I'll ready yer chambers."

Chambers? "I hadn't planned on staying the night."

*But, I have often thought of staying the night—with ye beside me.*

She straightened. "Nonsense. It's late and there is no reason to ride in this storm. We would be pleased if ye would favor us with yer presence."

"Aye, ye don't want to venture out in this downpour," Alastair added.

Heather

Alec studied his men. They would willingly leave, trudge through the cold rain, if that was his command, but he might not see Heather again for quite a long while. He longed to bask in her warm companionship, hear her carefree laughter, and absorb her unfettered innocence. Before he knew what he was about, he said, "We would be most pleased to stay."

Did her eyes light up…just a wee bit? A smile stretched across her soft lips, and she excused herself. Her hips swayed. Shite! His trews grew tight at the mere thought of enjoying her company.

Serving girls brought out trays laden with smoked fish, steaming vegetables and warm bread. Alastair shuffled to the long trestle table. "Gentlemen, will ye join me?"

Alec and his men followed the old laird and sat on the benches. Eric rubbed his hands together. "It smells wonderful."

After the evening meal, Heather joined them next to the fire while his men offered stories of their adventures.

Eric nudged Ralf with his elbow. "'Twas a good hunt, but when that hog turned and charged, Ian jumped into the loch!"

Ian puffed up. "Laugh all ye want, but ye did not have that tusked monster chasing ye."

Heather laughed, the tinkling sound uplifting and somehow soothing. She welcomed them with the warmth of her smile and cheerful demeanor. Alec relaxed, the strain of death and destruction for once, set aside.

~~~

Da grasped the sides of his chair, struggled to his feet and straightened his bent frame. "Gentlemen, I have enjoyed the evening, but it's time for me to retire. Goodnight, daughter."

He ambled toward his chamber.

When Heather rose from her chair, Alec stood. He took her hand in his warm palm and his strong fingers closed over hers. "May I have a word with ye…in private?"

137

In private? She swallowed as if thick gruel stuck in her throat. Her nerves stood on end. Just the sweep of his gaze in her direction caused her insides to tremble.

She nodded at him, then addressed his men as they stood and stretched. "Please let me know if ye need anything."

"We will, mistress." Eric bent at the waist. "Thank ye for yer gracious hospitality."

Alec clutched her elbow and guided her to the solar. What did he want to talk to her about that could not be discussed in front of her father or his men? After disclosing the painful truth of his betrothal, what could he possibly have to say to her?

She stepped into the room and Alec closed the door behind them. Thunder rumbled in the distance and rain pelted the side of the castle. A window stood ajar, curtains flapping in the tempest. She weaved around the desk and chairs to the opened portal, tugged the shutters closed and latched the hook.

Alec stepped up behind her. She turned to him and smoothed trembling fingers down the front of her gown. Why did she let him affect her so? He leaned against the desk's edge and crossed his thick arms over his chest. He had cropped his dark hair short, highlighting his face's chiseled features. Whiskers hid his upper lip, covered his cheeks and strong chin. Curls peeked from the opening of his brown tunic, and she longed to glide her fingers through their softness. His piercing eyes, the grey outlined in onyx, stared at her, and her heart fluttered.

"I saw yer sister, Cameron." His deep voice rumbled in his chest.

"Ye did? She's well? Robert and the baby?"

He chuckled. "They're all well. Little Douglas is quite a handful."

An image of the little boy, a head full of black curls, scurrying down the hall on his hands and knees with Cameron chasing behind him flashed through her mind and she smiled. "Aye, he's a sweet laddie."

Lightning flashed through the room and thunderous vibrations rattled pottery lining the solar's book shelves.

"I missed ye," he whispered.

Heather

*He missed her?* Words from their last meeting echoed through her ears. Her body stiffened. What of his betrothed? Driving rain battered the windows, and a cold breeze swirled through the worn slats, matching the bleakness creeping into the corner of her heart. She tugged her wrap tighter around her shoulders.

Like her nerves, tension strung taut between them. He grasped her hand and tugged her toward him. She longed to lean into him, feel his strong arms around her and lose self-control for one night. Shame heated her cheeks. Where was her pride? He belonged to Robena.

She shook her head and placed a hand on his chest. "No, Alec…"

The earthy scent from his day in the saddle and the warmth of his body engulfed her. His calloused thumb stroked the back of her hand as she struggled to break the spell he cast.

"I have to carry out another assignment and I don't know when I'll be back this way."

Her chest tightened. Not another mission. Although she had no claims on him, she dreaded the loneliness of his absence and worried over his safety. He was a warrior and would always return to battle. That was his way of life.

His intense gaze held her's. "I would have ye as my wife."

Her eyes widened. What kind of a cruel joke did he play? Did he dangle a carrot in front of her face, only to yank it away with words of his betrothal? "Yer wife?"

"Aye, if ye will have me."

Stunned, her pulse pounded in her chest. "What of Robena? I thought ye were betrothed?"

"We were."

"I don't understand."

He stepped away and raked a hand through his dark hair. Torchlight from sconces in the wall highlighted his strong chin. "Had I not been so reckless three years ago, I would never have agreed to marry her. When I arrived home to find Da in bed after the weight of his horse crushed his legs, it

139

changed my life. I had been too busy tupping a village lass to be bothered with responsibilities to Da or to my clan."

Heather studied him, pondering his first words uttered about the accident. While she had not wanted to believe he had anything to do with the cause of it, his absence had let his clan down.

He exhaled and glanced at the ceiling. "I assumed Da would be fine leading the men in a skirmish without me. But that was not the way of it." Pain radiated from the dark depths of his eyes. "If I had been there, perhaps things would have turned out differently. At the time, I would have done anything to undo what happened and I swore I would never shirk my duties again. So when Da asked, I felt compelled to atone for my indiscretion by agreeing to wed Robena."

"What happened to yer da was not yer fault. Had ye been there, what could ye have done to prevent his fall?"

He snorted. "While I did not push him from his horse, I was not there to thwart the attack, watch over and protect him."

She could not dispute his words. He had failed his people.

He cupped the side of her face. "I severed the sham of betrothal with Robena, and I want ye for my wife, ensconced in my clan, part of my family. I want ye to bear my children. I want to grow old with ye, Heather."

Her heart flew into her throat. How she had longed to hear him speak those words, but she could not marry him and leave MacDougall Castle. Images of Da, Beathan and Lindsey flashed before her eyes. What would become of them, of her clan? She would not leave them vulnerable.

Nay, she must remain steadfast, marry a man she could trust without question, someone whom she could count on to defend and protect her family, and not let herself be swayed by words she longed to hear.

Not to mention the acts she committed, fighting and killing soldiers. Alec would be horrified if he knew the truth. He must not discover what she had done. She could not stand his scorn.

She covered his hand with hers. "Let's see how things are when the conflict with the English ends."

Heather

Alec reared back. "While I admire yer confidence, I don't see this battle ending any time soon. I would have ye as mine long before that day arrives."

She stepped away from him and wrapped her arms around her waist. What was she to say? She would not divulge the true reasons she could not marry him. "It's too soon, too sudden."

He grasped her shoulder and spun her to him. "I would see ye safe with my name. I would know ye're protected while I'm away."

How ironic he spoke of protection when his own clan had not been able to count on him. How she wanted to believe he had changed, but she couldn't risk the security of her people. "I'm safe behind MacDougall walls. Ye need not worry."

"Ye don't know the kind of men this war has brought out. They rape and pillage under the name of Edward. He sends his forces deep into our lands to bring us under his control. Did ye know the English force Scottish brides to succumb to their mauling on the night of her wedding?"

Oh, my, God. "No," Heather breathed out, her face scrunching. "Why would they do such a thing?"

"For control. The Sassenachs refer to it as their right of the first night. They deflower the woman, humiliate her before she can be with her husband."

Heather shivered.

"They're brutal with no concern for those they hurt." Alec kissed her forehead. "For God's sake, Heather, I worry about ye."

Thunder clapped and she jumped. His eyes darkened, and he tugged her into his strong embrace. She buried her face in his shoulder and closed her eyes. Savoring the feel of him, she eased her arms around his back. He untied her ribbon and combed his fingers through her hair, her scalp tingling from his touch. An earthy smell mingled with leather clung to his body, and she inhaled deeply, her head reeling from his closeness.

She longed to halt time, remain forever enveloped in his embrace, savoring his strength and basking in the security of his arms. He straightened, and his lips brushed her forehead, down to her eyes, and cheeks. He cupped her face, and she tilted her lips to meet his. Whiskers scraped her skin as he slid his mouth over hers and she ascended into heaven.

His tongue slipped into the recesses of her mouth and a jolt shot to her core. Her tongue tentatively touched his, tasting ale on his breath. Her breasts tightened and she leaned into him. She was engulfed by his essence, his strong arms, his heated body.

Incoherent thoughts drifted through her mind. She should not be kissing him. She should…stop, but her resolve to stay detached shattered.

His lips left her mouth and he leaned his forehead against hers. "Heather," his whisper a feather's touch on her skin.

She froze for fear he would break away, once again leaving her to lament over his absence.

He captured her mouth once again. His hands roamed through her hair, down her back, and cupped her bottom.

Her head reeled. How she longed to scream *yes*, she would be his, now and forever. To be his wife, sit by his side, raise his children. Ach, it was a dream she would never attain.

As he slid his hand to the side of her breast, a rumble emanated from his chest. His thumb rubbed her sensitive peak, and she moaned into his mouth, molding her body to his. A hard shaft pressed into her abdomen and the area between her thighs tightened in a dull ache.

With a strangled sound, he straightened, his breathing labored. "Promise ye will wait for me. Promise ye'll be mine when I return."

She wanted nothing more, but how could she agree? The weight of defending her clan crushed her shoulders. "Come home safely and we'll see how ye feel then."

He placed his hands on either side of her face and whispered against her mouth, "I'll be back, Heather. I will be back for ye."

# *Chapter Ten*

*Battlefield near Perth*
*March 1299*

"Hold," William Wallace shouted. "Hold firm!"

The ground rumbled and shook as massive warhorses thundered down the grassy knoll. Sweat trickled down Alec's face. Could they hold their ground? He had ordered his men through the attacking forces knowing they scarcely stood a chance once Edward brought in his archers. With Wallace resorting to a frontal attack, Alec feared the worst.

Blazing arrows filled the stormy afternoon sky with barbs raining down on the Scottish warriors. Wretched screams of dying men and animals surrounded him. Smoke and the stench of burning flesh filled his nostrils.

A soldier charged, sword over his shoulder. Grim eyes glowered through grey armored slits, the metallic monster bellowing a battle cry. The man swung. Alec sidestepped and deflected the blow. The attacker's momentum propelled him forward.

Both hands gripping his blade, Alec slammed the soldier's back. Vibrations reverberated down his arms, and he struggled to maintain a grasp of his weapon. The man dropped to his knees, and Alec drove his sword into the soldier's side.

He spun to face another. This one wielded a wicked, curved blade. Alec ducked and weaved to the right, but the weapon grazed his forehead. With a solid thrust, he sank his sword into the man's belly.

Alec wiped his brow and scanned the battlefield. Mutilated remains littered the hillside with arrows protruding from lifeless bodies. Dying and injured men groaned and cried out in pain. A black river of rain mixed with blood oozed through the grass. He snorted. He would forever smell death. It permeated his soul.

"Retreat! Live to fight another day!" The surprise command came loud and clear.

Hundreds of Scots scattered like leaves in a windstorm, the English in pursuit. Alec searched the field for his men. Eric and Ralf ran beside Ian.

"This way." Alec led them through the forest dodging brambles and hurdling over fallen tree stumps.

He rounded a boulder. An English soldier took aim, his arrow sighted on Alec's chest. A piercing war cry rent the air as a Scottish warrior dropped from a tree, landing on the soldier's back, a large dagger clutched in his fist. The Scot wrapped his legs around the man's waist and plunged his blade into the soldier's thick neck. The man clutched his throat and crumpled to the ground.

The lad straightened, blood dripping from his blade. A black cloth covered his head, but blond strands escaped around his dirty, blackened face. It was the MacDougall lad, the young warrior.

Beathan ran up the hill and grabbed the boy's arm. The warrior flipped his dagger and slid it into the sheath. Alec wrinkled his brow. He had seen that gesture before. Flashes of Heather in the garden flicking her knife, passed through his mind. Movement to his left caught his attention as a soldier advanced on Eric.

"Watch out!" Alec grabbed his blade and threw it, planting it deep into the attacker's chest.

Eric rotated, sword in hand. His head bobbed and he grinned.

A deafening war-cry resounded. English soldiers swarmed the woods, their numbers vast. Alec's stomach plummeted. The Scots would sooner die than let the enemy advance farther. They fought for their freedom, their very way of life. But Edward's numbers were too great, his forces too strong.

Eric ran beside Alec, stopping only when they were safely away, hidden in the thick trees. Alec skimmed the woods for the young MacDougall warrior, but the lad was nowhere in sight.

Out of breath, Eric leaned over, hands on knees. "That…was close. We could have held them."

Heather

Alec wiped his face on his sleeve, not surprised to see smeared blood. "Aye, but Wallace was right. It will be far better to live and fight another day."

~~~

Heather raced through the forest with her men behind her. Tears cascaded from her burning eyes, her lungs filling with pungent smoke. She choked and coughed, gagging on the putrid smells of death. Pain spread from her ribs. "I can't go on."

Beathan gripped her wrist. "Aye, ye will. Hurry!"

Shouts and the clanging of swords rang in her ears. Da's men surrounded her, sheltering her as they raced to their horses. Her calves burned, and her muscles screamed in protest.

She stumbled, but Beathan grabbed her arm. "Hold on! Just a little longer."

Arrows whistled through the air. One of the barbs struck the tree she passed. "Look out!" she screamed as more rained upon them, several landing at her feet.

Panic welled through her as Beathan propelled her forward. Finally, their hiding place was in sight. The horses stirred nervously. The captain hoisted her onto the saddle before he swung onto his mount. Heather dug her heels into her horse's sides and bolted through the thick forest, her men following.

Two hours later and miles from the battlefield, they reached a secluded spot. Heather weaved through a strand of thick trees down a worn path opening into a clearing adjacent to a river. A purple hue covered the sky as the afternoon sun dipped low and its light dimmed.

To the right, immense boulders created a waterfall that must span fifty feet. On either side of the flow, a rocky ledge jutted, creating a shelf that disappeared behind a curtain of water. The deluge cascaded into a pool before rushing through a narrow gap and continuing down river. Although they had not seen the English since fleeing, they remained vigilant and cautious. The surrounding dense woods and shrubs created the perfect shelter.

Her men dismounted and led their horses to the water. Other than an angry cut traversing David's forehead, the warriors appeared unscathed.

Her ribs were a different matter. When she had dropped from the tree, her chest slammed into the soldier's shoulder, and pain radiated through her torso. Now her clothes, soaked with the man's blood, stuck to her skin, the smell sickening. She shivered, still feeling the resistance her blade found and his lifeless body crumpling beneath her.

Bile rose in her throat and spittle flooded her mouth. Gagging, she fought not to retch. She scrambled off her horse, and her fingers trembled as she opened her water skin. The cool liquid slid down her throat and eased the choking sickness.

Beathan jumped to the ground. He strode over and stopped in front of her. His arms crossed his massive chest. "Ye took a great risk dropping onto that soldier."

She swiped a cloth across her grimy face and neck. "I had no choice."

"Aye, ye did."

"It was Alec, Beathan. The man had him in his sights." She winced and grabbed her side. "I could not let that happen."

He frowned, his eyes darkening. "Are ye hurt?"

"It's only my ribs. I'll be all right."

"Ye should take a break from this conflict, lass. I can lead the men. It's getting too dangerous."

She shook her head. "No, I need to do this for Da, for the clan." She paused. "And for myself. I won't be forced to marry a blackguard conqueror or subject the clan to one."

Several of her men drifted back up the bank and awaited orders. Blood splattered their clothing and drizzling rain dripped from their hair. They were a sorry-looking lot with mud and dirt smeared from head to toe, but yet a wondrous sight. She thanked the Lord everyone had survived.

Emotion clogged her throat. "We'll stay here tonight."

Heather

Beathan reached for the animals' reins. "William, take Jonathan and gather wood. Brian and I will care for the horses."

Heather followed Beathan and Brian to the burn's edge. She stooped beside the water, dipped her hands in the freezing liquid and scrubbed her arms. Goosebumps rose on her skin as she glanced around the site. Rocks, smoothed from the flow, lay scattered beneath the falls before disappearing into a deep pool. How she longed to dive into that basin and rid herself of the battle stench.

She straightened and shook her hands, flinging cold droplets. Draping a cloak across her shoulders, she grabbed her satchel off her horse and stepped to a clearing secluded behind large shrubs. As she brushed back pine needles, her thoughts turned to Alec. She had barely escaped his detection. He had been only a few paces away, his questioning grey eyes searching her face. Did he recognize the young warrior? What would he think if he knew it was her?

Men's voices and the clop of horses' hooves caught her attention. Other Scots, battered and bruised, joined their campsite. The warriors dismounted. Some led their horses to the river while others tugged saddles onto the ground. One turned toward her and swiped his forearm across his face.

*Eric.*

Her pulse pounded in her ears. If he was here Alec must be as well. She tugged her scarf farther over her head and wrapped the heavy cloak tighter as her gaze shot around the surrounding woods. More men on horseback drifted from the dark forest and entered the encampment. She recognized the neighboring McCarthy clan. Buford called greetings and Eric rotated toward him, grabbed the laird's hand and slapped him on the back.

She hurried away from the incoming group to the safety of the concealed spot she had chosen for her bedding. Glancing over her shoulder, she spread a blanket on the cold ground and eased down, careful to remain hidden behind the shrubbery.

A cold breeze blew around her and shivers racked her body as she peered through the bushes at the arriving throng.

William and Jonathan dropped sticks while Randall started a fire. Her men acknowledged the other clans with a wave before shuffling about, shoulders hunched. Subdued and disheartened, they stoically set up camp.

Thunder rumbled in the distance, while rain sprinkled the bedraggled group. Beathan tossed his satchel next to her and she jumped.

"What has ye so skittish?"

"Alec's men just rode into camp." She tugged a branch down and peeked through the leaves again.

Beathan glanced at the clearing. "Ye'll be safe enough."

Her head jerked toward him.

He shrugged. "He's not expecting to find ye here. I doubt he'll notice the MacDougalls amongst the clans gathered."

"Aye, perhaps ye're right." She dropped the branch and it sprang into place, obscuring her from sight. Rubbing her forehead, she fought to ease her apprehension. Deep breaths in and out of her nose helped steady her nerves as she tried to convince herself that dressed as a warrior, Alec would not notice her. Before long, her body relaxed. She must act normal and not do anything to draw attention to herself. The MacDougalls would leave before daybreak, and he would never know she had been among the deflated warriors.

Beathan picked up his wineskin and drank in eager gulps while she rummaged through her cloth bag. Her fingers closed around a clean tunic. If she could find a wee bit of privacy, she would scrub away the remnants of battle and don the fresh clothing.

Beathan dropped beside her. "We need to talk."

Heather folded the tunic and placed it in her lap. "What is it?"

"Ye cannot continue."

She stilled, then glared at him. "Just what do ye propose I do?"

"Let me lead the men."

"No. We have gone over this many times, Beathan."

"Who would know?" He shrugged, his palms held up. "Everyone sees the MacDougalls in battle, not ye or yer da."

Heather

"I must be there to understand what's going on for the clan's sake."

Beathan shook his head, his shaggy hair brushing his shoulders. "If William Wallace resorts to frontal attacks, ye will be no use to us. In fact, ye hamper us." He touched her arm. "We have to fight while keeping an eye on ye."

Heather swallowed past the lump in her throat, her world closing in. Memories of Randall and Blake throwing their bodies in front of her as Beathan sprinted her to safety flashed through her head. They were always there to protect her. "I'm tired. We'll discuss this later."

Beathan mumbled under his breath and stalked off.

Tears flooded her eyes and she buried her face in her hands. Her chest tightened. What was she to do? He was right. She had become a hindrance. She dried her eyes and curled up on her pallet.

Images and sounds of battle played in her mind. Bloodied, mutilated men had begged for help, their screams unbearable. Burnt flesh, an odor of copper and rotten eggs, lingered in her nostrils. Her stomach churned.

The Scots were no match for King Edward's soldiers. Time and again frontal attacks proved deadly. They had made progress striking food shipments and disbanding the English processions. Why had Wallace changed strategy? How could she lead the men into this type of warfare? Hidden in the trees, her bow skills had proven valuable, but for a woman, hand-to-hand combat was impossible.

The drizzle finally stopped, and the moon peeked between drifting clouds. She longed to loosen the binding around her sore ribs and rid herself of the stench swathed clothes, but did she dare leave the safety of her hiding place? Snores and grunts of the men clustered together sang out. She eased onto her elbow and peered through the shrubbery at the still forms sleeping close to the blazing fires scattered throughout the camp. With the exception of their lookout, everyone slept.

She slipped the blanket off, stuffed the clean tunic under her arm, and sneaked close enough to grab a stick from

149

the fire. It blazed in the night air. She cupped her hand, sheltering the flickering flame and made her way to the river.

Her gaze skimmed the bushes and trees at the top of the waterfall. The hidden shelf would provide privacy. She inched up the side of the hill. Her foot slipped and she grabbed a thorny branch. A sting coursed her palm and little finger, and she winced. After gaining her footing, she sucked on the side of her hand and resumed her climb.

She held the flaming stick out, peering around the space. An open dirt area, surrounded by enormous boulders, fed a trail to the right and disappeared through thick trees and shrubs. To the left, the path wound behind the falls.

She surveyed the ground below. Firelight blazed in the wind and shadows danced across lumps of men huddled near its warmth. Treetops swayed with blustery weather creeping in.

All was quiet.

She stepped behind the waterfall.

The roar of water cascading over sheer rock drummed in her ears and a cold spray wafted against her face. She crept forward, the grey, wet ledge slippery. A curtain of water fell to her left, and a shelf opened into a cave at her right.

Darkness enveloped its vast opening.

Did she dare enter?

She peered in, her eyes squinting into blackness. Thrusting her blazing stick forward, its light flickered across the cavern walls. She edged inside, her fingertips scraping the walls' rough stones and icy water seeping through crevices. As she descended into the recesses of the cave, the noise of the falls abated.

She swung her stick to the right, the flames glimmering in the cold breeze. A small pool collected a trickle's overflow. After jabbing the limb into a crevice, she stooped beside it, reached underneath her large tunic and loosened the fabric holding her breasts. Her ribs throbbed, but the reprieve from the bindings was a welcome relief. She tugged the material from her side, dipped it in the freezing water and dabbed her neck. Goosebumps rose as she cleaned away the dirt and grime. Although she did not want to erase the disguise of soot and ash, she was utterly miserable soaked in the soldier's blood.

150

Heather

Her body ached, her soul torn asunder. Could she continue this farce? How long would it be before someone discovered she led the MacDougall warriors? How long before her clan was attacked again? After each job, she feared she would return home to find the castle overrun, defeated by unscrupulous louts.

But no matter how many times she assessed the situation, she always came to the same conclusion. She had no choice but to continue if she wanted to remain in control of Da's warriors. Not to mention neighboring clans must not suspect the MacDougall's vulnerability. Symon and Lowrens would be storming their gates at the mere mention of Da's illness.

A light caught her eye. Her head jerked around as she dropped her tunic in place. She sucked in a breath.

A man stood at the entrance to the cave, a torch in his hand. He held the flame to the side, shadows concealing his face.

Heather doused her stick in the pool, shrouding herself in darkness. Had he followed her?

The man swung the light and stepped into the cave.

Her pulse pounded. She straightened and clutched her blade, her grip tightening on the hilt.

"Ye need not fear me." He held the light aloft so she could see his face.

*Alec.*

~~~

Finally, Alec faced the young warrior. Would his suspicions of Heather playing the lad's role prove correct? His stomached clenched. He didn't want to consider the possibility, but he did not believe in coincidences.

The lad backed into the shadows.

Alec secured the torch between two rocks. "Are ye hurt?"

"It's nothing, only bruised ribs." The lad's voice was a mere whisper in the drum of the falls.

151

Alec nodded. "That was quite a feat, jumping onto that soldier like ye did. I wanted to thank ye."

The boy remained silent.

Alec stepped closer. "May I have a look? They might be broken."

"No." Blue eyes flashed in the torchlight.

*Heather.*

Soot, ash and dirt could not hide her beauty. Fury burned through his gut. He advanced on her and plucked the black scarf off her head. Blonde waves fell down her back.

The image of her dropping from the tree onto the soldier flashed through his mind. Fear struck his core. His barely leashed anger threatened to explode. He wanted to grab her. Shake her. Wrap his arms around her and protect her. "What the hell were ye thinking? Ye could have been hurt. Raped. Killed, for God's sake!"

Restraining his rage, his body shook uncontrollably. He could only utter one word. "Why?"

She squared her shoulders, and her chin jutted forward. "To protect my clan."

His hand fisted around her scarf. "Where is yer da? Why does he send his daughter to fight in his stead?"

"He did not *send* me. The decision was mine."

Teeth clamped together, his chest heaved. "I ask ye again. Why?"

She shook her head and turned from him.

He grabbed her upper arm and twirled her around. "What are ye hiding, Heather?"

Moisture gathered in her eyes, her stubborn chin wobbling. A tear trickled down her cheek. "My da can no longer lead. He's not well."

"I thought he'd recovered from his wound."

Her hands balled into fists. "It's his mind, Alec. He's losing his mind."

Her words punched him in the gut. Memories of Alastair looking to Heather coursed through his head—his daughter always answering for him, his reluctance over selling the horses.

## Heather

Heather's frame sagged and she rubbed her eyes. "Mum begged me to care for him, step in and run the castle. She saw his deterioration. She knew it was only a matter of time before he became feeble and helpless." She paused. "I will continue to lead the men, to protect him from being cast aside and my clan from tyrannical miscreants."

"No, ye will not." If he had to lock her in her bedchamber for the rest of her life, she would never again lead *any* men or take part in *any* battle!

Her arms crossed her chest. "Ye have no say in what I do."

"As my wife, ye will learn I do."

She thrust her hands to her sides and stepped forward. "How dare ye assume we will wed? I have not consented, and if ye think I will marry ye just to become a disengaged bystander, ye are sorely mistaken."

"We *will* wed. Ye will be involved in running the keep and seeing to the inhabitants' needs. The men will fight, defend and protect the clan. Not ye."

"Ye don't seem to understand. I cannot marry ye. I can't leave the clan exposed."

How she must worry over the safety of her clan, commitments to the rebellion, and men swarming around her like vultures ready to devour her. Responsibilities weighed heavily on her slim shoulders. While she faced them head on, they had to be slowly breaking her back.

The sound of rushing water and spray off the falls drifted around him. Comprehension of her predicament replaced his anger. He slid his hand down her arm. She trembled, and his chest squeezed. "Is that why ye refuse to promise me yer hand?"

"I cannot…"

"Do ye not want me as yer husband?"

Her head snapped up, the pain in her eyes intense. "Nay, it's not that."

He cupped the side of her face. "Months ago I told ye I would strive to earn yer trust. I want ye to confide in me. Had I known, I would have taken steps to protect yer clan. *After* we wed, I'll reside at MacDougall Castle. Ye need not worry for the safety of yer da, yer clan...or yerself."

Her eyes widened. "Reside at MacDougall Castle? What of Glencara?"

"I expect my cousin to return soon. Logan's quite capable of running the castle. We will work together to ensure the safety of both clans."

Heather wrenched out of his hold. She wrapped her arms around her waist and turned away. "No, it won't work. Ye're needed there."

The sound of rushing blood roared through his ears. Time stood still. His heart pounded. "We can manage until Logan arrives."

She rubbed her forehead. "Nay, I cannot, Alec."

He touched her back, his large hand dwarfing her small frame. "What is it? What is the reason ye refuse?"

Silence.

"Look at me, Heather."

When she turned, her shoulders slumped, and anguish traversed her face. "I'm sure ye can imagine the things I have done. Ye can't want the mother of yer children to be a woman who wields a sword. Ye must see me as a monster."

Alec grasped her chin and raised her face, her blue eyes shiny with unshed tears. "What I see is a courageous woman risking her life to protect her family." The pad of his thumb stroked her bottom lip. "What I see is the passionate and caring woman I want by my side."

~~~

Heather's breath caught. After discovering her secrets, he still wanted her by his side? He claimed he had learned his lesson, would never disappoint his people again. Could it really be true? If she surrendered to him, no longer would she fear losing her clan. No longer would she fear leading Da's men. Alec would protect her and her family. She would have children of her own. *Alec's* children.

She searched his dark eyes and found only steadfast truth. Joy and relief burst through her. The dreams she assumed

154

would always remain out of her reach had a chance to come true.

Alec's thumb rubbed her cheek, his warm hands caressing, comforting. He bent and brushed his lips against hers. "Say ye will be mine, Heather."

She wanted to scream, *I will be yours now and forever*.

"Aye," was all she uttered before he tugged her into his embrace.

He held her tight, nuzzling her neck. "Ye will no longer lead yer father's men."

"I only did so because I had no other choice."

He straightened and grasped her upper arms. "Promise me."

She swallowed. "I promise."

"There will be no more secrets between us." He searched her eyes. "Agreed?"

She nodded. "Agreed."

Rough whiskers scraped her skin, and a hint of ale on his breath wafted as he lowered his lips to hers. She eased her arms around his neck, and he deepened the kiss, his tongue sliding into her mouth. Her unfettered breasts pressed into his chest and her sensitive nipples pebbled.

His hands slid down her sides and across her back. He squeezed her bottom, pulling her against him. Pain shot through her torso and she moaned.

His hold eased. "I'm sorry. I forgot about yer bruised ribs."

She rested her head on his chest, the steady beat of his heart thumping against her ear.

"Ye need to bind them. The fabric will give ye support while they heal."

"I had them wrapped, but I needed relief. It was too tight."

He chuckled, the sound rumbling deep in his chest. "Ye should tie it to give support, not to cut off yer air. Give the wrap to me. I'll help ye."

She straightened, and her brow rose. "Indeed?"

"Ye can put yer back to me."

Did she trust herself, scantily clad, to be so close to him while she ached for his touch?

"It's dark in here, Heather. I won't be able to see yer..."

She held up the worn fabric, and he ran his hand down it, unwinding it. She turned and tugged the large tunic over her head and held it against her breasts, glancing over her shoulder at him.

He grinned, and she hesitated.

"Come on, drop the tunic on the rock, and hold yer arms over yer head."

She let the oversized shirt fall. Gathering her hair in her left hand, her arms rose, and rested on top of her head.

He stepped closer, his chest brushing her bare skin. His arms circled her, and he placed the first wrap around her breasts. She arched, her nipples straining for his touch. His fingers brushed the sensitive peaks through the thin fabric and a strange tightening shot to her core.

His lips nibbled her upper arm. "Hold this in place."

She clutched the wrap with her right hand and tilted her face toward him over her shoulder. He kissed her temple, and she leaned back against his chest. Butterflies tumbled in her stomach. She played with fire, but she didn't care.

His hands stilled.

"Lass," he whispered, placing kisses along her sensitive skin. His palms slid underneath the fabric, and his warm hands cupped her naked breasts.

She sucked in a breath and closed her eyes, relishing his caress.

He kneaded her fullness, his rough fingers brushing her nipples as he groaned. His chest expanded against her with each deep breath before his palms eased away, and cold air enveloped her skin. He stretched the fabric across her bosom, around her back, repeating it several times before tucking the ends under the binding.

"Turn around," he whispered, his voice husky in her ear.

Heather twisted to face him, and her hair fell around her shoulders. Alec's eyes darkened, and his nostrils flared. His

156

hands slid down her arms, and he placed a kiss on her palms, his gaze never leaving hers.

"We must return. Beathan will search for me if he notices I'm not on my pallet." She pulled away and tugged the clean tunic over her head, then bunched the soiled one.

Alec grabbed the torch, and she followed him from behind the wall of water. He stopped abruptly, and she bumped into his back.

"What is it?" She moved to his side, but his arm swung out, and he held her back.

Six men surrounded the opening, their swords pointed at Alec's chest.

~~~

"Well, well...What have we here?" Robena's brother stepped forward and Alec's gut tightened. Daniel McMillan's coarse dark hair, a bushy mat surrounding the edges of his face and curling under his chin, hung to his shoulders. Dirt and dried blood smeared his skin, and his disheveled clothing reeked of sweat and excrement. "I thought that was ye slinking around camp, Laird Campbell. Da demanded yer head for humiliating my sister, and he'll reward me for having ye drawn and quartered."

"Ye have it wrong, McMillan."

Daniel leered at Heather. He licked his beefy lips and assessed her from head to toe. "What I *have* is entertainment for me and my men tonight." Daniel laughed, his men joining the taunts.

Alec ached to wrap his hands around the swine's neck and squeeze the life out of him, watch blood vessels burst in his beady eyes, but he would not do anything to endanger Heather. "Ye had best not start something ye can't finish."

Daniel held his arms out, exposing yellowish-brown sweat stains covering his tunic. "Are ye daft? Can ye not see ye're surrounded?" He took a step closer and sneered. "Say yer farewells to the lovely miss."

Movement from the trail behind the McMillans caught Alec's eye. Heather's men sneaked forward. Beathan, David,

Brian and Randall drifted from the shadows, their arrows aimed at the McMillans. Eric, Ian and Ralf emerged from behind the MacDougalls, swords in hand.

"It's ye who should be saying farewell," Beathan said.

Daniel spun around, his head jerking right, then left.

"Drop yer weapons, and no one gets hurt," Alec demanded.

One of the McMillans yelled, raised his sword and advanced on Alec.

*Sfit!*

An arrow pierced the man's shoulder. He bellowed and grasped the shaft.

Beathan nocked another, the next target in his sights.

Daniel's eyes narrowed. He spit a brown stream on the ground. "Ye'd better watch yer back, Campbell. Ye won't be so lucky next time."

"On the contrary, I won't be so lenient next time."

The McMillans lowered their weapons.

"Eric, see these men find their horses and get on their way." Alec's glower was fixed on Daniel. "If we meet again, ye'll regret it."

"Let's go." Eric nudged Daniel with the tip of his sword. "Move!"

Daniel sneered before he and his group stormed down the trail with Alec's men and the MacDougalls behind them.

Heather stepped beside Alec and placed her hand on his upper arm.

His heart pounded. He had underestimated the McMillan threat. Perhaps he should have taken them out and left them to rot. Revealing Heather, his weakness, placed her in danger. His lips grazed her velvety hair, and he kissed the top of her head. "Ye will not venture off on yer own. Ye must stay vigilant. McMillan is not a man to trifle with. He'll be furious. His pride is wounded."

"I'm not worried about him."

Alec straightened and grasped her shoulders. "Damn it, Heather. Ye should be." The unspeakable things the McMillans would have done to her struck terror in his soul. What would he do if something happened to her? He clasped her tighter. "Ye mind my words. I want someone with ye at all times."

Her eyes widened. "Aye, I'll be careful."

He had scared her. Good. Perhaps she would heed his warning before she ventured from the safety of the castle. Clutching her hand, he led her down the hill to the encampment. As they entered the clearing, horses thundered out of the campsite with the last of the McMillans disappearing into the darkness.

David, Brian and Randall followed Beathan and Eric to the clearing with Ian and Ralf close behind.

Eric stopped in front of Alec and Heather. His eyes narrowed, and he cocked his head to the side. "Mistress Heather, I didn't expect to see ye here."

Her grip on Alec's hand tightened. "Nay, I'm sure ye didn't."

Alec placed his arm around her and nestled her soft body against him. "It's a long story. One I'll share later. For now, I thank ye."

Eric saluted. "Anytime."

Beathan's gaze dropped to their joined hands and he frowned.

"I asked Mistress MacDougall to become my wife, and she agreed," Alec announced to the group.

Beathan's gaze swung to Heather's face, his brow knit. "That is what ye want?"

"It is. Alec and I discussed Da's predicament, and he understands the difficulties we face."

"Then ye have my blessing." Beathan looked at Alec. "'Tis good news. I worried I would have to call ye out."

Alec chuckled. "Ye should have been worried. I would have hated to take out a good man."

With a hearty laugh, Beathan clapped Alec's shoulder.

"Congratulations." Eric grasped Alec's hand and nodded at Heather.

The MacDougalls and Campbells offered good wishes, laughing and clapping each other's backs.

Alec glanced across the men. "Get some rest. We leave at first light."

The warriors dispersed and Alec escorted Heather to her pallet. He placed his knuckle under her chin and raised her face to his. Her lips parted. The simple gesture struck his gut. He slid his hand around the back of her neck, stroking her smooth skin. "Ye need sleep. We have a long day ahead of us tomorrow."

Heather stretched out, and Alec draped her cloak over her lithe body.

"Sleep well," she whispered.

He strode to his bedding and grabbed it off the cold ground. Bunching it along with his saddlebag, he marched back to Heather and rolled it out behind her.

She rose on her elbow to glance over her shoulder.

Alec stretched out and tugged her down, snuggling against her back. No one would dare bother her with him there. Not to mention, this position afforded him an opportunity to nestle against her luscious curves.

She brought his arm across her waist and held his hand. "Goodnight."

Alec rested his chin on her head and closed his eyes. He would protect her and her clan. Their world swarmed with unsavory characters, both English and Scottish. Defending two castles miles apart would be difficult. He prayed for Logan's safe return and looked forward to ensconcing his cousin at Glencara.

Heather shifted in her sleep, dropping his hand. Although her cloak lay between them, the curve of her breast rested against his arm. He inched his fingers higher, cupping her bounded bosom. A lump stuck in his throat with memories of her naked breasts in his hands, her nipples pebbling against his palms. She sighed, and he placed his lips on the side of her face.

When she looked over her shoulder, her sleepy eyes sparkled in the glow of the campfire. She kissed him playfully. "Neither of us will get any rest this way."

He sighed audibly. His hand slid off her breast, but his throbbing manhood objected. "Goodnight, m'lady."

160

Heather

He snuggled against her, forcing his wicked thoughts at bay.

~~~

Hues of rose spanned the horizon, lighting the sprawling grasslands and surrounding forest. Heather breathed in the cool morning air as her mount trotted down the dirt road behind Alec. The route home wound through tall pines and up a steep hill.

The corners of her mouth tugged up as her thoughts turned to waking in Alec's arms, nestled against his broad chest, his hips cradling hers. Her pulse beat erratically envisioning the nights to come, lying in his arms when no one was around...just the two of them.

Joy flooded through her. Although he had not professed his love, his worry over her safety and the way he held her showed his care. She could not believe she would become his wife. Everything had happened so quickly. Within a few short hours, she had swung from worry over her clan to happiness unlike any she had experienced.

She wanted to giggle, shout her elation.

Alec led the group with Beathan by his side. He sat high in the saddle, the knuckles of his fist resting on his muscular thigh. His cloak opened, exposing brown trews hugging his long legs and disappearing into dark boots. He would be a powerful laird, a leader for her clan.

"Riders heading this way," Eric called from ahead.

Traveling through the forest, they had managed to dodge English patrols, but now on the open road, they risked detection and an ensuing battle. The sound of horses' hooves grew loud and several men appeared over the hill.

*Hamish.*

Her stomach dropped.

"Good day," the rebel commander shouted and waved as he slowed his horse.

Alec held up a hand and their group stopped. "Hamish, it's good to see ye."

161

"And ye." He nodded in acknowledgement to Heather. "Mistress MacDougall, I did not expect to see ye here. Eric, Beathan, ye appear well."

"We were lucky to escape unscathed," Eric said.

Hamish crossed his hands over his saddle. "Aye, and the bloody Sassenachs are still on the march." He glanced across Heather and Alec's men, then back to Alec. "Brandon asks to give ye word he heard from yer cousin."

Alec straightened. "Logan?"

"Aye, he's well. Last week, he stopped a shipment coming up the River Eden into Carlisle and confiscated documents outlining plans of attack near Glasgow."

"Thank God." Alec exhaled loudly, and his body relaxed.

"Brandon requests ye travel to Glasgow and head off the invasion."

Alec's eyes darkened, his jaw jutting forward. "When?"

"The first of next week."

Alec rubbed the back of his neck and paused. "I'm escorting the MacDougalls home. I'll alert Robert on my way back to Glencara."

No sooner had her heart soared with joy, it plummeted with thoughts of another risky assignment, another possibility of losing Alec.

"Tell Brandon he can count on us to take the scum out."

Realization sunk in—she would replace one worry with another. She was marrying a warrior. She would forever fret over his safety. Would he return to her? Would they ever live a life of peace?

~~~

*MacDougall Bailey*

The next morning, Heather handed Alec his satchel and he tied it to Aeton's saddle. Black whiskers lined his cheeks and chin. The wind blew wisps of his dark hair, and she longed to touch its softness.

162

## Heather

"Mount up," Eric shouted as he strode across the bailey to his horse with his bow slung over his shoulder and his sword knocking against his leg. He swung onto the saddle.

Ian and Ralf positioned their horses behind Eric, and the other warriors fell in line.

When Alec turned, her heart hitched. His smoky grey eyes held concern. His hand cupped the side of her face, and she turned into it, placing a kiss on his palm. He hissed and drew her face to his. Whiskers scraped her skin and a lingering hint of sandalwood wafted past her nostrils as he lowered his lips to hers.

She refused to shed tears, but it was almost her undoing when he melded his body against hers, wrapping her in his strong embrace. Too soon, he straightened. "Ye remember yer promise," he whispered against her forehead. "No more fighting. I have talked to Beathan. He'll be in charge until I return."

She nodded, unable to speak for fear her voice would crack and she would fall into a fit of tears.

"Ye must be strong. I will return for ye."

"I look forward to that day." Her throat clogged.

He slowly released her and stepped back. "I'll miss ye, Heather."

He leapt onto Aeton's back. The horse pranced and tossed his head. Alec nodded to her, tugged the reins and galloped out of the bailey, his men following behind.

A tear escaped her eye as he disappeared from sight. "Come home to me," she whispered.

# *Chapter Eleven*

*MacDougall Keep*
*April 1299*

Heather stacked her ledgers on Da's desk and sighed. Three weeks passed with no word from Alec. While the mission could take twice that time, she had hoped to at least receive a message. Perhaps she should be content with the knowledge that if Alec had been injured she would have heard something, but she worried for his safety. With the Scots having successfully stopped large caravans over the past year, the English were alert, the ambushes expected.

"Merchants arriving," a lad shouted from the main hall.

Clyde and his son, Edan, must be here. She rifled through her documents and extracted a list of ordered items. Throwing her wrap around her shoulders, she hurried from the room.

The midmorning sun greeted her as she stepped out of the keep and tilted her head to the ramparts. Da's men patrolled, forever gazing beyond MacDougall walls. They paced back and forth, swords strapped to their sides, quivers at their backs. The clanking of metal reverberated through the yard drawing her attention to Beathan, Jonathan and Randall sharpening long-handled scythes. Sickles, flails and other crop gathering tools lay to the side as the men prepared them for the upcoming harvest. Several women, arms loaded with laundry, strolled past them as Lindsey led a chestnut mare with a long dark flowing mane into the stables.

The sound of horse hooves clattered over the wooden bridge as Clyde's wagon came into sight. The old merchant steered the animals past the guardhouses and into the yard.

"Whoa!" He stood on the toe board as he tugged on the reins, and the creaking wagon rolled to a stop in the middle of the bailey.

Blake and two other stablehands ran from the barn and grabbed the harnesses to steady the beasts.

Heather descended the stairs. "Good morning, Clyde."

He straightened, his old hazel eyes sparkling. Black and white whiskers traversed deep wrinkles in his cheeks, and the beam of his snaggletooth grin warmed her insides. He removed his grey woolen cap, bent at the waist and reached down to her. His weathered hand grasped hers.

"Good morning, m'lady."

She shaded her eyes from the sun and inspected the barrels and crates in the wagon's bed. "I see ye have a full load today."

"Aye, I brought everything ye ordered." He climbed from the cart and shuffled to the rear.

She followed and unrolled her parchment.

Edan lifted a large carton and tossed it to Blake. "Here's yer material."

Blake opened the wooden container and Heather peered in. Folds of brown and tan linen lay inside. She picked up a cloth and rubbed it against her face, the softness ideal for undergarments. "It's lovely."

"And I brought the wool ye requested." Clyde flipped up the wrap covering a mound. Bundles of fleece crowded beneath.

She ran her hand over the much needed wool. There was plenty for blankets and clothing. Envisioning the happy faces of the MacDougall women, Heather smiled. "This is wonderful, Clyde."

Edan threw another crate to Blake. "And this one has herbs."

Blake removed the top as Heather crouched beside him. She examined the contents of the containers, mentally checking off the items. "Everything appears to be in good order, as usual." She glanced at Blake and Tavish. "Take the fleece and materials to the ladies in Mum's solar."

"Aye, Mistress," Blake responded. The lads hoisted the heavy containers onto their shoulders and carried them up the stairs while she opened her pouch and counted out several coins.

Clyde beamed, his eyes wide.

She handed him the money, and his fist closed around it. "Now, what may I bring ye on my next trip?"

Heather raked her teeth across her bottom lip. "I have a special request."

Clyde smiled and clutched his hat. "Anything fer ye, Mistress."

He was such a dear man, but she paused wondering how quickly word of her upcoming nuptials with Alec would spread. "Are ye familiar with the Campbell crest?"

"Aye, Laird Campbell proudly displays the red lion on the blue background of his shield."

"I would like a brooch made in its likeness."

Clyde's eyes widened. "Ye're in luck, m'lady. I know the blacksmith that created the Campbell coat of arms." His head cocked to the side, and his brows rose. "The ornament is fer a special occasion?"

She smiled. "Aye, we are to wed and I would like to gift the broach to him."

Clyde straightened and clasped his hands before him. "'Tis wonderful news, m'lady. Young Campbell is a lucky man."

She handed him a parchment. "Please ask the blacksmith to inscribe these words on the back."

Clyde nodded and accepted the document. "I will, Mistress."

With thoughts of Alec's face when she presented him with her wedding gift, joy welled through her. "Thank ye, Clyde."

~~~

Late that afternoon, Heather and Muire finished treating several patients from the village and strolled back up the dusty road to the keep. The wind stirred with an approaching storm, thunder rumbling in the distance. Pounding horse's hooves caught Heather's attention. A cloud of dust billowed behind a rider galloping toward her.

"Mistress Heather," the man shouted.

Heather

When he neared, she recognized Blaine, the messenger. Her breath caught. Did he carry news of Alec? Had he been injured?

The horse skidded to a halt.

"What news do ye have?" she asked.

He jumped to the ground, his fist holding a wrinkled stained parchment. "A message about Elsbeth."

"Elsbeth?" It had been months since her baby sister traveled to establish a new abbey. Fear struck Heather's core, and she motioned frantically. "Quickly, let me see."

He handed her the letter. She braced herself for bad news and unrolled the sealed document.

*My Dearest Loved Ones,*

*I miss ye terribly and pray this missive finds ye well. My work at the abbey keeps me busy. Time passes quickly as with each day children and displaced families find refuge in our church. Sister Mary worries we will not be able to care for everyone, but the Lord always provides a way.*

*The English get closer to the convent, but so far they have respected our sanctuary. We continue to pray for a miracle that will bring peace to our countries.*

*I anxiously await the day we meet again.*

*Fare thee well,*
*Elsbeth*

Heather hugged the note to her breast and grasped Muire's hand. "Elsbeth is safe."

"Oh, child, thank goodness we finally heard."

Happiness bubbled inside Heather. "We must hurry back and tell Da." She turned to Blaine. "Thank ye for bringing this joyous news. Please come in and rest."

Fat raindrops splattered the ground as Heather hurried into the bailey with Muire and Blaine. She ran up the stairs and into the great hall ordering food and drinks to be served to the messenger before she dashed to Da's bedchamber.

She rounded the door to find him sitting before the hearth, a book in his hands. "We received a letter from Elsbeth."

Da scooted to the edge of his seat, his eyes wide. "Elsbeth?"

He grabbed the parchment and quickly read the letter. His old frame sank against the back of the chair, tears clouding his dark eyes.

Heather knelt beside him and embraced his shoulders. How many times had they discussed rumors of Edward's forces burning towns and monasteries? They had worried no one was safe from Edward's wrath...not even the sisters of the abbey.

"We must celebrate." Da clutched Heather's hand. "Plan a feast, and we'll rejoice in this good news."

~~~

Lowrens chuckled. In the excitement, no one noticed him mingling in the crowded yard, listening and gathering information. Women bustled about, laughing and hurrying to finish chores. Two lads raced past him, weaving around a wagon full of hay and disappearing in the growing throng. A man led a horse, hauling a cart laden with large barrels, toward the keep where the celebration would be held.

Brown hood pulled low over his face, Lowrens slipped from the bailey and strode to his horse. Within a few days, he would be ensconced in the castle as Laird of the MacDougall clan. Heather would be his. He licked his lips imagining her naked, writhing beneath him. His cock swelled and he rubbed his crotch. He wouldn't have to wait much longer.

He swung onto the saddle, kicked his horse and galloped down the road. Stinging rain pelted his face as he made his way to camp several miles away. As he entered the hideout, he guided his mount past the lowlife mercenaries Symon had amassed. The slovenly group had grown in size after promises of grandeur and riches gained with the overthrow of Laird MacDougall.

## Heather

Lowrens dismounted and strode past the men huddled around a large fire awaiting his return. One man drew a blade across a sharpening stone. Another straightened. His cold eyes narrowed as his gaze followed Lowrens' path to Symon's tent.

Lowrens shoved the canvas flap back and stormed inside the shelter. A damp, musty smell mixed with the stench of unwashed bodies met him. If things went as planned, this time tomorrow he would be out of this pit of hell and comfortably settled in the warm keep.

Symon lounged in a chair next to a three-legged wooden stand he used for a table. Thin blonde hair lay plastered to his scalp, and his beefy arms crossed his chest. The bastard thought he would run MacDougall Castle, as if being Alastair's relation meant anything.

Symon would find out differently soon enough.

"They plan a celebration tonight." Lowrens pushed the hood from his head. "This is our opportunity to get into the keep. They'll be unsuspecting and unaware of our imminent strike."

Symon threw back his head and roared with laughter. "Tomorrow, I'll be the new Laird of the MacDougall clan!"

~~~

Heather held the dancers' hands on either side of her as the circle of men and women twirled in time with the music. Children skipped around revelers, and the great hall resounded with merriment. Ale flowed freely, and everyone helped themselves to the drink.

A man weaved on his feet. He steadied himself against a chair and raised his mug into the air. "Here'ssss to Elsssbeth and good times ahead."

Boisterous laughter and cheers rang out over toasts to her sister.

Heather strolled to the wooden tables against the back wall. Two serving girls entered the hall from the kitchen carrying a platter of roasted venison and smoked fish. Another held a tray of Rena's sweet cakes.

"Place them at the end of the table," Heather instructed as she moved two half-empty trenchers to make room for the fresh food. The lasses eased the heavy meat and tempting treats onto the surface.

Rena handed Heather a cup. "Would ye care for some mulled wine?"

"Aye, thank ye," she answered and took a sip.

Poignant melodies hushed the crowd as Jonathan blew into his bagpipe. The man forced air into the sheepskin bags and squeezed them hard, causing wind to rush through the reed pipe. Heather closed her eyes. How she wished Alec could be here with them to celebrate the news of Elsbeth. Where was he tonight? Would he return safely?

The front door banged against the wall.

Startled, her eyes flew open, and she gasped.

Randall ran into the room. Sweat dribbled from his mud streaked face. "Mistress MacDougall!"

She set her wine on the table and dashed to the front of the room. "I'm here. What is it?"

He advanced, his face strained. "It's yer cousin. He and his men have come over the walls."

Her heart slammed into her chest. "What?"

Randall swiped his arm across his sweat-streaked face. "They sneaked in the back of the castle. We didn't know they were there until it was too late."

A piercing scream rent the air.

Heather whirled toward the clamor.

*Symon.*

He stormed into the great hall and plunged his sword into the stomach of the man in front of him. The reveler fell to his knees, and her cousin jerked the blade from his body. Blood dripped from the weapon as he turned and swung the sharp edge across another man's belly. Shrieks and shouts resounded through the hall as Symon's band of miscreants swarmed through the door like ants upon a scattered mound. The clanging of swords rang out as the MacDougall men fumbled with their weapons, desperately trying to fend off the attackers. Several women tried to flee with crying children, but the assailants surrounded them and prevented their escape.

## Heather

Heather grabbed at her hip, but her hand grasped air. Damn it! She had left her sword in her bedchamber.

Wails and frightened voices filled the hall as more of Symon's men rushed into the keep. Two advanced on her. Pulse racing, she ran to the stairs while jerking her blade from the sheath tied to her waist. Rough hands seized her upper arms, their hard fingers painfully biting into her flesh. She managed to secure the dagger up her sleeve and prayed it didn't drop. With the weapon concealed, she would bide her time and wait for the opportunity to inflict the most damage.

"Where do ye think ye're going? The party is jes beginning." A burly men laughed and dragged her to the center of the room.

Two men hauled Beathan through the front door. His head dangled between his shoulders. A flap of skin across the back of his brown hair hung open, and blood smeared his dirty, torn clothes. Two more shoved Fergus through the door and into the great hall. The old captain's foot caught the leg of a table and he plummeted to the floor. Symon's man grabbed Fergus' upper arm and hauled him to his feet.

The clang of steel clashed to her right. Da swung his sword, both hands clutching the hilt. Two men circled him, their blades thrusting perilously close to his chest. Her father lunged. One of the men slammed his shield on Da's arm, causing Da's sword to clatter to the floor. The raiders grasped her father. He fought against them as they brought him to stand beside her.

Her chest clenched and she gasped for air. How had this happened? How had Symon broken through their defenses?

The room quieted as her cousin marched across the floor and stood in front of Da, a sneer plastered on his dirty face. His matted blond hair hung to his shoulders in greasy strands. Disheveled filthy clothes clung to his bulky frame. "Well, well, Uncle, we meet again."

"Symon?" Da's brow furrowed, his dark eyes questioning. "What are ye doing?"

"Relieving ye of yer duties, old man." He stopped inches before Da's face. "MacDougall Castle is now mine."

171

"By Satan's hairy arse, ye are a pig!" Da shouted.

Symon sneered and punched him in the stomach.

"Umph!" Her father bent forward, his arms held taut by two of Symon's men.

"Pick yer damn head up!" Symon grabbed Da's thin hair and yanked.

Da's face scrunched in pain.

"No! Stop!" Heather screamed and struggled against the men's strong grip. Her stomach plummeted. Da could not withstand Symon's bare fists.

The jeering miscreants held her father while Symon pummeled him. Blood splattered his clothes. His head reeled back. Cuts and scrapes crisscrossed his paper-thin skin. His beaten body sagged to the floor.

"Leave him!" Fury shot through her core. Her chest heaved, and her breathing rasped through her nose.

*I will see Symon dead!*

"Ye're not in any position to be issuing orders, Mistress MacDougall," a man shouted as he sauntered into the main hall.

Her head turned to the familiar voice. *Lowrens?*

The blackguard smirked and stopped in front of her. "This is all yer fault. If ye had only cooperated, none of this would have happened. But, now Symon and I have joined forces. Ye're just a means to an end, lass."

Rubbing his knuckles, Symon approached her and shoved Lowrens to the side. Her cousin's filthy calloused palm cupped her cheek. "Ah, Mistress Heather, it is so verra nice to see ye again."

She jerked her head away and spat at him.

He swiped his sleeve over his grimy chin, his dark eyes glaring. His meaty fingers grabbed her face and squeezed.

She inwardly winced, but she would die before she would show it.

"I'm going to enjoy taming ye," he breathed. The smell of rotting meat pervaded her nostrils.

She wrenched from his grasp, but he grabbed her head with both hands and crushed his mouth against hers. His thick tongue squished through her tightly closed lips, the stench of his unwashed body repugnant. She slammed her booted foot into his shin and bit his lip.

Symon cried out, but she would not let go. Her teeth clamped tighter. She yanked, and a metallic taste oozed into her mouth. As he shoved her from him, her fingers tightened around the handle of her blade and she extracted it from her sleeve. Anger billowed inside her, and she thrust the dagger at his torso.

His eyes widened, and he lurched to the left.

She missed his heart, but the weapon lodged deep in shoulder.

"Shite! Damn ye!" He grabbed the protruding knife, his chest heaving. The men holding her rushed to him as he dropped to his knees. Blood gushed from the wound. Hands gripping the handle, he tried to extract the slippery shaft.

She turned and ran toward the stairs, but two hulking brutes grabbed her around the waist and hauled her back.

Lowrens advanced and slapped the side of her head. Pain shot through her ear. Knocked off balance, she reeled to the side, but the men held her up. His beefy paw reared back and whacked her face again. Agony ricocheted through her head. One of the men holding her arms lost his grip at the powerful blow, and she fell against a table, her ears ringing.

"Ye had best start praying he doesn't die, bitch." Lowrens jerked her up by her hair and slapped her again.

A sharp jolt sliced through her head. Blackness pervaded her senses, and she crumpled to the floor.

~~~

Lindsey followed Blake into the kitchen and grabbed a fresh scone off the worktable. "It won't be long before Bess delivers. I'm hoping for another colt like Blaze —"

A piercing scream silenced her. Lindsey's eyes widened. She ran to the curtain covering the entrance to the kitchen and peered into the room.

Bodies lay scattered about the great hall, some alive, but bleeding and badly wounded. Food, platters and crockery littered the floor. Men, women and children were huddled

173

against the walls, guarded by filthy assailants wearing dark animal skins and leather trews. Clanging and crashing sounded through the room as the attackers pillaged the keep. Half-dozen men rushed around another lying on table in a pool of blood.

A man hauled Muire into the room and shoved her toward the group. "Ye will treat Symon or die."

Lindsey's hand flew to her mouth. "Symon!"

As she lurched forward, Blake grabbed her shoulders and tugged her back into the kitchen. "Wait, Lins," he hissed in her ear. "We can't overtake them by ourselves. We need help. It wouldn't do any good for us to become captives, too."

"Get water from the kitchen," a voice ordered.

Blake motioned for her to follow. "Hurry!"

He grabbed her hand and thrust her into a storage room off the kitchen toward the trap door they'd played in as children. Why hadn't she thought of that?

He snatched a torch out of the sconce in the wall as she opened the small wooden door. They crawled inside and quickly shut the entrance behind them. Fetid air buffeted her face as Blake straightened and motioned with his hand. "This way."

When she did not move, his head jerked to her.

"I can't just leave them," she whispered.

"Ye don't have a choice, lass. We have to leave to get help."

A loud crash and another scream sounded overhead.

"We're wasting precious time." He tugged on her arm. "We must go now."

She nodded. "All right."

"Watch yer step." Blake jogged down a long flight of stairs and through a narrow corridor to an exit leading outside the castle walls. After shoving the rusty grate aside, he stuck his head out.

Lindsey placed her hand on Blake's side, trying to peer around him. "Do ye see anyone?"

He turned back to her. "No, be quiet, and let's get out of here."

He inched through overgrown brambles and grabbed her hand as they ran, escaping into the surrounding woods.

## Heather

"Where are we going?" Lindsey asked.

"Glencara."

# Chapter Twelve

Heather awoke in darkness, her head throbbing and cold penetrating her bones. Her body trembled uncontrollably. She opened her mouth and worked her sore jaw back and forth—not broken, thankfully. With only one eye willing to open, she tried to focus.

Pitch black.

Where was she?

A musty smell permeated the stale air surrounding her, but she caught a whiff of spices. Her fingers eased to her side and ran along a lumpy straw mattress.

Men's voices rumbled nearby. A moment later, a door swung wide, and a shaft of light spilled into the room illuminating crates and cartons along the walls. The storeroom. She lay in the small chamber that contained the keep's supplies.

Shadows drifted across the back wall as shuffling footsteps neared.

Her pulse pounded in her ears. Reaching for her knife, she felt her bare thigh. Not only did she not have her blade, she was clad only in her thin chemise. Near naked, her body shook with tremors.

"Heather, it's Muire. Are ye awake?"

"Oh, Muire." Relief poured through her. She tried to rise, but her head swam.

The aging healer knelt and set her basket beside her. "How do ye feel?"

"I'm freezing. My head hurts, and I'm sore all over."

Muire draped a blanket over Heather's body. "Lowrens would not let me cover ye, but I convinced him if he were to keep ye alive, ye must have some protection from the cold. I brought the heaviest blanket I could find." Muire rubbed her hands up and down Heather's arms. "I'm relieved to see ye awake."

"How long have I been in here?"

"Two days. Ye're lucky to be alive after the way that monster beat ye. I worried ye would not awaken." She rummaged in her basket, extracted a vial and twisted off the cork plug. "Drink this. It will alleviate yer pain."

Heather rose on her elbow and sipped the draught. Her mouth stung. She touched her face and winced. Her lip was twice its normal size. "Have ye seen Lindsey or Da?"

Muire shook her head. Flickering light cast moving shadows on her drawn face as she dug through her basket again and withdrew another jar.

"I have not seen Lindsey, but yer da and his men are held in the dungeon. Lowrens will not let me tend them." She opened the container, dipped her finger into the contents and applied a salve to the ragged cuts on Heather's cheek.

Heather's nose wrinkled from the pungent odor. Her breath hitched. Da would not survive long in that damp hole. "Where could Lindsey be?"

Muire glanced at the door and whispered. "She's not in the keep. Blake is not here either. I pray they escaped to get help."

"What happened to my gown?"

"Lowrens had ye stripped, ranting ye could not flee near to naked." Muire smoothed the hair from Heather's face. "Ye delivered a severe blow to Symon. He's in bed with a raging fever."

A trickle of hope flickered. "Will he recover?"

"I fear so, but regardless, his injury has bought us time."

A shadow crossed Muire's form as a large man paused at the door's threshold. "Ole woman, enough. Yer time's up."

"I'm coming." She gathered her supplies and slipped Heather a small wrapped bundle and wineskin. "Take this bread and cheese. Eat what ye can."

Heather nodded. "Thank ye."

"Be strong." The healer squeezed Heather's hand and left.

The guard closed and locked the door, once again shrouding her in darkness.

She eased back on the pallet, praying for a miracle. What happened to Lindsey and Da? Were they alive? Were they suffering at the hands of her malicious cousin? Her gut churned, and she put her face in her hands. The salt of her tears stung the cuts on her face. She touched her lip and winced.

"Alec, where are ye?"

*Ye must be strong. I will return for ye.*

Recalling his words, she straightened. Determination welled through her. She swiped tears off her cheek. "If I die trying, Symon will regret this!"

~~~

*Forest South of Glasgow*
*March 1299*

The warning whistle sounded. A rider approached.

Alec sat in front of the campfire discussing their last job with Robert. It had been dangerous stopping the large caravan of weapons and food, but they had successfully attacked, dispatched the soldiers and confiscated the shipment. Although they were victorious, two of his men, William and Bryce, were badly injured. It was time to head home and lay low.

A few moments later, Kirk rode into camp. There was only one reason the man he left in charge of the castle would travel from Glencara.

Trouble.

Kirk dismounted and strode over to Alec and Robert. His face was pale, his cheeks drawn. "It's the MacDougalls."

Alec's heart leapt into his throat as he stood.

"Symon Fraser attacked. Blake and Mistress MacDougall traveled to Glencara looking for ye."

"Heather?" Alec held his breath. "Heather MacDougall?"

"No, m'laird. Lindsey."

"Shite!" Alec tossed the remnants of his cup in the fire. "What of the MacDougalls—Heather and Alastair?"

"I understand Symon overcame them."

Lord, no. Alec's worst nightmare materialized. "That's a hard two day's ride from here."

Lachlan, Eric, and Kendrick crowded around.

Alec addressed Robert. "I could use yer help."

178

Robert nodded. "I'd like nothing better than to crush Symon once and for all."

"We'll split off at the north fork. Once ye get yer wounded home, meet me at the MacDougall's south border." Alec hesitated. "If ye're willing to bring yer wife, her services would be appreciated."

Robert's back straightened.

"I'll understand if ye don't want her there."

Robert scoffed. "I doubt my wife would let me live if I did not allow her to attend her family."

Alec nodded. He hoped Cameron had a family left to attend.

The men broke camp. William and Bryce could ride, but barely. Leaving the seized shipment behind, Alec led his men down the dirt road. He fought the urge to race headlong to the MacDougalls. He had to control his emotions. Glencara was on the way. He would secure fresh horses, question Blake and Lindsey, and formulate a plan.

Was she all right? Had Symon harmed her? Ideas of what the man might be doing to her ripped through his gut.

God willing, he would get to Heather in time.

~~~

*MacDougall Keep*

Another day had passed. Heather gingerly sat and eased her legs over the side of the mattress. Her head swam. She must gather the strength to face Symon and Lowrens. She placed her hands on either side of her thighs for balance. The darkness didn't help her disorientation. Only the light seeping through wooden slats in the door gave her a sense of direction.

There was a chance she would find a weapon stored amongst the crates and containers. With the bottoms of her feet planted on the cold dirt surface, she straightened. Her aching muscles screamed. Oh Lord, she had to make them move. She crept to the back of the storeroom, fingering shelves on the wall.

Pottery hit the floor with a crash. She sucked in a breath, whirled toward the door and froze. Shadows passed through the light filtering into the room. When no shouts of alarm sounded, she exhaled and shuffled along, her tender, bare feet inching forward. Frantically, she stuck her hands in and out of cartons, searching the contents for the knife she used to cut string just days ago. She was about to give up when her fingers closed around the large dagger. "Oh, thank ye, Lord."

Clutching the weapon, she traced the length of the blade with her fingertips. Would she be able to conceal it? Clad in her chemise, she had few hiding places.

She hobbled to the mattress and grabbed her blanket. Throwing it around her shoulders, she leaned against the back wall, then sank to the cold floor. She placed the blade under her left arm. Hugging herself, she maintained a death grip on the dagger. She would be ready when Symon or one of his minions strolled through that door.

~~~

"Unlock it, and ye can take a break," a man's deep voice boomed.

The lock rattled, and the door swung open. Light streamed into the room as a man entered holding a torch in front of him.

"I'll be back directly," the guard said.

"Take yer time, take yer time. I plan to spend a while between her lovely thighs. Ye won't be needed for hours."

The guard laughed and shut the door behind him.

"No need for concern." The man turned toward her.

Lowrens.

"It's just me."

Trembling, she willed herself to stand and face him.

He secured the torch in a support on the wall and turned to her. "Well, well, Mistress Heather. What were ye doing on the floor when ye've got a nice bed over here? Mayhap ye were lonely in it without that bastard, Campbell? Symon told me ye were spreading yer legs for him. Now ye're going to spread them for me." He continued to chuckle as he tugged off his boots and untied his belt. "Yer cousin is waiting in that bed of

180

yers right now, but I figure I'll enjoy ye first since him and me are partners." He dropped his trews to the floor and stepped out of them. "I won't bloody ye up past him getting his use out of ye."

Her heart slammed against her chest, her fist clenching the knife.

He sauntered toward her, his manhood swinging between his stocky legs. "What's wrong Mistress? Are ye not happy to see me?" His hand pumped his flaccid member. As it grew, he chuckled. "Maybe *now* ye're happy to see me." He stroked himself and licked his puffy lips. "And…" He advanced. "*I* will be happy to see those tits ye've been hiding under yer gown."

He grabbed the front of her chemise and yanked.

The material ripped. She jerked the knife from under her arm, and with both hands, she thrust it into his belly.

His beady eyes widened.

Blood spewed from his gut.

He grabbed the protruding knife and fell over, knocking her to the floor with him.

His body twitched, smothering her under its weight.

She pushed and shoved his shoulders. Warm blood soaked her shift. Her fingers slipped in the gore as she heaved him off her legs and scrambled from beneath him.

Heart racing, she froze and stared at the closed door. When no one sounded an alarm, her trembling fingers snatched his trews and scrubbed the blood off her hands and face. She had no time to lose. She grasped the protruding dagger's handle and yanked. As she extracted the blade, a sucking sound came from the wound. Her nose wrinkled, and she swallowed the bile rising in her throat.

His lifeless eyes stared unblinking. She nudged him with her foot, and his head rolled to the side. *Thank God, he's dead.*

Wiping the dagger on his clothing, she quickly wrapped it, along with Muire's sack of food and wineskin, in her blanket and grabbed the torch in the holder.

She hobbled to the door and eased it open. Hinges creaked. The sound pierced the silence. Holding her breath, she cringed.

All was quiet.

After glancing to the left and right, she staggered down the corridor to the far end of the hall and into another storage room. Weaving around crates and containers scattered about the floor, she made her way to the back wall and slipped through the trap door leading to the rear of the keep.

Thrusting the torch in front of her, she peered through her good eye and shuffled into the narrow passageway. Sharp rocks cut her feet, cold numbing the pain. Cobwebs grabbed her head and she ducked, waving the torch at the sticky substance. Her skin crawled with thoughts of spiders and other creatures living in the dark bowels of the castle. Something skittered past her foot, and she gasped in stale putrid air.

Taking steady breaths, she calmed herself and little by little, crept forward until she reached the exit. She shoved the rusty grate with her shoulder. It scraped across the dirt and barely opened. *Oh, please, Lord.* She threw her body against the gate, and it opened another inch. She rammed it again and again. Pain streaked down her arm and back. She shoved the grate once more, and the rusty bars finally gave way.

Relief swept through her.

Now, to get out of here without being seen.

Night had fallen. She'd have to leave her torch. Fear welled through her at the idea of stumbling in the darkness, but someone would spot the light. Reluctantly, she snuffed the flame in the dirt. Darkness enveloped her, and she squeezed through the opening.

Holding her chemise closed at the neck with one hand and her blanketed bundle in the other, she slid along the rocky wall, her back scraping the rough stones. Laughter and raucous shouts drifted from the bailey. Symon's men continued their celebration. Flames leapt into the dark night from torches lining the castle walls. The MacDougall Crest had been torn from the flagstaff. A purple pennant flew in its place. She seethed. She would see Symon's banner burned.

Heather

Several men patrolled the ramparts. One slapped another on the shoulder. His head reared back, his wide girth shaking with laughter.

If she could make it to her secret hiding place in the cave, she could rest until she was strong enough to go for help.

No one would find her there.

She inched her way to the back of the keep. Torches lit the grounds. She would have to make a run for it. Could she get past without being seen?

She peered around the corner.

No one was in sight.

Glancing to either side, she took a deep breath and sprinted over the wet grass. She plastered herself against the bailey wall, her chest heaving. No alarm sounded, no men ran to search for her.

Keeping to the shadows, she crept to the back gate. Just as she suspected, the old hidden door stood unguarded, but she would have to be quick.

A shout sounded in the bailey. Several men ran to the disturbance. She bolted through the door, across the hard-packed ground and into the forest, running into the thick trees, her aching legs pumping. Rocks and debris cut the bottoms of her feet, but she ran.

The familiar path opened into a clearing. She dashed to the wild thicket and wiggled between multitudes of spiny branches. As she thrust herself into the safety of her secret cave, thorns tore into her arms and legs. She shoved the bushes back in place, concealing the entrance.

Chest heaving, she leaned against the wall of the cavern and the bundle dropped from her fingers. Her body trembled. She sank to the floor and wrapped her arms around her legs. Her hands and face were sticky from Lowrens's blood. Her shift, ripped in two, provided little protection from the cold. Shivering, she grabbed the blanket and threw it around her shoulders.

Tears dribbled down her checks. What had Symon done to her family? Images of men falling under his blade, and women attacked and raped flashed through her mind.

Would she be able to get help in time to save her clan?

~~~

*Glencara Castle*

Alec and his men charged into the bailey. Lads from the stables ran to take their horses as Alec dismounted then lifted Bryce out of the saddle. "Ralf and Ian, help William inside. Eric, get fresh horses and ready the men. We ride for MacDougall Castle within the hour."

Alec carried the wounded man, taking the stairs two at a time as he raced into the keep. When he handed Bryce to Kirk and Roger, Blake and Lindsey bolted from chairs in the main hall and ran to meet him.

"Laird Campbell," Lindsey shouted. "Thank goodness ye're finally here!"

Maria issued orders to take the injured upstairs and followed the men from the room.

Dark shadows circled Lindsey's eyes—eyes the color of Heather's. He took a deep breath. "Tell me what happened."

Blake shook his head. "We don't rightly know. We were working in the barn while everyone celebrated news from Elsbeth. After we finished, we went inside and found Symon and his men had taken over. We escaped and raced here for help."

"How many men were with him?"

"I don't know…several dozen."

Lindsey grabbed Alec's arm. "They took Da and Heather. Ye've got to help them."

Alec's gut twisted. Lindsey's words struck terror in his heart and waves of tension rolled through his stomach. He had never felt so nervous about a battle, but then again, he never had so much to lose. "I need as much information as I can garner before we head out. Now, tell me everything ye saw."

A short time later, with his sword strapped to his side and daggers in hand, he stormed out of the keep.

Lindsey and Blake sat on their mounts amongst his men.

"Where do ye think ye're going?" Alec questioned Lindsey as he swung onto his saddle.

She squared her shoulders. "It's my family. I will not remain behind."

Alec seared her with a dark glare. "Ye will stay out of the way and at a safe distance from the castle. I'll not be concerned about protecting ye when the battle starts."

"Ye don't have to worry about me," Lindsey threw back at him.

Alec glanced at his men. "Let's ride."

~~~

*MacDougall Keep*

Symon's guards marched across the MacDougall ramparts. The main gate was closed, the castle secured and well armed. Shouts and jeers bellowed over the walls—raised voices, women's screams.

Alec and his men crouched at the tree line, concealed in the shadows. His blood boiled and his body strummed with tense anticipation.

"I can show ye a secret entrance," Lindsey whispered.

Alec's head snapped around. "What? Why did ye not tell me that earlier?"

Blake crouched next to her and shrugged. "It's a secret escape route, information we were entrusted not to divulge."

Frustration tested his patience, but with precious time slipping away, he tamped it down. "Show me. *Now*."

Blake jogged down a worn path through the woods, leading Lindsey and the others to the back of the keep. He stopped and knelt, Lindsey at his side. Alec stooped beside them.

Blake pointed to an area thick with brambles and undergrowth. "There. Through those bushes."

Alec inspected the thorny intertwined weeds, their branches providing a barbed thicket of protection. "Where does it lead?"

"Into the bowels of the castle. The dungeons are down there, but passageways run in a number of directions. Da has many escape tunnels." Lindsey wiped her face on her sleeve. "I can lead ye to a back room off the kitchen."

"Nay, ye will stay here. Blake will show us the way."

"But…"

"Don't argue," Alec ground out. "Robert, leave some of the men to watch over yer wife and Lindsey. This is as far as they go."

Lindsey's eyes narrowed.

Cameron clutched her shoulder. "We'll wait here."

"Michael and Randall will protect them," Robert answered.

Alec nodded at Blake. "After ye."

The men crouched low and ran from the woods. Upon reaching the castle walls, they pushed aside brambles and exposed a narrow overgrown path leading to a trap door. One by one, they made their way down the passageway and into the belly of the castle.

Blackness engulfed Alec, and he grabbed Blake's shoulder. "Take hold of the man in front of ye," he whispered to the men behind him.

With no torch to light their way, Blake shuffled along, his hands feeling the walls.

The smell of sewage and stagnant water assailed Alec, and he gagged on the stench. Cold air enveloped his body, and rats scurried past his feet. Pulse pounding, his grip tightened on the hilt of his sword.

*Heather.*

What would he find? Would she be alive? Had Symon raped her and passed her amongst his men? His legs could not move fast enough.

After trudging down one corridor then another, a light glowed ahead. The maze opened into a main section connecting tunnels running in different directions. Staying in the shadows, he searched the area.

Men's voices drifted down the hall. He signaled to keep quiet and crept forward. The smell of excrement assaulted him as he rounded the corner. Iron bars enclosed dark cells lining the walls with men inside, huddled on the dirt floor.

Several guards stationed outside the bars laughed. One tossed a pair of dice. They rolled to a stop next to the leg of a chair.

"Whoa!" Another slapped the man's back and grabbed the cubes. "My turn."

At Alec's signal, the men charged from the shadows.

The stunned guards scrambled for their weapons.

Alec thrust his sword into a man's belly before the scum could extract his weapon. Another clutched a dagger in his fist. He swung. Alec ducked. The edge ripped his tunic.

The man's powerful thrust knocked him off balance, and he stumbled forward. Alec twisted to the side, planting his elbow in the man's face. With that blow, Symon's man collapsed on the floor.

The clash ended as quickly as it began. Breathing heavy, Alec skimmed the room. Robert, blood oozing from a slash on his cheek, straightened over a lifeless body. Eric, Blake, Kendrick…all standing.

Alec snatched the torch from the bracket in the wall and swung the flame toward the cells. Light filtered through the grates and shone on the bedraggled men. Their dirty and bleeding faces lifted. Their eyes, squinting from the bright light, peered at him. Alastair hung by his wrists from iron hooks secured in the back wall. Beathan dangled beside him.

Fergus grasped the bars and hauled himself to his feet. "Laird Campbell?"

"Aye, we're here to get ye out."

Several prisoners struggled to stand and helped others from the filthy ground. "Thank the Lord ye're here!" one shouted.

Others chimed in with words of gratitude. "Ye're a sight fer weary eyes, lads."

Alec grabbed the cell gate. "Keep yer voices down. We don't want to alert the bastards upstairs."

Robert, crouched over one of the fallen guards, searched the man's clothing. "I found them."

He held up keys, then rattled the lock and opened the iron doors. The captives rushed the opening, and Eric and Colin helped them into the dark corridor.

Alec handed Blake the torch, marched into the cell and severed the ropes binding Alastair's wrists. As the old man slid to the ground, Alec caught him. "Thank God, he's still breathing."

Robert cut the MacDougall captain's ties and the man's limp frame sagged. "Beathan, as well."

Ian ushered more wounded men into the hall as Alec carried the old laird out of the rank cell and laid him on the ground. Dried blood and black bruises mottled his swollen and distorted face. A large cut sliced his cheek, and a ragged flap of skin hung loose. "Alastair, can ye hear me?"

His eyes fluttered, and his mouth moved as he tried to speak.

"I need water," Alec demanded.

Eric tossed him a wineskin, and Alec poured a small amount into the laird's mouth. He gulped at the liquid. Droplets escaped, dribbling down his rough chin.

"Alec?" Alastair's voice croaked. "Is it ye?"

"Aye, rest easy. Ye're safe. I'm leaving men down here with ye while I kill that swine."

"Take care. My Heather is up there."

Aeton's kick to his gut could not have hurt more than those few words. "Lindsey waits out-of-doors with Cameron."

The MacDougall Laird closed his eyes. "Thank ye, lad."

"Colin, Ian, stand guard." Alec nodded to Blake. "Lead the way."

The men followed Blake through dark narrow passages and up the stairs to the kitchen storage room. After easing the trap door open, Alec's gaze skimmed the room for signs of Symon's men. No one was about. He signaled for Robert to follow and slowly the large men filled the room.

His fist tightened around his dagger. "Ready?"

"More than ready," Robert muttered.

## Heather

As they rounded the corner, a serving girl standing across the room jumped, her eyes wide, her hand grasping her chest.

Alec held a finger to his mouth.

She peered over her shoulder and quickly ran to him. "Symon and his men are eating in the main hall."

"Get yer healer to the dungeon. Laird MacDougall and his men need her attention."

"Aye." She bobbed her head and moved to leave, but he caught her arm.

"Where is Mistress Heather?"

"I believe she's held a floor below, in the main storage room."

He cursed at the thought of her locked away, but at least she would not be in danger when the fighting started. "See to yer Laird." She raced off as he turned to Robert. "Take yer men and go around to the front hall. I'll wait until ye're in position, and we'll move in."

As Robert stepped away, Alec grabbed his forearm. "Symon's mine."

Robert's eyes narrowed. "I have waited a long time to end his miserable life."

"I understand, but he's mine."

Robert inhaled and nodded before leading his men through the narrow serving hall.

Alec peered through the curtain. Men, with swords hanging off their belts, lined two trestle tables, their loud rambunctious laughter echoing against the walls. Symon sat at the dais, as master of the keep.

Not for long.

He grabbed a serving girl. She screamed as he jerked her onto his lap, his dirty hand groping her breasts. Another man ran his hand up a woman's gown. She kicked and punched at him as he grabbed her, hoisting her over his shoulder.

Symon's blond head reared back, his loud burst of laughter resounding.

Blood rushed in Alec's ears. Where the devil was Robert? Struggling against the urge to storm in and lay waste to Symon, his fist clenched the hilt of his sword. He craved the blackguard's hide.

Finally, Robert appeared at the entrance to the main hall, and Alec and his men charged into the room.

Stumbling backward over benches, Symon's men grabbed their weapons. Clanging swords and men's shouts reverberated off the walls.

Alec had Symon in his sights. He stalked the beefy man. A bloody bandage crisscrossed Symon's chest. His face flushed and he sweated profusely. The fiend spun to flee, but stopped when he faced Eric and Blake.

Symon spun toward Alec. "I should have known ye'd come for yer whore."

His taunting words struck a blow, and Alec bore down on him, his sword poised to strike.

"Ye might have ridden her first, but that was all right. It smoothed the way for my big cock," he shouted and lunged, his blade slashing wildly right, then left.

God's blood, but he would rip the bastard's black heart out. Alec struggled to maintain control of his emotions. He darted to the side, easily deflecting the blows.

Symon leapt, striking again, but Alec effortlessly sidestepped his attack and brought his weapon down on the fiend's arm.

The man roared and jabbed his blade. "Too bad ye will never see her again. Seems my man Lowrens did away with her."

He tried to close his ears to Symon's taunting words, but images of Heather's lifeless bloodied body flashed through his mind. Rage billowed through him, strengthening him.

Symon nicked his side. A sting spread.

"Ye're tiring, Campbell." Symon panted, out of breath. Blood oozed down his shirt sleeve. He screamed and crazily swung his sword. "Fight, ye sniveling coward!"

With a powerful swing, Alec knocked Symon's sword from his hands and thrust his sharp blade deep into the blackguard's gut. A look of utter astonishment plastered Symon's face.

Heather

Elation coursed through Alec's body, and he jerked his blade upward into Symon's chest. The beast made a gurgling noise and fell in a heap, blood pouring around him.

Symon's men ran in the main hall from the bailey to join in the fight, but the Grahams and Campbells made quick work dispatching the invaders. Bodies lay crumpled amongst overturned and broken furniture, smashed pottery and eating utensils littering the floor. Eric wiped blood from his forehead. Robert jerked his blade from a man and straightened.

Lachlan, from the Graham clan, ran into the hall. "The bailey's secured."

Alec addressed Robert. "See that the men are helped from the dungeon, and take care of the women."

"Kendrick, bring my wife and her sister into the keep," Robert shouted. "David and Brian, come with me."

Alec sheathed his sword, spun to the back of the room and raced down the stairs to the storeroom. One of Symon's men sauntered down the hall. Alec lunged and planted his fist in the man's face. With a satisfying crack, blood spurted from the man's nose. He bent over, grasping his face and howling. Alec brought his knee up and slammed the man's head. Bleeding and unconscious, the assailant slid to the floor.

A large lock dangled from brackets in the storeroom door. Alec backed up and kicked the doorframe off its hinges. Wood splintered, flying in every direction, exposing a darkened room. He snatched the torch from a support in the hall and shoved through the opening. "Heather? Heather, where are ye?"

He waved the flames from side to side, peering into the shadows.

"She's no longer here."

He spun around at a woman's voice. A young lass stood in the doorway wringing her hands. "Symon and his men searched, but no one found her."

"What do ye mean?"

"She just vanished."

Memories flooded his mind.

*I hid in my secret place when I did not want to be found.*

He burst from the room, ran through the keep and bounded down the stairs and into the bailey. Lachlan and Eric dashed behind him.

God's blood. He prayed she was alive.

Alec led the men through the woods, down the path to the water. Rounding several large boulders, he waved the torch toward the thick bushes and thorny brambles and searched for the opening Heather had shown him weeks earlier.

Lachlan and Eric glanced at each other. "Laird?" Eric asked.

Alec slashed his sword at the prickly overgrowth. "She has to be in here."

After opening a passage, he squeezed through the narrow hole and entered a large cave with Eric and Lachlan thrusting through the entrance behind him.

Swinging the torch to the right and left, Alec shouted, "Heather? Are ye here?"

A muffled, strangled sound drifted from deep within the cave. He ran forward, ducking and weaving around bulging rocks and boulders. His light finally settled on a huddled form crumpled against the wall.

*Heather.*

Pain pierced his soul.

He rushed to her side, dropping the torch on the floor. He stooped next to her and touched her shoulder.

She flinched, and one eye flew open.

"Lass, it's me, Alec."

Her glassy eye focused on his face, and her breath caught. "Alec?"

"Aye." He stood, tugging her before him. Her small frame bent, vulnerable.

"Oh, Alec. Ye're here."

He wrapped his arms around her and held her against him as Eric and Lachlan stepped back to give them privacy. She cried into his chest, his heart breaking at the sound of her sobs. Kissing her forehead, he ran his hand down her hair. "It's all right. He'll never hurt ye again."

## Heather

When her tears subsided, she raised her head. Dark bruises marred her beautiful face. One eye remained swollen shut. Her torn, bloodied shift hung in rags. She trembled, her skin frigid.

He jerked his tunic over his head. "Let me put this on ye."

She slid her arms in the sleeves. It hung well below her knees, giving her some measure of warmth. "Alec." Her teeth chattered. "My father...."

"Is safe. Muire's with him." He rubbed her arms up and down.

Her breath hitched. "Thank ye."

He scooped her up and cradled her in his arms. "We need to get ye inside where it's warm."

She rested her head against his chest. Lachlan and Eric had widened the opening, and Alec stepped from the cave.

*Thank ye, Lord. At least she's alive.*

He carried her through the dark forest, her weak body clinging to him. Bile welled. Never had he experienced such a searing pain of fear.

Cameron ran to meet them with Robert and several of his men following. "Let me take her."

"Nay. I'll tend her. See to yer father and the others."

"But...." Cameron started to protest.

Robert clutched her arm. "Let them be."

Heather turned her face into Alec's bare chest as he brushed by the group and carried her up the stairs, down the hall and into her bedchamber.

Cameron called for hot water along with a tray of food and wine to be sent to Heather. The room filled with lads struggling with the old wooden tub and sloshing buckets. Cameron rummaged through her basket and extracted a vial. She opened the container and shook some of the contents into a mug, then filled it with wine.

Alec sat before the popping and hissing fire with Heather snuggled in his lap. Cameron placed the brew on a table next to them and ran her hand down Heather's hair. "This will help ye rest."

193

Heather lifted her head from his shoulder. "Thank ye."

Cameron's gaze traveled over her sister's face. "I left a salve next to the potion. See that her cuts are treated."

Alec nodded. "I will."

After Cameron ushered the lads out the door, she slipped from the room and the chamber fell silent.

What should he say? How could he comfort her? He had not been here to protect her. Guilt flooded him, and his chest tightened. He ran his hand up and down her arm, remembering Symon's taunts.

Had he raped her? Did she suffer humiliation and pain from his bestial attack? His chest squeezed painfully. Her shift had been bloodied and torn to her waist. Obvious signs of rape. How would he heal the horror she had suffered?

He reached over and picked up the goblet off the table. "Here, drink this. Yer sister put something in it to help ye relax."

She hesitated.

He nudged her. "Come on, ye need it."

Heather straightened and took the cup. Her hands trembled.

"Careful. Let me help ye." He gently held the mug to her lips as he studied the blackish-purple bruises and cuts marring her delicate skin.

She sipped the brew, her small fingertips on his hands. Her gaze lifted to his, her swollen eye still closed.

He set the cup on the table, and emotion clogged his throat. He stroked her hair, afraid of what she had been through, and too frightened to ask. "Would ye like to bathe? It might make ye feel better. I can ask one of yer sisters to tend ye."

Heather's head turned to the steaming water. "I would love a hot bath, but please don't leave me."

Alec traced the side of her face with the back of his finger. "Verra well. I'll stay right here."

He stood with her in his arms and stepped to the tub. When her feet touched the floor, she cringed. Cuts lined her skin.

194

"Ah, lass. Ye're hurt all over." He tugged the hem of his tunic up and lifted it over her head. Her blonde tresses, matted and dirty, hung down her back. Her bloodied and torn shift gaped open from the neck to her waist. He pushed the remnants down her arms and onto the floor before picking her up and easing her into the tub.

She winced as hot water seeped into her abrasions.

Alec lifted her hair off her slim shoulders and poured water through it. "I know it stings, but it will be good to wipe away the dirt and grime."

He lathered soap through her thick locks and rinsed the suds. She laid her head against him as he attempted to wash away the filth and memories. Firelight danced across her bare shoulders, her breasts peaking above the water.

He ran a slice of soap down her arms. He wanted to be tender and show her respect, but he longed to hold her and erase the nightmare.

The sight of her naked body marred with cuts and abrasions struck fear in his core. An overwhelming urge to make love to her swathed him. He wanted to show her the act could be loving, not brutal.

Her long hair hung over the back of the tub. The wet tresses grazed his bare chest as he leaned over her. Her skin, bruised as it might have been, was soft as he ran his fingers down her arms and held her hands.

She laid her head against his upper arm. "Thank ye for once again coming to my rescue."

His throat constricted. He could not speak. He sat in silence, at a loss for words.

Once the water cooled, he released her, stepped to a trunk at the foot of her bed and removed a clean shift. He grabbed a drying cloth and held it open. "Come. Let's get ye in bed. Ye need rest."

When she stood, water sluiced off her luscious curves, droplets trickling off her pink erect nipples down her abdomen to her long legs. She stepped into the cloth, and he wrapped it around her, picked her up and laid her on the bed. He slid the clean shift over her head, then sat against the back of the bed and pulled her into his arms.

She snuggled next to him, her head resting on his chest, her eyes closed.

"Try to sleep. I'll be beside ye."

The light from the fireplace danced across the bed, clearly displaying the abusive marks Symon left. Alec clenched his jaw. What he would give to have Symon alive. How he would have enjoyed making the bastard suffer so much more.

What was it about this lass that had his gut churning? What was it that constantly drew him to her?

*Spirit.*

*Loyalty.*

*Compassion.*

He closed his eyes and swallowed. Heather scared the hell out of him.

~~~

Heather woke with a start and cried out. For a moment, she was back in the dark storeroom.

Strong arms embraced her. "Shhh, it's all right. Ye're safe."

Flames in the hearth slowly came into focus. A steady heartbeat sounded against her ear. She exhaled and closed her eyes.

*Alec.*

Once again, he had rescued her and her family from Symon. She gazed up at him and touched his bearded cheek. "Thank ye for coming."

His dark eyes searched her face, his brow knit. He rubbed his knuckle across her cheek. "I wish I had arrived sooner."

"How did ye know?"

He huffed. "Lindsey and Blake. They escaped and made their way to Glencara. Kirk got word to me."

"They're safe?"

"Aye, they're well."

"And Da?" She cringed remembering his crumpled form lying at Symon's feet.

196

Heather

"I think he'll recover. Muire and Cameron are taking care of him and Beathan. They were badly beaten, but I have faith in the ladies' healing ways."

A tear slipped from her eye, and his thumb wiped it away. She snuggled against his bare chest, his warm embrace comforting. They lay in each other's arms, watching the fire, listening to the popping and crackling of the flames.

"I want ye as my wife, if ye will have me."

She stilled. "Oh, Alec," she whispered.

How she longed to marry him, care for him, raise his children. How many nights had she dreamt of becoming his wife? But he did not know about Lowrens. Would he still want her if he knew she had no feelings of remorse over killing the man? Would he still want her if he knew she rejoiced in his death? Her former betrothed's sneering face loomed before her. She could not withstand Alec's scorn.

"What is this?" Alec placed his hand under her chin and gently lifted her face toward him. "Why does that make ye cry?"

She shook her head. "Ye don't have to..."

His eyes searched hers. "I don't feel obligated." His rough thumb stroked her cheek. "I *want* to marry ye."

"Ye don't know all that happened." Her breath hitched. Upon learning how she gleefully killed Lowrens, relishing the feel of her blade plunging into his soft belly, disgust would fill his eyes, just like Richard's. "Ye would not want me if ye knew."

Silence.

"I won't force ye to talk about it, but when ye're ready, I'm here and will understand."

Reliving the nightmare, she buried her face against his chest and shook her head. "It's too terrible to speak of."

Alec's torso swelled with a deep breath. "Then, let's not speak of it tonight." He stroked her hair. "Whatever happened, ye must know these evil men thrust it upon ye. Ye had nothing to do with their depravity."

The fire popped and crackled as a log rolled in the grate. The red glow of coals flickered, and flames blazed around the charred wood.

"I killed Lowrens McLaughlin."

Alec stiffened.

Heather went cold. What was he thinking? She could not withstand his derision, his antipathy.

"Lowrens?" His voice rumbled in his chest.

"I had no choice. He attacked me."

"Symon wanted me to believe Lowrens killed ye. I thought he lied about Lowrens being involved." He rested his cheek against her head. "I'm sorry for what ye experienced, but it doesn't change anything. I still want ye as my wife." He tugged her chin up. "I'll help ye get through this."

She peered up at him through watery-eyes, her nose running. "Are ye sure?"

"Aye, I'm sure."

She ran her hand across the side of his handsome face, his dark beard rough against her palm. "I would be honored to have ye as my husband."

He lowered his head, his mouth lightly brushing her swollen, split lips. "I promise to protect ye and yer clan." He stroked the side of her face and looked into her eyes. "No one will ever hurt ye again."

Her heart swelled, and she prayed, someday when she revealed how she had killed Lowrens with no remorse, he would not turn from her, but instead she would hear him utter words of love.

# *Chapter Thirteen*

*MacDougall Keep*
*June 1299*

Two weeks had passed since Symon's attack. The resilient clan, albeit battered and bruised, rallied behind Alec, determined to put their lives in order and move on. Heather glanced at Da sitting before the solar's hearth. A blanket draped his lap and a splint held one leg stiff before him. Remnants of yellow splotches replaced his black bruises, the cuts not as aggravated.

Beathan leaned back in the chair next to her father, his right arm resting in a sling. An angry slice traversed his face, the red line running from his cheekbone to his chin. He was fortunate the strike had not taken his eye.

Alec strode into the room and tossed documents on the desk. He poured a mug of ale, dropped in a chair and gulped the contents. Dark wavy locks graced his forehead and swept to his heavy eyebrows. The shadow of a beard spanned his cheeks and strong chin. His cream-colored shirt, left untied at the neck, gave a glimpse of thick muscles working the liquid down his throat.

He set the tankard on the table and swiped the back of his sleeve across his mouth. He leveled his gaze over his forearm. Grey eyes locked with hers, eyes she had rarely seen since her rescue. "Mistress. Ye're well?"

Her heart squeezed. "Aye."

His brow rose. "Yer injuries have healed?"

"I'm fine."

His head bobbed imperceptibly. Perhaps he considered her answer terse. What did he expect? He had ignored her. At first, she'd considered his absence due to ensuring the safety of the clan. But two weeks later, with the castle secure, she could no longer ignore his lack of attention.

Beathan cleared his throat, and Da gazed at the floor. Had she made a mistake? Once he gained acceptance into MacDougall Castle, did he have no more need of her? But, she had felt his love. He had been gentle and kind, attentive the night he saved her and her clan.

Eric sauntered into the room and plopped onto the bench next to her. Dust clung to his brown boots, and his trews carried stains of grease. He swiped a cloth across his face, his wet hair dripping on his tunic. "Sorry I'm late."

Alec leaned forward, his muscular forearms resting on the desk. He turned to Da. "I've inspected the grounds and had my men repair the damage. Since Symon gained entrance with no opposition, the structure of the castle suffered little destruction."

"That's good news."

"As discussed, I'll assume responsibilities in yer place." He paused. "Is that what ye want, Alastair?"

"It is," Da answered with no hesitation.

"Verra well. Eric will manage Glencara until Logan returns. It won't be easy to control both castles, but I have ideas on combining efforts and will soon put those changes in place."

Eric's arms crossed his chest. "I'll leave in the next few days."

"We'll discuss my plans for Glencara this evening." Alec addressed Beathan. "Once ye've recovered, I want to work with ye on training yer men. They require skills to fend off future attacks."

Heather sat forward. "Da's men fought bravely. Aye, we did not anticipate Symon's attack, but it had nothing to do with the men's lack of fighting skills."

Alec's dark gaze bore into her. "I realize the castle was taken by surprise, but my observation of their fighting techniques stands."

Beathan exhaled loudly. "He's right. While we have men with good, strong skills, we have quite a few who need improvement."

No one argued the point further. Alec's eyes softened. "Mistress Heather and I will marry in two days time, making the transfer official."

How she had longed to hear the words, but she had envisioned more. She wanted him—his attention. Had she imagined his endearing affection? Had he whittled his way into her heart in order to gain her father's land?

Da clasped his hands. "The clan will welcome ye, lad."

Eric stood and touched her shoulder. "Aye, it'll be a good match."

When she offered no words of agreement and didn't giggle in bliss, Eric cleared his throat. "Well, if there's nothing else, I have duties to attend."

Beathan glanced between Alec and Heather. He stood and patted Da's back. "Let me help ye to yer chambers so ye can rest."

"Rest? But it's early evening. The sun has not yet set."

Beathan placed his hand under the pit of Da's arm and tugged him up. "Aye, but Muire says ye need to lie down and stay off that leg."

Da grumbled as the two injured men shuffled from the room. Beathan shut the door behind him.

The room fell quiet. Stilted moments passed.

"Where do I fit into yer plans?" Her voice sliced the tension between them.

Creases crisscrossed Alec's forehead, and his eyes darkened. "Ye will become my wife and run the castle as we agreed."

"As we agreed? I told ye I want to stay involved."

"And I told ye, ye will not engage. I do not need yer help commanding *my* men."

Her chest tightened, his words cutting. Was he shutting her out already? Had she jumped into his arms too easily? Relinquished her position too quickly? Her chin jutted forward. "I want ye to keep me informed."

Alec's stony demeanor ripped through her soul.

"Do ye not ask yer da's opinion?" she asked. "Do ye not involve Eric in yer plans?"

"Aye." He clamped his teeth together, and the muscles in his jaw bunched.

"I would be yer counsel as well."

His eyes narrowed slightly. "As ye wish."

Regret filled Alec. Heather's blue eyes pierced his soul. Unwittingly, he had hurt her feelings. She fancied herself a leader, and he must humor her—let her think she had a say. But how would he get used to her inserting herself in his business? She was a woman, fragile and vulnerable. A man's world of war was no place for her gender. They could not be trusted to make logical conclusions. They ruled with their hearts and lacked the fortitude to make difficult decisions.

The castle's safety was the laird's responsibility. He would have the final say.

He bit the side of his cheek. Perhaps he would pacify her with tidbits of information. Once she accustomed herself to his role and accepted she was no longer needed to lead her da's men, she would lose interest and concentrate her energies on managing their home, raising their children.

Thick blonde hair lay in wisps around her face, caressing her creamy skin. Her bruises had faded, and her eye and lips were no longer swollen. Her brown woolen gown hugged her breasts, and she clutched her fingers in her lap. His gaze lifted to hers, anguish and distrust emitting from the depths. His heart clenched.

She invaded his every thought. He missed being near her, hearing the gaiety of her laughter, seeing the sparkle of her eyes. He longed to watch the children absorb her tales, envisioned her holding their child...*his* child. But, her traumatic experience weighed heavy on his mind. The thought of Symon and Lowrens—what they had done to her—gripped his stomach in a vice. He grieved over the misery she'd endured and the possibility she would abhor their marriage bed.

He'd had to stay away since finding her, give her time to heal. When she was near, he longed to grab her and whisk her away to his chamber. She required patience and understanding. All of which he was willing to give, but he was a man, with needs. He was not strong enough to resist the tempting morsel constantly within reach. However, now that two weeks had passed with his nerves strung tight, he needed time alone with her. To hold her, be near her.

He stepped around the desk and extended his hand. "Will ye join me for a ride?"

Deep azure eyes searched his face before Heather placed her fingertips in his palm. He intertwined his fingers through hers and led her out the solar, through the keep and down the steps into the bailey.

A warm evening breeze blew in as the golden sun set, sending streaks of red and pink splashing across the sky. Alec blew two shrill whistles. Aeton whinnied and tossed his black head, his full tail held high as he pulled the lead Blake held. The lad dropped the rope, and the horse trotted to his master.

"Whoa." Alec patted Aeton's sleek neck.

Heather stroked the horse's soft nose. "He's a beauty."

"Aye, Aeton and I have been partners for many years." He turned to Heather, grasped her small waist and placed her on Aeton's back. With reins in hand, he swung onto the saddle and settled her across his lap. He hugged the horse with his knees, and Aeton lunged forward, galloping out of the bailey, past the guardhouses and through the castle gates.

He held her against his chest as they cantered across a green field toward the loch. When he reined Aeton in, they wound through thick trees, down a narrow path leading to the water. Large boulders lined the edge of the lake, opening into a small, secluded clearing. He tightened his hold on her as Aeton slowly came to a stop at the water's edge.

She relaxed against his chest. "It's lovely here."

Lilac wafted from her blonde hair. With her legs resting over his left thigh, Alec turned her face toward him and cupped her cheek. He searched her eyes. She didn't flinch or cringe from his touch. He lifted her chin and placed his lips on hers. She sighed, and his hand slid to the back of her neck.

Her tongue tentatively touched his and a bolt struck his gut. She welcomed his caresses. His heart exploded. Wrapping the red ribbon holding her hair around his fingers, he tugged and released her long tresses. He straightened. Her eyes had darkened, her kiss-swollen lips begging for attention.

God, she was beautiful.

He swung down and lifted her off Aeton's back. "Come, let's walk."

Holding her hand, he led her down a small path to a stream emptying into the loch. The cold water trickled across several large stones creating a noisy waterfall. He placed his arm around her shoulders and hugged her to his side. She eased her arm around his waist, and he smiled.

While he wanted to discuss her days in captivity, he dreaded the subject for fear of what he would hear. "I'm happy yer wounds are healing."

She stiffened slightly. "Aye."

"Yer bruises have all but disappeared. Now I worry about yer injuries inside." He touched her chest with his knuckle. "In here. Wounds I cannot see."

"Do ye?"

His brow scrunched. "Why do ye question my concern?"

Her head turned back to the water. "Because I have not seen ye. I thought ye didn't care."

Alec grasped her chin and angled her face toward him. "I stayed away from ye to let ye heal, give ye time to get over the attack, not because I did not care."

Eyes narrowing, her head tilted slightly. "Truly?"

"Truly." He captured her soft lips and tugged her into his embrace. How could she have misunderstood his absence? She should have known the reason he stayed away.

He stepped back, taking her hand in his. They strolled around the loch, the moon casting its light across the lake. Shimmering ripples rolled to the water's edge and treetops swayed in the breeze.

Heather stepped away from him and scooped up a handful of the cold liquid, letting it slip through her fingers. "I used to come here for a swim from time to time." She glanced over her shoulder at him as he leaned against a boulder watching her. "That was when I thought it was a safe, secluded spot."

He pushed away from the rock. "It's safe with me here." *Always.*

Heather

"On the contrary, I think it's most *unsafe* with ye here."
Cupping a handful of water, she splashed him and darted past,
the tinkle of her laughter enchanting.

Cold droplets sprinkled his face before he launched
himself at her. He caught her around the waist and rolled onto
the grass, dragging her down on top of him. Heather's eyes
sparkled, her smile bright. His pulse hammered as he pulled her
head down and kissed her gently before flipping her on her
back underneath him.

He stroked the side of her face, thankful Symon and
Lowrens had not destroyed her spirit. "Lass, in two days' time
I'll have ye as my wife. I want ye to know I'll be patient. I'll
understand if ye don't want to—"

Heather shook her head and placed her fingertips
against his mouth. "I welcome becoming yer wife in every
way."

Could that be true? Would she really welcome his
lovemaking? He bent and placed his lips on her soft mouth.
Wrapping her arms around his neck, she deepened the kiss, her
breasts molding against his chest. How he longed to release
them into his palms. He could not help himself from sliding his
hand across one of the mounds. Her nipple pebbled, straining
against the bodice. Desire heated his blood, and his shaft stood
rigid. Nuzzling her neck, he inhaled her fresh scent. With eager
hands he explored her lush curves, then boldly shifted lower
and pressed his hips against the apex of her legs.

Something pushed Alec's back. He jumped to his feet,
jerking his dagger from his belt as Heather scooted away, her
eyes wide, chest heaving.

Aeton snorted.

Alec hung his head and chuckled. Heather wrapped her
arms around her legs and laughed as Aeton snorted again and
nudged Alec's shoulder.

"All right, all right. I know we need to get back." He
grasped Heather's hand and pulled her to her feet. He kissed
her palm before lifting her onto Aeton's back.

As he reached for the reins, he adjusted his trews to accommodate his stiff cock and groaned. The next two days couldn't pass quickly enough.

# *Chapter Fourteen*

Heather's wedding day finally arrived. She opened her eyes to bright rays of sunlight filtering through the bedchamber's wooden shutters. Her insides tightened with anxious butterflies as she thought of the dark handsome man she would marry. She closed her eyes and relived the glorious sensations his touch invoked. How she longed to feel his hands on her bare skin.

Her pulse thumped loudly remembering his strong embrace, imagining what their night together would be like… *Alone.*

A knock sounded on the door before it burst open. Lindsey, Cameron, Ainslee, and Muire bustled in.

"It's close to noon, child. Time to get out of that bed," Muire ordered as lads prepared a bath. They filled the barrel and the old healer sprinkled in rose petals. As the boys were ushered out the room, a loud commotion of voices and laughter drifted from below stairs.

Ainslee plopped onto Heather's bed. "We need to get ye ready."

"What's going on down there?" Heather asked, holding a blanket to her neck while propping against the headboard.

"Everyone is excited about yer nuptials," Ainslee replied. "Rena has been preparing a feast."

Cameron and Lindsey held a beautiful cream-colored linen gown layered in silk. Lace flowers adorned with little white beads trimmed the bodice. The skirt flared under a gold belt at the hips. "This was Mum's gown," Cameron said. "Would ye like to wear it today?"

Tears filled Heather's eyes. She slid off the bed and fingered the soft material. How she wished Mum could be here. A teardrop trickled down her cheek, and she wiped it away. "I'd love to."

She spent the afternoon with her sisters and Ainslee preparing for her special day. Cameron affixed a lace veil over Heather's face. It hung down her back, covering the curls hugging her waist.

Ainslee grasped Heather's hands. "Ye look beautiful."

A loud thump knocked on the door. Muire opened it and Beathan stuck his head inside. A smile broke across his rugged face. "Yer da is ready."

The women left the chamber and hurried down the corridor. Da waited at the base of the stairs. His eyes lit, and with a sharp gasp of air, he beamed at Heather. "Ye remind me so much of my Rosie." He grasped her fingers in his weathered hands and placed a kiss on her knuckles. "And I know she would be verra proud of ye, Daughter."

He clutched her arm and escorted her into the main hall. Servants rushed around the room. Rena issued orders to place platters of roasted boar and leeks on the long wooden tables, and Fergus directed several lads struggling with vats of ale.

The old cook turned, and her hand clutched her chest. "Oh, my. What a bonnie bride ye make."

Heather smiled. "Thank ye."

"Ye must hurry," Fergus added. "Everyone awaits ye in the kirk."

Nerves stretched taut, she inhaled deeply. Da patted her hand. "Ye've nothing to fear. Alec is a good man and will provide well for ye, but I'll miss ye when ye leave."

She squeezed his gnarled hands. "I'm not going anywhere, Da."

His eyes widened. "But what of yer husband? He'll want ye to reside with him."

Her chest constricted with his continued loss of memory. "Alec and I have decided to remain at MacDougall keep."

"Ahh, that is excellent news, Daughter!"

~~~

The small chapel, crowded with friends and family, grew warm. Alec stood with his back to the altar. Sun streamed in from a side window and highlighted intricate wooden carvings of Jesus with his hands opened to saints at his feet, and little children frolicking with lambs, rabbits, fawns and other baby animals. Benches on either side of the aisle were filled with anxious MacDougall and Glencara residents, their restrained voices respectful of the Lord's house.

He faced the sanctuary, with Eric positioned to his left, and admired the three beautiful women to the right of Brother Michael. Ainslee, Cameron and Lindsey whispered while awaiting his bride.

The harmonious sound of lutes began, and his gaze swung to the back of the room. The angel of his dreams stepped into the sanctuary. Heather's long wheat-colored hair flowed around her shoulders, a lacy veil shrouding her face. She clutched her father's arm as he escorted her down the aisle. Images of her telling spooky stories, passing out sweet treats and overseeing the children's games flashed through his mind. Her fighting spirit to protect her loved ones surpassed most men. Indeed, Heather's beauty blossomed from the inside out, and he thanked the Lord for such a compassionate, caring wife.

Alastair placed her fingers in Alec's palm. She gazed at him, her smile radiant. Mesmerized, his hand rose to her face, and he cupped her soft cheek.

Brother Michael cleared his throat. "Laird Campbell?"

Alec kissed the back of her hand, turned to the man and shrugged.

The brother winked and the ceremony began.

Heather repeated Alec's words, her voice clear and confident. He slid a silver band etched with his family crest on her finger, and Brother Michael ended the service with, "I pronounce they be Man and Wife together. Amen."

Alec lifted her veil. A fresh scent of roses wafted past his nose before he leaned down and gently kissed her lips. He wrapped his arms around her and molded himself against her. When she slipped her arms around his neck, he groaned and deepened the kiss.

Cheers roared from the congregation, jolting him back to the moment. He straightened as the crowd rushed forward offering good wishes. Eric slapped Alec's back and grabbed his shoulders. "Let's celebrate! Everyone to the main hall!"

With Heather's fingers intertwined with his, Alec led the boisterous group from the small chapel. As they stepped onto the landing, he stopped dead still.

*Commander Taylor.*

Beathan, Eric and Robert stepped to Alec's side.

"Commander." Alec dipped his head toward the English officer, his gaze sweeping past the man, observing enemy soldiers filling the bailey.

"Laird Campbell." Barclay glanced at Heather then back at Alec.

"Let me introduce ye to my wife, Heather MacDougall Campbell."

Barclay bowed. "Lady Campbell, my congratulations to you and Laird Campbell."

"Thank ye," Heather barely whispered, her hold on his hand tightening.

The commander peered at his second in command. "Take the men, and wait beyond the gates of MacDougall Castle. We will be respectful of the wedding celebration."

The man stared for a second before answering, "Yes, sir!"

He then ordered the men to file out behind him.

Once the bailey cleared, Barclay's gaze turned to Alec. "I do apologize for this most inopportune timing, but might it be possible to have a word with you?"

Alec's eyes narrowed. He placed his arm around Heather and held her against his side. "Take our guests into the hall and begin the celebration. I'll join ye in a moment."

"But—"

"It's all right." He kissed her temple, then addressed Cameron and Lindsey. "See yer sister to the keep. I'll be along directly."

Heather's eyes held concern, but she smiled as the women clutched her arms.

"Be strong, sister. Alec will take care," Cameron whispered, and her sharp gaze caught his eye as she turned and strolled down the chapel stairs with Heather.

"Commander, if ye'll join me." Alec extended his arm toward the keep. What did the commander want? The hair on his neck rose with suspicion. "Ye're welcome to bring along yer second in command."

"That will not be necessary."

"As ye wish." Why would the officer and his soldiers arrive on the day of his wedding? If Taylor thought to have Heather in the 'right of the first night', the man would die. King Edward's minions would not bed his wife in an act of control over his clan.

Alec marched into Alastair's study with Barclay following. The late afternoon sun shone into the room, displaying dust flitting through the air. Alec poured ale in two mugs, handed one to Barclay, and motioned for him to sit before the fire.

Alec dropped in the chair across from the commander and pointedly glared at him. "What can I do for ye?"

Barclay took a swig of the amber liquor. He squinted at Alec then balanced his cup on his thigh. "I had no idea it was you marrying the MacDougall lass."

Alec's blood simmered. If it had not been him marrying Heather, would Barclay have demanded the King's rights? Would he have forced himself upon her? "What is it to ye who she marries?"

"Nothing. Nothing at all." Barclay stared through the window overlooking the back of MacDougall keep. He then looked back at Alec. "King Edward demands all Scots pay homage to him and that we establish these lands in his name."

Alec stiffened. "Yer king has a lot of damn nerve coming onto our soil, butchering and destroying anyone opposing his path and demanding our reverence."

Barclay leaned back in the chair. Silence stretched between them. His arms crossed his chest. "I owe a great deal to you. I have been in touch with Skena. She fairs well and I have you to thank. She's to have my child any day now, and I ask that you see to their protection. In return, I will turn a blind eye to MacDougall and Campbell lands and leave you to live in peace."

Alec considered Taylor's words carefully as he swirled the contents of his mug. "How can ye ensure that?"

Barclay's eyes narrowed. "I have contacts in the king's service that owe me, but that is not yer concern."

To have this exclusion was certainly not what he expected to hear. "Verra well. I'll agree with one slight change. I would request ye include Graham lands."

Alec unrolled a map outlining the boundaries and pointed out the lands' borders.

"Agreed." Barclay downed the contents of his glass. The men stood and shook hands.

"Skena resides in the keep and works beside her mum. I'll send the MacDougall's healer to ensure she and yer child are healthy."

"Thank you, Laird Campbell. When the fighting is over, I'll come for them." Barclay held out the decree with his stamp, officially establishing these lands off limits.

Alec escorted the commander to the bailey. Barclay mounted, his horse prancing, tossing his head. "Laird Campbell."

He momentarily locked eyes with Alec before trotting out the gate. Soldiers filed in behind him, and they disappeared down the road.

Alec exhaled, dropping his head back. The strange alliance could prove advantageous. He studied the darkening sky. Would the English stay off their land? Enable them to live in peace, no longer fearful of attack? Although he did not trust the commander, he would take the offer for what it was worth.

Cheers and shouts of merriment drifted through the main doors. He glanced at the keep. Heather waited. What would the night bring? Would she cringe from his touch? No, she had responded at the loch. His heart thumped with cautious optimism, and he jogged up the stairs.

Men, women and children danced to loud music. Alastair, Robert, Eric and Beathan eagerly awaited him inside the door.

Robert stepped in front of him. "What happened? What did he want?"

Alec motioned for them to follow, and the men slipped out of the hall and into the solar.

"A number of months ago, I caught him in a compromising situation." Alec stepped to the side table, grabbed the wine vessel and held it up. Alastair nodded and handed him an empty mug. Robert, Eric and Beathan did the same. Alec filled the mugs and replaced the container on the table.

"At the time I questioned my sanity for granting the man leniency." He leaned against the corner of the desk and took a swing. "Seems that might have set us in good stead."

Robert's eyes narrowed. "In what way?"

Alec set his mug on the desk and crossed his arms over his chest. "Commander Taylor is expecting a child. The mother is a young lass who lives at Glencara. In exchange for her safety, the man has signed a decree officially protecting our lands from English incursion."

"Do ye trust him?" Beathan asked, his brow drawn.

"About as much as any Sassenach." Alec reached in his tunic, extracted a rolled parchment and spread it on the desk.

Eric bent over the document and whistled low. "It appears in order."

"It even has the king's stamp," Robert pointed out.

"The way I see it, we have nothing to lose." Alec drained his mug.

Eric laughed and slapped Alec on the shoulder. "A toast, my friend." He refilled the men's empty mugs with more ale. "May we live in peace, and may yer marriage to Mistress Heather be blissful."

"Here, here!" The men clanked their mugs and drained their ale.

"I think ye had best find my daughter now, lad. She'll not take kindly to ye sitting in here drinking with the men while she's entertaining yer wedding guests. My Rosie would have flayed me alive."

Robert laughed. "Aye, if she's anything like her sister, ye'll not want to keep her waiting long."

He clapped Alec on the shoulder as they made their way back to the main hall.

Alec searched the room for Heather and found her surrounded by family.

*Ye're beautiful.*

She turned as if she had heard his thought. Her eyes appeared expectant, worried. Weaving through well wishers, he made his way to her. When he finally reached her side, she stepped into his arms, and he twirled her onto the dance floor.

Holding her tight, they swayed to the music, circling around and around. She looked up at him and he smiled, then kissed her plump lips.

She pulled back slightly. "Is everything all right?"

"Aye, everything is fine." He lowered his mouth to hers again, ran his fingers through her thick hair, down her slender back, and over her bottom. He groaned into her mouth. "Ye're killing me, wife."

~~~

Heather reveled in the feel of Alec's strong embrace, but she longed to know what the English commander wanted. Did Alec avert the commander's right of the first night? Was that why the soldiers arrived, or did Barclay divulge information she should know? Could she trust Alec to inform her as he had promised? Once again, he'd shut her out. She resented his secrets, but would not press the issue. Not on the night of their wedding.

As the hour grew late, Cameron tugged her arm. Lindsey and Muire stood behind her, knowing grins slinking across their faces.

"It's time to get ye ready for bed." Cameron looked at Alec. "Ye don't mind if we borrow her, do ye?"

Alec kissed Heather's knuckles. Her heart hammered at his captivating dark eyes. "Until later," he whispered.

The women ushered her from the main hall, climbed the stairs and entered her bedchamber. A plate of wine and cheese was on the table next to the fire, and candles were set about the room giving it a warm, inviting glow.

Lindsey rummaged through the chest at the foot of her bed, tossing out undergarments. She held one up. "Do ye not have anything more…" She inspected the underclothes, turning them from side to side. "More *enticing*?"

"Lindsey MacDougall!" Warmth crept up Heather's neck and spread across her cheeks.

Cameron chuckled. "Ye have much to learn, big sister." She opened her basket and removed a white gown. "I brought ye something Alec will find *quite* enticing."

Heather's breath caught. The silky gown was adorned with only one tie at the neck. She fingered the sheer fabric. What would Alec think? Was it too wanton for their first night together?

"I don't know. It's beautiful, but…" She held it up to the candlelight. "I can see through it."

Lindsey giggled. "Exactly."

Heather stepped out of her chemise, and Cameron helped her into the scandalous gown. The ladies kissed her, then wished her a good night as they closed the door behind them.

Heather glanced around the room and poured a mug of wine to ease her nerves. She paced back and forth. How she wished Mum had told her what to expect. Her sister mentioned things went on between a husband and wife, but she had been a bit foggy on the details. How would she know what to do? Would Alec be disappointed in her lack of…skills?

Another mug of wine seemed to help. By the third, she was feeling quite warm and much more relaxed. She stood by the fire, the flames mesmerizing.

The door opened, and she turned as Alec stepped into the room. He had changed into brown trews and a cream-colored tunic. Her gaze traveled the length of him from his narrow hips up his wide chest to his cropped hair. Smoky grey eyes held a passion she longed to explore. Her pulse quickened. How many times had she dreamed of this night, of lying in the arms of the man she loved?

~~~

Alec marveled at the vision in front of the fire. He could see Heather's silhouette clearly through the light fabric.

He leaned against the closed door, and soaked up the sight of the angel before him.

Her golden hair appeared on fire, the flames from the hearth casting a halo around her form. The gown left little to his imagination. His gaze traveled across her breasts. The rosy peaks puckered, and he longed to touch them. His mouth watered as his eyes trailed over her taut stomach and lower to her most private area. Blonde curls cloaked her womanhood, and his cock pushed uncomfortably against his trews.

He stepped away from the door and strolled to her. An open wine flask sat on the table. Did she need the fortification? She had a death grip on a mug. Perhaps she remembered the brutality inflicted upon her. If given the chance, he would show her a loving act and teach her of the pleasures between a man and woman.

He held up the bottle. "More?"

She nodded and handed him her empty cup. Her hand trembled. He steadied the mug and filled it. She turned the wine up and drained the cup again.

"That's probably enough. Ye don't want to feel ill." He removed the mug from her hand and placed it on the table.

Her plump lips parted, and he bent and kissed her gently, his fingers coursing through her thick tresses. "Ye are truly bonny, wife."

Her hands grasped his shoulders, her gaze caressing his face. "As ye are handsome, husband."

His thumb rubbed her bottom lip. Her blue eyes darkened, but her expression held…what? Fear? Anxiety? He prayed she would accept him, that the nightmares of Symon and Lowrens would not destroy their first time together.

He untied the ribbon at her neck and opened her gown. His eyes feasted on her creamy breasts. He brushed the pink tips with the back of his fingers, and she inhaled sharply.

The longing in her eyes jolted him, thickened his aching need. Stroking his thumb across her sweet peak, he bent and kissed her cheek, her nose and soft lips. He slid the gown from her shoulders, letting it pool on the floor around her feet, then stood back and admired her naked body. Her hair was disheveled from his fondling, her cheeks rosy.

His heart pounded in his chest. "I have waited a long time for this."

~~~

Alec knelt before Heather, and his warm mouth closed around her nipple, his tongue playing havoc on the sensitive bud. She ran her hands through his thick hair and clasped his head to her breast, relishing his mouth's exquisite tease. He suckled each nipple, then trailed kisses lower, down her stomach. A hand splayed over her belly as his tongue dipped into her naval. Shivers tingled across her body, and chill bumps rose on her skin.

He stood and ran his hand down her back to her bare bottom then lifted her against his straining member. "I want ye," he whispered against her neck. "But I'm willing to wait until ye're ready."

Her eyes searched his face. "Nay, I want to be yer wife in every way."

His hot mouth slid to her neck as butterflies flittered around her stomach. With his warm palm cupping her breast, she leaned into him, relishing the feelings he awakened.

He nibbled her ear. "Ye are sure?"

"Aye," she breathed out.

Smoky grey eyes held her captive as he tugged his tunic over his head, kicked off his boots and untied his belt. When he stepped out of his trews, her eyes widened at the sight of his swollen member.

He was too large for her.

She swallowed hard.

His eyes darkened, and his nostrils flared. He pulled her body into his embrace, and his manhood pressed against her torso. The rough hair on his chest and abdomen grazed her virgin skin. With her senses heightened, the slightest brush of her nipples sent shivers to her core. Nuzzling her neck, he placed a hand at her back while the other roamed down her belly and lower. He touched the curls surrounding her most private area. His warmth cupped her womanhood and she squeezed her legs tight.

"Relax." He kissed her softly, whispering against her mouth, "I won't hurt ye."

He slowly ran his fingers through her curls. No one had ever touched her so…wickedly, so deliciously. She tentatively pushed her hips into his caress. His fingertip slipped between her folds, and she inhaled as he stroked her sensitive nub, circling, pulling her into oblivion.

Her legs buckled.

Liquid fire rushed through her quivering limbs.

He scooped her into his strong arms and carried her to the bed. She slid to the middle of the mattress. Her body trembled with desire, and she leaned back on her elbows. With the grace of a large cat, he climbed up as if he stalked her, his gaze holding hers as his lips trailed across her calves to her knees. He eased her legs open, and her eyes widened, her pulse pounding. His dark eyes gazed at the apex of her legs, and a dull ache tightened at his inspection. He reached out, and the back of his finger stroked her core. His tongue slid up her leg and traced circles on the inside of her thigh. Her stomach tightened as his mouth drew closer and closer to her womanhood.

"Alec?" She tried to scoot back, but his strong hands held her hips as his teeth nipped her quivering flesh.

"Ye taste so sweet." His dark eyes smoldered with desire. His scratchy cheek brushed her skin as his lips feathered kisses higher still. His hot breath blew over her mons, and she sucked in air. Her insides clenched. He couldn't mean to…

His tongue slid up her folds. She gasped, her legs trembling. Strong hands clutched her bottom as his tongue teased her heated flesh.

A moan escaped her lips. She wantonly raised her hips, desperate for more. His fingers spread her nether lips, and his mouth covered her sensitive petals. Her legs dropped apart, and she grasped the blanket, the fabric twisting in her fists. Her head rolled from side to side as he suckled and dipped his finger into her passage.

"Ye're body is ready for me, lass," he whispered against her moist flesh. "And I am more than ready for ye."

Alec climbed over her. His mouth captured Heather's as his member pushed at her opening. His heart beat wildly. The desire to sink into her overwhelmed him, but the thought of the brutal assault she suffered surfaced, and he tamped down his overwhelming urges.

She closed her eyes, and her body stiffened. What was she thinking? Was she remembering the assault?

"Lass, look at me."

Her eyes flew open.

"Breathe."

She exhaled.

"Are ye sure ye want to do this?" He kissed her tenderly. "I will wait for ye."

She shook her head. "No, please don't stop. I...I want to."

Although she spoke of her desire, her stiffening body conveyed a different message.

"There is nothing to be afraid of." He slowly pushed the head of his cock into her, stretching her to accept him. Her moist heat surrounded him in a cocoon of exquisite pleasure. "Ahh, Heather," he sighed, his eyelids drooping.

She tensed. "I worry ye will not fit."

His head lifted, and he kissed her cheek, then her soft lips. "Trust me, I will fit."

Her opening wept for him, but she was small. His hips rocked, inching his member a little farther into her sheath. A barrier blocked his passage, and his eyes sprang open. Confusion coursed through him. Her virgin barrier remained intact. How could that be? Each day since the attack, he had envisioned the horror she had endured and dealt with the guilt of not protecting her. He rose on his elbows.

"Lass?"

Her frightened eyes gazed up at him. "Is there something wrong?"

"Nay, but I...I feel yer virgin's barrier."

"Aye, but I'm ready for ye." Her limbs trembled. "I know it's painful the first time a woman is breached."

Her words brought such joy to his heart. He dropped his forehead to hers and closed his eyes. "I cherish I'm yer first."

"But of course. I've not lain with any man." Her voice was defensive. "Did ye think me unchaste?"

"I worried Symon or Lowrens…"

She placed her finger to his mouth and shook her head. "Nay, they did not defile me."

Those few words brought a wave of jubilation coursing through his body, a happiness he had never before experienced. Exhilaration pumped through his veins. She could not have gifted him anything more precious.

Her hips moved against him, and his cock pressed against her wall of innocence.

"Please…" she whispered. Her eyes, dark with desire, implored him.

"Ahh, Heather." He thrust his hips.

She cried out and grasped his shoulders.

He stilled, then placed his hands on either side of her face and kissed her eyelids. "Forgive me, lass. I didn't want to hurt ye." His mouth settled on her soft lips. "Once ye are accustomed to me, I will pleasure ye."

Moments passed with his manhood fully sheathed in her passage. His pulse pounded in his ears as he quelled his desire to pump into her sweet body.

She moved her hips against him.

His face nuzzled her cheek, her woman's scent engulfing him. "Ye're all right?"

"Aye," she breathed out.

He eased out of her and slid back in. They made love, slowly, lazily. He savored each stroke of his manhood plunging into her, filling her completely. His hand slid between them and found her swollen pearl.

Her intake of air and tightening muscles revealed her impending climax.

A building pressure mounted, but he strained to control his release. Sweat beaded his forehead. His fingertip circled, massaged her slick nub of pleasure.

Heather

She cried out, and her body convulsed around him, her muscles milking his member. Pleasure as he had never known poured through him. He pumped faster into her warm haven until he too reached a zenith and spilled his seed into her womb.

Collapsing against her, he kissed her face, her eyes and cheeks before devouring her mouth. Her limbs relaxed, her body sated. He rolled over and wrapped her in his embrace. They lay in each other's arms, and he stroked her side, running his hand up and down her leg.

The fire crackled and popped, the flames casting shadows across the room. He hugged her close and whispered, "I thank God Symon didn't take ye as he boasted, and Lowrens did not hurt ye as I feared."

Her face nestled against his chest, and her small hand caressed his torso. "I managed to thwart their intentions."

His fingers grasped her chin and tilted her face to him. Firelight caressed her skin, her cheeks pink from their loving. God, she was beautiful…and she was his.

He captured her lips once more, and his hand slid over her soft breast. His thumb rubbed her nipple, and she moaned while inching her hands around his neck. Raging desire flooded his core, and his manhood stiffened against her thigh. "Ahh, lass. I can't get enough of ye."

He rolled her underneath him and made love to her until they collapsed together in sheer bliss and exhaustion.

~~~

Later that night, she lay awake with Alec's dark head nestled against her breast. She raked her fingertips through his thick hair. Memories of their evening together played across her mind. His large calloused hands, accustom to wielding a heavy sword and lethal weapons, had been gentle, ensuring her pleasure.

Love for him poured over her, and her chest clenched. While he never uttered words of endearment, she *felt* his affection more than once. Would he ever admit his feelings?

221

Bring her into his trusted circle? Would she ever truly win his heart?

# *Chapter Fifteen*

*MacDougall Keep*
*July 1299*

Steel against steel resounded from a field outside the walls of MacDougall Castle. Shouts and grunts of exertion, comingling with Alec's brusque commands, pierced the morning air. Standing on the grey stone ramparts, Heather peered around the crenels. Her husband marched down a line of sparring men. He assessed each warrior's skills, issuing instructions and correcting moves. He turned to Beathan who helped illustrate blocking and lunging, then stood back and watched the men emulate his techniques.

Alec gathered the troops into a semi-circle. Sweat drenched their faces as their attention focused on him. He tugged his tunic over his head. Clad in buckskin trews and dark boots, he wielded his large broadsword over his head. The muscles in his sun-kissed shoulders and arms bulged with every swing of the blade.

His sword crashed upon a makeshift wooden enemy. Three men bellowed and ran into the middle of the ring. Alec spun, his sword positioned to strike. He lunged. A man jumped back. Alec's blade sliced his tunic. He advanced. The aggressor leapt to the side as Alec swung his sword. The weapon flew from his foe's grip. Shaking his head, the man stepped back and held up his hands in defeat.

"Argh!" a second yelled and charged. His saber aimed at Alec's back.

Heather sucked in a breath, her hand grasping her throat.

Alec whirled to face his attacker. The warrior backed up, tripping as he tried to fend off Alec's powerful blows. He knocked the challenger's sword out of position and plunged his blade, stopping a hair short of the man's chest.

A roar went up from the bystanders.

Shouts and bellowed cheers rent the air as more entered the combat. Alec relentlessly fought each warrior, displaying his dominance, strength, and expertise. Soon no others challenged him, and the mock-battle ended.

Heather sighed. Fortune had smiled upon her. Alec was brave and powerful, and she was lucky to have him as her husband.

Dust billowing from the road to the castle caught her attention. She shaded her eyes from the bright morning sun. Clyde and Edan drove a team pulling a worn cart laden with goods and supplies. Rena would be happy to receive the much needed spices, and Muire, her coveted herbs. Heather pushed away from the crenel, hurried down the narrow stone steps and into the bailey.

Lindsey, dressed in brown trews and a cream-colored tunic, led a grey mare from the barn. Auburn curls, stuffed under a cap, escaped around her face. "Is that Clyde?"

"Aye, he and Edan are finally here."

The old creaking wagon entered the bailey and rolled to a stop. A lad jogged out of the stables and grasped the horses' harness.

"Good morn," Heather greeted the men.

Clyde tugged the wooden lever brake and tied the horses' reins to it. "Ahh, 'tis indeed a fine morning."

Edan jumped to the ground and strode over to Lindsey. "This is the horse ye told me about?"

Lindsey stroked the animal's pink nose. "Her name is Josephine, and she's produced fine stock."

Edan ran his hand down the horse's honey-colored side and across her rump. "She looks to be in good form."

Lindsey guided the animal in a circle. The mare pranced, tossing her head, her long black mane bouncing. "She's in the best of health and has a smooth natural gait."

Edan glanced at Clyde. "What do ye think, Da? She appears to be what Laird McCarthy requested."

"That she does. Aye, we'll take her."

Lindsey extended her hand as Edan counted out several gold coins. "Did ye hear about the race, Mistress Lindsey?"

Heather's gaze darted to Lindsey's face.

Her sister's brow drew together. "Race?"

"The horse race in Dumfries. People are coming from miles around to enter. The winner gets a large purse. Ye would do good to be there with yer animals."

Edan extracted a wrinkled document from his satchel and handed it to her.

Heather peered over Lindsey's shoulder at the parchment.

He pointed to the announcement. "That shows ye when and where it'll be held."

Lindsey skimmed the notice. "May I keep this?"

Heather's eyes narrowed. What was she up to? Was she thinking to show off her horses? Dumfries was too close to the English border.

"Aye, we're spreading the word and hoping to sell our goods at the event."

Lindsey spared a glimpse at Heather and stuffed the parchment in her pouch, then handed Josephine's rope to Edan. "Treat her well."

The lad patted the animal's neck. "It's as I told ye. She'll live a pampered life. The laird purchases her for his overindulged daughter."

"Mistress?"

Heather turned to Clyde.

His hazel eyes sparkled as he handed her a small cloth pouch. "'Tis yer special order."

Excitement bubbled up. She loosened the string woven through the bag and extracted a three-inch broach intricately designed in the likeness of the Glencara crest. She ran her finger across the blue background signifying trust and loyalty while the red lion represented a powerful warrior. "Oh, it's perfect."

The merchant pointed to the ornament. "On the back ye'll see the inscription."

She turned it over and read the words. *To my husband with affection. Heather*. Joy coursed through her as she imagined Alec's face upon seeing it. "'Tis just as I wanted."

Clyde toyed with his worn grey cap and beamed. "It does my old heart good to see yer happiness."

Heather clutched his wrinkled, weathered hand. "Alec will be most pleased." She slipped it into the leather pouch at her waist. "What about the other items I ordered? Were ye able to bring Muire's herbs?"

The old man scrambled into the back of the wagon. He rummaged through a crate, lifted a wooden box and handed it to her. "I have them right here."

She opened the container, shuffled through jars and pouches, then ticked off the items on her register. "Wonderful, now for the rest of my list..."

The men delivered the promised goods, and she shook Clyde's weathered hand. "Thank ye. We look forward to yer visit next month."

"Good day, Mistress." The old man clucked and slapped the reins against the horses' rumps. The wagon lurched forward and plodded out of the bailey with Josephine trotting behind.

"Those poor fellows didn't stand a chance between the two of ye."

At the sound of Alec's deep voice, Heather straightened from examining the crate of spices. A breeze blew an errant lock onto her face, and she brushed it aside.

He kissed her forehead and held her hand, glancing at the cartons and cases of food and supplies. "I take it this is a normal activity for ye and yer sister?"

"Aye, Clyde and Edan come by every month, and I place orders for the next visit."

Lindsey sauntered past. "And they buy my horses."

She jogged up the stairs and into the keep, counting gold coins as she went.

"I see." Alec watched lads maneuvering the heavy barrels. He glanced at Heather, his gaze settling on her bodice. "I would like a bit of yer time this afternoon...."

His darkening gaze lifted to her face, their smoky depths conveying lascivious thoughts.

Her heart fluttered.

"...To go over the keep's accounts," he finished.

*Go over the accounts?* Disappointment rolled through her body, and she mentally shook herself, embarrassed at what had she thought he wanted. "Verra well. Let me record these items, and I'll get with ye."

He tugged her into his arms. A pungent earthy scent from his training wafted under her nose, and droplets from his sweat-dampened hair dripped on her shoulder. He ran his hands down her back, cupping her bottom.

Lads unloading the goods snickered, elbowing each other, their amusement encouraging Alec's outrageous behavior.

Heat spread across her cheeks. She scrunched her nose and wiggled out of his embrace. "I'll have the tub sent to ye while I finish here."

His hands circled her waist, drawing her against him again. He nuzzled her neck. "I'd prefer ye gave me a bath."

He scooped her up, and she shrieked. The lads laughed aloud. She grasped his neck as he strode up the bailey stairs and into the hall. "The mistress and I need a bath."

Serving girls stopped and stared, their mouths agape.

"Send a tub to our chambers."

Heather buried her heated face in the crook of his neck. He marched up the stairs, down the hall and into their room. When he slowly released her, she slid down the length of him.

"I've missed ye," he whispered against her lips.

"Och, we...*were together* just last night."

"Aye, *hours* ago."

Several lads ran into the room, each carrying buckets sloshing with steaming water. They filled the tub and left the room, closing the door behind them.

His fingers worked the ties on her gown. Cool air assaulted her skin, but he slipped his warm palm into her bodice and caressed her breast. He shoved her gown off her shoulders and lowered his head, his mouth capturing a nipple. One quick tug of her gown, and it pooled around her feet.

"Alec, it's still daylight...." her words drowned in his kiss.

He straightened and yanked off his trews. His manhood stood stiff against his stomach, and her eyes feasted on his glorious form. He swept her into his arms, carried her to the large wooden tub and placed her inside.

"What are ye doing?"

"We're going to take a bath." He sat in the barrel, leaned against the back and extended his hand to her.

She could not believe he wanted to bathe…together. A wanton thrill niggled its way through her insides. She grasped her hair and twirled it into a knot on top of her head.

Alec sucked in air. "Come here, wife."

When she gingerly knelt, he twirled her around and she squealed, water spilling over the sides. He positioned her between his muscular legs, her back against his chest. His arms wrapped around her, and he nuzzled her neck, trailing kisses across her shoulders.

"Ye'll not get clean this way." Heather grabbed the soap off the side table and lathered his legs and arms. Dark hair covering his limbs lay against his tanned skin.

Alec slipped the soap from her hands and skimmed it across her breasts. Her nipples stood stiff against his rough fingers. He nibbled her shoulder, sliding his sudsy hand down her abdomen to cup her mound. "Spread yer legs," his husky voice whispered against her neck.

Her knees fell open and his fingers eased between her nether lips. Her breath caught and she relaxed, resting her head against his shoulder. Oh, my. She would never get enough of his caresses.

He kissed the side of her face, then lifted her hips and eased his manhood inside her. He groaned when she sat, fully encasing his member. Her eyes closed at her fullness, and he guided her up and down his length, water sloshing over the sides of the tub. Waves of ecstasy wrought her body. At the same moment, Alec tensed and found his release.

His chest expanded against her back. When his breathing calmed, he lifted her slightly and eased out of her.

"Now, that's my kind of bath," he said and stood with her in his arms, placing her on the floor in front of him. Cold air swirled around her.

He kissed the top of her nose and wrapped her in a drying cloth before turning her toward her gown and swatting her bottom. "Get dressed and quit tempting me. We've got work to do. Ye have yet to explain the accounts."

Her jaw dropped in mock indignation. "I beg yer pardon?"

He chuckled and rubbed a cloth over his muscled, hairy torso.

How she loved his teasing and wished she saw more of his playful side. She slipped her gown over her head and picked up her pouch. Her fingers removed the gift, and she clutched it in her hand as she turned to Alec.

He had stepped into his brown trews. Water droplets dripped from his tousled hair as he reached for his tunic.

She stepped to him, and he paused. "I've something to give ye," she whispered.

His head cocked to the side, and his brow scrunched.

She took his hand and placed the little bag in his calloused palm.

He dropped his tunic on a chair and tugged on the dark corded string. The pouch fell open and as he extracted the brooch, his eyes lit. "It's beautiful." He fingered the ornament and turned it over. "Where did ye get it?"

"Clyde delivered it to me this morning. I had wanted to present it to you on our wedding night, but…"

Alec tugged her to him and wrapped his strong arms around her. "I will cherish it always."

~~~

Later that afternoon, Alec sat beside her and ran his finger over the levels of inventory and notes she had made on the inhabitants' needs. "Ye keep verra detailed records."

Her pulse thumped faster. She wanted his respect and longed to win his trust so he would include her in the strategies of the rebellion and how the clan would participate. She pointed to a row of numbers. "These are the purchases I made over the past year. And…" She turned the page. "These are the revenues I recorded."

"Yer da sold a hundred head of cattle?"

"And Lindsey sold a number of her horses."

Alec's brow rose, and he whistled low. "That's quite a sum."

"She breeds pleasure horses, work horses and race horses."

Alec's head turned to her, his eyebrow raised. "Race horses?"

Heather nodded. "Aye, the animals are beautiful with slightly longer legs and great stamina."

The corner of his mouth tugged up. "Humph, who does she sell them to?"

"Scoff if ye like, but she has made a name for herself through the traveling merchants. They buy them from her and sell them for a profit, just as this morning. A number of men have shown up over the years inquiring about her herd."

"Interesting." Alec's gaze narrowed, and he leaned back in the chair.

After finishing the paperwork, Heather took him on a tour of the stockrooms where they stored dry goods, linens and wool. "The ladies of the keep use the fabric not only to make clothes and bed linens, but also to supply bandages for Muire."

Once they finished inside, Alec whistled and motioned for Eric to join them as they made their way to the barn. His captain jogged over, and the three entered the barn.

The aroma of freshly cut hay and leather met them. Alec studied the area. Sunbeams shined through the large windows, providing fresh air and light. The wide dirt aisle lined with spacious stalls on either side traversed the length of the stables. Sturdy beams spaced roughly ten feet apart supported massive logs crisscrossing the expanse of the wooden ceiling and thatched roof. To their left, a lad backed out of a stall while he raked a pitchfork through soiled shavings. Blake nodded in greeting as he pushed a wheelbarrow, full of manure and dirty straw, past them. Another lad poured fresh water into the large paddock's trough.

Alec shook his head. "I'm surprised a stable of this size only has a handful of lads to manage it."

Lindsey, arms full of cloth sacks, strolled up the aisle toward them.

"I stand corrected—a handful of lads and a *female taskmaster*."

Eric laughed, but Heather's ire rose at his cutting tone, and she stepped forward. "Ye shouldn't ridicule her. She's well organized and strictly controls the goings on of the barn. She has her horses sectioned off by breed, and each has two lads responsible for their feeding and grooming."

Lindsey dropped the empty bags next to the tack room. "May I help ye?"

Alec inspected the horses corralled in adjacent stalls. "The animals are impressive, but there doesn't seem to be enough hands to handle them."

Lindsey's shoulders squared, and her eyes narrowed. "We manage."

Eric shook his head. "It cannot be easy with the number of horses ye have."

Alec glanced over his shoulder at Eric. "If we moved them to Glencara and comingled them, we would have more men to oversee their care."

"Aye, such a plan would make it easier to control both herds," Eric agreed.

Lindsey stormed before Alec, her stance rigid and her violet eyes accusing. "I said we manage fine. There's no need to remove *my* horses from *my* stables."

Alec glared at her. "Now that we have both Glencara and MacDougall Castles, it makes sense to combine the animals under one roof so we can better peddle them."

Lindsey's eyes widened, her hands firmly affixed to her hips. "*Peddle* them?"

"I'm aware of the revenues ye've generated, but it could be tenfold with the right man to get them to those who would purchase them."

"I don't need any help," Lindsey's voice rose. "Ye will not turn *my* horses over to some *man*."

Alec glowered at her before stalking off, calling over his shoulder, "Eric, we'll discuss my plans later this evening."

His captain fell in step behind Alec.

"Wait!" Lindsey caught up to Alec and grabbed his arm. "Ye cannot have my horses!"

Her voice was frantic, her eyes pleading.

Heather's breath caught in her throat, and she reached out to her sister. "Lins, please—"

"No, I won't let him take them."

Alec seared Lindsey with a dark glower. "Ye don't have anything to say about it. If I choose to move the horses, I will."

He turned and stormed from the stables.

His words held a tone of finality. Why was he being so obstinate? Couldn't he see how he upset her sister? And for what purpose?

Lindsey watched him leave with Eric trailing behind.

Heather placed her arm around her sister's shoulders, but she jerked away.

"Lins, he's only thinking of the common good of the clans."

"I don't care what he's thinking. He might be yer husband, but he's not mine." Her brow scrunched. "I'll talk to Da. He won't let anyone take my horses."

"Ye'd be wasting yer time. Alec is Laird now."

Water shimmered in Lindsey's eyes, and her hands balled into fists at her side. "Ye don't understand." Her voice trembled. "Ye have Alec. Cameron has Robert and Douglas. Elsbeth has her life with the sisters, and I have my horses. Why can't he leave them alone?"

She burst into tears and ran into the bailey.

"Wait!" Heather raced after her, but her younger sister dashed into the keep.

She shook her head. Why had Alec upset Lindsey? Perhaps she would talk to him and explain how her sister felt. Surely there was a way to keep them both happy.

~~~

Lindsey paced her bedchamber. Alec didn't think she was capable of managing and selling her horses…her *own* horses! She had to prove she could handle them as well as any man. He would then have no choice but to let her continue to

232

care for them. How had this dilemma happened? She had no way of knowing when that fiend married her sister he'd attempt to push her aside.

She tugged the wrinkled and worn document from her pouch.

*Dumfries Horse Race*
*15 August 1299*

Three weeks from today. She lowered the parchment. Hamish had requested she deliver word to the Scots' southeast stronghold of an incoming English ship. Perhaps she would take Blaze and several prize horses to the race after the rebel commander's assignment. Disguised as a lad, she would enter the competition. If she won, the MacDougall stock would become known far and wide. Men from all over would travel to purchase her horses.

She'd show Alec.

Her spirits rose. She packed a bag of her belongings and headed to the stables to garner support from her closest allies.

~~~

Alec yawned and rubbed the back of his neck as he studied the plans for the next ambush of the English caravan. They would depart at first light and rendezvous with Robert by mid-day. The hard part would be telling Heather he was leaving. He should've informed her earlier, but he was preoccupied with his plan of attack, and the time slipped by.

When he entered their bedchamber, Heather lay on her side with her back to him, her beautiful hair fanned across the pillows. Her hiked-up gown exposed a shapely calf. He would like nothing better than to climb in bed and make love to her, but he suspected when he informed her of his upcoming trip, she would not welcome his advances.

He stood beside the bed, tugged his tunic over his head and dropped his trews. He slid underneath the blankets and slipped his arms around her. A faint whiff of roses wafted off her hair. He kissed her shoulder, and she snuggled her soft, warm body against his.

They lay in each other's arms for a while before he finally broke the silence. "I have to execute another assignment."

Heather remained quiet as she grazed her fingertips along his arm lying across her waist.

"We'll be riding out at dawn."

She rose on her elbow. "Tomorrow? But, I had no idea. Why did ye not tell me?"

Alec's fingers traced circles on her back. "Ye've been busy running the keep."

Her blue eyes darkened, her glower penetrating. "Ye promised not to shut me out."

"I didn't intentionally shut ye out."

"The results are the same."

Alec took her hand in his and kissed her knuckles. Why did she have to insert herself into his business? He had promised to care for her and her clan. "I don't want to argue with ye before I leave."

Her gaze searched his eyes. "Nor do I, but don't keep me in the dark. I want yer word."

Alec's thumb caressed her cheek. "And I want yer trust."

"Ye will not gain it in this manner. When we married, we had an agreement. Ye promised to include me."

Alec withdrew his arm from around her and rolled over. "It's late and I grow weary of yer accusations."

She was sorely mistaken if she thought he would acquiesce to her unreasonable stance.

## *Chapter Sixteen*

Daylight broke, the sun barely peeking above the horizon. Pink splashed the morning sky and cool air swirled around Alec. He tugged his cloak tighter around his neck, trotted down the steps and into the bailey. A dozen men mingled in the courtyard, some securing their belongings, others saying goodbye to loved ones.

"Mount up," he commanded.

While his men made final preparations, he stepped into the dim barn. The smell of fresh cut hay and grain met him as he strode down the main aisle, horses lining the stalls on either side. "Blake?" he shouted.

The lad rounded the corner, wiping his hands on a cloth as he approached. "Aye, m'laird? What can I do for ye?"

Alec handed a sealed parchment to him. "Give this message to Maria when ye arrive at Glencara. It's important she receives it. Do ye understand?"

Blake stuffed the missive in his pouch. "I'll see she gets it."

Alec didn't like the party journeying to Glencara without him. Although Commander Taylor had given his protection from the harassment of enemy soldiers, hardened outlaws still roamed the area preying on unsuspecting travelers. He chose Blake and a group of his most trusted men to accompany Heather and Ainslee to his home. Alec owed the lad a great deal. If it had not been for him and Lindsey, the consequences of Symon's attack would've been far worse.

"Keep to the roads, and set up camp early so ye're not traveling after dark."

"We'll leave as soon as the women are ready."

"I'm counting on ye to protect them."

Blake straightened. His chest expanded. "I won't let any harm come to them."

Alec clapped him on the shoulder. "Wait for me at Glencara. I expect to arrive by midweek. We'll travel back here together."

Blake's head bobbed. "Ye need not worry."

Alec strode from the stables. His men had mounted their horses and lined up behind Aeton. Heather wrapped her cloak around her shoulders as she slipped down the steps. The cool air colored her cheeks pink and wisps of blonde hair blew around her face. His stomach tightened as she hurried over to him. He enveloped her in his arms and kissed her forehead.

"Be safe, husband." Her intense eyes searched his face. "I'll worry until ye return."

Alec bent and kissed her lips, then straightened and held her shoulders. "Don't take unnecessary risks."

"We'll be fine. I want to visit yer home and meet yer father."

He glanced at the men awaiting his orders before turning back to her. "I want ye to take Muire with ye. There's a lass at Glencara due to have a baby any day now. I want to make sure she's in good hands and nothing happens to them. Her name is Skena. Please ask Muire to take care of her."

Heather's brow knit. "Skena?"

"Aye, she lives in the keep. She's Maria's daughter."

"All right, I'll ask Muire to join us."

Alec cupped the side of her face. "Stay with Ainslee and Blake. I'll meet ye at Glencara as soon as I can."

Her blue eyes held concern. After exchanging heated words last evening, he worried how she would respond to him this morning. Her desire to be involved irritated like boots rubbing a boil. Why could she not trust him? What must he do to win her confidence?

~~~

Alec led the group out of the bailey and through the castle gates. Heather wiped tears from her eyes. She worried about the danger he was riding into. A part of her longed to be there, hidden in the trees with her bow and arrows as she had done so many times before. She prayed the Lord would watch over him and bring him home unharmed. She would travel to his home and wait for his return.

Her thoughts wandered to Glencara Castle and Skena. Who she was to Alec? Why was he so concerned about her welfare?

236

## Heather

Heather stoically entered the stables. Alec had promised she would have a voice in his decisions for the clan. After so many months of planning strategies with Beathan and Da's men, she couldn't simply revert to overseeing the keep's laundry and food preparations.

He had said there would be no more secrets between them. So why did she feel he was hiding something? *Like Skena.* A lass having a child was no strange or uncommon occurrence. He acted as if she and the child were special to him.

Her eyes adjusted to the barn's dim light, and she strolled down the long aisle to the back of the building. Lindsey brushed Blaze, a young stallion she'd bred and raised. His sleek black coat gleamed. He tossed his head. His dark, full forelock hung below his eyes, covering his white markings.

Heather slipped into the stall. "Good morning."

Her sister glanced over her shoulder, her lips drawn into a tight line.

Heather ran her hand over Blaze's loins. "I didn't get a chance to speak to Alec on yer behalf, but I will. I promise."

Lindsey faced Heather, her hand clutching the brush. "Yer husband is an overbearing lout."

Heather cringed at her tone. How was she to convince her sister Alec held their best intentions, when she herself questioned his purpose? "He means well."

"Humph, at my expense. Who does he think he is? He bullies his way into our clan and promptly takes over."

Heather flicked loose hairs off Blaze's rump. "Ye don't think I should have married him?"

Lindsey hesitated, and then exhaled loudly. Dark circles lined her puffy, red eyes.

Heather's heart squeezed. Lindsey's horses were her life—a life that appeared to be crumbling.

"Seems marrying him was about yer only choice at the time. Ye couldn't continue to lead Da's men. And…it was best for the clan." She shook her head. "I understand his decisions include two castles, but why must he take *my* horses? Ye know I've sold them and collected many gold pieces for our clan. It's

not fair he pushes me aside and replaces me with his men—
men who do not know my horses." Her gaze narrowed. "I'll
prove I can peddle my animals as well as any man."

"Ye don't need to prove anything. I'll speak to him
when he returns."

"A lot of good that'll do. He's set on replacing me."

Heather's teeth raked her bottom lip. A twinge pinched
her chest. Alec was set on replacing her as well. Actually, he'd
already replaced her with himself. Da's troops no longer
needed her guidance. Was her husband determined to ensconce
his men into positions of authority at MacDougall Castle?
Lowrens and Symon had also wanted to replace her and Da.
Her heart lurched. "I'll do what I can. I pray I have not made a
mistake."

"Well, at least he's not beastly to look upon."

Alec's dark eyes and sculpted body glistening in the
firelight flashed through her mind. "No, ye've got a good point
there."

*And ye've not seen him in all his glory.*

~~~

Midmorning, Heather scooted next to Muire on the
worn seat of a cart loaded with trunks and supplies being sent
to Glencara. Her heart, like a boulder, sat heavy in her chest.
Sleep had eluded her last night as she lay on her side, hugging
the mattress, staying as far away from Alec as she could while
still remaining in the same bed. Remembering the bitter words
she and Alec exchanged, sickness had spread through her body
upon awaking.

Now she worried over Skena. What other things did he
keep from her?

Alec's sister skipped down the bailey stairs and across
the yard to the horses lined up, waiting. "Good morning,
Blake."

The lad lifted her on top of a horse. "Ye have
everything ye need?"

She smiled. "I do, thank ye."

# Heather

Sitting sideways in the saddle, she smoothed her tan linen gown over her legs. Her dark, shoulder length, curly hair blew softly in the breeze.

He rotated to Heather. "Mistress, are ye ready?"

When she nodded, he called to head out. She flicked the reins and the horses started forward. The wagon jerked and rattled down the muddy road. Ainslee chatted amiably, Blake hanging on her every word. Her tinkling laughter and youthful inquisitive interest made Heather smile. Although her stomach was sick with thoughts of Alec and their future, the harmless prattle lifted her spirits.

She tilted her face to the sun and closed her eyes. The rays warmed her skin. It had only been a little over two months since she wed Alec, and he'd asked that she give their arrangement time. She sighed. How she longed for a true partnership.

Perhaps he was right. It would take time.

Their uneventful journey lasted two days, but finally the tired group made their way into the cobblestone bailey at Glencara. Darkness descended on the keep. Massive grey walls surrounding the interior yard were lined with torches, their flames blazing in the cold wind. Warriors patrolled the stone ramparts surrounding the top of the castle and connecting towers at the structure's four corners. The vantage point not only provided a clear view of attackers, but a strong fighting platform. Compartments for the blacksmith, barracks for warriors and various dwellings lined the walls. Light shone between slats of shuttered windows, the glow inviting.

Lads ran from the stables to help Muire and Heather off their wagon as a middle-aged woman stepped from the keep. Her white braided hair, wound in a tight bun, was affixed atop her head. Wrinkles furrowed her leathery skin and several missing front teeth created her snaggletooth grin. She wrapped a brown woolen cloak around her slumped shoulders. "Come in, come in. It's miserable out here."

Blake helped Ainslee dismount, and she bestowed a pretty smile on him. "Thank ye." Her hands lingered on his shoulders for a bit longer than necessary before she stepped back and turned to Heather. "Let's get inside."

Heather clutched Muire's elbow, and they followed Ainslee up the steep stairs to the landing before a large oak door.

Blake carried one of Ainslee's trunks on his shoulder and turned to her. "Where would ye like this?"

"Oh, come with me." She led him across the main hall.

The old woman ushered Heather and Muire into a comfortable room off the main hall. Dark wooden benches lined the chamber and a thick rug warmed the stone floor. A spicy fragrance filled the air, and several chairs faced flames blazing in a large hearth. Light twinkling from candelabras filled the room with a welcoming glow.

The woman tugged Heather's cloak from her shoulders. "Ye must be the new Lady Campbell. We received word yesterday of yer visit, and everyone is excited ye've arrived."

"Aye, I'm Heather." She extended her hand, and the woman grasped her fingers. "And this is Muire, our healer."

"I'm Maria." The woman curtsied. "'Tis nice to meet ye both."

Maria—Skena's mother?

The servant squeezed Heather's hand, her soft brown eyes shining. "Our Laird certainly chose a beauty. Please make yerselves at home. I'll have refreshments brought in."

She returned Maria's smile, slipped into a chair next to Muire in front of the hearth and held her fingers to the blaze. Perhaps she had been mistaken. Surely, Maria would not have offered such a warm welcome if there was a relationship between Alec and her daughter.

Blake marched into the room. "Maria, I have a note for ye from Laird Campbell. He said I should give it to ye as soon as I arrived."

A note? Why had Alec given the message to Blake instead of her? She glanced at the Maria and then at the lad as he fished out the document from the pouch at his side.

The older woman grasped the parchment and blushed as she studied it. "I don't read," she whispered.

240

Heather

Blake looked at Heather and Muire. He shrugged, his brow lifting.

Heather extended her hand to Maria, her fingers trembling. "I can read it for ye. Let me see."

Maria handed her the missive. "Thank ye, mistress."

Heather broke the seal and examined the correspondence addressed to Maria in her husband's handwriting. She read the note aloud.

*I'm sending Muire, the MacDougall's healer, to Glencara.*
*I want to ensure Skena has all she needs*
*and that she and the child are well cared for in my*
*absence.*
*Please let Kirk know if Skena should need*
*anything and he will get word to me.*

Heather swallowed past a lump lodged in her throat and lowered the parchment. She sank in the chair before the fire. Why was Alec so concerned about this maid and her child? He wanted Kirk to get word to him…while on an assignment?

Her belly roiled.

Blake stepped to Heather's chair. "Laird Campbell is a most gracious and caring overlord."

Maria wrung her hands. "I appreciate his concern about my daughter and for all the people of Glencara."

Stunned, Heather's mind raced. Who was Skena to her husband? Body numb, she stared blindly in the fire.

Maria cleared her throat. "Mistress, I…I'll have yer belongings brought in and escort ye to yer chambers so ye can rest."

Muire clutched Heather's hand. "Ye're overly tired. Perhaps it would be best for ye to lie down."

Heather couldn't move. Why had Alec not told her about Skena? While he asked for her trust, he kept secrets. He must've thought her a fool.

"Mistress?" Maria clasped her hands before her waist. "Let me show ye to yer room."

Heather took a deep breath and followed the servant up the stairs, down the dim corridor and into Alec's bedchambers.

She stood inside the doorway and wrapped her arms around her waist.

Candles flickered in candelabras set against the walls, lighting a massive bed covered with thick woolen blankets. A large fur positioned underneath dark wooden chairs absorbed the heat from the fireplace. Two swords crossed over the mantle, the Campbell emblem carved in pewter proudly displayed above the apex.

A copper tub full of steaming water had been placed before the flames. Firelight dancing across the walls cast shadows through the room. A chill engulfed her and she trembled, her emotions strung tight. She strolled to the bed while shedding her clothes.

Maria placed a drying cloth and fresh gown over the back of a chair. "Is there anything else I can get ye?"

Heather shook her head and eased into the hot water. "No. I'm fine. Thank ye."

"I'll send someone to check on ye shortly." Maria slipped out of the door.

The room fell quiet. A log rolled in the hearth, and the fire popped and crackled. Heather leaned back and closed her eyes. It had been a long day, and she was tired. She wanted to climb into bed and pull the blankets over her head. However, Ainslee was going to introduce her to Alec's father, and she must manifest a cheerful façade.

The door opened and closed. A cool breeze swept her back. She straightened and looked over her shoulder. A woman with shoulder-length russet hair, wearing a form-fitting grey gown displaying her ample bosom, strolled across the room. Her hazel eyes focused on Heather.

Naked and feeling vulnerable, Heather drew her knees up and crossed her arms over her breasts while gazing up at the woman.

"So ye're Lady Campbell." She slowly circled the tub. "I do feel sorry for ye."

She stopped in front of Heather and stooped at eye level. She dipped her fingers in the water, swirling circles. Her dark eyes lifted to Heather's face, and her lips pursed. "He's using ye for yer ties to MacDougall Castle."

Heather

Heather's pulse pounded in her ears. She glared at the woman. "Who are ye? What do ye want?"

"My name is Megan. Let's just say I know from experience how Alec treats women. He used me, too." She gazed longingly over Heather's shoulder. "He lay between my thighs time after time right there in that verra bed, pledging his love for me. Then, once he had what he wanted and no longer needed me, he tossed me aside." She sighed and clutched Heather's hand. "I've come to warn ye."

Heather extracted her fingers from the woman's grasp. "Warn me of what?"

"He loves another. She carries his babe, and he will be warming her bed when he returns." Megan straightened and circled the tub again. "Tsk, tsk. I do feel sorry for ye. Don't say I didn't give ye forewarning." She laughed as she strolled from the room.

Her chest constricted at the thought of Alec with another woman, let alone bearing a child with her. Did Megan tell the truth? Her stomach flipped over. After little sleep over the past few nights, she continued to feel sickly and exhausted. Her emotions were fragile, and she couldn't think straight. She must get rest and pull herself together.

She climbed out of the tub and dried off, stiffly going through the motions of dressing. Sitting before the fire deep in thought, she brushed her hair dry.

A knock sounded at the door. Ainslee stuck her head into the room and slipped inside. "Ye look lovely."

Heather smoothed the front of her green linen gown. "Thank ye."

"Da's looking forward to meeting ye."

Heather placed her hand on Ainslee's arm. "Before we go, may I ask ye something?"

She had to know if Megan spoke the truth.

Ainslee clutched Heather's hand. "Aye, what is it? Ye seem distressed."

Heather swallowed and raised her chin. "I'm aware of Alec's leman."

Ainslee's shoulders sagged. "Oh, Heather. I'm so terribly sorry."

Her few words sliced through Heather's belly. Well, there it was. Skena was Alec's leman.

Ainslee hooked her arm through Heather's. "I begged him to remove her. She's nothing but trouble."

"I see."

"Come, let's go visit Da. It'll brighten yer spirits."

Heather nodded, and Ainslee escorted her from the room. They walked down a long hall that opened into a common area with one staircase going up and another below. They climbed the steps and continued down a damp corridor. Candlelight from the sconces lining the cold stone walls flickered at the women's passing.

With thoughts of Alec's mistress plaguing her, Heather's stomach clenched. Why had he not told her about his leman? Although it was common place for a man to bed many women, she had not considered the possibility of Alec's indiscretions. While he asked for her trust, at every turn she found he kept her in the dark.

Ainslee stopped before a worn oak door and knocked loudly, then stuck her head inside. "Da, are ye awake?"

"Aye, come in, come in," a raspy, deep voice called from the dark chambers.

Holding Heather's hand, Ainslee led her into the room and over to the bed. Alec's father sat propped against the back of his bed, a parchment in his lap. Sparse white hair stood out in tufts around an otherwise bald scalp. His thick, bushy eyebrows framed his grey eyes—Alec's eyes. Her insides knotted at the resemblance.

"Da, this is yer daughter-in-law, Heather." She turned to Heather and held her hand out to her father. "And Heather, this is yer father-in-law, Grant Campbell."

Heather reached out and grasped his wrinkled hand. "It's so nice to finally meet ye. My da has regaled many interesting stories about the two of ye growing up."

He chuckled. "Ah, the pleasure is all mine, lass. Ye're every bit as beautiful as yer mum." He beamed at her and patted her hand. "Please sit and visit with me." He motioned to the bench beside the bed. "Tell me, how is yer father? I miss seeing my old friend."

Heather fell in love with her father-in-law. His quick wit and charming personality welcomed her into the family. Her spirits rose, and she forgot about her troubles. They talked for quite some time, but it soon became apparent he was tired. The ladies made their excuses and left him to rest.

Ainslee grasped Heather's hand, and they strolled back down the long corridor and into the main hall. The aroma of roasting meat and freshly baked bread wafted past Heather's nose. She inhaled the scrumptious smell, and her stomach rumbled.

The evening meal of roasted boar, fish and hot vegetables lined the table. Maria had worked hard to make Heather's first dinner at Glencara pleasurable. Heather ate her fill while enjoying Blake and Ainslee's company. As the hour grew late, she excused herself for the night.

A servant was bent over, adding wood to the fire when Heather entered Alec's chamber. The woman straightened and placed her hands on her lower back, her extended stomach protruding.

Heather's breath caught.

Was this Skena?

With her light hair and soft hazel eyes, she resembled Maria. What was this maid doing tending to her? She had some kind of nerve, flaunting her swollen belly—swollen with Alec's child.

The girl smiled. "Good evening, m'lady. I was just getting the chamber ready for ye." She busied around the room, turning back bedding and laying out a nightgown.

Heather stepped up to her and took the gown from her hands. "Ye don't need to do that."

Skena's brow raised, questions reflected in her eyes. "M'lady?"

"I can handle my things. I don't need yer help."

"Uh, aye, Mistress." Skena stepped toward the door.

Suddenly, she grabbed her middle and doubled over. Crying out, she sank to the floor.

Heather hurried to her. "What is it? Is it the bairn?"

Skena hollered, and water gushed from under her skirt.

Heather grasped the maid by the shoulders and helped her stand, then guided her to the bed. "Ye rest. I'll get Muire."

Skena gripped Heather's hand. "But m'lady, this is yer bed."

Heather's chest squeezed. Alec's leman was giving birth to his child in their bed. What more could she take? She gazed at Skena's wide eyes, her pale face strained with pain. "I'll be back directly."

She covered the maid with a blanket and raced from the room in search of Muire. She ran down the stairs and into the main hall where she found the healer sitting next to the fire. "Ye must come quick. Skena's having the babe in my chambers."

"Let me gather my things. I'll be right there." Muire called for hot water and blankets and climbed the stairs to her chamber.

A few moments later, Skena cried out as Heather entered the room with Muire and Maria following. Muire began preparations to deliver the baby.

As Skena yelled, Maria took her hand. "It's all right, daughter. Muire will help ye."

The healer examined Skena. "The babe's head's in position."

She gently coaxed the maid as Heather and Maria held Skena's head and shoulders, trying to give support. Skena pushed and strained, but the babe refused to enter the world. Hours passed with Heather wiping the servant's brow and softly encouraging her.

Finally, late into the night, she gave birth to a tiny lass. The women laughed and cried at seeing the little pink bundle. She already resembled her mum with a head full of light brown curls. Muire helped Skena as Heather cleaned the baby. Maria cried tears of joy while gazing over Heather's shoulder at her new granddaughter.

Heather held the little one in her arms and gently bathed her face and body. The babe kicked and cried while Heather spoke softly, soothing her as she wrapped her in a blanket and cradled the bairn.

Alec's bairn.

Her heart broke. The little one began to cry. She patted her back as she carried her to her mum. "Shhh, it's all right."

Skena smiled and reached to take her daughter.

Once the babe was settled, Heather excused herself and slipped from the room. With her stomach in knots, she had to get away.

The keep was quiet. No one was around as she hurried down the stairs and into Alec's solar. She closed the door and leaned against it, gasping for breath. Tears slid down her cheeks. Emotions wrecked from exhaustion, she swiped at the moisture and tried to bolster her resolve. She would not let Alec make a fool of her. After all, she had her pride. Skena and their child were not part of the marriage agreement.

She took a steadying breath, her gaze sliding through Alec's solar. Wooden panels lined three of the four walls. A massive stone hearth and ornate timber carved with hunting scenes filled the back wall. An oversized desk positioned before the fireplace held scattered documents, an ink well, a carafe of wine, and a small candelabra. Melted beeswax drippings had splattered, frozen in time along the yellowed candles. Bulky, dark wooden chairs placed on a thick rug faced flames barely flickering around several large logs.

Sighing, she pushed away from the door and added wood to the fire. Soon the flames blazed. She sat in one of the chairs, wrapped her arms around her legs, and stared into the orange glow. Megan's words haunted her, and she closed her eyes trying not to picture Alec with Skena. She poured herself a mug of wine and sipped it well into the night.

Sometime later, Heather awoke to a soft knock. The door slowly opened, and Maria quietly padded across the floor. "M'lady, please come to bed. Kirk has moved my Skena to her quarters, and I have freshened yer chambers."

Heather rubbed sleep from her eyes. Dozing in the chair left her stiff, and she stretched her tired muscles as she stood. "I must've fallen asleep."

"Aye, it's been a long day. Come along." Maria ushered Heather up the stairs and into her chambers. She bustled across the room. "Mistress, I thank ye for yer kind soul, helping with the delivery of my grandchild and placing my daughter in yer own bed. Most ladies of the keep would have sent her to another chamber. Ye're truly special. Sleep well."

She padded across the room and out the door.

Furs and blankets lined Alec's bed, but she objected to the thought of lying where Skena had given birth to his bairn. Heather tugged the covers off the mattress and sank before the fire. She wrapped the thick blankets around her and settled on the cold floor.

If Maria knew Heather's true feelings, she would not have uttered those words. How dare Alec leave this matter unsettled for her to discover on her own!

Too tired to think clearly, she drifted off to sleep with troubling thoughts of Alec and Skena. If he thought Heather would accept this relationship, he was mistaken.

## *Chapter Seventeen*

The scratching of Heather's quill broke the silence in Alec's solar. She brushed the feather against her chin.

*I want to ensure Skena has all she needs and that she and the child are well taken care of in my absence.* Alec's torturous words repeated through her mind. Had he plunged his dagger into her heart, he could not have hurt her more. While she understood a past liaison, she could not accept his amorous attention toward Skena and their child. Had he truly used Heather to garner MacDougall properties? While she fretted over Symon and Lowrens, was Alec yet a third conniver using her as a pawn to enrich his holdings?

Dust flittered in the morning sun shining through the windows. She stared at the rays warming the chilly room, their presence somehow comforting. But nothing could console the emptiness pervading her soul. After spending the night tossing and turning, she had thrown her blanket aside and immersed herself in learning Glencara's accounts and household chores.

A loud rap on the door startled her. She had relished the quiet solitude. Her study of the thick ledgers provided a distraction from her troubled heart.

Another knock vibrated the door. Good heavens. What was the urgency? "Aye, come in."

Skena, cradling a bundle in her arms, slipped inside the room. "Mistress?"

*What did she want?*

The maid padded across the floor and stood before the desk. Her brown wavy hair had been secured into a leather thong, and several curls sprang free around her face. She raked her teeth over her bottom lip. "I would like to thank ye for all ye did for me and my bairn."

Heather's chin rose slightly. "It was nothing."

Skena shook her head. "Oh nay, it was verra kind of ye."

Heather stacked several parchments on the desk and opened the castle ledgers. She began reviewing the recorded transactions.

"Ye're fortunate Laird Campbell married ye."

Heather's gaze shot to Skena's face. Heart pounding, her fingers trembled. How dare she speak of their *fortunate* marriage? "I beg yer pardon?"

"I mean to say…I don't have that comfort." She hugged her daughter and kissed the tiny head of brown curls. "To lie in my man's arms and cherish his embrace."

Visions of Alec holding Skena flashed through her mind. Her body shook, and her insides twisted, but she would be damned before she would let her emotions show.

Skena's eyes shimmered with tears.

"I want him to know about our daughter. He'll be relieved to hear we're both well. He was so verra worried when he left." Her lips grazed the babe's head. "Would ye send word to Laird Campbell?"

Heather fought to control the tremors racking her body. Holding the edge of the desk for support, she stood on shaky legs. "I'll see he gets yer message."

"Thank ye, Mistress. I know once my love hears the news, he'll come for me and our bairn."

Did she have no shame? Heather fixed Skena with the harshest glare she could muster. "Leave me."

The maid's eyes widened. She bobbed her head, turned and fled the room.

Heather's legs wobbled, and she sank onto the chair. Anger billowed through her. No wonder Alec eagerly agreed to live at MacDougall Keep. He could keep his wife there and his concubine and child here. How conveniently Heather had played right into his plans.

She snatched the documents before her, shoved them into the ledger, and slammed it shut. Tugging her brown woolen wrap around her shoulders, she strode from the room and hurried down the corridor toward her chamber.

Megan stepped in front of Heather and blocked her path.

"Ye poor dear," she said, red lips pursed, her hazel eyes conveying concern. "I would get her out of here before Alec returns. I wonder whom he'll greet first? Ye…or her and their child? My wager is on his new family. Ye'll be waiting in line

250

for his affections. But he is a *big* man, and I'm sure he'll have something left over for ye."

Heather brushed past and continued down the hall. The harlot's caustic laughter echoed through her ears.

She reached Alec's bedchamber, slipped inside and closed the door. She was exhausted. With fragile emotions strung tight, her pulse hammered in her chest. She forced her weighty limbs to move and made her way to the hearth. A book of poems lay on the mantle. She grasped it and flipped it open.

The door opened with a squeak. Prepared for battle, she whirled to face her adversary.

Muire stuck her head inside the room. "Heather?"

Relief poured through her, and her shoulders sagged. "Oh, it's just ye."

The healer's brow rose. "It's *just* me?"

Heather dropped the book and rubbed her forehead. "I'm sorry. I did not mean that as it sounded."

The old woman shuffled across the room. Her white hair was secured in a bun at her nape, and a tan shawl cloaked her dark gown. She placed her arm around Heather's shoulders. "Ye will be fine, my dear."

Heather's gaze shot to Muire's face. Did she know of Alec's leman? No doubt, Skena informed her of how she longed for his embrace through the night. *Argh!* How can Muire make light of this situation? Heather's heart was breaking, and Muire acted as if it were nothing.

The older woman touched Heather's cheek with the back of her fingers. "Ye need to lie down and rest."

"Rest? What has that got to do with anything?" she snapped.

"'Tis the best thing for keeping yer strength." The healer patted Heather's back. "Ye're tired and overly distraught. It's expected in the first few months."

"In the first few months?" Had the woman gone daft? Heather didn't care if they had been married for fifty years, she would never accept this arrangement.

"Aye, but within a month or two ye'll be feeling much better."

Heather's mouth fell open, and she shook her head. Did Muire expect her to embrace Alec's paramour and bairn? "What are ye saying?"

"I believe ye're with child, my dear."

Heather's heart lurched. "What?"

The word sounded sharp, even to her ears.

Muire patted Heather's arm. "It explains yer illness in the early morn and yer unusually *sensitive* emotional state."

Heather narrowed her eyes. "Unusually sensitive?"

The old woman grinned and patted Heather's arm. "Did ye not expect it?"

Her hand drifted to her abdomen. "Well, no. I mean, I did not think on it."

"Have ye had yer monthly bleeding?"

*When was the last time?*

"I…I…no. Not since before my wedding day…." Her voice trailed off in a whisper.

Muire squeezed her hand. "Ye'll be fine, but ye must lie down for a bit."

"A baby?"

Muire guided Heather to the bed. "I'll wake ye in time for the midday meal."

She stroked Heather's hair, then hobbled from the room and shut the door.

Heather caressed her abdomen. Her breasts had been tender, but they often were before her monthly bleeding. She had not considered the possibility of being with child.

A wave of protectiveness descended, cloaking her in unbridled love for her babe. Self-pity be damned. She snuggled down in the blankets. With proper rest, she would regain her strength and thrust herself into her role as the laird's wife.

~~~

Ominous clouds billowed in from the north and a strong wind from an impending storm whipped around Alec. The tempest battered treetops, their branches swaying, leaves, dust and debris swirling. He tugged his cloak tighter around his shoulders and squinted, searching the countryside for shelter.

Heather

Robert reined in his mount beside Alec and held up a hand to protect his face from the gusts.

"If memory serves, there's a large cave ahead," Robert shouted over the tumult.

Alec and his men followed Robert down the road. As they rounded several boulders, he spotted the cavernous hole in the side of the mountain. He dismounted and led his horse up the steep slope, picking his way through thorny thickets and brambles. A blast of air buffeted him, pushing him backward. Loose pebbles rolled under his boots, but he gained traction and trudged up the hill with his men behind him.

When he stepped into the cave, the sound of the roaring wind abated. Water trickled down the cavity walls and a cold damp breeze swirled from a gaping void at the back of the cave. Tunnels traversed these ancient caverns, a converging and intersecting maze of darkness—the desolate atmosphere matching the bleakness of his soul.

The men pulled saddles from their mounts. Eric brushed a cloth over his horse's back, and Beathan shoved his overcoat from his shoulders and brushed sticks and debris from the cave's floor.

Alec found a dry patch of ground. He jerked his satchel off Aeton's back. Rummaging through his belongings, he thought of the day before when he and his men had come upon Edward's aftermath. Soldiers had ransacked and destroyed a small town. There had been little opposition from the helpless villagers. Bodies of old men and boys lay scattered on the ground. Women picked through the rubble or stared, traumatized and confused, their faces blackened from smoke.

A heart-wrenching wail had caught his attention. A middle-aged man sprawled in the road, clutching a woman's beaten and burned body. Her blonde hair was matted with a mass of blood, a wedge carved in the back of her head.

Images of Heather, battered and bruised, flashed before his eyes. Gut-wrenching pain shot through his core. Witnessing the man's anguish, Alec's stomach clenched as if Aeton had kicked him. He suddenly realized how important Heather was to him, to his sanity. He longed to be near her, to feel her soft, nourishing embrace. She kept him strong and resolute, gave him purpose.

He had let his stubborn pride rule. Regardless of her desire to be involved in the clan's business, he kept her at a distance, hurt her without cause. Would it be so hard to include her, seek her counsel? After all, she had managed and cared for her own clan before he arrived.

He extracted a flask and dropped his bag on the ground while gulping the much-needed ale. The refreshing liquid slid down his parched throat and began the numbing, healing process he desperately craved.

Eric started a fire, the tenuous flames flickering around burnt remains of a campfire long ago extinguished. Several men tossed in sticks and larger pieces of wood and before long, warmth emanated from the growing blaze.

Alec leaned against a cold grey boulder and swiped a cloth over his grimy face. Robert dropped on the ground and rummaged through his bag. The man had married Heather's sister, an equally challenging and stubborn MacDougall daughter. How did he manage the willful woman?

Robert stretched his legs and crossed his ankles. "What has ye so quiet?"

Alec stared at flames and shook his head. "I grow weary of the brutality."

"Aye, 'tis hard to stomach." Robert turned his flagon up and gulped the contents.

Eric handed Alec a piece of dried beef and hard bread. Alec nodded his thanks as his captain and several others gathered by the fire. The howling wind beyond the cave's entrance and wood popping and crackling in the flames broke the silence. More of their men joined the circle, each quiet, absorbed in thought.

Alec swallowed a mouthful of ale. "Do ye ask for Cameron's advice?"

Robert's head turned toward Alec. His brow rose as he considered the question. "I do."

Alec tossed a stick into the blazes.

"Cameron is my greatest confidant, and I seek her opinion on many topics." Robert took another drink of ale.

## Heather

Perhaps Alec had been wrong. Although he would have the final word, he could ask his wife's opinion and include her in the clan's decisions. He longed for her trust. What better way to gain it, than to work closely beside her?

Lustful thoughts of working beside Heather materialized.

Perhaps he could bend…a wee bit.

Now that he was married, things were different. He no longer needed to shoulder burdens and responsibilities alone. He had a partner with whom to share them. Relief coursed through his body, and with thoughts of a new beginning, his spirits rose. When he returned home, he would bring Heather into his bevy of advisors, show her his trust and prove his…love…for her. His mind stumbled over the word.

His gut clenched.

When had she wheedled her way into his heart? The compassionate comfort she offered to families huddled in MacDougall's hall, and her fighting, protective spirit invaded his thoughts.

God, how he missed her.

His resolve hardened. They would start fresh, together ensuring the safety and well-being of both clans. He only hoped his pig-headedness had not destroyed any chance of reconciliation.

~~~

Two days later, Alec climbed a large boulder perched on top of a ridge and peered into a clearing at the base of the hill.

*Barclay Taylor.*

Squatting, balanced on the balls of his feet, the enemy soldier held his hands over a small campfire. His head turned, and his stare skimmed the surrounding forest. A brisk wind swayed trees and kicked up swirling dust. He stood, wrapped a brown scarf about his neck and tugged his dark cloak tighter around his shoulders. His head swung to the left. Eyes narrowed, he scrutinized the countryside.

After dispatching Edward's soldiers and their food shipment, Alec had sent the confiscated bounty ahead. No need to rub the commander's face in their brazen victory.

Eric scrambled up the rock beside Alec. "We didn't see any others. He appears to be alone."

After one last glimpse at their meeting place, Alec jumped to the ground and strode to Aeton. "Let's go."

He led his men down a steep embankment and through dense woods. They entered Taylor's camp, and the man spun toward them, his dark eyes wary. His gaze darted across the Scots surrounding him.

Alec rested his hands on Aeton's saddle and eyed the soldier. "I see ye received my message."

Barclay's arms crossed his chest. "I appreciate the escort to your keep."

Cautious trust stretched thin between them, their abnormal alliance tenuous. While their relationship remained advantageous, it hinged on a single maid. Taylor risked his life to be with Skena and their child, and Alec prayed he did not make a fatal mistake bringing the man into Glencara. "Mount up."

The commander kicked dirt into the fire and doused the flames. Smoke curled from the charred wood and dissipated in the breeze. He marched to his horse and swung onto the saddle.

Alec nudged Aeton toward home.

~~~

Alec's breath caught at the vision above him as he and the men trotted into Glencara's bailey. Heather stood on the ramparts, her long wheat-colored hair blowing in the breeze. With her arms hugging her lithe body, she raised her chin, her eyes unwavering. From this distance, he struggled to detect her emotions.

She turned abruptly and disappeared behind the stone wall. He hoped she would descend the stairs to greet him.

"Alec, ye're home!" Ainslee skipped across the yard to him. Her eyes settled on Barclay, and she froze.

Alec clutched her arm and turned to the man. "Commander Taylor, my sister, Ainslee."

256

The man cleared his throat. "It's a pleasure to meet you."

With wide eyes, she accepted his extended hand.

"The commander is here to see Skena and meet their daughter."

If possible, Ainslee's eyes enlarged farther. "Oh…welcome to Glencara. Ye have a most beautiful babe."

He bowed. "Thank you."

Randall stopped in front of Taylor and addressed Alec. "Should we board his horse?"

"Aye, he'll be visiting for a few days." Alec turned and addressed Barclay. "Gather yer belongings. Randall will have a lad rub down and feed yer mount."

When Taylor stepped out of hearing range, Alec glanced around the bailey and back at his sister. "All is well?"

Ainslee's face stilted. She nodded, but her eyes averted to the ground.

"What is it?"

"Did ye not see Heather on the battlements? During the day she spends time up there, observing yer warrior's training. When she returns at night, I assume she waits for ye."

Alec inspected the ramparts. Men patrolled, swords strapped to their belts, but Heather no longer stood watch. "Why?"

Ainslee huffed. "The verra night we arrived, Megan confronted yer wife."

"Megan?"

His sister nodded. "Heather told me she was aware of yer leman."

"Shite." Alec's fingers stabbed through his hair.

Ainslee shook her head. "I told ye to get rid of her, brother. She's nothing but trouble."

He rubbed the back of his neck. "It's not as if we…continued our liaison."

"Perhaps not, but I doubt Megan informed yer wife of that fact."

A lad took Aeton's reins, and Alec strode toward the bailey stairs. He took the steps two at a time. What the hell had

Megan said? That was all he needed, just when he hoped to reconcile his differences with Heather. His ire rose. By God, he had nothing to atone for. He had not taken the wench to his bed in years.

He marched across the landing and grasped the door handle. What would he find on the other side? Had Heather sharpened her sword, prepared to rid him of his head?

He took a deep breath and opened the door.

~~~

Alec was home. Heather smoothed her hair and ran trembling fingers down her gown. Her heart thumped wildly. She wanted to throw herself into his arms, tell him she loved him, and that they would have a babe of their own.

But there would always be Skena and Alec's daughter. Somehow, she would have to come to terms with that fact if she and Alec had any chance of a future together.

She hurried down the stairs and into the main hall. The front door swung wide, and Alec led his men into the keep. A squeal rent the air and Skena sailed past Heather, running straight for Alec.

Did she dare race the wench to her husband, knock her to the ground and stomp on her? She watched in horror as the maid ran into the arms of…another man…an English soldier. He grabbed Skena and swung her in a circle.

Heather froze. Who was this man? Why did Skena run to him? A babe cried, and Heather turned toward the sound. Maria, cradling her granddaughter, stepped up to the happy couple. Skena took the wee one in her arms and handed the child to the English commander. What was this about?

Could she have been wrong about the baby? Could this soldier be the bairn's father?

Her throat constricted. How foolish she had been! But, what of Alec's missive? And Ainslee had sympathized with her over Alec's leman…and Megan had said…

Boisterous laughter echoed through the hall. Megan cackled and pointed at Heather. Holding her middle, the woman bent over in guffaws.

## Heather

Heat crept over Heather's cheeks. How could she have been so daft?

"Enough," Alec's deep voice boomed. The harlot shrank and her laughter died instantly. He turned and stepped in front of Heather. His dark hair curled on either side of his rugged face, and a leather band wrapped his forehead, the thongs brushing his broad shoulders. A red, irritated scratch traversed his right cheekbone, and dried blood smeared abrasions over his eye and down the side of his face.

She gasped and cupped his cheek. Dark whiskers lay soft under her fingertips. "Ye're hurt."

"'Tis nothing." His warm hand covered hers, and he placed a kiss on her palm. His arm circled her waist, and he tugged her against him.

She shook her head and broke out of his grasp. While elated the child did not appear to be Alec's, there was still the matter of him keeping her in the dark. Why had he not told her about Skena? What else was he hiding from her?

"No…I…we, that is, we need to talk." She peered at the men and women milling in the great hall and back to Alec. "In private."

She backed away, spun on her heel, and marched up the stairs and into their chamber. Candlelight flickered from the candelabras positioned against the walls. Her interlaced trembling fingers fidgeted as her gaze slid from Alec's large bed stacked with grey woolen blankets to the dark wooden chairs in front of the fire.

The bedchamber door closed. Alec stood behind her. She felt his presence. Resisting the urge to throw herself in his arms, she took a deep breath and faced him.

He stopped inches from her. Without touching, his large body engulfed hers. The essence of his allure emanated from his solid frame. She couldn't think straight. His earthy scent, leather, and ale filled her nostrils. Heat radiated from him, and she closed her eyes, her resolve slipping.

She must gain control.

He placed his knuckle under her chin. "Look at me."

Her eyes fluttered open.

He searched her face. "Ainslee explained what happened, and I'm sorry. I assure ye, the woman means nothing to me. I'll send her away first thing tomorrow. I should have made her leave months ago."

"I don't understand. Send who away?"

His eyes narrowed. "Megan. Who else? I thought that is what ye'd want."

"Are ye still bedding her?"

"No. The last time was over three years ago."

Even the harlot admitted their relationship was in the past. Heather's pulse raced, her mind a muddle. She had imagined the worst, worried unnecessarily and lost hours of sleep all over a misunderstanding. Emotions fragile, she wrapped her arms around her waist. Her shoulders shook, and tears dribbled down her cheeks.

Alec's hand slid down her arm. "Lass, why are ye crying? I'm trying hard to understand. If Megan is not the problem, I have not quite grasped yer concerns."

She blinked watery eyes and sniffled. "For days I have thought ye loved Skena and that she gave birth to yer daughter."

He straightened. "What would give ye such an idea? I've never laid a finger on the maid."

"I read yer note to Maria."

Alec tilted his head to the side. "I fail to see why that would lead ye to this preposterous conclusion."

"Ye told Maria to get word to ye about Skena and the child …while ye were away. They were obviously important to ye." Her body shook and her chin wobbled. A fat tear dropped on her gown.

He gripped her shoulders. "Do ye remember the English commander that arrived as an unexpected guest at our wedding?"

"Aye."

"In exchange for my protection of Skena and *his child*, the commander guaranteed English soldiers would not patrol MacDougall, Campbell or Graham lands. Our property would remain off limits. We could live in relative peace, or at least breathe a bit easier."

260

Heather

Her back stiffened and she inhaled sharply. Heart hammering, she struggled to keep from pounding her fists on his broad chest. "And ye did not tell me this?"

"I didn't think to tell ye."

Her fingers splayed in front of her. "Did not think? Did ye not *think* it was important for me to know? All of this could have been avoided if ye had only kept me informed. Instead, ye kept me in the dark."

His thumb stroked her face, and he kissed her forehead. "I should have told ye."

"I did not even know of ye leaving until mere hours before ye were to go."

"I promise to share more with ye. I didn't mean to hurt ye." He gazed into her eyes. "I'm sorry, Heather."

"Ye're sorry? Is that all ye can say? How dare ye? I will not tolerate ye withholding things from me."

"I said I'd keep ye informed, and I will," he ground out.

Her shoulders shook with her sobs. "If I had known about yer arrangement with the commander, I could have helped, watched out for Skena and her child."

"I was wrong."

She studied his eyes. Sincerity emanated from the grey depths. She wanted to believe him, wanted their marriage to work.

She loved him.

She rose on her toes, eased her arms around his thick neck and kissed him.

His lips softened, his body relaxed, and he wrapped his arms around her. He picked her up until her feet no longer touched the floor and nuzzled her neck while whispering against her ear, "Will ye give me another chance? I want yer trust, and I will endeavor to gain it."

Over the past week she had endured sleepless, distraught nights, but in truth he had given her no reason not to believe him. Her fear of betrayal had gotten the best of her, and her imagination had run wild. Her head bobbed against his shoulder. "Aye."

"We'll start anew, and not withhold information or harbor secrets between us."

"Well...there is one more thing I need to tell ye," she whispered against his neck.

He eased her down. His eyes darkened, in what...annoyance? Impatience?

She prayed her news would be well received.

"And what would that be?"

"I'm with child."

~~~

Alec's heart slammed against his chest. His jaw dropped, and his shoulders fell from his rigid stance. *What?* He grabbed her upper arms. "A child?"

She nodded, her fingertips brushing his chest.

"A bairn. *My* bairn," he whispered. He placed his hand over her abdomen. A slight rounding met his palm. "Ye're well? Do ye need to lie down?"

"No, I'm fine." Her small hand covered his. "Ye're happy?"

"Oh, lass, I couldn't be happier."

Heather wrapped her arms around his neck, her soft breasts pillowing his chest. He groaned and grabbed her bottom, lifting her against his hard cock. When she gasped, he murmured, "I'm more than ready for ye, but I don't want to hurt ye or our babe."

"Muire assures me there is no danger of that happening."

"Ah, verra good. Ye inquired about it, then?" He nibbled her ear. His mouth trailed her soft neck. "Were ye anxiously awaiting my return to yer bed?"

"Alec!" She punched his shoulder and tried to wriggle free.

He chuckled and tightened his arms around her, bending her over backward. "Well, I anxiously awaited returning to yer bed, but...I'm wet and dirty."

"Aye, ye are." She wrinkled her nose and slipped out of his embrace. "The lads were heating yer bath water when I came upstairs a moment ago."

Heather

She hurried to the door and called down the corridor for the old worn tub. Alec watched her beneath hooded eyes as she poured a tankard of ale and handed it to him, then ushered the lads in with his bath. He guzzled the brew, his gaze fixed on his bonny wife. After the boys finished filling the tub, she escorted them out.

She strolled across the room, took his arm and guided him to the steaming water. When she tugged his tunic over his head, her breath caught. "Another gash."

Her fingertips traced a long ragged cut traversing his torso.

Alec jolted from her touch and caught her hand in his. "Leave it."

She searched his face, then dropped her gaze to his chest. Her soothing fingers spread over his skin, across his ribcage and lower. She knelt before him and tugged off his boots. When she rose on her knees, her face was level with his manhood.

His pulse raced and his member strained against his trews, anticipating, longing for her attention.

She untied his belt and the head of his shaft jutted through the opening. Her intake of breath and eyes examining him caused his impatient cock to jerk. He gritted his teeth and sweat peppered his brow as he watched her forefinger draw circles in the bead of glistening moisture on his sensitive tip. He steeled himself to her exploration, but his nerves, subjected to her sweet torture, stood on end.

She peeled his trews down his hips, and his anxious shaft sprang free, standing stiff against his abdomen.

"Come," she whispered and guided him to the bath.

That one word stretched his limits, but he restrained from grabbing her and sinking into her sweetness. He submerged in the heated water and relaxed against the back of the tub, his mouth dry in anticipation of his wife's ministrations.

Heather ran a slice of soap across his chest. Her fingers stroked his tired muscles, the grime of his trip sliding into the bathwater. Her gaze settled on his manhood. He raised his hips, his cock aching for her touch. Her slippery fingers encircled his throbbing member. He gritted his teeth, straining not to embarrass himself.

His eyes closed as he relished the exquisite feel of her grasp. She eased her palm up and down his length. When her touch roamed lower and she cupped his sack, he emitted a bestial growl. How much could he stand before he flipped her into this tub and sank into her honeyed chamber?

Her hand left him, and his eyes sprang open. Holding a large drying cloth, she coaxed him from the water. She rubbed the fabric over his chest and torso, working her way down his abdomen. When she knelt before him, he sucked in a breath. Once again she studied his stiff cock. Did she know the effect that simple act had on him?

Sweat beaded his brow. He could not withstand her tortuous inspection much longer. Finally, she stood and led him to the bed where he stretched out, crossed his arms behind his head and watched her, his painful stiffness craving the release only she could provide.

She stepped back from the bed and began removing her clothes. Did she attempt to seduce him? Hips swaying provocatively, she clearly reveled in the power she held over him. Her breasts appeared heavier, the pink tips darker, and her waist was a wee bit thicker. His body smoldered by the time she let her gown slide past her hips and pool on the floor.

That was it.

He'd had as much as he could take.

He launched himself toward her, and she squealed as he toppled her over and onto the furs in front of the fireplace. He covered her with his body, his tongue mating with hers. Her plump breasts filled his palms, and he tweaked her nipple. Longing to capture the pebble between his teeth, he raked his lips across the tops of her breasts, and lower, licking the dusky tips. She tasted so sweet.

He gently suckled as she arched her back. With his cock throbbing, he nudged her knees apart and slid in between them. Positioning her legs around his waist, he sank into her haven. He closed his eyes, savoring her tight sheath. God's blood, her sanctuary engulfed him.

Heather

In the age-old rhythmic dance, he slid in and out of her warmth. His muscles strained to go slowly, relish each stroke. He held himself up on his elbow and eased his hand between them. Finding her special nub, he watched her lust-filled eyes as he pleasured her.

Her face flushed, and her breathing heightened. She cried out, her body convulsing in tremors. Lost in the exotic sensations, Alec thrust into her until he too reached a pinnacle.

He rolled off her and nestled her head in the crook of his arm. Firelight danced off their naked bodies, as they lay entwined in each other's embrace.

His hand inched across her belly. His child lay beneath. Euphoria rushed through him.

He kissed the top of her head. "Wife?"

She stroked his forearm. "Hmmm?"

How could he disclose his feelings, expose himself, and leave himself vulnerably opened wide? His gut wrenched.

"I love ye," he croaked.

Heather rose over him, her blonde, silky tresses falling onto his chest. Her eyes widened. "What?"

He touched her cheek with his knuckle and cleared his throat. "I love ye. I think I always have."

A tear slid down her face. "I love ye, too, and I *know* I always have."

# *Chapter Eighteen*

Heather slipped into Alec's bedchamber and shut the door just as the glimmer of dawn's light crept through the wooden window slats. Chilly air swirled around her, and fine hairs rose on her skin. She rubbed her arms, tossed a log on the grate, and stirred the amber coals. Flames flickered around the wood, casting warmth into the room.

She turned to the bed and paused. A glow bathed Alec's muscular frame stretched upon the crumpled linens. Fallen blankets exposed his broad sun-kissed chest dusted with dark hair. Her gaze traveled down his torso. Memories of his gentle caresses evoking fevered passion caused warmth to slither up her neck and over her face. He had introduced her to a world she had never dreamed of experiencing, love she had never dreamed of attaining. She couldn't get enough of him, of his intimate cuddling, of his warm embrace.

Her limbs quivered from the stress of empting the contents of her stomach. She tugged her wrap off her shoulders and dropped it on a chair, then padded to the bed and eased beneath the warm blankets.

Alec's arm snaked out and snuggled her close. He kissed her clammy forehead. "Ye're well?"

She snuggled next to him and rested her head on his chest. "Aye, I'm better now. Muire assures me this sickness is normal and will soon pass."

She prayed the healer was right. How could she survive this affliction every morn until her bairn arrived?

They lay in each other's arms, enjoying the quiet solitude of the morning. Alec's hand stroked her hip. "I would like some of yer time today. I have ideas I want ye to consider."

Heather stilled. "Ideas?"

"Aye, we need to make plans for both keeps and I would like yer opinion."

Her insides fluttered, and she rose on her elbow. Her hand splayed on his brawny chest.

His arm pillowed his head, and his face turned to her.

She cupped his cheek, his dark beard soft against her fingertips. "I'm ready to discuss any ideas ye have."

A grin spread across his full mouth, and he rolled her beneath him. He nuzzled her neck, his warm palm covering her breast. "Let's start with this one…"

~~~

After they broke their fast, Alec led Heather across the bailey. They entered the barn where the smell of freshly cut hay and grain from bins lining the walls, wafted in the air. Horses nickered and an occasional snort greeted them. With Alec's fingers interlaced through hers, they made their way down a center aisle. Her neck swiveled right, then left. Magnificent beasts housed in wooden stalls lined the passage. An intersecting walkway opened into a large paddock where several men worked with the animals.

Alec stopped and faced her. The corners of his mouth tugged up. "What do ye think?"

"It must be twice the size of Lindsey's. It's wonderfully spacious with plenty of room for the horses."

"I want to discuss combining the MacDougall and Campbell horses under one roof."

Oh, no. Lindsey would never agree to move her animals here. He could not expect Heather to go along with his plan to do so. She shook her head. "Alec, I don't think…"

He held up a hand. "Hear me out."

She crossed her arms over her chest. "Verra well."

As he paced a few feet from her, he interlaced his fingers behind his back. "With both keeps to manage, we need to consider merging the animals to more easily care for and peddle them. Glencara stables are the largest in the territory, so it makes sense to bring them here. My thought is to ask Lindsey to manage the combined group, using her knowledge to enhance and enlarge the herds. It would be better for her if they were in one location." He paused and turned toward her.

He was not replacing Lindsey. He was placing her in charge. Her mind raced. She had not expected that. "Lindsey would live here? At Glencara?"

"If she's willing."

While she would understand Lindsey's reluctance to leave her home, she also knew her sister would jump at the opportunity to work with more horses. "What of Logan? I thought he cared for yer herd?"

"He did, but I would now have him manage Glencara. He'll no longer have time to devote to the horses."

She took in the bright, airy stables. Sunlight streamed in the open windows, and a delightful breeze wafted through the barn. Large warhorses, and the lightweight animals Da gave Alec, milled around the stalls. Lindsey would be in heaven amongst these majestic creatures. Alec's thoughtfulness for her sister caused Heather's heart to swell with love. "I think it's a perfect plan."

His smile turned her insides to mush. "I'll inform her when we return."

The air slammed out of her chest. Lindsey had gone on a job for Hamish. Oh dear, she should have told Alec her sister was a runner for the rebellion. Her chest clenched.

He touched her shoulder. "Do ye feel well? Ye appear pale."

She nodded. "Aye, I'm fine." She cleared her throat and smoothed her gown over her abdomen. Her teeth raked her bottom lip as she considered her words. "Lindsey is not home at the moment."

His brow knit. "Not at MacDougall Castle?"

"No." She swallowed past the lump in her throat. "She's on an assignment."

His shoulders squared. "An assignment?"

"Aye, she's a runner for Hamish."

With his gaze focused on hers, he stepped back and rubbed the back of his neck. "Ye are one to preach about me keeping ye in the dark."

She moved toward him, her hands clenched before her. "I'm sorry. I meant to tell ye."

His grey eyes darkened, then narrowed. "*Meant* to tell me? Did ye not think it important I know assignments are being run out of MacDougall keep? Did ye think I would agree

268

to yer sister risking her bloody neck to deliver messages, when I have many capable men to handle it?"

"I did not purposefully withhold the information from ye. She has been doing this for quite some time."

"Shite!" He stormed through the paddock. Several men stopped working and craned their necks at Alec's raised voice. When he rotated back to her, his eyes radiated fury. He advanced. "When did she leave? Where was she going?"

"She planned to leave shortly after we departed last week." Heather wrung her hands. "She only told me it was somewhere in the southern territory."

"Ye don't know her plans?"

"Not exactly."

He stopped several feet from her, his size overwhelming. *Laird Campbell* stared down at her. "How in the hell did ye expect to find her if she needed help?"

Her chest heaved and her pulse pounded in her ears. "I…I did not think."

"Damn it, Heather, do ye not know the consequences of a Scottish lass traversing English-infested land, carrying missives to our warriors? Do ye have any notion of what the Sassenachs will do to her if she's caught?"

Tears stung her eyes. How could she have been so careless? "Travis and David rode with her. They promised not to take chances—to deliver the message and return home."

Alec crossed his arms over his chest and glared. "If two men accompanied her, why did she have to go?"

"She would not have taken them if I had not insisted." When his brow rose, she continued. "Lindsey feels it's her duty, her part in the rebellion. She prides herself on her riding skills to outrun—outmaneuver—the soldiers. When I learned of her involvement, I demanded she stop, but I had little ground to stand upon as I led Da's men."

Stilted moments passed. "She's a fool. I'll end her activity in this man's war. It's no place for a woman."

He was right, but Lindsey would not readily agree or welcome his interference.

"Is there anything else ye wish to impart? Any other *revelations*?"

"No." She didn't blame him for being angry. Hadn't she just yester eve railed at him over secrets? "I, too, want yer trust, and will strive to keep ye informed."

His eyes narrowed imperceptibly. "From this day forward, I will not tolerate ye withholding *anything* from me."

"I promise to keep ye apprised."

Another moment of silence passed before he dropped his hands to his hips. "I'll send word to Hamish to find yer sister and escort her home. I forbid her to continue this dangerous game."

"She'll be most pleased with the changes ye plan and will immerse herself in her duties."

Skepticism caused her voice to squeak. Lindsey fancied herself a rebel—a warrior in her own right. Heather could only hope to convince Lindsey of the importance of dropping this perilous business.

His piercing eyes brooked no argument. "I will not abide her impertinence or disobedient behavior. She'll adhere to my rules, or as with any other member of our clan, she'll be punished." He paused. "If we're to be partners going forward, we stand together. I have yer word?"

*Partners.*

"Aye, ye do."

~~~

Heather leaned her elbows on the solar desk and flipped through the pages of scattered scribble. Did that read a carton of food or fabric? The handwriting was sloppy, the notes illegible. How did they keep track of goods ordered and delivered?

A knock on the solar door interrupted her thoughts. Alec stuck his head inside. "Are ye busy?"

She peered at the ledgers spread across the desk and back at her husband. "Well, I'm not making much progress."

He stepped into the room and moved behind her. He picked up a document, and his brow scrunched. "What are these?"

270

"They appear to be purchases, but I'm having a hard time deciphering the handwriting."

He pushed several papers around, studying the contents. "The ledgers are not the same quality or detail ye're accustomed to reviewing." He ran his finger across the page. "Would ye be willing to help Ainslee, teach her how to keep the accounts straight?"

He wanted her help? "Of course."

"Perhaps we'll visit once a month so ye can work with her. Yer records are verra revealing. Ye know the revenues the clan collects and the expenses ye incur. I never have a good feeling for what we need, what we have ordered, or if we're making money on the sale of our goods."

"I can tally the figures for ye."

He sighed. "My sister does not work well with numbers."

"She'll feel differently once we've gone over them."

Alec rolled his eyes. "Ye might reconsider after working with her. She turns green when I merely mention the accounts."

He turned and strode to the door. Before he left, he said, "Once ye total the transactions, ye can advise me if it makes sense to share goods between the clans."

Heather beamed. Once again, he requested her opinion. "I'll work on it straight away."

His smile warmed her. Their shaky start this morning gained solid ground.

~~~

Heather strolled into the main hall as Ainslee hurried from the kitchen carrying a large platter of turnips and leeks. Alec and his men had gathered at the long oak table. Their conversation and laughter filled the hall.

"Oh, Heather, there ye are." Ainslee placed the tray on the table and turned to her as she wiped her hands on a cloth. "How are ye feeling? Muire tells me ye've been poorly in the mornings."

"I'm better. She prepared a brew that soothes the sickness."

Ainslee threw her arms around Heather. "I'm so thrilled we'll have a little one."

Heather giggled, her happiness near to bursting. "And I cannot not tell ye how happy I am."

The women joined hands. Serving girls wove around them, their arms full of trays laden with meat and leeks. Another carried a platter of freshly baked bread.

Heather tugged Ainslee to the side. "Where is Commander Taylor? I have not seen him this morning."

Ainslee's eyes softened. "I told Skena to take the day and enjoy what time she had to be with him and their daughter."

Heather owed the maid an apology. "That was verra nice of ye. When ye see her, would ye ask her to come to me?"

"Aye, I will."

Strong fingers slid down Heather's arm and she turned. Alec kissed her temple. "Will ye join us?"

She placed her fingers in his palm, and he guided her to the chair beside him. She slid into the seat of honor—her role as his partner solidified.

Several women placed trenchers of meat and tankards of ale before the men at the table.

Eric sat in front of her. "Mistress, ye're well?"

"Aye, thank ye." She sipped her ale and picked at the roasted venison. While her sickness had settled, her appetite suffered. The normally tempting food did not appeal to her.

Clanking of utensils filled the room. As the meal wore down, Alec addressed the men. "We received a summons from Brandon. He requests all clans be represented at Kilmory next week."

Taking her cue to leave, Heather rose from the bench, but Alec grabbed her hand. "Please stay."

Glancing around the table at the warriors focused on her, she composed herself and sat back down. "Verra well."

Eric placed his tankard on the table. "Brandon has another assignment for us?"

Heather

"From what I understand, we'll meet with Wallace. I expect he'll try to garner our support in a new strategy."

"I hear the McCarthys suffered a bungled assignment," Ian said. "They lost a number of men in a skirmish last week."

Alec rubbed the back of his neck. "Aye, the English are on to us. They're prepared for our ambushes."

Heather leaned forward. "What more can we do? Time after time the frontal attacks destroy us."

Alec drummed his fingers on the edge of the table. "Aye, we cannot match their numbers, and we can't survive another Falkirk. I'm anxious to learn of our new battle plans."

He addressed Eric. "Ye, Ian and Ralf will accompany me." His head turned to her. "Who would ye recommend from MacDougall keep?"

He asked her advice, in front of their men. "Beathan and Randall. I would like William and Jonathan to protect the clan while ye're away."

"Verra well, and Kirk can manage Glencara until we return. We'll ride to MacDougall Castle tomorrow and prepare the men."

She touched Alec's arm. "What about the commander?"

"I'll ask him to travel with us to the border."

Eric angled his body toward Alec. "I don't like having him around."

Other men grumbled in agreement.

"Nor do I, but 'tis necessary." Alec pinned each man around the table with a glare. "I don't want to hear any more protests about him. Do ye think I like consorting with the enemy?" When no one spoke, he continued. "He can protect our clans. He does not ask questions and turns a blind eye concerning us. So keep quiet, and be on yer best behavior until he leaves."

Alec grasped her hand. "Are we in agreement?"

She squeezed his fingers. "Aye, we're in agreement."

~~~

The next day, Alec and Heather descended the stairs and strolled into the bailey. They were returning home. While

Alec gave last minute instructions to Eric, she glanced around the courtyard.

Blake held Ainslee's hand as they walked to his horse. He cupped her chin and gently kissed her. When had they become so friendly? He ran his thumb across her bottom lip and spoke to her. She beamed at him and kissed his cheek.

Feeling as if she intruded on their privacy, Heather moved toward the stairs. Commander Taylor and Skena descended with Maria, her arms cradling her bundled granddaughter. After their rough beginning, Skena had graciously accepted Heather's apology, and the two had come to enjoy each other's company.

"Ye come back soon, Mistress," Maria said.

"We'll not be away long." Heather tugged the brown woolen blanket away from the babe's little face. Dark eyes peered up, and her little mouth worked in a sucking motion. Heather ran the back of her finger over the bairn's soft, pink skin. "She's precious."

She tucked the wrap around the little lass and turned to Skena. "Take care of yer beautiful daughter."

"Thank ye," Skena replied, tears pooling in her sad eyes.

Heather's heart broke for the young maid saying goodbye to her beloved soldier. Although he was English, there was no doubt of the love between them.

Alec clutched Heather's elbow. "Are ye ready?"

She nodded, and he escorted her to his horse then lifted her onto Aeton's back.

Kirk handed the reins to Alec. "Safe travels."

They shook hands, and Alec swung up behind her.

Heart squeezing, Heather waved, and the group departed for MacDougall keep.

The trip home was uneventful, but it was late the following evening before they entered the bailey. Alec grasped her around the waist and lowered her before him. He brushed a stray lock from her forehead and peered into her face. "How do ye feel?"

She patted his hand at her side. "A little tired, but I'm fine."

Heather

"Let's get ye inside to warm up and rest." He intertwined their fingers and led her up the stairs and into the keep.

Laughter met them when they entered the main hall. Cameron and Robert sat at the long trestle table with Da and little Douglas.

Heather made her way with Alec to the group. "Sister, I didn't know ye'd be here. What a pleasant surprise."

Cameron hurried to Heather, and the two embraced. "Robert told me he had business with yer husband so I joined him."

Heather straightened and squeezed Cameron's fingers. "I have good news."

Cameron's brow rose. "And that would be?"

"I'm with child."

Cameron's eyes grew wide and her mouth fell open. "I'm so happy for ye." She placed her hand on Heather's abdomen. "Ahh, I feel a slight bulge. It will not be long before ye feel its kick."

Heather eased her hand over her sister's. "Oh, Cameron, I never dreamed I would someday feel a babe's movement inside me. The father of my child, a man I love."

Cameron's green eyes softened. "I know, and I'm thankful ye will experience the joy of having yer own bairn."

A strong arm slipped around Heather's shoulders.

"Congratulations, Laird Campbell. I'm most pleased to hear the good news." Cameron turned to the group. "Heather and Alec will have a little one soon to keep Douglas company."

Da beamed. "Praise be! Another grandchild."

Lasses brought ale and food for the arriving party. Alec and Heather joined the group and enjoyed the roasted boar and freshly baked bread. After dinner, with the exception of Lindsey and her baby sister, Elsbeth, Heather's family gathered around the hearth. Robert sat beside Cameron, their small son in her lap. He wiggled out of Cameron's arms and toddled over to Da.

"Well, that's a sweet laddie." Da picked up the bairn, and the little boy rested against his grandfather's chest while sucking his thumb.

Alec informed the group of their plans for MacDougall Keep and Glencara and discussed their ideas for consolidating the herd of horses.

Da liked the consideration of having Lindsey in charge and thanked Alec for his thoughtfulness. "She'll be pleased to hear of yer plan."

Heather leaned back in her chair, her gaze traveling across her loved ones. Alec's deep laugh vibrated off the walls at something Da said. He clapped her father's back, and Da's face beamed with mirth. No longer did she see the worry and stress her father had carried for so long etched in his face. Alec treated him with respect, included him in the workings of the keep—made him feel important.

Her heart swelled.

The pieces of her life had fallen into place. She married the man who held her love and kept Da's secret. No longer did she worry about leading men into battle, or miscreants storming the castle and threatening her clan's existence. Alec exhibited his love for her, and every day their relationship grew stronger. He kept his promise to include her, bring her into his counsel. She had a say in their future.

She thanked God for bringing Alec to her. Her world was now complete with her husband—her partner—by her side.

Thank you for reading Heather! I hope you enjoyed her story. I would love to hear from you.

Email me at mcfarland.lane@gmail.com.

Please check out Cameron's story, *The Daughters of Alastair MacDougall* ~ Book I. And look for *Lindsey* to be released in 2014 with *Elsbeth* soon to follow.

## *Cameron*

Determined to band Scots together against English tyranny, Laird Robert Graham seals a truce with his feuding neighbor, the MacDougalls. But after his brother is nearly killed in a treacherous attack, Graham kidnaps the laird's daughter in an act of revenge.

Cameron MacDougall has devoted her life to the healing arts. She's long rebelled against her father's feuding ways, but when Robert Graham abducts her, she's finds herself at the center of the dispute between their families. She expects the anger she feels, not the simmering attraction to the powerful warrior, or the love she develops for his clan.

Can she stop further violence between the clans with her escape? Or will she find her surrender leads to a lasting peace and her own heart's desire?